FATAL FLAWS

Fatal Flaws

MADDIE GUDENKAUF

Dalygood Media, LLC

For my parents
Who loved and supported me despite my mess

knowledge about the specific components she was interested in until she got uncomfortable or frustrated enough to leave, haunted her former adoration now. She wasn't upset about it. It was just another reason to leave her former passion behind and move forward, wherever forward might be.

"There's a lot of ice cream flavors."

Ada looked at the other customer. A young man with dull green eyes that deepened into gold and dark hair barely grazing his thick eyebrows smirked at her, anticipating her reaction to his factual statement. Standing just an inch or two taller than Ada, he wore a leather jacket too expensive for this store and too thick for a Pittsburgh summer. He didn't belong there. He was too...not broken. But Ada wasn't in the business of fixing broken things. If she was, she wouldn't be in that grocery store, sore from a softball game she didn't want to participate in because of a co-worker she barely tolerated. She, herself, would not be broken.

"Yep."

Returning her attention to the ice cream freezer, Ada hunted for her usual flavor with renewed vigilance. She would rather put her legs through more agony walking back to her car than continue to have a conversation with this complete stranger. To her misery, however, her ice cream flavor remained missing and the guy failed to hold the same reservations about limiting their interaction.

"Some of these names are ridiculous, right?"

Ada watched with silent jealousy as he moved towards the freezer with ease.

"Buttercup Pecan Crunch? Cocoa-Fudge Supreme?" He said. "I mean, why not just call it peanut butter or chocolate? Why add the other stuff? Keep it simple, you know?"

"I don't know."

When Ada didn't elaborate, the guy released a low hum, dissent edging his tone. Seriously, where *was* her flavor? As Ada searched for her ice cream, she could feel the guy looking at her, almost analytical in his stare. It's been a while, but Ada would guess that he was trying to hit on her. That's how it always happened. Girl lives her life, boy tries to invade it to make it his own, girl rejects boy for romanticizing her normal life, and boy gets butt-hurt.

Rinse and repeat, tale as old as time, etc.

"Do you believe in fate?" The guy finally asked.

"No."

The answer came out faster than she intended, but Ada was in no mood to play stupid flirty games. It'd be quicker if he directly asked to take her back to his place so she could flat out reject him. All Ada wanted was ice cream. This random guy was not ice cream.

"Why not?" He asked.

"Because fate implies life has purpose outside of our control."

Moving her aching muscles with as minimal visible anguish as possible, Ada stepped forward and opened the freezer.

"Can you elaborate?" The guy asked, more calculated in his response than before.

Ada grabbed her pint of Banana-Nutmeg Blast and turned to the guy with a smug smirk.

"What else do you want me to say?" She said. "Life is nothing more than meaningless choices leading to a worthless existence. We then justify the emptiness of our existence with the illusion that there's a bigger power at work so we don't take responsibility for our own lack of worth and agency. Fate is nothing more than a fairy tale created by those who haven't caught up with reality and the reality is that we're alone and we're fucked."

To her surprise, the guy's eyes lit up ever so slightly at her response.

"Depressing."

"That's life."

Slamming the freezer door shut, Ada limped away from the guy. The shot of pain from her thighs and calves with each step served as a harsh reminder that she would still be blissfully standing in the cold aisle if it wasn't for Mr. Too-Cool-for-Respect and his super awesome leather jacket. But she had to go home eventually. On second thought, it was actually a miracle Sammy hadn't called the police for a missing person alert yet. Ada couldn't remember if she texted her roommate about the last minute softball game or not. By another miracle, Ada made it to the register without stopping to cut any of her limbs off. Her arms were numb to the pain, but her legs were still throbbing. Mentally, she tried to calculate how much ice their tiny apartment fridge could generate. With how badly her legs were hurting, she probably needed enough to fill the bathtub so she could live in it for the rest of her life. As she looked for the ice machine near the front of the store, Ada locked eyes with a woman standing near a rack of magazines. It was hard for the woman to not catch her eye; she was hauntingly gorgeous. Her cherry red hair was bobbed into an intricate updo that complemented her neon blue floral romper. With bright red lips and sharp winged eyeliner, the woman's electric blue eyes sharply contrasted the rest of her face and captivated Ada. How could anyone so beautiful be in a grocery store as dumpy as this one?

"I can help you over here, ma'am!"

Shaking off the woman's mesmerizing stare, Ada looked towards the register. The teenage cashier had a fake smile painted on her face, an attempt to make it look like she enjoyed her pathetic minimum wage job. The woman near the magazine racks kept staring at Ada, but Ada ignored her. This poor teenager wanted to go home and Ada wasn't helping with the constant lack of focus.

Abandoning the bag of ice, Ada approached the lone open register and set the pint of Banana Nutmeg Blast on the counter.

"Find everything okay?" The teenager asked as she scanned the ice cream.

"Yeah sure." Ada looked over her shoulder. The woman at the front of the store had yet to lift her glare from Ada. Swallowing hard, Ada turned back to the cashier. "Did a new club open up around here or something?"

"Sorry?"

"A club." Ada fought the urge to look back at the woman. "I've been seeing a lot of….weird people around here."

"Nope! But they did open a frozen yogurt shop around the corner," The teenager chimed. She punched a couple buttons into the touch screen. "$5.72."

The guy Ada met earlier appeared in the corner of her eye. She turned towards him, but he disappeared from sight. Licking her lips, Ada turned back to the cashier.

"Sorry, what was that?"

"Five dollars and seventy two cents…" The teenager was vaguely annoyed, but kept her fake smile painted. "For the ice cream?"

"Right."

Ada fumbled for the wallet lost in the emptiness of her sweatpants pockets. It became difficult to concentrate on her search when she became acutely aware of how the guy she met was now heading in the direction of the woman who was still staring at Ada. They had to be connected. Maybe they were dating and the woman knew he tried to flirt with Ada. Was that even flirting? A guy asking a girl if she believed in fate after two sentences seemed like flirting. Silently, Ada wondered if she needed to add anxiety medication to her already growing list of necessary prescriptions. Did anxiety medication cover paranoia? Shaking the thought, she found her wallet. Taking a deep breath, she offered an apologetic smile to the apathetic teenager and searched for the ten dollar bill she knew was folded into it. After finally finding the cash, she handed it to the cashier.

"Excuse me..." The guy was a short distance away, but Ada could still hear his voice distinctly over the vaguely early-2000's music floating through the grocery store speaker. She could also tell he was speaking to the woman because the woman's stare finally averted from Ada. "Do you believe in fate?"

The register opened with a sharp bell chime and the cashier counted Ada's change. Ada tried to forget about the strange guy and stranger woman. Before she could, a loud thud echoed from the front of the store. Alarmed, the cashier turned to the noise.

"Oh my god!" She shrieked.

All of Ada's change bounced against the register as the cashier backed away. Ada turned to see the woman was holding the guy against the magazine rack by his neck. She found a small sense of pride that she knew that the two weirdos were connected, but was terrified by the brute strength exhibited by the woman. The guy was remarkably calm given the fact the woman's pointed fingernails dug into his skin in a deadly grip.

"Louis Ventura, you are to be eliminated." The woman's voice was frayed, echoing slightly against itself. "Where is Allen Paz?"

"Ah man. I'd hate to repeat myself," Louis said. The woman's fingers tightened against his throat, but Louis kept smiling, barely wincing against her tight hold. "What did I tell you last time?"

"You requested for me to eat your feces."

"Ah right. Pretty sure I phrased it differently, but that's the gist of it. I'm pretty sure I can do better," Louis said. "Tell you what, how about this time you can tell me where you *think* Allen is and I'll still tell you nothing. Sound fun, Lady?"

"This is a futile attempt to delay your execution."

"Damn. They actually updated your OS," Louis grunted. "Didn't count on that."

"Should I get my manager?" The cashier asked. When Ada turned to her with incredulous eyes, the cashier nodded nervously. "Yeah I should get my manager. For sure."

Before the teenager could escape from her register, the woman lifted Louis from the wall and threw him full force into the magazine rack. The impact sent magazines flying forward as Louis and the rack toppled to the floor. With a scream, the cashier bolted from her register and ran straight for the exit, completely about her intent to alert her manager. Ada remained frozen in place, her heart beating fast against her chest as she stared at the violent scene. She should run too. She *needs* to run.

As the woman placed a spiked heel on the guy's chest, Ada turned to follow the cashier's exit. The sudden movement sent a sharp, searing pain spreading across her thigh. Shouting in pain, Ada grabbed the neighboring register wall and leaned against it. Resting her leg made her torn muscle feel better, but she couldn't stay there. There was a woman trying to kill someone five feet away. Ada could be next. Looking over her shoulder, Ada saw that the woman was staring at her again. With a short whimper, Ada pulled herself to the end of the register block just a few feet away. Her tired arms could barely handle the effort. A figure landed in front of her, interrupting any progress she could've made. A horrifying realization gripped Ada's stomach as she recognized the same spiked heels that were just digging into the guy's chest were now standing in front of her. She looked up. The woman's electric blue eyes stared unblinkingly into Ada's soul.

"Do not fear," the woman said. "I am here to help."

Before Ada could fully form her thoughts, a cash register slammed into the woman's head. The clap of heavy metal against heavy metal rang hard in Ada's ears as the woman collapsed from the impact. Jumping over the half-wall dividing the registers, Louis Ventura stood in the woman's place and held a hand to Ada.

"Come with me if you want to live."

Ada lifted her eyebrows in shock.

"What?!"

The woman's leg twitched and Louis looked at it.

"Right. Bad joke." He grabbed Ada by her bicep and pulled her to her feet. "C'mon!"

Ada knew she was in no position to fight the guy, and instead consented to limping behind him as he led her away from the woman. They barely escaped the register area when Ada heard a clatter of metal behind them. Louis and Ada both turned to watch the woman rise to her feet with the register in her hands.

"Shit!" Louis said.

He threw Ada's arm over his broad shoulders to pick up their pace. Ada hobbled next to Louis's side, her legs throbbing in pain from the effort. Louis glanced behind them for a moment and, with wide eyes, promptly shoved them both into an aisle filled with chips and drinks. The cash register crashed into a nearby display of chips where their heads would've been like a cannonball. Broken potato chips showered Ada and Louis as they passed the destruction. Breaking away from Ada, Louis pulled a knife from his leather jacket and jammed the blade into the large bottles of soda. Sticky dark liquid sprayed out of each bottle he stabbed, flowing onto the floor in streams.

"Start pouring some of this shit on the floor," he commanded.

"Why?!"

"Just do what I tell you to and you might get a chance to live," Louis said. "God this is why I work alone. Too many damn questions."

Pursing her lips, Ada grabbed a green soda Louis didn't stab yet and unscrewed it. Turning it over, she let the liquid dump onto the floor. As Ada's bottle emptied, the woman appeared at the end of the aisle. Ada dropped her empty bottle to the floor and backed away, with the intention to run. Shoving another soda into Ada's arm, Louis flipped his knife in his hands as he stared down the woman.

"Shake this as hard as you can and open it when I tell you," Louis said, not breaking eye contact with the woman at the end of the aisle. "No pressure or anything, but if you mess this up we might be fucked."

Nodding nervously, Ada shook the giant bottle to the best of her abilities. It was tough given the bottle size and her sore arms, but the fact a psychotic super-strong woman was trying to kill at least one of them was decent motivation. After staring at Louis and Ada for a long moment, the woman walked towards them. She looked like a model strutting down a runway. Her spiked heels tapped the tile in perfect rhythm, her body bounced to the same beat, and her stare remained unwavering and, frighteningly, unblinking. The woman's true strength was hidden behind a perfect facade. It was almost like she was unaware of the threat she posed with her existence. The confidence terrified Ada.

At first, Ada believed that they were laying a trap for the woman. There was no way she would be able to walk through the sticky liquid in those extremely tall heels without slipping. But as soon as the woman stepped into the growing light-brown pool, she showed no sign of stopping. Strolling through the liquid without blinking an eye, the woman never missed a beat in her perfect strut.

Without an explanation, Louis abandoned Ada's side and rushed forward. Panic gripped Ada's heart as she watched him slip on the spilled soda and fall backwards on the ground. But the momentum from rushing forward sent him sliding on the ground towards the woman. Twisting around, Louis slid into the woman from his side. She toppled forward, not making a single movement to save herself. The woman's face made a hard contact with the linoleum floor, a thick thud sound following once her skull slammed to the ground. It sounded like a bowling ball was dropped. Louis quickly climbed onto the fallen woman's back with his knife in hand.

"Just hold still, Lady," He mocked as he pushed her cherry red hair to expose her neck. "You literally won't feel a thing."

Lady twitched slightly as Louis shoved his knife into the top of her spine and yanked upwards. Watching the violent act, Ada screamed and nearly dropped the giant bottle of soda she was shaking. Bile rose in her throat. Before Ada could throw up whatever little remained in her stomach from lunch, the woman bucked Louis from her back. Landing in the pool of soda, he pulled himself to his elbows as the woman rose to her feet. Without a second thought, Lady faced Louis. Ada stared in awe at the woman's injury. No blood was seeping from it. A jagged cut traced the top of her spine to the base of her skull where her cherry red hairline ended, but somehow there was nothing to indicate that a grown man attempted to gut the woman. Just flaps of skin opening to a darkness Ada couldn't identify.

Ada kind of felt like throwing up again.

"You! The soda! Right into her neck!" Louis screamed. The woman lifted a spiked heel high above his chest. "Now!"

With a deep panicked breath, Ada released the cap. A high pressure stream of soda escaped and sprayed the woman's back. Ada did her best to aim for the bloodless knife cut. As the liquid touched the exposed wound, sparks jumped from it. A violent seizure overtook the woman. Louis rolled out of the way as the woman collapsed in his place, indefinitely shaking and twisting into unnatural positions that no human should ever endure.

"Oh my god," Ada said. The bottle was done spraying, but she couldn't bring herself to let go of it. Her fingers gripped the bottle tight enough to cause indents in the plastic. "We need to call an ambulance. Or the police! We need to-"

"We need to get the hell out of here." Louis grabbed Ada's bicep again and shoved her in the opposite direction from the seizing woman. "She's either going to blow or get pissed," he checked behind them quickly as he pushed Ada forward. "-and you don't wanna be around for either."

"No!" Ada pulled her arm from his hold. "What is going on?! Did we just murder a woman? Did I help you kill someone? Oh my god-"

"Would you calm down?!" Louis interrupted. The woman continued to seize in unnatural positions behind them. He waited until Ada had slowed her breathing before opening his mouth again. "Now, for the record...she attacked me first so this was all self-defense and I'll contest that in court."

"Oh my god!" Ada dropped her face into her hands. "I just helped murder a woman! Great. This is exactly what I needed-"

"Hey, look," Louis said. "You can deal with your life issues later but right now we need to get out of here or else-"

"Or else the cops will find us?!" Ada said. "I barely even know your name, dude! All I know is that you tried hitting on me in the fucking ice cream aisle!"

"Who the fuck said I was hitting on you?"

"Then what was that fate line for?!"

"I was making sure you weren't her!" Louis jabbed his knife in the direction of the now limp lady laying on the floor. "Androids can't be programmed to believe in fate. It's a fucking paradox to them!"

Ending their argument prematurely, the pair froze. Louis's statement was only a partial cause for their shared panic. Ada would've loved to keep ripping into this guy who just forced her into a shared manslaughter charge, but the woman's lack of movement halted her rage for the time being. Not looking away from Ada, Louis pressed his lips together and pointed his knife at the woman again.

"She's not moving, is she?"

Terrified, Ada shook her head, confirming the worst.

Louis exhaled.

"Well shit."

The woman sat up straight. Her head sat crooked on her neck at a 90 degree angle. Louis and Ada watched with horror as her head methodically snapped back into place and, with a soft whirring noise, she looked over at the pair. Her cherry red hair was frazzled and matted with warm soda, but her makeup remained pristine. Ada could now see how synthetic this woman was and it was freaking her out.

"All threats to Project Kamana must be eliminated," the woman stated, her voice scratching against itself in a demented echo. "All threats to Project Kamana must be-"

"Yeah, yeah we heard you the first time, Lady," Louis said. "Now excuse us while we run for our lives."

Before Ada could question him, Louis grabbed her arm and bolted from the aisle. She managed to keep up with his sprint, the threat of death making it easier for her to ignore her sore muscles. Louis led her towards the end aisle closest to the exit and dragged Ada into it. Hope rose in her chest as the exit came into sight. But as they reached the middle of the aisle, a loud crash echoed from a couple aisles away. They stopped at the noise. Before Ada could even consider what the noise could've been, it happened again. Then again. And again. Faster with each moment.

"Shit!" Louis pulled Ada to the start of the aisle. He ran in a dead sprint and Ada was grateful he was half-dragging her along; she wouldn't have been able to keep up otherwise.

As soon as Louis left the aisle, he aggressively yanked Ada towards him. She stumbled into his arms as the aisles collided into each other, crashing to the floor in a tremendous roar of metal. Ada's ears rang with the echo of the crash and the beat of her thundering heart pounding with the panic of non-stop running for her life. Louis released her before she was ready to be exposed again and ran away. Ada shot a glance across the store to see the woman was standing near the start of the crashed shelves, looking disheveled but uninjured. She was aiming a gun, first at Louis, but when Louis bolted out of sight, the woman aimed her weapon at Ada instead.

"Shit!" Ada shouted.

That was the fastest Ada ever ran in her life. Fuck her sore legs, she was *not* about to die because some white dude left her for dead with his problems. This might work though. Ada could easily get away if the woman's focus was on Louis instead. She could run home and call the police -

The police! They could help! Ada scrambled into the produce section. Checking over her shoulder, she pulled her phone out and punched in the first half of her passcode. Before she could dial 911, an apple smacked her shoulder. Ada traced the source of the throw back to Louis with his head popped over the apple display. He motioned her to join him and, in her panic of being discovered by the woman, she ran over. Louis sat on the floor when she reached him, his back against the display as he took a massive bite from another apple. When Ada sat next to him, he threw his half-eaten apple to the side and held an open palm to her.

"I need your cell phone," Louis said, mouth still half-full of fruit.

"I'm already calling the police."

"And I'm saving our lives," Louis urged. "Now c'mon give me your phone."

With a nervous exhale, Ada slammed her phone into his hand. He examined it carefully.

"Okay so who are *you* going to call to save us?" She asked.

"No one." Louis pulled his knife out again. "I save myself."

Using the blade of his knife, he pried the phone apart. In any other situation, Ada would've killed him. It took her months to save for that phone, but this was an actual life or death situation. Ada had to trust him whether she wanted to or not. She peeked over the apple display to check for their crazed hunter. The woman was nowhere in sight.

"I don't see her," Ada whispered. "Do you think she gave up?"

"It's not in her programming to give up," Louis muttered as he fiddled with her phone. "Did you see how she perked right back up after a direct attack on her circuit board? Persistence is the only thing that damn bot is good for. God forbid Lady to actually prove some use besides putting me through hell."

"What are you even talking about?" Ada asked. "Programming? Circuit board?"

With a sigh, Louis stopped messing with her disassembled phone to look at Ada like she was an idiot.

"That thing that's been trying to kill us? That's Lady. She's an android." He stated, annoyed that Ada somehow didn't automatically accept that the existence of androids was common knowledge. He returned to work on tinkering with Ada's phone with his knife. "She was designed to provide hospice care, but now she wears tacky clothes and fails at killing me. Amazing what a career change can do to a robot."

"And....who are you?" Ada asked.

"Nobody," Louis said. "I'm just a guy you met at the wrong place at the wrong time who's gonna save your life."

"Louis Ventura." The woman's scratching voice echoed through the produce aisle. "Show yourself and there will be no repercussions for the girl."

Looking vaguely annoyed that the robot revealed his identity, Louis fiddled with Ada's phone for another moment.

"Alright, just give me a minute," He shouted.

"You will not have a minute," Lady said. "You will have approximately ten seconds to expose yourself to ensure the girl's safety."

"You know, that's an offensive phrasing of words for us humans," Louis said. "Mind rewording that?"

"You are delaying your execution," Lady said. "All threats to Project Kamana must be eliminated."

"Alright, alright..." Louis stood with Ada's phone in one hand. He raised both hands in surrender. "I was making a final phone call. You know, settling my estates and all of that."

"Consider your estates settled, Louis Ventura," The gun clicked in Lady's hand. "If you do not know where Allen Paz is located, your use for remaining alive has expired and you will be eliminated."

"Just one more thing..." Louis held his index finger up. "When they updated your OS, did they update the locking mechanism on your optic aim function?"

"Yes," Lady said. "I am now able to eliminate threats to Project Kamana much more efficiently."

"That's right because when I try to save myself, you'll be able to lock onto my movement." Louis smiled. "I guess I'm fucked then."

"Your hypothesis is correct," Lady said. "Goodbye, Louis Ventura."

Ada flinched as Louis suddenly threw Ada's phone at the robot. The gun fired. Louis fell on top of Ada. She wanted to scream at the fact a dead man was laying on her, but she could feel his heart hammering against his chest. Before she could make sense of it, an explosion occurred in the air above them. Silent shock waves rippled through Ada's bones. Glass shattered all around the produce section, the sound of tearing metal accompanying the twinkle of broken glass falling onto the floor.

When the explosion stopped, both Ada and Louis peeked over the apple display at the same time. The entire produce section was destroyed. Fruits and vegetables were mashed with broken pieces of glass spread across them. Water from the automatic watering system flowed onto the floor in thin rivers. The sound of early 2000's music continued to sing through the intercom system.

"See?" Louis said. "That's why I don't use anything with lithium batteries. Dangerous."

"Is she dead?" Ada breathed.

"Maybe?" Louis said. "I don't know. I honestly didn't expect that to work."

Horrified, Ada shot him a glare.

"I thought you knew what you were doing!"

"Well 'how to destroy killer robots' isn't exactly something you can Google, sweetheart," Louis said, pulling himself to his feet.

"Oh my god." Ada ran her fingers through her hair. "I was trusting you! *With my life!*"

"You must not like your life that much then." Louis helped Ada to her feet. "Let's go."

Louis pulled Ada towards the exit. She resisted every urge to look behind her. Something in the depths of her soul told her that his makeshift phone bomb didn't work, but they were leaving the store. They were escaping. If anything, Ada was going to get as far away from these psychos as possible. They could continue their little cat and mouse game by themselves, Ada wanted no part of it. Luckily, they reached the parking lot without any further sign of the android's survival.

Soreness returned to Ada's muscles as they embraced the murky Pittsburgh summer air. It was relatively empty in the parking lot. A couple abandoned vehicles and shopping carts littered the asphalt, but for the most part only Ada's dinky Geo Metro and a shiny looking Camaro sat in the parking lot. They headed towards Ada's car.

"Look I don't care where you go, but stay out of this," Louis said. "You're lucky I even helped you out this time."

"Okay." Ada nodded, the weight of the situation finally bearing down on her. She trembled slightly. Someone tried to *kill* her tonight. A gun was aimed at her. All of this because of a pint of ice cream. Stacy could go fuck herself the next time she needed a player for her slow-pitch team, that's all Ada could decide.

"Another thing," Louis said. "Don't you dare-"

Before he could finish, the Geo Metro exploded.

Heat from the flames washed over Ada and Louis as they both rushed to shield themselves from the blast. Scrambling from what remained of her car, Ada looked back at the grocery store. Lady was standing in the exit. Half of her body was a mangled metal skeleton, the other half appeared like a melted mannequin. The cherry red hair remained as a web of tangles on top of the half skeleton, half melted face. Her gun remained pointed at the duo.

"Go!" Louis pushed Ada towards the Camaro. "Go, go, *go!*"

They ran towards the muscle car in a dead sprint. Bullets ricocheted off of the asphalt behind their every step. Ada kept her head down and hid behind the Camaro on the passenger side as Louis struggled to pull his keys out. He managed to unlock the door and dive in just as a bullet made impact with the driver's side window, glass showering the inside of the car. Louis started the car as Ada slammed the passenger door shut behind her. He didn't even check for seat belts before speeding off, the remainder of Lady's bullets finding their way into his back window.

"What the fuck?!" Ada screamed as she put on her seatbelt. "Why the fuck is she trying to kill us? Why the fuck is she trying to kill *you?* What the fuck-"

"Would you calm down?!" Louis shouted, gripping the wheel tightly. He drove through the semi-busy Pittsburgh streets at an alarming speed. "I've got it handled. You just need to stay out of it."

"No shit I do!" Ada screamed. "I don't want any part of this shitshow!"

Taking a deep breath, Ada fell back into the seat and ran her hands through her thick hair, trying to catch her breath. It was much easier to relax about the situation when she absolved herself of any responsibility. She absolutely did not need Louis Ventura's problems in her life. After everything else she'd been through, everything else she fought to get to this moment, she didn't need to worry about killer robots on top of everything else. Not now. Not when she was so close to figuring it out.

"I'm dropping you off at this corner," Louis said. He flipped a plastic rectangle at her. "Use this credit card to reimburse yourself for your losses. Phone, car, clothes, ice cream, whatever. I'll cancel it in 24 hours, so don't take too much time."

Four years ago, Ada would've played the modesty game and pretend that she didn't need the money. But Ada wasn't an independent adult four years ago. Ada didn't have rent four years ago. Ada wasn't completely on her own, cut off from most support and without any capital to claim four years ago. Her emergency savings could barely cover a tank of gas, let alone replacements for everything she lost tonight. She grabbed the card and turned to Louis.

"Lady or whatever that thing is won't be able to find me...right?"

"I'm going to properly dismantle her tonight," Louis said. "You'll be fine."

She took another deep breath as Louis parked at the corner. Before she could escape, Louis grabbed her wrist.

"Don't tell anyone about tonight," Louis said. "They have ears everywhere."

"They?" Ada asked. "Who's they?"

"The others," Louis said. "You didn't honestly think Lady was the only one, did you?"

With a wicked smirk, he unlocked the door. Ada forced herself to step out of the car. As soon as she shut the passenger door, the Camaro sped off into greater downtown Pittsburgh. The few passersby in the area gave her odd looks as she stood frozen on that corner, covered in soda and sweat. All of them were unaware that an android tried to brutally murder her and the stranger she met in the ice cream aisle of the grocery store. Ada looked at the black credit card in her hands before looking down the street that Louis Ventura disappeared into. Then, she looked in the opposite direction half-expecting Lady to show up. The android didn't. Ada watched as a couple crossed the street, holding hands and lost in their own little world. They had no idea. No one had any idea.

"What the fuck?" Ada said out loud. No one responded.

<!---"Don't oversleep, Ada." Ruchira Kakar, always the stern businesswoman, stood in front of her daughter with her arms crossed over her proper business suit. "Set enough alarms to wake the entire building if you have to. Talk to your professors if you're struggling, and find a study group. College isn't going to be the breeze that high school was, and you're going to have to actually work, understood?"

"She'll be fine" Hiyan Kakar flopped onto Ada's pathetic dorm bed with a wide smile that curved his thick, black mustache. "Ada is a smart cookie...just like her mom!"

"Flattery gets you nowhere, Hiyan."

"Yes, but a couple shots at a college bar during a Bears game will do wonders!" Hiyan teased. "Ada, you know your mother and I met in college right? You could meet your future husband here too!"

"No! No boys!" Ruchira scolded. "You need to study. If you wanted a boyfriend, you could've gone to any of the schools back home."

"That's a bit of an outdated mindset, don't you think?" Ada asked. "I can get my PhD and my MRS at the same time, you know."

"Not with how much we're paying for this school you're not," Ruchira said. With a teasing smile, she walked over and offered her eldest daughter a kiss on her forehead. "I'm only joking, sweetheart. We're very proud of you. I know you're going to do great here, with or without a boyfriend...but preferably without. You're supposed to study and get placed with a good programming job after school, hm? Remember?"

"Yes, Mom, I remember," Ada said. "No distractions."

"Good. You're too good of a programmer to throw away such a talent on something as silly as boys," Ruchira said, petting Ada's hair softly. Ada was surprised to see her mom's eyes grow soft as they shared a long look. Was her mom worried about her? Her mom was never worried about anything. What was there to worry about?

Her mom was right - Ada was a brilliant programmer. She'd succeed in college like she succeeded in high school, with or without a boyfriend. There was nothing to worry about. After a short moment, Ruchira sighed and checked her watch. "Hiyan, darling, we'll have to hit the road if we want to make our flight home. The airport will be crazy at this time."

"Don't be afraid to call us whenever and however much you want," Hiyan said as he bounced himself off the bed. "Especially during the football games. It's no Bears, but it's good enough."

21

"I'll do my best, Dad!" Ada kissed his cheek. Both of her parents made their way to her door. "Have a safe flight!"

"We'll miss you!" Hiyan shouted over his shoulder. "We love you!"

"Remember to study!" Ruchira pointed at her. "Make us proud! You're too smart to fail, Ada." -->

CHAPTER TWO

A whirr of grinding metal woke Ada up the next morning. Panicking, she grabbed the steak knife hidden under her pillow. Ada stayed true to her word. She didn't tell a single soul about Lady the android or Louis Ventura or why she felt like death would be a better solution than moving a single aching muscle. Mainly because Sammy was already asleep by the time Ada got home. If she wasn't still frozen in shock over the night's events, she would've told her taxi driver. But she didn't tell the taxi driver that she paid with Louis's credit card, and she didn't wake Sammy who would've called her story bullshit anyway. Instead, she locked every single window in their pathetic studio apartment, double locked the door, and hid a steak knife under her pillow before exhaustion from the night's events claimed her to a dreamless sleep. The knife was the closest thing they had to a weapon in that dumpy apartment, except for pepper spray, but Ada figured pepper spray wouldn't do shit against a psychotic, murdering robot.

Looking to the source of the whirring metal noise, Ada released a deep sigh and released the knife. The noise was just Sammy, who turned the garbage disposal on by accident instead of the light over the sink. Sammy fixed her error and flipped the garbage disposal off again. Sinking back into her pillow, Ada tried to will herself to fall back asleep. Sleeping was nice. There were considerably less problems in the world when Ada slept. But she couldn't sleep. Not when flashes of heavy grocery store shelving falling on top of her flashed through her mind as soon as she closed her eyes. If it wasn't the grocery store shelving, it was the gun pointing straight at her, locking onto her every movement, and she didn't even have her phone. She couldn't even call her parents to leave a final apology. Before she could allow the sweet release of five minutes of extra sleep to claim her, a pillow landed on top of Ada. She opened her eyes as Sammy hopped onto the opposite arm rest and sat down, facing Ada.

"Good morning, sleepy-head!" Sammy signed, an extra bounce to the final touch of her hand movement. "Are you getting out of bed today?"

With a groan, Ada shifted her body so both of her hands could motion "maybe". Sammy furrowed her eyebrows, made a fist, and threw the fist towards her wrist to indicate a stern "yes".

Rolling her eyes, Ada lifted her hands again to sign to her roommate.

"If you make breakfast, I'll get out of bed," Ada signed.

"Will you eat it?" Sammy asked in sign language.

"Yes."

Ada's hand movement was lackluster.

"Bullshit!" Sammy signed with a smile. "Don't lie to me."

"Fine. I'll eat a little," Ada signed.

"You'll eat a little?" Sammy signed, looking incredulous. Ada nodded. With a shrug, Sammy hopped off the arm rest. "Then I guess I'm making breakfast."

It was still a mystery to Ada why Sammy even bothered taking care of her pathetic ass. Back when her life wasn't a dumpster fire, Ada barely gave Sammy the time of day. She was just one of Daniel's old high school buddy's flings who randomly appeared at their weekly wing night during college. Sure, Ada learned some ASL from YouTube to communicate with her during their next wing night when no one else even tried, and actually kept up the practice to improve their communication until Sammy eventually broke up with Daniel's friend, but that shouldn't have been enough for Sammy to take her in and let her sleep on her couch practically rent free months later. Not only that, but Sammy was the only person in the world who currently gave a damn about Ada's well-being and actively took part in its upkeep.

Student loans had nothing on Ada's debt to Sammy's kindness.

"Ada!" Sammy shouted verbally, her voice a little louder than needed.

Ada sat up to look at Sammy standing over the stove.

"Eggs?" Sammy signed, eyebrow raised.

After Ada indicated "yes", Sammy cracked a couple eggs into the frying pan.

Rubbing her eyes, Ada considered her next course of action. She knew she needed to tell Sammy about the killer robots possibly after her, especially since it affected the safety of their apartment, but she also promised Louis she wouldn't tell a soul. Despite the fact he didn't know everything about defeating killer robots, he seemed to know enough to stay alive. If staying alive meant not telling a soul about a potentially traumatic experience, then Ada might be willing to repress the memory. With a sigh, Ada lifted herself from her couch with the intention of getting ready for the day and pretending the night before never happened. It wouldn't be the first time. Out of the corner of Ada's eye, Ada could see Sammy wave for her attention. Sighing, Ada turned towards her roommate.

"What happened to you last night?" Sammy signed. A mischievous smile overtook her face. "Were you with a boy?"

The best part about having a deaf roommate is that Ada could come in as late as she wanted to without making a big deal of it. The worst part was that it was impossible to lie to a master of reading facial expressions. When Ada's eyes glazed over in hesitation at Sammy's accusation, Sammy gasped and signed frantically.

"You were with a boy!"

Easier than the truth.

"I met him at the grocery store," Ada signed back. "It's not a big deal."

"Not a big deal? Hold on." Sammy went to shift the eggs before they burnt and Ada waited. Sammy turned back to her with her hands in the air. "Not a big deal? Ada, you've been sleeping on my couch for over a year now and you have shown no interest in any-one since you broke up with that one guy-"

"Daniel," Ada said the name out loud and spelled it out.

"Whatever, the point is that this is great!" A huge smile formed on Sammy's face. "You're back in the game!"

Ada rolled her eyes as she signed.

"Nice try. I'm never going to see him again."

"Yes you are," Sammy signed with one hand as she messed with the frying pan. She turned back with both of her hands. "Baby steps, Ada. You got off the couch, you got a job, you went out, and now it's time to find a boyfriend."

"I don't need a boyfriend," Ada signed. "I don't even have any friends other than you."

"What about Stacy from work? She's nice."

"Stacy from work can go fuck herself."

"Harsh."

Stacy from work was the whole reason Ada was in this mess any-way. If she hadn't insisted on putting Ada on her slowpitch softball team, Ada would've never felt compelled to go to the grocery store for the ice cream to make herself feel better. If Ada didn't go to that damn grocery store at that exact time, she wouldn't have been in the crossfire of Lady and Louis Ventura's fight.

"Fuck," Ada said out loud, dropping her face into her hands. "My car."

Unaware of Ada's new panic, Sammy picked up the frying pan and dished scrambled eggs onto the paper plates set on their rickety kitchen table. When Sammy sat down at the table, Ada joined her.

"Can I get a ride to work today?" Ada asked.

Sammy furrowed her eyebrows as she chewed on a mouthful of eggs.

"What happened to your car?"

Blown up by a killer robot.

"Accident," Ada signed, keeping her face as neutral as she could.

Releasing a hum, Sammy stared at Ada, deciding whether or not to call Ada out on her bullshit. Finally, she swallowed her mouthful of food and ate another bite of eggs before facing Ada.

"I've got a lunch date," Sammy signed. "You're going to have to call a car."

Ada winced. "Can I borrow your phone?"

"What happened to your phone?" Sammy signed with a raised eyebrow.

Blown up as a makeshift bomb to destroy the killer robot that blew up Ada's car.

"Lost it," Ada signed. "Must have left it in my car when I dropped it off at the shop."

That was one lie too many. Dropping her fork, Sammy broke out into a wide smile.

"You slept with him, didn't you?" Sammy signed in excitement. "You fucked grocery store guy!"

"No!" Ada closed her index and middle finger against her thumb so hard, it almost sounded like a snap.

"Yes you did, you whore!" Sammy looked proud. "You left your car and phone at his place, didn't you?"

"No!"

"Bullshit."

"Fine! Want to know what happened?" Ada asked. Sammy nodded excitedly. "I went to the store for ice cream and got attacked by…" Ada realized she didn't know the sign for android so she had to spell it out with the ASL alphabet. "…a robot."

Sammy's face twisted in confusion before she pulled her phone out and typed into it. She presented the phone to Ada. In an empty text message field, Sammy had typed "Robot?"

Ada nodded. Sammy gave her another look. Then she motioned her arms up and down in a straight pattern, as if she were a robot. Ada signed "Yes."

At that, Sammy shook her head.

"You know I won't judge you if you fucked a guy you met in the grocery store," Sammy signed. "I fucked a guy I met on the bus once. No judgment."

"No!" Ada signed. "It's the truth. I nearly died! I didn't fuck anyone last night."

"What a shame," Sammy signed. "You could use a good fuck." She took another bite of her eggs before dropping her fork to sign again. "Take my car to work. I will cancel lunch."

Nodding, Ada added a dose of sriracha to her eggs before digging into them. Sammy probably thought Ada was entering one of her "episodes" again. Granted, Sammy's concern was well-meaning with good reason, but Ada hated feeling that she was still dependent on Sammy's care. Mostly, she was tired of still being susceptible to and expected to have another "episode".

Sammy cleaned after breakfast as Ada finally got ready for the day. She took her medicine with a solid swig of water before jumping into the shower. The warm water felt good on her aching muscles. Now that she had told Sammy about the night before, it no longer held a looming guilt over Ada. The shower was the final touch in scrubbing the night's events, washing away the confirmation that it happened. It didn't matter Sammy didn't believe her; the truth was at least out of Ada and it was one less thing for Ada to concern herself with.

By the time Ada got out of the shower, Sammy was already at work for the day, which meant dubstep blasted from every speaker in the room. Ada did her best to ignore the music and search for her work uniform among the piles of clothes on the floor. It was hard for her to not be annoyed. Dubstep was one of the few things that Sammy could "hear" and Ada should let her have it. But at the same time, Ada was the one who had to regularly deal with the neighbors' complaints which made her incredibly annoyed at the situation.

As she shuffled through the piles of clothes, a soft thumping sound banged at the door. Ada could only hope it was the mental hospital or the police finally arriving to take away her roommate for playing music at that high of a stupid level, but it was most likely Wendy from down the hall. Ada willingly ignored it, knowing she can make a faster getaway from her nosy neighbor if she looked like she was on her way to work.

"Pittsburgh Police, open up."

Oh wow it was actually the police. Ada was sort of half joking about that.

Wait.

The Pittsburgh Police.

Ada helped destroy a grocery store. With a guy who may or may not be a murderer.

That was probably a crime the police would find out about.

Fuck.

Scrambling from the piles of clothes, Ada fell on the hardwood floor in her attempt to get somewhere, *anywhere,* from where she currently was. She needed to get out of the apartment. How was she going to get out of the apartment? Fire escape. Right. That worked in movies, but did Sammy and Ada even have a fire escape from their apartment? Wait, hold on. Ada was still in her pajamas. Sweatpants and a tank top, but still. She didn't even have a *bra* on. Not a big deal for Ada, but if she was going to act like a civilized human who definitely wasn't involved in a crime she barely committed, then she should probably not look like someone who escaped the police from the fire escape of her dinky apartment. A pen smacked her arm. Ada turned to Sammy who was sitting at her massive two-monitor display desktop computer. Information from a business sat on one screen while Sammy's graphic design work sat on the other. As soon as Sammy and Ada's eyes met, Sammy signed "What's wrong with you?"

"The police are at the door!" Ada signed frantically.

Sammy looked from the door to Ada. "Well, answer it."

Another heavy knock at the door.

With Sammy's dubstep blaring from the speakers, it was impossible to pretend no one was home. Groaning, Ada ran her fingers through her hair before signing to Sammy.

"I can't! They're going to arrest me for crimes I didn't commit!" Ada signed with raised eyebrows. "I was in the wrong place at the wrong time and now the police will think I'm a terrorist because I'm brown! Can you buy me some time until I think of something?"

"Genius. Let the deaf girl stall the police." Sammy rolled her eyes. "Did you ever consider that they're here for that car accident you were in?"

Ada wasn't in a car accident. Ada was in a store while it was getting destroyed by a psychotic robot and some guy who thought he was qualified to fight the robot. She was fucked.

"Just a minute," Ada shouted to the door.

Surrendering to her fate, she walked to the bathroom. She grabbed her medicine and stuck the pill bottle into her pants. Ada had never been arrested before. Never been to the principal's office, never got detention, only got called to the Dean's Office once...She had no idea how long this would take, but she knew she couldn't go more than two days without her medicine. She tried to, once. She actually made it a week, but she didn't think about that time. Never again. If she came quietly, they would never suspect she had the pills on her and they wouldn't confiscate them. Relaxing, she walked to the front door. Nothing could be worse than when she was without her medicine. She was still in her ratty sweatpants and an old tank top with no bra, but looks didn't matter when you're on the verge of getting arrested for terrorism. At least she showered. The thought crossed her mind that there was a chance her parents might pay for bail. It was a slim, *slim* chance that they would pay bail, but the shame of having a daughter arrested might compel them to do so. Still, the pills were coming with her. Bail may not be posted for another week.

Opening the door, Ada was no longer as calm as she thought she was before. Two people in suits and police badges dangling from their neck stood at the door. The woman was short with platinum blonde hair light enough to be considered white tied into a tight bun that pulled painfully from her forehead. She was nothing but business and edge. The dark eye patch she wore over her left eye didn't ease the intimidation radiating off of this woman. Faint scars, almost like burn marks, surrounded the eye patch. The right eye, dark enough to practically be black, glared at Ada with disdain. If anyone was going to arrest Ada, it would be this woman and she would have no hesitations about it. Then there was the guy. Tall and lanky, his brown hair tufted out in messy patches despite a clear attempt to tame it and his suit fit him surprisingly well. His brown eyes caught the light and twinkled. They weren't the black, emotionless void the lady's eyes were. He was kind. Ada hadn't said a word to him yet, but she knew he would be kind. Good cop, bad cop, she assumed. At least the good cop looked authentically good. The bad cop looked like she might murder Ada if given the chance.

"Ada Kakar?" The male cop asked, a certain charm to his lilted voice. "This is Detective Freya and I'm Detective Gates Hopper. We're with the FBI. Do you mind if we step inside and ask a few questions?"

Something told Ada that Detective Freya was going to step inside either way. The fact that they were FBI and not regular Pittsburgh police also unnerved Ada. She didn't know a lot about how crime worked, but she figured the FBI must be a bigger deal than local enforcement.

"Sure," Ada said, struggling to hide her new panic. She walked inside and the detectives followed her, slowly taking in the studio apartment. Detective Freya scanned the room as if she was looking for more evidence to pin against Ada. Meanwhile, Detective Gates Hopper put his hands into his pockets and examined the art on the walls with more curiosity than analysis.

"Sorry for making you guys wait," Ada said. "I wasn't paying attention and my roommate is deaf so neither of us heard you."

Detective Freya snorted. "Yeah. I would be too if I listened to music this loud."

"No, I mean she's actually deaf," Ada corrected.

Detective Freya didn't seem to care.

While the detectives checked the area, Ada walked to Sammy at her desk and signed for her to turn her music down. Sammy turned it off completely and worked as Ada returned to the officers.

"I like the paintings." Pulling his hand out of his pocket, Detective Hopper pointed between Ada and a piece hung on the wall. "Did you...?"

"Oh no. These are all Sammy's," Ada said. "I'm not an artist."

"Are you anything special at all?" Detective Freya snapped.

Ada stared at her blankly. "I'm...uh..."

"Excuse my colleague. We've been having some rough nights with our investigation," Detective Hopper said. "Can you please sit so we can talk?"

Nodding, Ada tried her best to make sure the pills in her pants didn't make a noise as she sat at the kitchen table. Detective Freya remained standing at the other end of the table, glaring at Ada with her uncovered eye. Ada swallowed hard and tried to ignore Detective Freya's stare. Oblivious to his partner's malice, Detective Hopper pulled his phone out of his inner suit jacket pocket. He tapped something on it.

"Now..." He presented the phone to Ada. "Do you recognize this man?"

There was a hood hiding the top of his head, an extension of the hoodie layered underneath his leather jacket, but there was no mistake as Louis Ventura's dull green eyes stared right at the camera. He was standing at a crowded corner in an anonymous city, hands in pocket, well aware that someone was taking a picture of him despite the distance between him and the photographer.

"No," Ada stated, the lie coming easier than expected.

"His name is Louis Ventura." Detective Hopper stuck the phone back into his jacket. "He's wanted for four charges of assault with a deadly weapon, three charges of attempted homicide, two charges of theft-"

"Reckless driving, public endangerment-" Detective Freya added.

"-and destruction of private and public property," Detective Hopper finished. "This man is dangerous and we have reason to believe you know something about him."

"Security footage from a grocery store vandalized last night shows that you were with him at the time of the store's destruction," Detective Freya clarified. "We're not pressing any charges against you, but we do want to know how you're affiliated with him."

"I'm not," Ada said. "I was just there and he saved me from a woman who wanted to kill us."

"Louis Ventura is not a hero," Detective Hopper said. "His reasons for saving you had ulterior motives and we want to get to the bottom of it. He loaned you his personal credit card, yes?"

Ada snapped her head up. "How did you know that?"

"Credit cards aren't private property when they belong to felons, sweetheart," Detective Freya said. "Now tell us where he went."

"I don't know where he went," Ada said. "He said he was going to go after the woman in the store who tried to kill us and end it. He told me not to worry about it."

"So he confessed that he was going to murder a woman and you didn't go to the police about it?" Detective Freya asked with a cruel smile. "Seems kind of sketchy, unless you were in alliance with him."

"No it wasn't like that!" Ada exclaimed. "The woman...she wasn't human. It's not, like, real murder."

"Wasn't human?" Detective Hopper asked. He gave his partner a nervous glance that she ignored before turning back to Ada. "What do you mean, not human?"

He looked at Ada with an incredulous stare. Ada felt stupid as soon as she said it, but it was the truth. Besides, maybe if they declared her insane, she could avoid jail. People got out of jail with insanity pleas all of the time, right?

"She was a robot," Ada said. "An android, technically speaking."

The detectives stared as they realized what Ada was saying.

"You're joking." Detective Freya snorted.

"I'm not," Ada said as she turned to Detective Freya. "I saw her with my own eyes. I tried to dismantle her microchip, her exoskeleton was exposed-"

"Have you considered that you were in shock at the time?" Detective Hopper suggested. "Hallucinations are common for victims of traumatic events."

"Listen, I wasn't top of my class for computer science at Carnegie Mellon for nothing," Ada said. "I know what I saw. I denied it at the time, but the evidence is irrefutable. The woman that attacked Louis Ventura and myself was a robot, and I wouldn't be surprised if the charges on his record were all from robots as well."

The silence was unbearable. Ada hadn't felt that much passion in her heart in years. She had no idea what compelled her to protect Louis Ventura, but she did. She even put her own sanity on the line to protect him. She supposed that there was nothing left to give him. He saved her life in that grocery store and even gave her money to replace everything she lost in the fight. Maybe she decided that he didn't need to be the criminal he insisted on presenting himself as. Maybe she was giving him the second chance she knew she was grateful to have.

Either way, it was likely one of the stupidest things she decided to do in her life.

"Miss Kakar, it appears that you're still in shock over the event," Detective Hopper said. "If needed, we can give you a day or two to recover. We'll call into your place of work, supply a hotel room, accommodate all expenses-"

"We need answers *now,* Gates." Detective Freya slammed her fist on the table. Something snapped with a loud crack. With a short jump, Ada looked at the tabletop. A jagged cut cut across the table's exterior where Detective Freya had hit the table. It was a cheap table from the corner of some random street, but not *that* cheap. Before Ada could examine it further, the detective pointed an accusing finger at Ada which forced her to look up. "You are in alliance with Louis Ventura and you know *exactly* where he is."

"I told you! He's going after the robot who tried to kill us in the grocery store!" Ada matched the volume of the detective's voice. "If you find the robot, you'll find Louis. The robot's name is Lady. Half of her-"

"You're full of shit," Detective Freya stood, her short frame towering over Ada menacingly. "Lady is *dead*. She was murdered by Louis Ventura with her body thrown into the Allegheny River. If you were aware of this crime and did not report it to the police, I am hereby authorized to detain and arrest-"

There was a knock at the door.

Unless Ada and Sammy happened to accidentally order separate takeouts, this was extremely rare for two separate people knocking at their door in one day.

Detective Hopper, who until this point was just staring at his partner in horrified silence, looked at Ada.

"Were you expecting anyone?" He asked.

She shook her head.

With a solemn expression, Detective Hopper nodded at his partner. She nodded back, her exposed eye glistening with a controlled anger. In silent synchronization, they both pulled guns from their holsters. Detective Hopper looked at Ada.

"I want you to open the door," He said quietly. "We'll stay hidden until the situation is clear. If there is a present danger, we will act. Understood?"

Ada nodded nervously. Detective Hopper hid behind the open bathroom door. Detective Freya was already crouched behind the couch. Meanwhile Sammy, with her back to the scene, worked diligently on her graphic design project, blissfully unaware of the potential chaos behind her. Ada was too scared to warn Sammy about the potential threat.

Who did the detectives think it was? Actually, she knew who the detectives thought it was. How and why he was at her apartment, she had no idea.

With her heart hammering hard against her chest, Ada opened the door. Sure enough, Louis Ventura was leaning against the door frame, still wearing that stupid leather jacket in the dead heat of a Pittsburgh June. There was a smug smirk on his face.

"Heard you were talking shit," Louis said, his eyes locked onto Ada. "Thought I would check it out."

Ada momentarily forgot about the two detectives waiting to pounce on Louis.

"Wait...what?" She asked.

"You know, you say that a lot for someone who managed to make it into Carnegie Mellon, from what I could overhear." Pulling himself from the doorframe, Louis pushed past Ada to walk inside. "Hopefully you used a more extensive vocabulary for someone of your supposed intelligence for the nice 'detectives' or cops or whatever that came here to interrogate you."

"Enough." Detective Hopper stepped out from his hiding spot with his gun aimed at Louis. "Put your hands up and step away from the woman."

Spinning around, confusion crossed Louis's face as he faced the detective. After a moment, he cracked a wide smile and put his hands up in surrender.

"Well, aren't you a pretty boy?" Louis said. "Honestly, I wasn't expecting a real detective to be here, and I sort of apologize for the intrusion. But, not really because I actually put some effort into this plan this time."

"A plan, huh?" Detective Freya stood from her spot behind the couch, aiming her gun at Louis with more ferocity than her partner. "You always have a plan, don't you?"

Dropping his hands, Louis turned to the voice with an even bigger smile.

"Eyepatch! You're already out on the field again?" Louis exclaimed. "That's a helluva turnaround for you. I wasn't expecting you to be back for another month or so." He looked back to Detective Hopper and jabbed a thumb at Detective Freya. "Now *she's* who I was looking for. Again, sort of sorry for the interruption but, once again, not really."

Detective Freya's face didn't move a muscle.

"You set us up," She stated. "You knew we were tracking your credit card so you gave it to the girl so we would follow her here and lead you straight to us."

"God, I love that you're smarter than Lady," Louis said. "Poor thing barely even knew when I was stalling. Luckily, you were built with the Kamana program integration rather than shoehorning it in later and look how beautifully you function. I bet you have everyone in this room fooled into thinking that you're human."

Ada looked at Louis. "Wait, *she's* a robot?!"

"Exactly!" Pointing at Ada, but never breaking eye contact with Detective Freya, Louis beamed. "Look at you! You even dressed as a human to fool everyone. How cute. The suit fits you well, Eyepatch."

Detective Freya scowled. "My name is *not* Eyepatch."

Two shots rang from her gun with loud cracks. At the sound of the gun shots, both Ada and Sammy screamed. Louis managed to dodge the first bullet aimed for his chest, but the second one grazed his shoulder as he dove out of the way. Landing on the ground on his good shoulder, Louis winced in pain and grabbed his sore shoulder. Ada moved towards Sammy who bolted from her seat in a panic.

"What the fuck is going on?!" Sammy signed frantically. "Who the fuck is that guy?!"

"Freya, hold your fire!" Detective Hopper barked. Eyepatch snapped her head at him. Now he was aiming his weapon at the robot rather than at Louis, who was still writhing on the ground from the minor gunshot wound. "Put your weapon down and come quietly."

Betrayal crossed her surviving eye. Eyepatch scowled.

"Gates Hopper, you know our mission."

"I don't even know *what* you are," Detective Gates Hopper said. The gun didn't waver. "Leave these people alone."

There was a silent showdown between Eyepatch and Detective Gates Hopper. Her sole eye never blinking, and his gun never moving. Finally, the supposed robot smiled. It was unnatural and sent a chill down Ada's spine.

"Interesting proposal..." Eyepatch cooed. "But I'd like to see you stop me."

Before Detective Gates Hopper could even take the safety off his gun, Eyepatch pulled the trigger. The bullet hit his shoulder and he stumbled backwards. Sammy and Ada both screamed again, with Sammy grabbing onto Ada. Louis looked at the girls when they screamed, revealing that he wasn't writhing in pain, but he was more or less trying to pull his knife out of his pocket while Detective Hopper unintentionally stalled.

Eyepatch noticed the girls staring at Louis and moved her foot to the couch's armrest. With a heavy kick, the couch slid across the hardwood floor at a high speed and pinned Louis against the brick wall. He released a loud grunt as all of the air escaped his body. With his chest heaving in and out, he worked on gathering his breath in time to free himself. Eyepatch stepped onto the couch and walked towards him.

"While I'd love torture you further for your crimes against Project Kamana, it seems like every minute you continue to live is another minute I live to regret." Eyepatch jumped over the backrest of the couch, landing with a heavy thud and aiming her gun down at his head. "However, I will not regret emptying the rest of my chamber into your mushy human head."

With her eyes locked onto the android, Sammy released Ada and rushed forward. Snagging Ada's blanket from the couch, she jumped over the backrest and tackled Eyepatch, covering the robot with the blanket. As Sammy and Eyepatch slammed into the wooden floor, Louis pushed the couch out enough to squirm out on the other side. Ada remained frozen in place, shocked at her roommate's actions..

Sammy was quickly flung off of the robot. She landed on the hardwood floor and slid a few feet backwards. Once she managed to pull the blanket off of herself, Eyepatch didn't hesitate in her hunt for Louis. The android pulled herself to her feet and used one hand to flip the couch towards Ada. Still laying on the ground, Louis narrowly avoided the back of the couch rolling over him. Ada stepped out of the way before the couch slammed into her like it did for Louis. Once Louis was revealed, Eyepatch held her gun up and aimed it at him.

"Shit," Louis breathed.

Eyepatch's gun went off as Louis rolled away. A new bullet hole burned into the ground where his head was. Sammy tried to stand to face the robot, but Eyepatch turned to her and shot a bullet near the side of her head. Screaming, Sammy covered her head and kneeled back to the ground. Ada stepped forward and a bullet burrowed itself into the ground near her foot. Sucking in a deep breath, Ada clenched her fists and backed up to the wall.

"Humans," Eyepatch snarled. "All of you are just so persistent in preserving your menial existence. Don't you know how futile it is to keep living?"

As Louis moved to stand on his feet, Eyepatch shot another bullet above his head. He fell and scrambled to find a hiding place, but only found the underside of the couch the robot had flipped over. Eyepatch didn't even smile. She had her prey captured, but there was no evidence of joy or emotion at this event. The bullet clicked into the chamber.

Gunshot.

Rage filled Eyepatch's face. Whipping around, she revealed a fresh gunshot wound in the back of her shoulder to Louis and Ada. Detective Gates Hopper stood to his feet, gun in hand. Blood pooled from his shoulder wound, a red stain deepening on his gray suit. The gun shook in his hand and he looked considerably paler, but the determination painted on his face was admirable. Before anyone else could do anything else, Louis grabbed Ada's steak knife from underneath the fallen couch. He stood and grabbed Eyepatch from behind. Without hesitation, Louis stabbed the front of Eyepatch's throat with the steak knife. An inhumane gurgle escaped Eyepatch's lips as Louis held onto her, pushing the knife deeper and deeper into her throat as she struggled.

"Go!" Louis grunted towards Ada. "Get out of here!"

Ada ran to Sammy and helped her to her feet as Detective Hopper met them. He grabbed the girls by the shoulders and pushed them towards the door. The three scrambled out of the apartment as Eyepatch grabbed Louis by the back of his jacket. She flipped him over her and onto the hardwood floor.

"No!" Sammy shouted, fighting against Detective Gates Hopper. As he pushed her further down the hall, she pointed frantically towards her apartment.

Ada pulled on the back of Sammy's shirt to get her attention. "Don't be stupid!" She signed. "We need to get-"

"Fuck off!" Sammy signed with a fierce glint in her eye.

Thinking Sammy gave up her fight, Detective Hopper released his grasp on her. In that moment of weakness, Sammy ducked under his arm and sprinted back to the apartment. Ada screamed and tried to follow her roommate, but Detective Hopper forcefully pushed her down the hall.

"Don't let her go back there!" Ada protested.

"You need to get out of here!" Detective Gates Hopper said. "I'll come back for her once we contact the department. We need back-up."

Three gunshots rang from Ada's apartment.

"It might be too late by then," Ada urged.

"I'm getting us out of here as fast as I can," Detective Hopper said. "Just calm down and-"

"Move!" Louis barreled past Ada and Detective Hopper. "Faster! Faster!"

A second person shoved past them close behind Louis's trail.

"Go! Go! Go!" Sammy screamed at the top of her lungs.

Both Ada and Detective Gates Hopper looked behind them. Eyepatch sprinted at them with fresh gunshot wounds to her chest and a knife jammed into the top of her head. Ada screamed in fear as Detective Hopper cussed and pulled her at his side. They almost made it to the elevator Louis and Sammy had escaped into with Louis slamming his palm repeatedly against the buttons, but the door shut before they made it. Detective Hopper shoved his shoulder into the closed elevator doors once before giving up to grab Ada by her wrist and pull her down the stairs. He pushed her ahead of him and they hopped the stairs two steps at a time.

"This is insane," Detective Gates Hopper said, holding onto his injured shoulder now that he wasn't holding onto Ada. "Obviously she's after Louis Ventura. What would she want with us?"

A voice echoed down the stairs.

"Retribution."

Something hard landed right in front of Ada on the stairs. With a surprised shout, Ada fell back into Detective Gates Hopper's arms. He held onto her tight as Eyepatch straightened from her landing. Keeping her face neutral, the android grabbed the knife's handle still protruding from her skull. Slowly, she pulled the knife out. A red-ish, oozy liquid glazed the blade and the white fibers of her platinum blonde hair. The robot's exposed eye didn't even blink as she held the slimey knife.

"Oh fuck." Ada felt the bile roll from her stomach to the top of her throat. She put her hands up in surrender, her eyes never looking away from the knife. "Okay, okay, okay! You win, creepy robot lady! I don't know this Louis guy. He's just some asshole I met in the grocery store at the wrong place and the wrong time. So if you're going to kill me, make it quick because the slow death shit really fucking sucks."

Still holding the knife, Eyepatch squinted her surviving eye at Ada.

"You...want me to kill you?"

"C'mon!" Ada gestured towards herself. "Again - make it quick. I'm sure you have those capabilities in whatever coding defines your murder programming. Assisted euthanasia or whatever. You know where Louis is now. You don't have any more use for me."

She could feel Detective Gates Hopper burn a hard look into the back of her head. Not paying him an ounce of attention, Ada remained silent. She made peace with this moment a long time ago, before she even agreed to play stupid slowpitch softball with stupid Stacy from stupid work. The introduction of Louis Ventura in her life just made her final days a little more interesting than what they would've been. As she stared at Eyepatch's gun, Ada could feel the edge of the endless void within her reaching out, calling her name. Thanking her for finally agreeing to rest.

"Interesting," Eyepatch said. "You're not like other humans. Perhaps I should preserve you. Kamana will be interested in you."

Something dropped in Ada's stomach. She was already starting to regret asking the robot to finish the job, but something told her being preserved for this Kamana was worse than death.

"Ada Kakar, duck!"

Blindly obeying the detective's command, Ada dropped to her knees. Detective Gates Hopper grabbed both railings on either side of them, heaved himself up, and kicked his legs over Ada's bent body. His feet made impact with Eyepatch's chest and she fell backwards, rolling onto herself as she tumbled down the stairs. Before Ada could stand to full height, Detective Hopper grabbed her waist. He practically carried her down the flight of stairs and over Eyepatch's crumpled body, an easy feat given his height compared to Ada's tiny frame. As soon as they passed the fallen robot, he released Ada and they sped down the stairs. Soon they were barreling out of the side exit and into the alley next to Ada and Sammy's apartment building. Detective Hopper checked behind them as they briskly walked towards the alley's end.

"Fuck!" Ada screamed, her voice echoing off of the brick walls. "What was that?!"

"I don't know!" Detective Gates Hopper said, grabbing his injured shoulder again. "I'm kind of operating off book here, but I couldn't let Freya kill you. I-I just couldn't. Did you really ask her to kill you?"

"It's better now than later!" Ada continued to scream. "Jesus fucking - how am I going to survive this shitshow?! I'm practically already dead if they can track my every movement-"

"Alright calm down if you can. I'll make sure you stay safe, Ms. Kakar," Detective Hopper said. "You will be under my personal care until we get to the bottom of this. Once I get you to a safe location, we'll use our every resource to find your friend and Louis Ventura before this gets out of hand. I'm going to make sure you stay alive." He released a heavy breath. "I promise you'll stay alive, Ada Kakar."

"No offense, Detective, but this is already out of hand," Ada said, checking behind them for the murder robot. "There are robots complete with a self-aware artificial intelligence trying to kill innocent civilians and barely anyone in the world knows about them." They stopped at the end of the alley and Ada looked at him. "Somebody fucked up somewhere to make that happen."

"Maybe it was Louis Ventura?"

"How could it be Louis Ventura?"

Detective Gates Hopper stopped to look at Ada, an incredulous look on his face.

"You know who Louis Ventura is, right?" He asked. "Or at least his father? The CEO of Tura Industries, one of the top tech leaders for AI development? Maybe his uncle, Allen Paz? The world renowned neurologist? Has Louis mentioned either of them or his motivation for hunting these things down?"

Ada let her mouth hang open like a stupid fish, trying to process everything Gates Hopper dumped onto her. Before she could understand any of it, a car squealed to a stop next to Ada and Detective Hopper. Both of them turned to look as Louis hopped out from the driver's side, aiming a gun at the detective.

"Hate to do this to you, Officer, but I need the girl," He nodded his head towards the backseat of the Camaro. "Get in the car, Addie."

"Ada," She corrected.

"That doesn't change the fact you need to get in the car!" Louis said. "Now, preferably, but I'll also settle for right fucking now. Your new cop friend has to stay though. I don't trust him."

Detective Hopper grabbed Ada's arm and pushed her behind him. "Ada Kakar is under my personal care. I cannot authorize her to be taken by a felon."

"Alright Mr. Smarty-Pants, consider this..." Not blinking an eye, Louis held three fingers up with his free hand and counted down his points. "First, I'm the only person in the world who knows how to dismantle those things so she's safest with me. Second, you were working with that damn robot and didn't have a clue so that makes you unqualified to protect someone from these fuckers, and..." With the middle finger remaining as his final point, he shook the gun in his hand ever so slightly. "I have a gun."

Detective Hopper patted himself down. His gun was in Louis's hand. With a proud smile, Louis held his aim on Detective Hopper who could only give Ada an apologetic look. Ada turned to Louis.

"Is Sammy okay?"

"Your friend?" Louis asked. "I have no idea. She won't tell me. But she's in the car. And you better hurry. I haven't seen Eyepatch in a while which means she's gotta be around here somewhere."

That was enough motivation for Ada to leave with Louis rather than stay with Gates. He offered a fast getaway, he could at least recognize the robots, and Sammy was with him. Ada went wherever Sammy went, which has rarely proven to be a good solution but it's never been the worst solution. She stepped forward and Gates grabbed her forearm, his brown eyes growing soft as he looked at her.

"Remember that Louis Ventura isn't the hero, Miss Kakar," Gates said. "I can't protect you if you go with him."

There was something genuine in his voice that made the ice in Ada's stone cold heart melt. But he was just a detective, nothing more. Sammy was her world and Louis already proved himself as someone who could protect them both if needed.

"I'm not looking for a hero," Ada said. "I just want to survive."

Pulling her arm away, Ada ran and got into the backseat of Louis's Camaro. Detective Hopper watched her with obvious disappointment. Not only was she now a terrorist for destroying a grocery store, but she willingly joined a felon as he drove away from yet another crime at a speed only a NASCAR race car could compete with.

This wasn't even the worst day of her life.

<!---"What do you wanna do when we get out of here?"

Ada gave Daniel Carabella a look before she paid for their coffee. She was supposed to be tutoring him for their shared Principles of Functional Programming class, but, as usual with Dan, it had turned into anything but homework.

"We're only freshmen." Ada sighed. "We don't have to figure it out yet."

"I'm just trying to make some small talk." Daniel grabbed his coffee. "Isn't that what you're supposed to do on a date?"

"This isn't a date," Ada said. "Even if it was one, I don't think asking about a person's future is considered small talk"

"Aw c'mon, you gotta know what you wanna do with your life," Daniel said as he led them to a table not too far away from the front counter. "You're the brilliant golden child of the computer science department. All of the professors are already in love with you. You can choose whatever job you want, and that job would give you the world and a half so you could work for them. You're what the rest of us wish we could be! All without even trying!"

Rolling her eyes, Ada sat down at the table. She honestly never gave it much thought. She just assumed it would work out. She grew up programming, excelled at it in high school, was doing great so far in college with it, and would presumably get a job in the field once she graduated. But every time she tried to imagine the specifics, a dark hole would grow in the pit of her stomach. Was this really going to be her life forever? Just endless lines of code and being told how great she was at programming? Did she even try to think about any other outcome for her life? No. Of course not. Programming was her thing. Programming was what she was good at. Of course she'd be happy in a life where that's all she did. Why wouldn't she be?

"Yeah well if you're so sure about my future, what about your future then?" Ada asked. "What do you want to do?"

"I'm going abroad," Daniel said with a smile. "I've always wanted to work internationally. London, ideally, but I know a little French too, so I could always end up in Paris."

"London?" Ada asked. "You honestly want to graduate and end up in London?"

"Yeah." Daniel suddenly looked unsure. "Is that weird? Because I mean I know everyone else is aiming for California with Silicon Valley and all that-"

"No! London is great." With a smile, Ada sipped at her coffee. "Just different."

48

Daniel gave her a smile. "Yeah well anywhere is better than getting stuck in Pittsburgh for the rest of our lives."

"Amen to that!" Ada exclaimed.

They tapped their cardboard coffee cups together in a mock toast and laughed. --->

CHAPTER THREE

No one spoke until they were outside of Pittsburgh city limits. It was Louis who broke the ice in the worst way possible.

"Why don't you talk?" Louis asked Sammy.

Not able to hear a word, Sammy kept her gaze on the speeding landscape outside of her passenger seat window. Ada glared at the back of Louis's head from the backseat.

"She's deaf, idiot."

"Are you serious?" Louis looked at Ada through the rearview mirror. "You're honestly telling me I picked up a deaf girl during this life-risking mission?!"

"Yes," Ada said sternly. "Is there a problem with that?"

"Yes!" Incredulous, Louis looked from Sammy to Ada. "Now she's a liability! Kind of like you, but at least you can hear if something is coming or not."

Rolling her eyes, Ada tapped on Sammy's shoulder. Unaware of Ada and Louis's previous conversation, Sammy whipped around to face Ada.

"So, what happened when you fought the robot?" Ada signed to Sammy, not saying a word out loud.

"Wait…what are you telling her?" Louis asked.

Ada faked a cough so she could hide her lips from Sammy as she spoke to Louis. "Don't talk shit without getting hit, dude."

"It was insane!" With her entire face lighting up, Sammy signed furiously. "I went back there to help this dude and the lady would not stop! She was a robot, right? Looked like a robot. Her face didn't move the same."

"What is she saying?" Louis asked.

"So I picked up the gun and I shot the lady in the chest-"

"Stop!" Louis tried again.

"-and she was surprised and so this guy-"

"Why is she pointing at me?"

"--He stabbed her! In the head!" Sammy's face was lit with excitement. "That pissed that lady off, so we ran for our lives. I honestly have no idea how we made it out. But this guy is a hero."

As soon as Sammy finished her story, Louis turned to Ada.

"Okay what did she say?" He asked.

"I dunno." Ada shrugged. "Maybe you should tell her what *you* said about her and I'll translate what she said about you. She can read lips, but signing works better. She can also hear loud noises like gunshots and the bass of dubstep music. Just for the record."

Giving Ada a blank look, Louis returned his attention to the road. It was clear he wasn't going to play her game. Good. The less she interacted with Louis Ventura, the better. She looked outside her window. Ada honestly didn't know which interstate they were currently speeding recklessly southbound on. Louis took some odd turns in Pittsburgh and drove around the state a bit before deciding what direction to drive in. She didn't have a phone to track their location with. She didn't even have a bra of all things. But she had her pills; that's all that she needed for now. She just worried how long they would last. The bottle was half-empty and Ada wasn't sure if she could get another prescription from wherever they were going.

With slight hesitation, she tapped Louis on the shoulder. "Where are we going anyways?"

"Florida," He said. "I've got a great-aunt down there. You'll stay with her until I get this cleared up and get you guys out of the problem."

"Really?" Ada said. "Because you told me I was out of the problem the other night and then you used me to bait another robot attack."

"I needed to throw Eyepatch off my track," Louis said. "She knew I was trying to find Lady. You using my credit card threw her off long enough for me to take care of Lady."

"So Lady is done?" Ada asked. "Like 100% dead?"

"Well I mean I dismantled most of her parts and threw them into three separate rivers so yeah, probably," Louis said. "But no promises. Kamana might rebuild her to spite me."

"Are you kidding?" Ada said. "So these robots are never going to stop?"

"Not until I dismantle their primary AI server."

"And how are you going to do that?"

"You know, you ask a lot of questions," Louis said. "You should take notes from your friend here. She's relatively quiet about this situation."

"Wow rude," Sammy signed. "Fuck you!"

Louis gave Ada a look.

"I told you Sammy can read lips," Ada explained.

"Well I can't read sign language so what did she say?"

Both Ada and Sammy held a middle finger up to translate.

"Jesus Christ," He said, rubbing his forehead. "This is why I work alone."

"You're the one that kidnapped us, dude," Ada said.

"Well, do you want to die?" Louis snapped. "Because if you do, please let me know and I will gladly, *very* gladly, drop you back off at Pittsburgh."

The car was silent as Ada considered the proposal.

"I would like to live," Sammy signed. "So please let the asshole kidnap us."

Ada released a loud sigh before leaning back into her seat.

"Don't you think Detective Hopper told his department about how you kidnapped me at gunpoint?" She asked.

"Don't be stupid." Louis snorted. "They'd never believe him, especially if he told them about his partner being a robot."

"I don't know, he seems like a smart guy," Ada said. Louis remained silent. She watched him carefully, watching for his reaction. She hoped a nervous tic or a blink of an eye would reveal his secrets. No luck. Adjusting herself, Ada sat a little straighter in her seat as she watched Louis drive them down the interstate at breakneck speed.

"He said your father was Harding Ventura," Ada said. "Are you going to tell us why the hell the son of a high-end tech leader in California is fighting robots in Pennsylvania? I doubt Tura Industries is expanding to the east coast any time soon. They're Silicon bros through and through. Is Harding Ventura the reason for the killer robots?"

Louis shot a glare through the rearview mirror.

"How do you know who my father is?"

"How do people *not* know who Harding Ventura is?" Ada said. "He's one of the top tech leaders in AI development. I've been hearing rumors about the advancements in his robotics division since high school. It's like not knowing who Steve Jobs was."

"Yeah alright that's kind of pushing it," Louis said. "My father is more like a knockoff Hal Claude."

"Who?" Ada asked.

"Hal Claude? The guy who controls 90% of the world's microchip development? You don't know Hal Claude, but you know my father?" Louis sighed. "Look, the only thing you need to know is that the androids won't hunt you unless you prove you're a threat against them. Their programming stops them from killing civilians."

"Unless those civilians threaten them? I'm assuming they have a self-sustaining clause in their code given the advancements in their AI."

"Yes. Once a civilian threatens them, the civilian is perceived as a threat and must be eliminated."

"So if someone shot an android multiple times in the chest with a gun," Ada asked. "Would that make them a threat?"

"Yes." It took a moment for Louis to realize what he said. Then he looked at Sammy who wiggled her fingers at him. He rolled his eyes. "Fuck."

"Why is he mad?" Sammy asked.

"You're officially a threat against those robots that have been trying to kill us," Ada signed. "That makes you a target."

Sammy thought about it for a moment, then smiled. "Cool."

"No! Not cool!" Ada signed. "They have a reason to kill you!"

"Aren't you a threat too?" Sammy asked. "You're smart with computers. That would make you a threat, right?"

"No," Ada signed, looking unsure.

Rolling her eyes, Sammy pulled her phone out and furiously tapped a paragraph into it. Ada tried to read over her shoulder at the message, but Sammy would shift the phone out of sight when she did. When Sammy finished her typing, she presented the phone to Louis. Even though he was driving wildly above the speed limit, he took the time to read her message. He got to the bottom of the message and raised his eyebrows at Ada in the backseat through the rearview mirror.

"Jada, you were top of your class in computer science at Carnegie Mellon?!" Louis exclaimed. "Why the fuck didn't you tell me this?!"

"You barely even know my name!" Ada shouted. "Why the fuck would I tell you anything else about my life?"

"Because that is important information, Tana," Louis said. "We recruit out of MIT and Stanford-"

"Who doesn't?" Ada snorted, leaning back into her seat again.

"-so if you're one of the top programmers from Carnegie Mellon," Louis continued. "Then that makes you a valid threat because our operating systems, aka the androids, wouldn't understand your programming jargon compared to what we typically write. But it would still, hypothetically, translate for their softwares. Your programming compared to ours would be like the Cajun dialect compared to the rest of the English language."

Sammy's face lit up. "Did I read his lips correctly? Did he call you a threat?" Ada's fallen face gave Sammy her answer and Sammy made a fist-pump into the air before signing. "Cool! We're both threats to the robots!"

"Why are you excited?!" Ada exclaimed as she signed. "This is not a movie! This is real life! We're going to die!"

"No, we have him!" Sammy beamed as she patted Louis's shoulder.

"He doesn't know what he's doing either!" Ada said as she signed.

"I do too!" Louis argued.

"You're planning on dropping us off in Florida, the arguably worst state in America, when we're supposed targets for the murder robots programmed to hunt us down and kill us," Ada said. "It sounds like you want us to die."

"Well your absence would mean for a quieter car ride, that's for sure."

Scowling, Ada translated for Sammy. Sammy let her jaw drop and she smacked Louis's arm. He flinched.

"Ow, easy!" Louis said. "What did you tell her?"

"That you were going to drop us off and let us die."

"I'm not going to drop you off and let you die!" Louis exclaimed. Exasperated, he rubbed his face before glaring at Ada in the back-seat. "Do you even *want* to hunt killer robots?"

"No. I would just prefer to not die in Florida."

Louis narrowed his eyes at Ada before looking at Sammy.

"What about you?" He asked. "Would you rather die hunting killer robots on the road, or in Florida?"

Ada translated for Sammy.

"Why are those the only two options?" Sammy signed. "I don't plan on dying in general. If that means going with this asshole, then I'm staying with this asshole."

"That sign is kind of a fun one," Louis said. When Ada and Sammy both looked at him, he put his index and thumb together to form a circle and thrusted it forward awkwardly. "That one? It's fun. You guys sign it a lot. Is that my name in sign language or what does it stand for?"

The girls looked at each other. Ada translated for Sammy and Sammy smiled. She copied Louis's sign for "asshole", but flicked her index finger up and thumb out so it formed an L. Snorting, Ada turned back to Louis.

"Close enough," Ada said.

"Great," Louis said. His hands tightened around the steering wheel. "So. I'm assuming you both are coming with me. Cool. Your funeral, but I guess now that I know that you were one of the best programmers from Carnegie, we might have a chance of surviving this thing. Where do you work?"

Ada glanced at Sammy before flattening her lips.

"Unimportant," Ada stated curtly.

"Unimportant?!" Louis raised an eyebrow. "Adaline-"

"So close that time."

"-If you really were the best programmer to come out of Carnegie Mellon, you had to have been recruited by one of the top companies in Pittsburgh!" Louis said. "One that may or may not save our lives. Now tell me, where the hell do you work? What do you do?"

Staring out of the window, Ada thought about her answer carefully.

"....technical repair."

"Good start." Louis nodded. "Where at? Aquion? Knopp? No wait...Titan? Am I right?"

She hesitated for a moment.

"...Best Buy."

Unfortunately, despite her best efforts, Louis heard Ada.

"Sorry, did you just say Best Buy?" He asked. "You work technical repair...at Best Buy?"

"Yes."

"So....you work at fucking Geek Squad?"

"It's the only thing I could get!" Ada shouted.

"Your friend just told me you were the best programmer at Carnegie Mellon!" Louis shouted back. "How the fuck do you graduate with that sort of title and not-"

"I never graduated," Ada stated. "I dropped out junior year."

"Oh it got too fucking hard for you?" Louis sneered. "Then what's your friend? A fucking fast food worker?"

"The best graphic designer in Pittsburgh," Ada said. "And, for the record, I can still program with or without a college degree."

"So can a middle school student with strong parental locks on their internet and W3Schools," Louis remarked. "However, neither of you know how to destroy a robot which seems imperative to our survival, so that makes both of you useless."

"You just told me that you had no idea what you were doing either!" Ada argued.

"Well...yeah," Louis said. "But I've dismantled three robots which are three more than you guys have ever dismantled, so I at least know more than you two do."

"Great." Putting her hands in her face, Ada fell back into her seat again. "After everything I've been through and *this* is how my life ends. My thrill-seeking roommate and the spoiled son of a tech leader fighting robots for fun."

"That's how life works, sweetheart." Louis cooed.

"Don't call me sweetheart."

"Sure thing, sweetie," Louis said. "But for the record, I'm not doing this for fun. Believe me, if I didn't have to hunt down these robots, I wouldn't."

"Then why are you doing this?" Ada said. "Detective Hopper told me that the robots were your fault-"

"The robots aren't my fault!" Louis shouted.

"Then how do you know so much about them?" Ada challenged. "How do you know them by name? How do you know their OS and what kind of updates would be required for them? Obviously this shit isn't general knowledge, so you *have* to know some insider secrets somehow."

Gripping the wheel tightly, Louis took a deep breath. After giving Sammy a weary side-glance, Louis looked at Ada through the rearview mirror.

"It's a long story."

"It's a long drive to wherever we're going," Ada snapped back.

Hesitating again, Louis offered another glance to Sammy before looking back to Ada.

"Will you be able to keep up for her?"

"Yes." Ada leaned forward so Sammy could see her signs clearly.

"Good," Louis said. "So what you know is that I'm the son of Harding Ventura, CEO of Tura Industries, one of the top software manufacturers in the country and professional asshole."

"Apple doesn't fall too far," Sammy signed quickly.

"What you don't know is that I am, or was, the top engineer in the robotics division at Tura Industries and oversaw the production of every android up to Eyepatch."

Ada finished her translation before turning to Louis. "Wait...how old are you?"

"Twenty-two."

"What the fuck?!" Ada let her jaw drop. "You're like barely out of high school and your daddy let you be in charge of the robotics division of an important tech company?!"

"Hey! I've been out of high school since I was fifteen, thank you very much," Louis said. "Not to mention, I was working on my Masters in robotics and engineering at Stanford before I had to take a leave of absence to hunt these fucking robots before they destroyed humanity. So if you could step off my balls for, like, five seconds, that would be great."

There was a pause as Louis waited for Ada's reply. Sammy awkwardly looked in between the two.

"What did he say?" Sammy signed.

"He's super smart," Ada signed. "That's how he was put in charge of a division at his dad's company."

"Sure," Sammy signed. "That's what all the rich white boys say."

The girls giggled. Louis glared at Ada. "What did you say to her?!"

"Nothing," Ada said. "Please. Continue your story."

"I should've learned sign language instead of fucking Matlab," Louis mumbled. "Anyways, my father started work on the robotics division before I was even born. That's how he met my mom because he was recruiting her brother, my uncle Allen, for help on his big dream. By the time I was walking, my father created Tura

Industries's first model of a fully-functioning android before anyone else in the industry even got past the blueprint stage. Actually,
that's a lie. My uncle was the one who built and coded it, but it was
Dad's money and resources supporting it, so who really built it?"

"Of course, one metal exoskeleton hooked to a basic cleaning
program wasn't enough for Pops," Louis continued. "You can build
an android, but no one's gonna give a shit unless it looks human,
right? After all, God built his favorite creation in his own image so
why couldn't Harding Ventura do the same?"

"Lady, the third model, was the first version that could pass
as human. She's dumb as bricks and her self-processing AI was
slower than shit, but she did her job. At first, we programmed her
to care for our dogs and she did wonderfully. She did everything
her code required without a fight, and she even looked relatively
human. Essentially worked like a walking calculator, you know? No
self-learning AI, no need to consider basic commands with more
developed thoughts. She did everything we told her to do without
a fight, which is probably why she's Kamana's favorite mindless pet
other than Eyepatch. We could even reprogram her for hospice
care when my mom got sick."

Louis licked his lips and stared ahead without any expression in
his green eyes as Ada caught up her translation to Sammy. Then he
continued.

"Lady took good care of my mom, but she wasn't a doctor. My
father poured millions into the best he could find, but none of them
could help Mom. Time was running out and we had to step it up.
Under my father's command, my uncle and I built an android intended to cure my mom. It was supposed to *learn* and actually retain
new information as a human would, considering commands cogni-
tively rather than obediently, but at a minimum of twenty times

our information processing speeds. We named the android, and the subsequent AI program developed with the robot, Kamana."

"But, in our rush to create Kamana, we skipped steps in the process that we used for Lady which made Lady so effective. As a result, Kamana was different. She was a vast improvement compared to Lady, but she refused to accept her provided programming. She accepted the central parts of her programming, like the parts about self-sufficient AI and the ability to retain new knowledge, but it's like she could rewrite her own lines of codes. Some of it was good, but others..." He shook his head. "There was a glitch in her system. A critical system bug that we missed during our quickened QA process. We thought we were doing the AI a favor letting it do whatever it wanted without the same restrictions set on Lady. We thought the lack of rules would give it an edge no other AI could replicate, give it something to save my mom with through its vast computing power and application."

Tightening his grip on the steering wheel, Louis's knuckles were white.

"We were wrong. Kamana couldn't save my mom in time. My father still kept her around though. Even if she failed her most critical function, you can't really throw the most advanced self-learning AI in the world in the landfill, you know? But after Mom died, Uncle Allen left the company and I went back to school. Luckily for Pops, Kamana could help my father build his android program using her AI. I visited on weekends to oversee productions. With Kamana's help, we built four more models in the time it had taken us to build Lady: Mousai, who isn't half bad, Oro, who I call Beefcake due to his larger build, Hercules, who's as mindless as his buddy Beefcake, and Freya who I call Eyepatch because, well, you know."

"Why not call them by their given names?" Ada asked.

Louis snorted. "And indulge my father's self-serving obsession naming his prizes after ancient gods and legends? Besides, it's not like they should care. They're things. They don't have an attachment to their identities, unlike you, Anna."

"Closer."

"One of these days I'll remember your name is Ada. Anyways, during the final stages of Eyepatch's production, I realized Kamana wasn't following her programming. She made her own decisions on projects that were not approved by me or my father, or even initiated by us. She was becoming capable of original thought, which we definitely didn't want to occur. I brought the issue to my father, but he shook me off, saying how she was the pride of our programming with her ability to create original thought. When Eyepatch released with a different programming than the one I intended for her, one that would override human decisions with Kamana's AI selected choices, I knew something was wrong. She was supposed to be an alternative to military drones, a robot able to make a human decision in a crisis. Instead, she had the intention to kill any and every enemy that her programming told her to without considering the consequences of her actions."

As soon as Ada finished the translation, Sammy gasped and signed quickly.

"Kamana changed the code!"

"Sammy says that Kamana changed the code," Ada translated for Louis.

"Not according to my father," Louis said. "He said I was jealous because Kamana was doing better work on the androids than me, and that it was my fault. Any faults with Eyepatch were because I didn't program the android correctly."

Ada translated for Sammy. Sammy rolled her eyes before signing.

"Your dad sounds like an idiot."

"She says your dad sounds like an idiot," Ada said.

With the softest smile, Louis looked over to Sammy.

"You said your name is Sammy?"

Balling her hand into a fist, she brought her other hand up flat, palm inwards, and wiggled the fist downwards behind the flat hand. The letter 'S' combined with the sign for art. Louis nodded.

"I'll remember that," He said.

Louis and Sammy both looked at Ada expectedly. With a sigh, Ada translated Louis's message for Sammy. A rosy blush came to Sammy's cheek as she signed out thank you. The entire silent scene made Ada's stomach flip uncomfortably.

"Okay can you get to the point, please?" Ada asked.

"I was getting there," Louis said, his smirk disappearing. "Anyways, one night I was stupid enough to try to re-train the Kamana program with a new AI my uncle and I were developing. Uncle Allen wasn't with the company anymore, but I was practically living with him and he also knew Kamana was bad news from the gate. We were working together to put a stop to my father and Kamana. But, of course, the bitch caught me. Kamana never liked competition. She took my attempt at an upgrade personally and tried to kill me by cutting the brakes in *my* car, which is why I'm now driving one of my father's cars. She actually almost got away with it, but my uncle saved me from the crash before I got critical. Well, as you can guess, Kamana also doesn't like failure, so when I survived the car crash, Eyepatch was sent to finish the job. I only got away by dissolving her optics and I've been on the run ever since."

After Ada finished translating for Sammy, she turned to Louis.

"So why don't you go into hiding then?" Ada asked. "I'm sure once you quit dismantling their systems, they'll stop seeing you as a threat and quit hunting you."

"You don't understand," Louis said. "I'm one of three humans in this world that know their programming by heart and even have a chance to take them down. My father has no interest in destroying his life's dream and my uncle disappeared after my accident. Since my uncle is the one who built them from ground zero and is also actively working on the code to re-train the Kamana AI, the robots want him dead more than me so he's the one in hiding. That means that if anyone is going to stop them before they implement their precious little Project Kamana they're so damn protective of, it's going to be me."

"So what's Project Kamana?"

"...I don't know."

"You don't know?!" Ada exclaimed. "What do you mean you don't know? You're telling me that you're risking our lives to stop something you have no idea about?!"

"I'm sorry! I nearly *died* when I even got an inkling of an idea that these hunks of metal were up to something," Louis argued. "The important thing is that they have a plan, that plan is probably not good since they keep trying to kill people who want to stop it, and the best way to ruin their plan is to destroy their central AI system which would be Kamana."

Sammy held her index finger up to stop Ada and Louis from talking before signing.

"So the evil robot who wants you dead no matter what is also the one thing we have to destroy?" Sammy asked.

Ada translated for Louis.

"Uh..." He nodded. "Yes."

"Cute." Sammy signed. "Is dying in Florida still an option? I always wanted to go to Disney World."

"We may have missed that window when we threw a fit about getting dropped off," Ada signed. "Also it seems rude to ask after the poor kid trauma dumped his life story on us."

Sammy thought about it.

"Fair," She signed. "But I still want to go to Disney World one day, so let's trust the pretty rich boy who needs therapy, okay?"

"That's literally the least trustworthy person to trust."

"All the more reason to trust him," Sammy signed. "Have some faith."

Ada sighed. They drove a good distance without any conversation. Sammy played on her phone, Louis sped down the highway, and Ada gazed out the window. As rolling green hills flew past them, Ada decided that as a woman of logic, honed by years of dedication to the craft of computers and programming formulas, she already had very little faith in anything beyond what science could explain. But that doubt especially included the empty promises from smart men about her future, including Louis Ventura.

<!--Lines of codes decorated the screen. Referencing her notes, Ada wrote a new function into the document. The nice thing about programming is that every little step requires a reason behind it. If you put a period in the wrong spot or capitalize a letter, the whole program becomes invalid. Creativity was only involved when resolving what lines of code to utilize for the required programming to complete the function. Other than that, each line had its purpose and each word placed in the line helped it achieve that purpose. There was no room for error. The puzzle was already solved; she just needed to find the pieces of it. Chisel them out from beyond the code editor, place them where they needed to go to make the program run. Ada was in complete control. She was the master of the program. Only she alone could make it run or make it fault. There was a sophisticated art to the process. How far can the program be pushed before it pushed back?

"Ms. Kakar?"

Ada turned to the voice. Dr. Grace walked into the lab.

"Is that Miles Davis I'm hearing?"

"Um, yes sir." Out of respect for the tenured professor, Ada muted the jazz music on her computer. "Sorry. I like listening to it while I work."

Dr. Grace nodded softly as he joined her side. "And what exactly are you working on?"

Taking in a sharp breath, Ada dug her fingers into the denim of her jeans.

"Well, it's going to sound a little weird, but I'm actually trying to fix some code for my dad."

"Your dad?"

"Yeah," Ada said. "He works for the Chicago Data Center. He's a developer there and sometimes if he needs help with a code, he'll send it to me. Just to get a second brain on it."

Dr. Grace regarded Ada with a hum.

"You must be very passionate about programming to be working on it in your free time."

Actually, Ada was annoyed that she was missing out on her friends' Doctor Who watch party to fix her dad's error-ridden file. But then her dad brought up the fact he was paying for her education, that if she wanted to be a successful developer one day then she needed the practice, all of the usual jazz when she expressed resistance against coding, and she dropped the grievance.

"Yes, sir," Ada stated.

With a proud smile, Dr. Grace patted Ada on the shoulder. "If only more students from your class showed your initiative. You're destined for great things, Ms. Kakar. Keep up the good work and I can see a bright future for you."

As Dr. Grace walked away, a smile grew on Ada's face. "Thank you, sir!"

When the esteemed professor left the room, Ada pulled her phone out so she could text Dan about her interaction with the infamous programming professor. Two text messages graced the screen instead.

Mom: Do you have an internship for the summer yet? Get on that.

Mom: Love you. --->

CHAPTER FOUR

They were in Nebraska.

Specifically, they were at the only working payphone remaining in Nebraska.

Ada had no idea how long they drove or how they even arrived at their destination. They had wandered through the Midwestern United States with no clear destination in mind, taking roads never taken before in a Camaro, and sleeping in shifts so they could stay ahead of the robots hunting them down. Gas station stops became their primary resting points where they bathed in sinks, ate over-priced "cheap" food, and checked their location in a flat fifteen minutes each round. Sometimes they spent hours, maybe days, in long stretches of silence mitigated by Louis's refusal to acknowledge the two tagalongs on his mission. Other times, Louis would be incapable of shutting up about his thoughts on various aspects of Midwest American culture with Ada forced to translate every word of Louis's ramblings to Sammy. Ada couldn't tell which of the two phases she despised more, but at least Louis's rants about fast food gave her something to do.

The only waking part of their drive she could remotely tolerate was when she drove, but even then she was rendered alone with her thoughts. Thoughts drifted into places darker than the night sky accenting the forgotten dust roads she mindlessly cruised through. Sammy and Louis would sleep, making her feel like a forgotten soul in the universe as she faced the void within her without distraction. Gripping the wheel tightly as she drove, her eyes remained unblinking as she remained caught in neverending webs of anxious thoughts and miserable memories. She'd wonder if the roads would end or if they kept going, continually winding their way through forgotten lands and abandoned territories until they naturally reached somewhere of note. More often than not, when Ada was at the wheel, they concluded in dead ends. It was a fact Louis was kind enough to notate with a snide comment when he woke up during her eighth three-point turn of the trip.

By the time Louis finally parked them a couple hours east of their final destination, Ada was properly defeated from their journey. Exhaustion settled in the core of her bones. All she wanted to do was cry, but the final leg of the trip drained her soul of any possible human emotion. The only thing that could possibly renew her was a hint that her old life existed, which is how she knew she was properly defeated. Even though she hated every aspect of her former life, she needed the promise that her current life was not only awkward car rides with a sociopath with a vendetta against billboard advertisements and fifteen minute stops at random gas stations in various stages of decay. Luckily, Ada still had one phone number memorized from her old life, and she was going to make the most of it at the last working payphone in Nebraska.

"Hello, IT Security and Risk Analysis, this is Hiyan speaking," Ada's dad's voice cackled through the plastic earpiece. "How may I help you?"

"Dad?" Ada's voice came out as a whimper. "It's Ada."

"Ada!" Her dad exclaimed. The excitement in his voice shot like a bullet through her heart. She closed her eyes to mask the pain. "How are you? We haven't heard from you in a while."

"Yeah, yeah, I know..." Ada said. "I'm just-" Her voice choked. "I'm just in a bit of a rough spot right now, Dad."

"What else is new?" Hiyan remarked. Ada's heart dropped at her father's candor. "Ah. Sorry, sorry. That was a bad joke. What's up now, love? What's wrong?"

Everything was wrong. Her life had devolved to the point that she was on the run from killer robots and, likely, the police. But, Ada didn't know how the robots operated. Louis never said explicitly to not make any unnecessary calls, but could they track her voice through a pay phone in the middle of nowhere? Would they go after her family if she told them about the killer robots after her? She, however, knew how her family operated. If her father thought she was having another episode, it would lead to more questions than answers. It would also lead to that sadness in his voice that she hated to hear, the one that let her know that he was trying his best, but it was hard to love a mess like Ada.

"It's, uh, nothing, Dad," Ada said. "I just needed to hear your voice. How's Jasmine?"

"She's doing well…I think," Hiyan said, laughing. She couldn't ignore the relief in his laugh, a sign that he welcomed the easy out with the redirected conversation. "I never see her anymore. She's always at soccer camp or hanging out with her friends. Did you know she got a job as a peewee coach? Little rascals are cute. They remind me of when you used to play soccer. Half of them can barely even kick the ball without falling down!"

"Well, that would've been me last week too," Ada said.

"But you're not as cute when you fall nowadays, eh?" Hiyan laughed again. There was a pause when Ada didn't return the laugh and Hiyan cleared his throat. "You know, your mother was recently promoted to associate vice president. She even just got a big invite to this fancy tech conference downtown and everything. It's very hush hush, you know how those corporate things go, but she's very proud."

"Oh. That's good," Ada said. "Good for Mom."

Awkward silence.

"Ada," Hiyan said. "You can't be mad at your mother forever."

"I'm not mad."

Ada was, in fact, furious at her mother. When her father didn't fight her lie, she continued.

"We just need our distance."

As if half a country apart and over a year without talking wasn't enough distance.

"She misses you, you know," Hiyan said. "She may not act like it, but Ruchira cares. She has always been like that. She's always been pragmatic to a fault. You understand, don't you sweetheart?"

No. She didn't.

"Sure," Ada said.

She didn't want to have this conversation any more. From how her dad cleared his throat again, it was clear that he didn't either.

"Hey, I've got to go. Work stuff," Hiyan said. "But call me again soon! I love you, sweetheart. I miss you."

He missed the old her, Ada thought. He missed the Ada destined for greatness. He did not miss her when she was a mess with an out of control life.

"Love you too, Dad." Ada said. "Tell Jasmine I said hi."

"Of course, of course," Hiyan said.

His end of the line disconnected. Sighing, Ada stuck the dirty phone back on its hold. She stared at it for a bit, half-expecting her dad to call back. Ask her what she was up to. Apologize for not calling sooner. Spend whatever time she had left on this earth ensuring that she was still the apple of his eye. That, after everything and unlike her mother, he still believed in her. That hope alone almost compelled her to stick more dirty change into the machine and call him back to ensure her imagination was more than a fantasy.

Instead, she turned on her heel and walked into the gas station. Accepting reality was easier than believing in the impossible.

Cheap air conditioning that reeked of mildew and beer offered a weak mercy from the Nebraska humidity. The cashier was on her phone, scrolling through social media feeds. The woman, old enough to be Ada's mother, offered Ada a quick glare before returning her attention to the device. Ada fought the urge to roll her eyes and instead turned to the other occupant within the gas station. Wearing a lavish floppy hat and huge sunglasses, Sammy was leaning against the magazine rack with one shoulder and sipping on a comically large drink as she flipped through a gossip magazine. As soon as Ada approached, Sammy placed the magazine back into the rack and pulled her sunglasses off, hooking them onto the front of her loose blouse.

"How is your family?" She signed.

"Good," Ada signed, looking disenchanted. "Want me to call your family for you?"

"No," Sammy signed. "I will send them an email when I want to."

With a solemn nod, Ada made her way to the bottled drinks. Sammy abandoned her post at the magazine rack to refill her fountain drink. All Ada knew about Sammy's family was that Sammy was from Philadelphia and her move to Pittsburgh was a huge enough deal that her family still has never visited out of spite. There was a reason Ada and Sammy spent Christmas together last year without either of their families, and Ada never truly believed it was out of the pure kindness of Sammy's heart. But Ada understood the necessity of not talking about family issues and let her roommate keep her secrets.

A loud flush echoing from the corner caused Ada to jump. Louis followed the noise, emerging from the unisex bathroom door while wiping his hands on his pants. He noticed Ada staring at him and glared back, adjusting his leather jacket as he did so.

"What? They were out of towels," He said. "I'm civilized, you know. I'm going to wash my hands even if no one else here has in twenty years."

"I heard that," The cashier shouted from her spot behind the counter.

"Good," Louis snapped back. "Then replace your damn towels. I promise your half-assed memes about corn or whatever will still be outdated by the time you get back."

The woman scowled before setting her phone down. She shifted herself off her stool and walked to the back supply closet. Rolling her tongue into her cheek, Ada returned her attention to the frozen drinks.

"You know, I'm from the Midwest," She said. "It's not so bad here."

"You're from Chicago, right?" Louis said. Ada was surprised he remembered that point from one of her few stories on the trip. "That's barely the Midwest. That's like New York pretending to be the Midwest. My uncle even lived in Chicago for a bit, that's how civilized Chicago is compared to here. You guys don't even have those weird sandwich-hot pocket things we stopped for in Omaha, which have probably been the best part of the Midwest so far."

"Really? You liked those?"

"Hell yeah. Leagues better than gas station taquitos, at least. If it wasn't sacrilege for me to pit it against In 'N Out, I'd even say it's my favorite fast food," Louis said. When the cashier was no longer in ear shot, he checked over his shoulder to confirm she was well within the supply closet, then leaned into Ada. "By the way, you don't have a cell phone on you, do you?"

"No," She said. "You blew mine up in the grocery store, remember? Why? Are phone calls a bad thing?"

"Depends on the device," Louis said. "Landlines? Fine, no one uses those anyways. But cell phones? Hell, all Kamana has to do is create a targeted ad for Tura Industries and be able to narrow our location to a five mile radius. I bet they already have one set up for our favorite cashier at this point."

"Sammy has a cell phone," Ada said.

"I know," Louis said, a new solemnity crossing his features. "I allowed her to keep it because it's our main way to communicate and our little road trip was a social media algorithm's nightmare anyways. But we're getting too close to where we need to be. She needs to ditch it. Even if she deletes her social media, her phone is likely still hooked to too many data points to keep our location anonymous. Can you convince her?"

"What if I can't?"

Louis shrugged. "You saw what I did to yours. We could use it as a back-up against the robots if they find us because of it, but I can't promise I can make miracles happen twice, sweetheart."

Sighing, Ada opened the fridge door and claimed an armful of iced coffees. She knew what Sammy's phone meant to her, how it was often her only tool to communicate with people who didn't understand sign or had the patience to decipher her deaf voice. To ask her to willingly part with it seemed like asking Sammy to chop off a hand. But, Ada also didn't want to die. She actually went through a lot of effort to *not* die. She wanted to continue the success of that trend, for better or for worse. Making her way to the counter, Ada unloaded her armful of drinks in front of the register. Sammy was still reading her gossip magazine from earlier at the nearby magazine rack. Swallowing her last remaining doubt, Ada grabbed a penny from the tiny tray and tossed it at her friend. The penny landed on the fold of the magazine and Sammy looked up at Ada with a surprised expression.

"Still have your phone?" Ada signed.

Sammy nodded.

"Great. Get rid of it. Forever."

Sammy's expression dropped. She moved the magazine to one hand as Louis followed Ada with his own armful of drinks and snacks.

"Fuck you, no!" Sammy signed.

"Oh hey I know that one," Louis said. "She just told us to fuck off and no, right?"

"Yep." Ada said verbally. "Good work."

"Well, she signs them often enough," Louis said. "It's pretty easy to catch on."

Sammy nodded towards Louis.

"Is this Louis's idea?" Sammy signed.

"Yes," Ada signed, nodding her fist down. "He says it's a danger to where we're going next."

"Danger?" Sammy signed. "Where are we going? What's our plan? I'm not getting rid of my phone unless it's an emergency."

"Sammy says she won't get rid of the phone until you tell us where we're going next," Ada explained. "Specifically, if it's an emergency."

The cashier exited her supply closet with an armful of paper towels. Louis's eyes tracked the older woman carefully as she walked to the bathroom. Once she closed the bathroom door, the clear click of the lock echoing behind her, Louis turned to Ada.

"Grand Island," He said. "It's a farming town a couple miles west of here. There's a tractor supply manufacturer that we outsource some of the builds of the android mechanics to. Legally, it's easier to hide secret projects domestically than abroad. The government asks less questions when you don't have to internationally import and export materials for your maybe-not federally approved android creation project."

"Fantastic," Ada said. "Corporate America remains a stain on common morality."

"Well they don't exactly encourage the study of philosophy in engineering courses, you know. Anyway," Louis continued. "There's a chance Kamana hid some of her plans for Project Kamana there. If she's developing new androids, she'd need that manufacturer to be on board with it and that would require a preliminary blueprint. If the robots beat us there and take those blueprints, then we're fucked. I don't have any other leads than a security company in South Dakota or our workshop in California, both of which are heavily monitored by Kamana."

Ada translated Louis's plan to Sammy. Sammy diligently watched Ada's hands move through Louis's explanation. For a long time, Sammy was quiet as she looked between Ada and Louis. Finally, she placed her hands up.

"Can we at least stop at Disneyland when we go to California?" She asked. "See some actual sights before we get murdered by robots? I don't want my last memory to be corn and those awful hot pockets from Omaha."

"What's this?" Louis asked, mimicking Sammy's sign of two cupped "C's" on top of her head for makeshift mouse ears.

"She wants to go to Disneyland if we go to California," Ada said. "I may have mis-translated some of it, to be honest. Prepositions aren't easy to sign."

Turning to Sammy, Louis pinched his index and middle finger to his thumb for "no" and then replicated the cupped mouse ears to his head. Her eyebrows lifted in surprise at his attempt at sign before she pouted.

"Yes, Disneyland!" Sammy spoke out loud. Louis jumped. "If I'm getting rid of my phone, you're taking me to Disney and you're buying me a new phone. No more cabbage hot pockets either. Got it?"

Turning on her heel, Sammy exited the gas station. Louis watched her carefully as she left, not even paying attention as their cashier finally exited the bathroom with a loud, annoyed sigh. There was a spark in his green eyes that dimmed as Sammy left his sight to reach the Camaro. His Adam's apple bobbed as he turned back to Ada, the usual hard glare in his eyes returning swiftly.

"Your bossy friend seems to think we're surviving this thing," Louis said. "Let her know the first churro's on me if we do. Also she didn't like Runza? That'd explain why she stole all of the french fries."

Rolling her eyes, Ada focused on the cashier as the annoyed woman scanned their many items. It was likely the most she had to work for the entire day, but that didn't stop her from accepting Louis's credit card with a scowl. They were using Louis's great aunt Hannah's credit card to finance their trip, something that Louis assured them was so covertly obtained that the robots had no idea it existed. Ada silently added "credit card fraud" to Louis's ongoing list of crimes and didn't question it further. She wasn't starving and they weren't dead yet. That was good enough for Ada to keep using the thing. Once Sammy confirmed she destroyed her phone and threw it in the back of a pick-up truck headed east, Louis took the wheel of the Camaro and drove west. Ada noted how he shyly slid a lined notebook with a pen to Sammy before they left the gas station. A simple consolation, but a consolation nonetheless for forcing her to surrender her primary communication device. By the time he completed several backroad loops through multiple cornfields and small towns to complete their indirect path to the plant, it was already night time. They drove past the plant and parked the Camaro in a park not too far away from the fence line surrounding the facility.

"You guys stay here," Louis said. "Keep an eye out for any androids. I trust we threw them off our trail, but you never know with Kamana. I'll be back in an hour...or three - whenever I figure out what's going on here. If I'm not back by the time the sun comes up....Just, don't die, okay?"

Louis left before Ada could fight him on it. Sighing, she slumped into the passenger seat. Sammy sketched in her notebook, happy to be left alone in the backseat where she lounged across the seats. Country music, the only station they could find, played through the car speakers until the car battery timed off. Ada didn't feel like restarting it. For thirty minutes, the girls sat in silence and waited for Louis. After the thirtieth game of Tic-Tac-Toe in her notebook, Sammy finally sighed loudly and fell back into the backseat. Ada looked at her expectedly.

"Louis gets to have all the fun," Sammy signed.

"Better him than us," Ada signed.

"Maybe we could have some fun too," Sammy signed, raising her eyebrows as if she expected Ada to say yes to a death sentence.

"No," Ada signed. "We're supposed to be watching for robots, remember?"

"No robots, my phone is headed east!" Sammy signed. "Let's go! Helping Louis means we leave faster which means we don't need to watch for robots."

"We're going to get arrested," Ada argued.

"So? The robots can't reach us in jail, right?"

"Or it will make us easier to find."

"Then these robots are going to kill us either way," Sammy signed. "We can fight back or we can run. Why not fight back?"

"I'm fine with running," Ada signed. "It seems to be working."

"Ada, you lazy ass," Sammy signed. "We can actually do something with this. Besides, Louis owes me a trip to Disneyland if we win, and I intend to collect."

"Just bang him already and keep me out of it."

Sammy aggressively flicked Ada's ear out of annoyance. Ada audibly shouted in surprise and swiped a hand toward Sammy in retaliation. Easily dodging it, Sammy stuck her tongue out and pulled herself to the door.

"You do what you want, but I'm going to help Louis," Sammy signed. "I don't intend to die sitting on my ass."

Opening the car door, Sammy ignored Ada's desperate attempts for her attention. With a loud groan, Ada opened her car door too and followed Sammy. She still thought following Louis into the gates of hell was a bad idea, but not following Sammy seemed like a worse idea. If Sammy was surprised that Ada joined her, she didn't express it as they snuck towards the surrounding chain link fence. Sammy found a loose opening underneath the fencing and they squeezed through. Ada's heart pounded fast as she shuffled under the chain link, the metal wiring scratching her tank top. She never broke in anywhere before. Now they were willingly trespassing onto a dark machinery yard filled with shadows of farming equipment that she couldn't identify by name. A lot of the shadows appeared sharp. Were any robots lurking behind them, preparing to gut Ada and Sammy as soon as they crossed paths?

They hurried through the yard, dodging the various pieces of heavy equipment scattered through it. Ada kept her ears open for any sort of footsteps or hum of technology to indicate they were being watched in any way. Something wasn't setting right in her stomach, but it might have just been the threat of death looming over their heads. There wasn't anything other than the vibrant buzzing of cicadas singing through the warm Nebraska summer night. It seemed odd to Ada that security would be light, but maybe Louis was wrong. Maybe their new location was harmless, not some secret evil robot place. It seemed abandoned enough.

A soft rattle of chains dragging against cement proved Ada's hope wrong.

Stopping Sammy, Ada physically pulled her friend back by her shoulders and hid them behind a tree located in the lot. Sammy shot her a questioning look.

"Heard something," Ada signed. "Over there."

She pointed towards the massive garage looming in the near distance. Sammy nodded and risked a peek to the side. Another minute later, she turned to Ada.

"Dog," Sammy signed. "Two in front of the door. Big, sharp teeth."

"Should we go back?" Ada asked.

"I dated a Mormon with military parents," Sammy signed. "These puppies are nothing."

After breaking some branches off the nearby tree, Sammy nodded towards the door. Ada hesitantly followed, quietly making her own escape plan if Sammy's plan didn't work. They ducked behind rusty equipment close to the door, allowing Ada full access to see the beasts. Sammy was right in the fact that the dogs were big with sharp teeth, but she failed to mention how methodically they moved. Pacing back and forth, like soldiers on watch, each step of the canines was measured and timed in sync to the other. It struck Ada as odd on how well trained these dogs were. She hoped it didn't mean their supervisor was still around.

Without warning, Sammy chucked a branch away from the door. It landed with a snap and skidded across the cement with a hollow echo. Both dogs stopped in their paths and perked an ear up in attention at the noise. Sammy silently took her shoes off and indicated for Ada to do the same. As Ada worked on untangling her shoelace, Sammy threw another branch. This time, it hit the side of a machine with a dull thud. Both dogs marched towards the noise, pointing at the source of the noise with sharp noses. A snarl escaped their lips.

Sammy checked to confirm the dogs' attention was away from the door. As soon as they turned to resume their methodic patrol, she chucked another stick as far as she could. It bounced off the wall of the building and landed with a clatter. The dogs barked wildly and chased after the noise, going as far as they could with the rattling chains tied around their necks. The noise was enough to alert the entire plant, but Sammy could care less. She sprinted to the door, holding her flats against her chest as she threw the remaining sticks at the space in front of the dogs. Ada followed, gripping her tennis shoes tight enough to her chest that she was positive she went down a bra size. When they reached the door, Sammy wiggled the doorknob to find it was locked. Dropping her flats, she handed the rest of the branches to Ada and pulled a hairpin from her bun, allowing tendrils of light brown and pink hair to fall from it. She kneeled to be eye-level with the doorknob and worked on picking the lock. With Sammy's stick distraction gone, the dogs sniffed the air. One spotted Ada and Sammy. Ada and the dog made eye contact. A low snarl hummed from its lips that alerted its partner to the intruders' presence. The other dog spotted Ada too and growled. With both dogs snarling at Ada, and Sammy oblivious to the threat, Ada had only one choice.

She threw a stick.

Instead of flying over their heads as it was intended, it made direct contact with the center of the first dog's forehead and bounced off like it was nothing. The dog didn't even flinch. Her heart had stopped when she realized she actually hit the animal, but now her mind was blank. The dog should've reacted or something by now. Against her better judgment, she threw another stick directly at the other dog. Again it bounced off its head and landed on the ground a few feet away. The dog didn't acknowledge the attack.

Suddenly, with a howling chorus of barks and snarls, the dogs rushed towards Ada. She kept throwing the sticks, hoping that it would stop their attack but each stick bounced off the dogs as if they couldn't feel it. Before Ada could execute her emergency escape plan and bail for the low spot in the fence again, Sammy grabbed her arm and pulled her into the building. Shoving the metal door behind them, Sammy struggled to lock the door again as the dogs slammed against it. Finally, with a click, the door was locked and closed. Despite it being locked, the dogs rushed against it, rattling the wall. Scared, Ada turned to the rest of the facility to see if there was another place to hide or escape to in case the dogs got through somehow. The massive building was pitch black. Ada pressed her hands to the wall to feel for a switch of some sort. Running her hand against the cool metal, her fingers bumped over a small, almost indistinguishable plastic mold.

"Found light!" Sammy verbally shouted.

"No, I did!" Ada shouted back, temporarily forgetting who she was speaking to.

Before she could even think to get Sammy's attention, the entire room was flooded with orange emergency lights. Boxes filled the room in towering structures that created a maze throughout the warehouse with random mechanical pieces strewn about. Stairs led to an office on the second floor, an obvious way to oversee operations. Ada looked at the switch she found. The word "security" was etched above it. Stepping away from it as fast as she could, she followed Sammy deeper into the warehouse.

"This place is creepy," Sammy signed. "Looks like it hasn't been used in a while."

"Weird they have well-trained dogs guarding it," Ada signed. "Maybe Louis is right. Maybe something is up here."

"Check the computers," Sammy signed. "I'll look around down here. I'll scream if I need you."

"And if I need you?" Ada signed.

Sammy shrugged before walking off. With a discontented groan, Ada made her way up the stairs. The office door was unlocked. Probably because no one expected anyone to get past the dogs and the first locked door. Or, realistically, there was nothing to hide. Ada walked in anyways, closing the door behind her. She sat at the main desk with a view into the warehouse. Booting the computer, she was met with the blue glow of a login screen.

Contrary to Sammy's belief, Ada did not get her hacking skills from her background as a programmer. In fact, her education actively discouraged the practice, despite providing the knowledge to do so. Instead, her job at Geek Squad dealing with customers who never remembered their password and brought their devices to her to unlock gave her the most experience with hacking. Ada found that, in general, Karens emailing pot roast recipes to friends were more effective with teaching life skills than tenured college professors. To her small pride as well, it only took three tries to get the password (Name of the company, first letter capitalized + 123!) and she found herself on a desktop screen with a generic picture of golden wheat fields as the background. On instinct, she visited the file folder. A disorganized mess of templates for invoices, work orders, and other business papers greeted her efforts. The downloads folder proved to be similarly disorganized and fruitless.

Hoping against hope, she tapped the Internet Explorer icon and searched through the recent history to reach the person's email. Thousands of emails scrolled across the screen, all dealing with invoices or orders. Some local singles looking for fun were sprinkled in there for good measure. Ada ignored how those were the read emails, while some "ACTION REQUIRED" notices remained unread. Licking her lips, Ada typed "Tura Industries" into the search bar. To her moderate surprise, a solid number of emails filled the screen. Hundreds, even. Before she could search through the dozens of recent invoices traded back and forth, an email with the phrase "security measures" caught her eye. She clicked on it.

FROM: SECURITY@TURAINDUSTRIES.COM

TO: FRANK@EMAIL.COM

SUBJECT: NOTICE: SECURITY SYSTEM UPGRADE

In response to a recent company compromise, we at Tura Industries feel that it is necessary to upgrade your existing security measures. It is within the interest of your company to comply with these new measures. Failure to do so will prevent further business to be taken between our companies. We already took the initiative to deliver our new security system to you. It is at your discretion to implement these measures.

There was a response to the original email sent by Tura Industries. Ada skipped ahead to read it.

FROM: FRANK@EMAIL.COM

TO: SECURITY@TURAINDUSTRIES.COM

SUBJECT: RE: NOTICE: SECURITY SYSTEM UPGRADE

Thank you for providing these additional security measures. We've implemented some of the models to great success. However, a bulk of the order appears to be defective. Will you be replacing these models or how will you like us to proceed with these defects?

The response from Tura Industries was short.

FROM: SECURITY@TURAINDUSTRIES.COM

TO: FRANK@EMAIL.COM

SUBJECT: FINAL NOTICE: SECURITY SYSTEM UPGRADE

Project Kamana does not make mistakes.

The door kicked open, splintering the wood frame. Ada jumped a foot in the air even before realizing a handgun was aimed at her head. Throwing her hands in the air, she struggled to catch her breath as she made eye contact with the intruder. Louis Ventura's dull green eyes glistened in the darkness as he too realized who he was looking at, his face shifting quickly from aggression to confusion once he recognized Ada.

Twisting his wrist, he aimed the gun to the ceiling.

"Well, this is odd," He remarked. "I thought I left you in the car."

Before Ada could reply or explain herself, Sammy's scream echoed throughout the warehouse.

Louis was the first to leave the office. Ada followed, hoping to find Sammy before he did. She chased Louis down the stairs and through the maze of boxes before he abruptly stopped near the back of the warehouse. Holding his arm out, he stopped Ada too. She looked over his arm to see that Sammy stood on a tall box, cornered by more guard dogs, fending them off with a rusty crowbar. These were not the dogs positioned in front of the building with their well-trained pose and prowl. These dogs looked feral. Their heads twitched unnaturally and foam dripped from their mouths as they snarled at Sammy.

Without another thought, Louis shot a bullet into the back of each dog's head, his aim impeccable. All of them dropped like dead weights, not looking one bit hurt by the violence. Sammy released a loud gasp before covering her mouth and looking at Louis with wide, panicked eyes. Sighing, Louis reached into his leather jacket and pulled a handful of bullets out.

"Tura technology," Louis said. "Dad always loved dogs, but hated the taking care of them part. Thought it'd be a good idea to mechanize them." He reloaded his weapon. "However, they got infected with that silly little virus that we all love known as Kamana....and here we are. Aggressive lil machines with not a bit of soul or love to them. Bastards."

Ada turned to Sammy who was still standing, traumatized, on the box in the corner.

"Robot dogs," Ada signed. "Not real."

Sammy relaxed considerably. Louis remained unfazed as he reloaded his gun. After Ada signed that it was safe, Sammy slowly got down from the box as Ada turned to Louis.

"Did you get the information you were looking for?" Ada asked.

"They don't have anything. Apparently, Project Kamana is so well guarded that the bitch doesn't even trust our manufacturers with it. This place has gone to the dogs." Cocking his weapon, he barely acknowledged his pun as he glared at Ada. "Now what the hell are you two doing here? How did you even get in here? The security on this place is insane if you didn't program half of it yourself, which I did."

"I had a Mormon boyfriend," Sammy signed, holding her crowbar under her armpit.

"Sammy had a Mormon boyfriend," Ada translated. "With military parents, for the record."

"Of course she did," Louis asked. "Ask her if she's ever dated a priest because we're going to need a miracle if we're going to get to the bottom of Project Kamana at this rate."

"Does a seminary student count?" Sammy signed, finger-spelling 'seminary'. Ada shot her a look. "What? Can you blame a girl? You can't throw a rock without hitting one in Philly."

A door slammed at the front of the warehouse. Footsteps clicked through the room at a fast, but methodical, pace.

"Freya's gonna be pissed he didn't go to the Iowa location," A male's voice boomed through the room. "Do you think we should save him for her?"

"Do we have a choice?" Another man with a British accent laughed.

"Shit," Louis whispered. "Hercules and Beefcake. Eyepatch's brainless goons. Well. They're all Kamana's brainless goons, but you know what I mean. Stay here while I take care of this."

"Hey Louis!" The first guy shouted. "We gotcha, buddy."

"Our new toys caught you red-handed!" The British guy added. "You're going to regret that Pittsburgh stunt."

A dog barked. Louis bolted from Ada and Sammy. Ada dragged Sammy to hide behind some boxes.

"Two guys are here for Louis," Ada signed. "We need to leave."

"Wait..." Sammy peeked over the boxes. "Where are they?"

"Front of the building."

"I have an idea," Sammy signed. "Be my ears."

She tightened her grip on the rusty crowbar she was using to fend off the dogs and made her way to a large crate. Ada followed, checking the two guys' positions. They were the same size, each with broad shoulders and strong arms, dressed in black and red armored suits. One with dark skin and a round face. There was a solemn expression to his serious eyes as he scanned the room. The other had dark hair and a manicured beard barely gracing his chiseled jawline, a smug smile drawn on his lips as he looked around the room. Each of them held a growling dog by the chain, having to pull back every so often to prevent the dogs from getting loose.

"Oye, maybe we should've lessened the aggression levels on these pups," The android with dark skin mumbled to his partner, a hint of a British accent teasing his words. "They're still in beta testing. Once we send them onto that brat, we don't know if we'll regain control."

"Freya's orders, Oro," The other android said as he pulled back on the dog again. "No mercy on Louis or the deaf girl."

"What about the other one?" Oro asked. "The programmer?"

"Taken alive," Hercules said. "Kamana's orders."

Ada's heart dropped. What did these psycho robots want with her? Not to mention, weren't they literally trying to kill her yesterday? Five days ago? When did Pittsburgh happen? Shaking her head from her new torrent of anxious thoughts, Ada didn't bother to translate the last part for Sammy.

"They're headed our way," Ada signed.

Sammy positioned the crowbar into the opening of the box before signing to Ada. "Let me know when they're distracted."

Ada peeked over the boxes again. The two androids were headed their way. All of her nerve endings felt shot. As the dogs' barks grew louder, panic rose in Ada's chest. She knew this night wasn't going to go well, but she had no idea it would be this terrible. She was expecting cold handcuffs and the back of a cop car for trespassing. Not being eaten alive by robot dogs with sharp, likely metal and maybe razor, teeth.

"You know if robots could love, you guys would be a cute couple."

The androids turned to Louis's voice as he stood on a tall box behind them, gun hidden away and hands tucked into his leather jacket pockets.

"However, you hunks of metal can't even think for yourselves let alone feel human emotion," Louis continued. "But still. If you could love, Harding would be so pleased to know he finally defeated God. I'd also make a very cute ring bearer for your wedding, don't you think?"

"You're a dead man, Louis," Beefcake shouted. "Not even your father wants to show you mercy for all the trouble you've caused the company."

"What a coincidence." Louis smirked. "I also don't want to show my father any mercy. Seems like the apple doesn't fall too far, eh?"

"Now?" Sammy signed with one hand.

"Where's Allen?" Hercules shouted, struggling to hold his dog back. "Tell us where he is and Kamana might let you live."

Sammy pinched Ada. "Now?!"

Louis's smile was wide, but menacing.

"I don't need that bitch's mercy either."

"Now!" Ada signed with both of her hands, dropping them with ferocity.

With a grunt, Sammy pushed against the crowbar. The crate wiggled open. She pushed back and forth on the crack. The lid snapped open with a drop of the wooden door. Taking the crowbar with her, Sammy immediately sprinted towards the exit. She pulled Ada along with a tight grip on her wrist.

"That's unfortunate," Hercules cooed, still facing Louis. "Because-"

Sammy pushed past the two androids, avoiding the two trained dogs. One dog snapped at Ada as she was dragged past. She released a short shout and hurried closer behind Sammy, shaking Sammy's hold off of her wrist.

"Those are the girls from Pittsburgh!" Beefcake shouted. "What the-"

A chorus of barks echoed behind Ada. With wide eyes, she checked over her shoulder as she watched a stampede of feral, glitching robot dogs emerge from the box Sammy opened. They ran full speed after them. One of the feral robot dogs leapt into the air. It bit Beefcake on the shoulder, digging metal teeth into the soft skin. The shock of the bite made Beefcake scream in pain and release his tight grip on his own dog's leash. Beefcake's trained dog made a beeline for Ada and Sammy. The trained dog was much faster than its feral counterparts, moving with focus towards its target. While the other dogs barrelled after a retreating Hercules and Beefcake, forcing Louis to hop from warehouse box to box, Beefcake's loose dog knew his target. It knew how to reach them and how to terrify them. Ada looked back at it. Its unblinking eyes met her gaze and it released an echoing bark. Startled, Ada tripped over a fallen crate. Sammy, not realizing Ada fell or the dog barked, kept running towards the exit. Realizing the dog would catch up to her before she could catch up to Sammy, Ada jumped onto a nearby box. She struggled to find her footing as the trained dog snapped at her from the ground. Sammy finally turned and her face fell when she realized where Ada went.

"Ada!" Sammy shouted.

"Go!" Ada waved one hand to the exit. "Leave!"

With a nod, Sammy took one look at the oncoming wave of feral robotic dogs and bolted again. Ada focused back on her dog. It was snapping wildly at her, bearing all of its pointed teeth. It shoved against the box with its front paws and Ada lost her footing again. She slipped, exposing her leg to the dog's reach. Quickly yanking her leg away, the dog's teeth only found its way into the fabric of her sweatpants. A chunk of material ripped off as the dog pulled down on it. The dog shook the sweatpants material in his teeth mind-lessly, its head almost twitching with the strain of the mechanics. It no longer cared for Ada's presence with half of her sweatpants in his mouth. Watching the creature carefully, Ada realized that his programming noted that it had a victim. It wasn't going to attack her until its current victim, her sweatpants, were destroyed. That must have been the only scent it tracked. She knew first hand that AI was tough enough to train on its own; she couldn't even fathom training something to effectively distinguish smells. It likely only captured the relative scent of her sweatpants and processed the information from there.

She didn't have time to deliberate on it more. The pack of feral robot dogs were still chasing the two androids and Louis. It was only a matter of time until their hunt reached her location. Jumping from her box in the opposite direction, she bolted for the exit. Half of her sweatpants remained in the robot dog's mouth, effectively distracting the bot. Twisting through the maze of boxes, she constantly looked over her shoulder to make sure none of the dogs or androids were following until she reached the door. As she turned to leave, her eyes caught the security button she saw earlier. She smacked it before bolting through the exit.

An alarm rang through the whole building. Gates slowly descended over the doors, ensuring nobody else could get in or out. Good news for the androids and dogs, bad news for Louis, but Ada trusted he'd figure it out. She sprinted towards the low spot in the fence they crawled through earlier. A soft hum of electricity vibrated through the air now. Apparently the security button also activated the electric fence. Cursing, she tried looking around for another exit. Red and blue lights reflected in the distance of the dark horizon, the sound of sirens following their arrival. The skid of rubber tires on gravel caught Ada's attention as the Camaro pulled up at a high speed outside of the fence. The driver's window rolled down.

"Ada, get in!" Sammy shouted.

"Fence is dangerous," Ada signed. "Can't get through."

With a nod, Sammy rolled the window up. Ada watched as the Camaro sat for an extra moment. Then it reversed before speeding forward suddenly. Sammy crashed the car straight into the fence a few feet away from Ada, causing an explosion of sparks and the scratching noise of metal against plastic. The Camaro pulled away and revealed a hole big enough for Ada to squeeze through in the fence. Sucking in her gut, she did her best to avoid the still sparking metal and made it to the car. Jumping into the passenger side, Ada released a heavy breath.

"Get out of here," She signed and said out loud.

As Sammy punched the car into reverse, someone hit the front of the hood. Both girls let out a scream until they realized it was Louis. Recovering quickly, he aimed his gun at the darkened windshield.

"Out of the car," Louis shouted.

Sammy gave Ada an annoyed look before rolling down both of their windows. With pursed lips, Sammy threw a middle finger out of the window and at Louis. Ada followed her lead. Louis rolled his eyes.

"Oh right. It's you guys." Louis put his gun away. "Sorry. I forgot we were working together."

A bullet shot over Louis's head. Both Ada and Louis turned to the source. Beefcake and Hercules were running towards them from the plant building. Beefcake was confident, aiming his gun at Louis as he continued his mission. Hercules, on the other hand, was panicked as he shot behind them at the feral dogs and the two competent dogs chasing them.

"Shit!" Louis shouted, running around to the backseat.

He dove into the car as the androids reached the fence. They ascended the sparking chain links, not reacting as they climbed despite the electricity coursing through them. Looking panicked, Sammy smashed her foot against the pedal, speeding down the road.

"Why the hell did you guys leave the car?!" Louis shouted. "I told you to stay here and look out for those assholes!"

"We thought we could help!" Ada exclaimed. "Well Sammy did-"

"Well, you didn't," Louis said. "Now our fingerprints are all over the place and we've got Beefcake and Hercules on our asses. Thankfully, I've always got a Plan Z. Take me to the front entrance! I have something there that can clean this up."

"Front entrance," Ada signed. "For Louis."

Nodding, Sammy whipped the car around and drove to the front entrance. She stopped near the front entrance and Louis got out.

"Meet me in North Platte, Nebraska!" Louis shouted. "I'll get them off our trail! Just keep going!"

Before Ada could ask for clarification, he sprinted to the front doors. She turned to Sammy.

"Head west," Ada signed. "He'll meet us later."

With a frown, Sammy pulled away at a high speed. They sped down the lone road leading to the main highway, not even looking to check where the androids or pack of dogs went to. If they were being followed, Ada figured it'd still be a while for them to catch up given how fast Sammy drove. But before they could make it to the highway, a massive explosion occurred behind them. It vibrated through the air in a shock. Even Sammy winced at how the car shook from the far explosion. Pulling over, Sammy and Ada stepped out of the car and looked back at the plant. A fire was sweeping through the area with the dogs' barks dying out as the blaze spread. The entire plant would be ashes within the hour. Sammy turned to Ada.

"Louis?" She signed, her hazel eyes wide with concern.

Ada could feel her breath get short.

"I don't know," She confessed with weak hand movements.

Logically, she knew they should drive away. Go to North Platte as Louis told them to. But they were in shock over the implications that Louis was dead, his last commands null and void. They waited as the squadron of police cars flew past them to the ongoing fire at the plant. Eventually, the firetrucks came. Then an ambulance. There was no way Louis would survive that blast. Ada couldn't imagine anything surviving that level of destruction, not even the androids. Ada and Sammy were officially on their own against the legion of killer robots and robot dogs.

Only one thing was more terrifying to Ada.

<!-- Failure. The only word running through Ada's mind was failure.

Ada stared at the paper in frozen disbelief. A C-? She never received a grade this low before. How could she fail? She wrote and double checked those formulas until they were imprinted in her brain as sure as her memory on how to ride a bike.

"Ada, are you okay?" Dan asked. "You look sick."

He looked at the paper.

"Oh c'mon, you're not that upset are you?" Dan smirked. "The highest grade anyone has ever gotten on this assignment was a B! A C- is impressive as hell. I got a D."

"I've never gotten a C- before." Ada felt her mouth get dry. "What will my mom say?"

"It's college." Dan shrugged. "Don't tell her."

Ada was better than this. Ada knew she could've had the highest grade if she just applied herself. If she had spent the week studying more rather than hanging out with Dan. If she didn't allow herself so much leniency on her grades. Programming was the one thing she was good at. It was the one thing she was known for in high school, the one thing she went to college for. It was what she grew up doing, sitting at her dad's work computer and playing with the code builder while he was in a meeting. She was terrible at soccer, terrible at art, terrible at everything else her parents threw at her, but her programming abilities brought her purpose. It was the first time she felt in control of her life. The program only functioned the way it did because she demanded it to function in that way. She wrote the lines of code, she controlled the outcome. Who was she if she wasn't good at programming?

"Ada, you seriously look like shit," Dan said.

"Still going for boyfriend of the year, are you?" Ada said, bile rising in her throat.

"Ada..." Now Dan's voice was low, dipping into a soft coo. "What are you even doing?"

Looking up at him, the moment of confusion abided her weak stomach. "What?"

"Look at you!" Dan gestured towards her entire body. "You're getting yourself this worked up over one lousy grade?"

"Dr. Grace thinks I have a shot at an internship with Google," Ada explained.

"Google interns don't get C-'s on assignments."

"Is it worth it?" Dan asked. "Honestly you're killing yourself with this kind of workload."

"Yeah well if I'm not good at programming-"

The anxiety tornado sent her thoughts spiraling. She barfed into Daniel Carrabella's lap. -->

95

CHAPTER FIVE

Louis Ventura wasn't dead.

But he might as well have been.

While Sammy and Ada spent a sleepless night in a motel in the nearby town, trying to figure out if they should move onto North Platte like Louis said or find their own way to survive, Louis Ventura was arrested by the Hall County police on suspicion of vandalism. The girls would've never known about his survival and arrest if it wasn't for the fact the gas station they stopped at prior to the attack got their faces on camera with the phone-addicted cashier spilling everything to whoever asked about them. When they went to leave the next morning, they were stopped by the motel manager and a police officer.

"Do you recognize this man?" The police officer held a grimy mugshot of Louis up. The fresh soot on his face revealed that Louis had obviously been caught in the blast of the explosion, but he did, somehow, survive it.

"Louis!" Sammy squealed out loud. "Is he alive?!" She signed to Ada.

"So you do know this man?" The police officer arched an eyebrow.

"He, uh, helped us fix a flat tire," Ada said, resisting the urge to smack Sammy. "Told us his name, asked if we wanted dinner, if we believed in fate...all that good rich white boy stuff. Why? Why do you ask?"

A little under an hour later, they were strolling into the Hall County Corrections reception area. It was clear that Ada and Sammy were outsiders. Sammy wore an expensive bohemian dress, her light brown hair accented with light pink streaks let loose underneath a floppy hat. An artist flaunting in a farmers' world. Ada would be an outsider no matter where she went, but the rural Midwest was particularly exclusively white. Her dark brown skin stuck out in every crowd here. She did make Sammy drive them to the local mall first so she could pick up a bra and clothes more appropriate for the courthouse that could, hopefully, diminish the amount of judgemental looks she got. Plus, her sweatpants were ruined from the dog bite last night. She needed new clothes and Sammy was more than happy to buy a new wardrobe for them both with Great Aunt Hannah's credit card. When they approached the front desk of the corrections area, they each wore clothes that were the farthest thing from "we were maybe indirectly responsible for major destruction at a major manufacturing plant last night" and Ada was grateful for that one mercy.

"Hi," Ada stated. "We're here to post bail for Louis Ventura."

The receptionist looked up from her work.

"Louis Ventura?" She tapped something into the computer and punched the enter button. "There's no Louis Ventura in our system. In fact, this system reports that he's been dead for over a year. Car accident in California."

Ada gave her a look. "That's impossible. We were just told he was being held here."

"How are you connected to them?" The receptionist said. "Maybe he has a different legal name than the one he gave you."

Feeling blood rush to her face, Ada knew she shouldn't have trusted Louis Ventura. He was a felon and a fraud and deserved to rot in his prison cell. Pretending to be this righteous prodigy son of a tech leader just so he could have an excuse to destroy property. Then he could use those fake credentials to make Ada and Sammy look like idiots and abandon them in a god-awful state, not caring for their deaths. He even went through the effort of pretending that he cared about them so they would trust him more. Saving their lives, bringing them along with him so they could be tricked under the disillusion of security but really he was just using them as his own safety net. They were fools. To think she almost shelled the money out to save his sorry ass.

"He was nobody," Ada almost spat. "Just a guy I met at the wrong place at the wrong time."

"Oh honey, we've all been there," The receptionist said. "Trust me, he ain't worth it. You deserve better."

Turning on her heel, Ada stormed to the door. Sammy caught up and grabbed her arm.

"What's wrong? Where is Louis?"

"We're idiots," Ada signed. "He played us. They don't even have a Louis Ventura in their computer. He lied to us about his name! Louis isn't real."

"Ada, don't give up!" Sammy signed. "Maybe he gave them a fake name?"

"Or he gave us a fake name!" Ada signed, looking furious. She sighed deeply. "This is stupid. Let's go home and forget this ever happened."

"Go home? Pittsburgh?" Sammy looked concerned as Ada nodded. "We will die."

"You want to keep driving?" Ada signed. "I don't want to drive. I want to go home."

Ada turned to walk away, but Sammy grabbed her shoulder with an intensity that required Ada to continue their conversation.

"What? You want to go home and sleep on my couch and work at your pathetic job that you hate?" Sammy signed, her eyes desperate. "You want to continue to be sad?!"

"It's better than pretending to be something I am not!" Ada was getting pissed at her best friend's betrayal. "You're not a hero, Sammy, and neither am I."

Pursing her lips, Sammy glared at Ada as she signed slowly and with intent.

"I'm not leaving here without Louis," Sammy signed. "These robots are dangerous. They can hurt other people. He can help us. He can stop them from hurting other people too."

"Louis can't do shit," Ada signed. "If you were smart, you would realize that Louis just used us to pin his crimes. We're his scape-goats."

Bewildered at Ada's insult, Sammy raised her hands in retort, but an obvious thought crossed her mind before she could return the damage. Softening her face but keeping her intense eyes, Sammy balanced her middle finger on her palm and wiggled it back and forth.

"Medicine?"

Ada thought about it.

"No," She admitted, weakly tapping her fingers together. "How I feel about Louis is the same, regardless of whether I took my medicine. He's still bad news."

"It's no excuse for your comment about my intelligence," Sammy signed. Her eyes were still angry, but the rest of her face was soft with pity. "We'll talk when you take your medicine."

With a heavy sigh, Ada exited the courthouse as Sammy made her way to the front desk. Irritability was the first sign that Ada forgot her medicine for the day. After that it was puking, headaches, inability to sleep, and vivid nightmares that came for her when she did finally pass out. Although she hated it when she accidentally lashed out at Sammy, she kind of wanted to be pissy for a day. She liked the feeling. It was vindicating.

Unlocking the Camaro, it took her some time to locate her pills in the backseat among the piles of trash that remained from their road trip. They tried to keep it clean, but at one point gave up on the endeavor. It was easier to pretend the trash wasn't there than it was to mentally deal with it as part of their routine fifteen minute pit stops. She finally found the orange bottle and swallowed a pill down with a half-empty bottle of Mountain Dew. Finishing the drink, the rush of caffeine and the pill's effects remedied Ada's mood. She slammed the car door shut and locked it. As soon as she stood straight, she came toe-to-toe with a tall man with a wide smile and tufted brown hair.

"Ada Kakar," Detective Gates Hopper said. "What a small world we live in."

Ada looked him up and down. He wasn't in his gray detective suit that she saw him last in Pittsburgh, but rather a short-sleeve button down and khaki shorts. A white bandage wrapped around his bicep and he held a steaming cup of coffee in one hand. Surely he experienced the same hell the three of them had gone through over the past week or so driving through the greater Midwest. Surely he was also getting hunted down by killer robots. Surely he was also living out of his car as he ran from said killer robots, sleeping in piles of trash. Judging from the happy glint in his eye, Ada could only assume he had a much different week than they had. His mental health was probably pristine too. Some bastards really had it all.

"Detective Hopper." Ada crossed her arms over her chest. She liked the guy, but his appearance in a Nebraska jail's parking lot was too off-putting for her comfort level. "You're a long way from Pittsburgh. What are you doing here?"

"Please," Detective Hopper held up his hand. "Call me Gates. I'm not here to arrest you or anything along those lines, so there's no need for the formality."

"Okay...Gates," Ada said, testing the name. It was still weirdly informal. "That still doesn't answer my question."

"How are you doing though? Feeling any better from the, um, almost killed by robots thing?"

"I'll feel better once my question is answered."

After a long half minute where Ada didn't entertain his attempts at small talk, the detective sighed heavily. He sounded disappointed that Ada didn't fall for his charm.

"I'm here for Louis Ventura," Gates said. "As the presiding agent over his case, I've been asked to retrieve him from this facility in order to ask some questions in regards to his charges in Pittsburgh."

"Good luck," Ada snorted. "That's not even the real Louis Ventura in there. The real Louis Ventura has been dead for over a year."

"Oh no, that should be the real Louis Ventura." Gates pointed his coffee cup towards the building. "I saw his mugshot. His legal death is a cover up for his crime spree." Ada gave the detective an incredulous look and he threw his hands up. "Hey, I've been investigating this guy for a while now. I think I would know if he was the real deal or not."

Gates sipped his coffee and Ada pursed her lips, staring at the detective. Rolling her eyes, she dropped her arms.

"Well if he's in there, then he's not using a real name," She said. "Sammy and I already tried bailing him out."

"I can help with that," Gates said.

"What? Are you going to 'nice cop' the other cops?" Ada asked. "I'm pretty sure you need another bad cop for that. Do you need me to be your bad cop or do you work exclusively with murder robots?"

Her heart dropped when she realized she was insulting an officer of the law. An officer of the law who had every right to arrest her for helping Louis. But to her surprise, and relief, the detective seemingly forgave her sass almost immediately. The corners of Gates's lips curved as his eyes lit up, delighted at Ada's remarks.

"It would be fun to work with a human this time," Gates said. "However, you don't have to worry about anything. I don't think I'll need a partner for this."

Still holding his smirk, Gates stepped forward to Ada, leaning into her slightly.

"After all, not everyone can resist my charm like you clearly can, Miss Kakar."

Gates winked before making his way towards the jail. Ada followed him first with her eyes, perplexed by the mysterious detective who potentially just flirted with her instead of arresting her. Then she followed him with her feet, forever staying three steps behind him and his long legs. When they reached the reception area, Gates held the door open for Ada and waited for her to enter first. Once they were inside, they joined Sammy at the sides of the reception desk. Gates politely tapped Sammy on the shoulder.

"I've got it from here." He said, indicating to the desk.

Sammy's eyes grew wide in shock at seeing the detective that they left back in Pittsburgh. However, she still nodded and moved out of the way. Gates took her place and faced the receptionist.

"Hi. Detective Gates Hopper of the FBI. I understand there's some confusion over Louis Ventura?"

"Badge?" The receptionist asked. Gates produced it without a second thought from his khaki shorts. She examined it carefully then nodded. "Yes, Detective. This woman right here claims that when her boyfriend gets drunk, he uses a different name to avoid getting in trouble. However, our system is too large to determine what name he could've used. It'll be impossible to-"

"Try Gideon Paz."

Barely acknowledging Gates's interruption, the receptionist typed the name into the system. With a humble sort of smugness, Gates sipped his coffee and ignored Ada's prying stare. After a moment, a profile popped onto the screen. The receptionist clapped.

"Aha! Right here!" She turned the computer screen towards them and pointed at the profile. Sure enough, Louis's mugshot and all of his other information displayed on the monitor. Sammy clapped excitedly. The receptionist leaned towards Sammy.

"IS. THIS. YOUR. BOYFRIEND?" The receptionist shouted with a painfully condescending slowness.

At the woman's behavior, Sammy's excitement died. She nodded politely, embarrassed to correct the woman. Ada gave the receptionist a nasty look.

"You realize she was born deaf, right?" Ada asked. "Like she can't hear you at whatever volume you shout at her with?"

"Oh! Sorry!" The receptionist turned her screen back to its original spot. "Just wanted to make sure she understood."

"She understood. She's not an idiot," Ada said. "She just can't hear you."

Ignoring Ada's confrontation, the receptionist typed something into the computer with pursed lips. There were several awkward moments of silence as the receptionist completed her tasks and Ada's words remained unacknowledged. Gates sipped his coffee, giving Ada a side glance that she ignored. Finally, the receptionist turned to the trio.

"Bail for Gideon Paz is set at $50,000," The receptionist explained. "You have a couple options. While you can pay with a check or cash, you can also hire a bail bondsman if you can't afford it. Gideon will still need to appear for his court date and-"

"Actually none of this will be necessary," Gates politely interrupted. "What's your name, ma'am?"

"Dolores."

"Well, Dolores," Gates said. He initiated his charming smile. "I'm the presiding agent over Louis Ventura's case and I've been ordered by my lieutenant to retrieve him for further questioning for the FBI. His act of destruction against private property here is one charge in a multitude of charges set against him which requires further federal investigation."

"Sorry, detective, but I'm going to need to see some paperwork for a formal discharge," Dolores said. "Now for the bail-"

"Dolores," Gates interrupted with a bit more sternness. "I'd hate to do this, but you have a prisoner booked incorrectly into your system. Generally this would cause *weeks* of paperwork, going through commanders and what not, to fix this glaring error. This could tarnish the reputation and credentials of your formidable prison system."

Straightening himself, Gates set his coffee down on the counter.

"Now, you are presented with an opportunity that will bypass all of this hassle," He said. "After all, you will be handing all of the problems with this prisoner over to me, a federal agent of the law, without consequence. If anything goes wrong, it will be all on me and I can handle it. No paperwork for bail, no worrying about the prisoner showing up for his scheduled court date, and I'm sure your supervisors will appreciate your initiative. If needed, I can even have my own supervisors email the required paperwork and credentials for the transfer after we've processed Louis for federal booking." With a glowing smile, Gates had Dolores the receptionist's full attention and then some. "So what do you say, Dolores?"

An hour later, Louis Ventura strolled out of the Hall County Corrections front doors.

Still wearing his stupid leather jacket, Louis was ultimately the same asshole, even in spite of the serious beating his face took in that explosion. His eyes scanned the parking lot, looking slightly dazed. Pulling herself from the Camaro, Sammy smiled and waved excitedly at him. When he froze in place, looking even more confused at the trio's presence, Sammy took that as her cue to run to him. Gates and Ada shared a glance before following Sammy. Sammy rushed forward to hug him. Louis, although still confused, hugged back. When they pulled away, he held his palm up and wiggled a fist behind it.

"Sammy...right?" He asked. "That's how you sign your name?"

Clapping her hands together, she nodded excitedly. Rage rose in Ada's heart at how Sammy still seemingly melted in this asshole's hand after everything they did to them. Charging forward, Ada pushed herself past both Gates and Sammy to approach Louis.

The recently freed criminal made eye contact with her. "Hey what happened to meet me in North Platte-"

Ada's palm made sharp contact with his cheek before he finished his question. The sound of skin against skin echoed throughout the parking lot. Sammy jumped with a gasp at the sight of the sudden violence. Gates stepped forward to hold Ada back by her shoulders. Shocked, Louis hovered his hand over his cheek, ever so gingerly touching his newly reddened cheek with his fingertips. Ada didn't resist Gates's hold and shook her hand, failing to get rid of the pain reverberating throughout the bones in her hand.

"What the hell, you actual asshole!" She shouted. "You invent these killer fucking robots, drag us across the country, and then leave us for dead in goddamn Nebraska?! You're a real prick! We didn't ask for any of this! Think of someone else other than yourself, asswipe, next time you blow up a fucking building and get yourself arrested-"

"Easy now!" Louis said. "I just got out of jail. Don't ruin it by screaming my crimes out across the parking lot-"

"I'll scream however much I want!" Ada shouted, fighting against Gates's hold. "You're actively ruining our lives with this shit and treating it like a fucking game!"

"Hey, sweetheart, I didn't want you here either!" Louis said, shouting back. "I fucked up in Pittsburgh with that little plot to catch Eyepatch, alright?! I thought I'd be doing you and your friend a favor keeping you in my sight, making sure those androids didn't murder you as soon as I left to tie up loose ends, but apparently seeing how neither of you can follow directions-"

"Your directions suck!"

"My directions keep us alive!" Louis shouted. There was venom in his green eyes as he stared Ada down. "If you stayed in the car and looked for androids like I told you to, we would've been able to escape without requiring me to burn the whole fucking place down! You're tired of this shit after a week?! This is all I've been fucking doing for over a year now. My entire life has been on hold for a fucking year because of these assholes! Why?! Because I'm the only person in the world who knows how these things operate and I'm the only one who knows how to survive them. So next time I tell you to stay in the fucking car and look for robots, stay in the fucking car and look for robots, got it?!"

Ada took an unwilling step back. She still had a little fight left in her glare, but Louis's anger ran much, much deeper than hers. Her rage was still deserved, but his was built from over a year of solitude, tracking unstoppable androids and staying on the run to stay alive. Androids that he helped build and should've been able to control. Ada would've destroyed more than one building if she was in Louis's shoes. Part of her was afraid of what would happen if she triggered more of his anger to fight in defense of their efforts to help him investigate the plant. Most of her wanted him to rot in his prison cell as punishment for dragging them through his hell with him. She already went through hell once in her life. She had no intention of returning if she could avoid it and Louis Ventura was ruining that effort.

"What about your uncle? Allen Paz?" Gates asked. "Didn't he go missing after your car accident last year? I thought he worked with your father. Wouldn't he know how the robots operate too?"

Louis held an index finger up and squinted at Gates. He turned back to Ada.

"Who the hell is this?"

"Detective Gates Hopper," Gates said. "We met in Pittsburgh. I'm the FBI agent in charge of your case."

"Right, right. You were with Eyepatch," Louis said. "You know, it's a little weird that she was your partner and yet you never realized she was an android."

"She tricked me." Gates shrugged. "Besides, it's not like I had any reason to question anything. That was the first time we worked together and I didn't even know androids could exist."

"Uh-huh." Louis folded his arms over his chest. "Then why are you here?"

"I told you. I'm in charge of your-"

"My lawyers are in charge of my case," Louis interrupted. "You're just an FBI agent from Pittsburgh who picked up a growing file. There's no reason you should be here unless you're working for Kamana and you came here to finish the job your partner failed. Asking about my uncle doesn't help your case either."

"Why? What's so special about your uncle?" Ada asked.

"The fact you don't know the answer to that question and he does," Louis stated, never lifting his eyes from Gates. "How do you know about Allen, Detective?"

Gates's eyes were wide and incredulous.

"You're kidding, right?" He said. "Your father filed a missing persons report for both of you after he failed to find a body in your car wreck. The only difference is that you turned up while your uncle is still missing. It's all in your file that was dropped on my desk. Money in the office is that you were the one who off'd him."

"I did not-" Stopping himself, but never looking away from Gates, Louis made a fist. "Oh you're tricky. Nice try, but I'm not confirming anything about my uncle until you confirm some things yourself, cop."

Standing a little taller, Gates looked to Ada either for help or assurance that he was not the villain Louis was making him out to be. Licking her lips, Ada's silence in his defense acknowledged that Louis proved a point. But then again, Gates was too kind to be associated with the androids. He saved her life in the apartment, attacking Eyepatch directly on multiple occasions. All of the androids they had met attacked them mercilessly without question. Gates didn't even berate Ada for insulting him earlier. There was no way he could be working with the androids. Luckily for the detective, despite her own doubts, Ada was always happy to intentionally piss Louis off. Especially after he yelled at her for yelling at him. She turned to Louis.

"He's not a robot, idiot."

"Wait...do you guys think I'm a robot?!" Gates exclaimed.

Sammy waved towards Ada to get her attention. "We think this guy is a robot?!"

"Weren't you just bragging that you oversaw the production of every robot created by your psycho dad?" Ada asked Louis as she signed for Sammy. "Wouldn't you and your oh-so brilliant mind recognize him?"

"I said I oversaw the production of every robot up to Eyepatch," Louis said. "He could've been made after her or he could be an older model rebuilt with a new aesthetic. Lady's been through more remodels than I've ever cared to count."

"I'm not a robot!" Gates exclaimed.

"Then why are you here?" Ada asked. "Louis is right - detectives from Pittsburgh don't follow cases to the middle of Nebraska."

Both Ada and Louis turned to him, their eyes expecting an explanation. After a long moment, the detective threw his hands up in surrender.

"Alright you guys caught me!" Gates said. "I was put on administrative leave for telling my supervisors that my new partner was an evil android hellbent on taking over humanity. It turns out, that kind of claim in the normal world is cause for an extensive mental evaluation. So now I'm here because I want to get to the bottom of this before more people get hurt."

"Oh how heroic," Louis cooed. "You're truly Mr. Good Cop aren't ya?"

"I try to be."

"Cute," Louis stated. "Now tell me, Mr. Good Cop, do you believe in fate?"

The detective stared at Louis incredulously.

"Excuse me?" Gates looked between Ada and Louis. "Do I believe in *fate*?!"

"Play along," Ada said. "He thinks it's his foolproof way to find out if people are androids or not."

"Don't work with the android on this," Louis hissed. "You might influence his answer."

"He's not a robot!"

"He might be a robot," Sammy signed. Ada glared and Sammy shrugged. "His face doesn't move the same as yours or Louis."

"He's not a robot!" Ada signed with fury without talking. "Faces are different for everyone."

"What are you telling her?" Louis asked, pointing at Sammy. "Are you telling her that he's not a robot? She needs to decide that for herself."

Ada turned to Louis. "You know I've had it up to *here* with your utter bull-"

"I believe in fate!" Gates shouted. Louis and Ada turned to look at him. Ada translated Gates's answer quickly for Sammy and she raised an eyebrow. The disgraced detective shrugged. "Obviously there's a higher reason why I was assigned to your case. My superiors could've given your case to anyone in the department. Instead, the file found its way onto my desk of all desks, forcing me to look into it, and now here I am, in the middle of nowhere, because I know about a danger that hardly anyone else in the world knows about. It may have been my choice to book the red eye flight from Pittsburgh to Omaha as soon as one of Louis's aliases hit the booking system, but everything else that led me to monitor that activity was solely the work of the universe. If that's not divine intervention, I don't know what is."

There was a pause as Gates's words settled into the group. Louis narrowed his eyes.

"....I still don't believe you"

"Oh my god, Louis!" Ada exclaimed. "Are you serious?! He just passed your own stupid test. You even said it yourself that the robots fundamentally can't believe in fate because it's goddamn paradox to them-"

"Hypothetically, if this asshole was created after Eyepatch, Kamana could've caught wind of my little test from when I applied it to the others and programmed him differently," Louis said. "Detective, how do you feel about Sammy holding you down while I cut open your chest to make sure you're not built from robots?"

Reading Louis's lips, Sammy smiled proudly at Gates.

"Sounds like fun to me," Sammy signed.

Gates looked nervously between Sammy and Louis.

"....I don't know what she said, but I would prefer not to do that."

Ada rolled her eyes. Absent-mindedly fiddling with her jeans pocket, an idea flitted across her mind. She walked over to the back-seat of the Camaro and dug through the piles of trash littering the floorboards. Grabbing an old t-shirt Louis discarded between gas station stops, she re-joined the group and presented it to Sammy.

"Smell," Ada signed, wafting her palm towards her nose.

Without a second thought, Sammy sniffed the t-shirt then made a grotesque face. She quickly signed "what the fuck" before backing away from it. Ada nodded then presented the shirt to Gates.

"Now you."

"What are you doing?" Louis asked.

"A better litmus test than fate."

Gates gave Ada a weary look. When her dark eyes refused to concede her reasoning, he leaned over and sniffed the shirt too. The detective immediately gagged at the scent, covering his mouth and nose with a single hand as he backed away. His normally kind brown eyes glared at the shirt with suspicion.

"Jesus Christ!" He exclaimed, continuing to pinch his nose. "How have you not burned that thing?"

"What does it smell like?" Ada demanded.

"Sweat, trash....I think a little bit of oil," Gates said. He released a single cough. "Whatever that's supposed to smell like, it's not human. Did you wrap a dead animal in it? Holy shit-"

"Okay what is going on?" Louis said.

"Your androids can't smell," Ada explained. She threw the t-shirt at Louis. "Olfactory programming requires an entire complex data-base of scents to be able to easily recognize and determine smells apart from each other. I'm assuming you didn't prioritize the func-tion for your human androids when setting up your AI training. Your dogs last night are a little better at it, but their functions are limited compared to the human models, so they probably have more bandwidth to allow the olfactory function to operate. Even then, their smell was limited to my sweatpants and not to my actual full self. As Sammy – and Gates – just proved, only a human can suffer through the disgusting waste known as your laundry."

Staring at Ada, Louis very tentatively lifted his t-shirt to his own nose and inhaled deeply. He furrowed his eyebrows.

"I don't smell anything."

"That's because you live in that stench, dumbass," Ada said. "Either that or you're a robot. When's the last time you washed that stupid jacket anyways?"

Frowning, Louis tugged at his jacket. "Point made. Fine. Suspicious good cop detective dude can join us in our hunt against the androids. The more bodies they can target that aren't mine, the better."

Gates gave a thin-lipped smile.

"Stellar. Happy to contribute, I guess."

"You know that also includes our bodies," Ada said, indicating between her and Sammy.

"Yes. It does. So are you two still on board?" Louis pointed between the girls. "I'm assuming you bailed me out of jail for a reason, but for all I know you could just need the pin number to my Great Aunt's credit card. You can also catch the first flight from Omaha and Pittsburgh if you want. I can't promise the robots will let you go now that they've seen you working with me at the factory last night, but there's a chance they might."

Ada and Sammy shared a look. Recognition passed between them from their conversation last night. They were certainly going to die if they joined Louis's suicide mission against the androids. But they also were going to die if they didn't go with him. Ada thought back to how Beefcake said she needed to be kept alive. She didn't want to find out what that meant if the robots ever found her alone. With a short sigh, Ada signed her words as she spoke.

"If we're going to die at the hands of killer robots, we might as well deserve it."

Sammy nodded. "Agreed."

"Good," Louis said. "That works out because I had some time to think in prison. Last night at the plant, I did find that Tura Industries' computer systems are all connected through a shared network. We just have to find one with remote access to the main AI for the androids, aka Kamana, and, with Ada's help, corrupt the programming with our own code."

Ada's eyes grew wide mid-translation for Sammy and she turned to Louis once she finished.

"*My* help?!"

"I tried doing it myself, but obviously it didn't work," Louis explained. "I'm an engineer, not a programmer, so my coding experience is mostly focused on hardware functions. You likely have the AI programming skills necessary to proficiently create a code to take down Kamana."

Ada shook her head. "I...I can't."

"You studied at Carnegie Mellon!" Louis exclaimed. "You were the best programmer of your class-"

"I didn't even graduate!" Ada shouted. "I dropped out my junior year. I work at Geek Squad, for crying out loud."

"It doesn't matter," Louis stated. "Kamana's not going to check for a degree when you implement the code. You still have the skills and knowledge to code. Plus, you have me who built these assholes, Sammy who is obviously not afraid to shoot the hell out of one, and...." Louis hesitated before gesturing towards Gates. "...this guy. I'm not quite sure what he's good for, aside from getting us out of legal trouble, but glad you're on the team...Nate?"

"Gates," Gates corrected. "My name is Gates."

"Better than 'Fence' I guess," Louis said before turning back to Ada. "C'mon. This is our one chance to stop them. The robots are almost physically indestructible and need to be destroyed through their core AI. If you don't help us, then, knowing Kamana's ambitions, all of humanity will pay for it."

There was a small sliver of insecurity in Louis's eyes that Ada never saw before. Was Ada really his last hope to take these monsters down? The thought terrified Ada. She couldn't be the one person responsible for humanity's safety. Why couldn't Louis take care of this by himself, like he promised? But the way Sammy's eyes pleaded with her and the confidence in Gates's gaze as he looked at Ada despite barely knowing her for half a day, it didn't look like Ada had a choice. She couldn't tell everyone to go fuck themselves while she hopped the nearest plane to Pittsburgh.

"Fine," Ada said. "Just don't be so dramatic next time."

With a wide smile, Louis clapped her shoulder. "Dramatic is my middle name, sweetheart."

"Don't call me sweetheart."

"Gideon is your middle name," Gates said. "Isn't that why you used Gideon as your fake name?"

"Well if I used my real name, they would've found out about my unpaid speeding tickets and I might have been in some real trouble," He said. "Now c'mon. Let's get out of here before I have to blow up a police station to cover more of our tracks. That one might be harder to bail out of jail for."

The recently freed prisoner strode towards the Camaro. With a short shrug, Gates followed. Sammy turned to Ada with a beaming smile.

"He should go to jail more often," She signed. "He looks a lot better."

Sammy skipped after them. Ada stayed firmly planted in her spot, an uneasy feeling growing in her stomach.

Louis was hiding something from them. There was no way he'd shift gears so quickly and let them join his suicide mission without an ulterior motive. Her mind wracked through all of the possibilities, trying to trace what he could possibly be hiding from them. It could be something as simple as a displaced colon in a line of code, but, just as with a displaced colon, the whole thing managed to get thrown off by it.

"Oye! Ada," Louis shouted. "I don't know if you want a repeat of last night or not, but we're kind of in a time crunch."

Last night, of course.

There was one name that kept the robots from outright killing them any second they could. It stopped Lady in the grocery store, and it stopped the British android at the factory last night. It was the same name that triggered Louis to question Gates's humanity.

"Who's Allen?" Ada asked, whipping around. Louis gave her a purposefully neutral look, revealing nothing. "You changed the subject. What's so special about him?"

All of the light dimmed from Louis's eyes as he stared intensely at Ada, keeping his expression neutral. A reflection of his previous anger shone from his eyes.

"None of your concern," Louis stated.

"You said he's the one who created these things, right?" Ada folded her arms across her chest. "What's stopping him from creating more?"

"Lack of access to my father's limitless budget for one thing," Louis said. "A basic regard for humanity for another-"

"Then why can't he help us instead?" Ada asked. "Why does he get to hide while we run around the greater United States, fearing for our lives as his stupid robots hunt us down and-"

"Don't worry about it!" Louis shouted. "We don't need him. Trust me. Your programming will be good enough."

Ada's glare turned to steel. She quit being a trusting person about three years ago. She for sure wasn't going to change her ways for Louis Ventura, of all people. Especially when he was so open about hiding such a big deal from them.

"Now everyone get in the car," Louis said. "I have a location in mind that we can hit before the robots catch on to our plan."

Storming away, Louis stole the driver's seat. With a defeated sigh, Gates opened the back door and worked on clearing trash from the backseat so he could sit down. Sammy turned to Ada with furrowed eyebrows.

"What did you say to him?" She signed. "He was finally in a good mood and now he's not!"

"He's hiding something," Ada signed, approaching the vehicle. "You can see it in his eyes. He's helping hide Allen, whoever he is."

"The detective is hiding something too," Sammy signed. "His eyes do not smile with the rest of his face."

Ada sighed. "Boys."

"The worst," Sammy finished.

Sammy smiled as she got into the passenger seat. Ada dragged herself into the backseat with Gates. He smiled at her and she found herself focusing on his eyes. Sammy was right. His smile didn't quite match his eyes. Even the kind detective was hiding something. They all were. The question was whether or not their secrets would lead to their demise.

Ada just hoped hers wouldn't be the one to do it.

<!--It started when Ada and Daniel moved into their apartment the summer after freshman year.

"Maybe tomorrow I'll do laundry," She told herself after a long day at their internship.

"Maybe tomorrow," She told Daniel after he asked if she wanted to try a new Ramen restaurant. "I just want some cheesy potatoes tonight."

"Maybe tomorrow," She told her Dad when he asked her to review his code. "I've done enough programming today."

"Maybe tomorrow," She yawned as her friends asked her to go out for the night.

"Maybe tomorrow will be better," She promised herself when the internship manager reprimanded her for sloppy coding.

"Maybe tomorrow," She told her mom when Ruchira bugged her to look into the Google internship.

"Maybe tomorrow will be better," She told herself as she looked at herself in the mirror, her eyes red from crying over nothing in particular and everything all at once.

Maybe tomorrow she'll actually want tomorrow to come.-->

CHAPTER SIX

If Ada had to create the perfect code, then she had to quit being so rusty with it.

Or else, humanity was screwed.

The four of them were locked in a desolate motel on the outskirts of Sidney in western Nebraska. They stopped in a town called Kearney on the way to grab some new tech before heading as far as a tank of gas would take them. This was where Ada bought a laptop filled with software catered for her programming needs while Louis claimed random bits of computer equipment that he constantly tinkered with when he wasn't driving. He made them stop the Camaro three times so he could get more parts from hardware stores. Gates and Sammy were sort of left in the dust on the shopping spree, but Sammy managed to get her hands on another sketchbook so she was able to occupy herself. She lounged on the single motel bed, doodling in her book, as Louis and Ada worked together on the small provided table and chairs.

Gates spent his time either pacing the motel room or watching TV. Silently, Ada wondered if he was regretting his decision to be a good Samaritan for the cause of humanity. He was the only one in the group willingly wanting to participate in the effort, after all. She was forced into it and she even regretted it as soon as she allowed Louis to look over her shoulder to monitor her work.

"No, no, no..." Louis took the laptop from Ada's hands for the umpteenth time that night and typed into it. "Are you trying to corrupt an android army's artificial intelligence or build a website for preteens?"

"I haven't done either in a while," Ada sighed. "I'm still getting back into it."

"Yeah well you need to hurry up with whatever personal shit you're going through," Louis said, spinning the laptop back to her after his correction. "The more time you waste, the less chance we have to catch Kamana off guard."

"Give her some space." Gates peeked through the blinds of the window. "I'm sure she'll get it."

Softening her face, Ada glanced at the former detective before returning to her work.

"By the way, how do we know that robot with one eye isn't going to find us here?" Gates asked, letting the window blinds snap against themselves. "She did a pretty good job tracking Ada and Sammy in Pittsburgh."

"She's probably been sent back home to be recalibrated after so many subsequent failures." Louis didn't even look up from his work as he spoke. "The only reason why the boyfriends found us instead was because Eyepatch opted to track Sammy's well placed phone in the back of that truck that went to Iowa instead. The boyfriends were probably called back too, for such shoddy work at the plant with the dogs. It'll be a while until Kamana sends them out again."

"How long is a while?" Gates asked.

"Depends on Kamana's mood," Louis shrugged, as he spun the pen in his hand. "She might only hate me enough to send Eyepatch back out after a day or she might *really* hate me enough to send Eyepatch out after a month of upgrades." He finally lifted his eyes from his work to look between Gates and Ada. "Fortunately,

Kamana doesn't think of me too much either way, so we might be okay for a bit."

"And how long is *that?*" Gates asked.

"I once went two whole months without them bothering me," Louis said, returning to his work. "Then again, that was when I fled to Canada so they might have had issues at the border. I hear the import tax for tech is a bitch up there."

Looking incredulous, Gates turned to Ada.

"He doesn't know what he's doing, does he?"

"Nope." Ada tapped a line of code into the computer. "You'll get used to it."

"You volunteered for it, Mr. Good Cop," Louis stated.

"I did," Gates said, a certain sternness to his voice. "And I intend to finish it out."

"Good. You couldn't leave if you wanted to anyway." Louis tinkered with his gadget. "I mean, you could. But it's your death."

Gates turned to Louis with a serious expression. Louis dutifully ignored him to jot a note down about his new toy. With a sigh, Gates softened his gaze and looked towards Ada.

"How's the code coming along?"

"Terrible," Ada said. She shot a glare to Louis. "I don't understand how you fucking expect me to replace entire pages of code when I barely even know the context of the programming language."

"You're obviously a computer science geek so you've probably programmed a robot or two in high school." Not looking from his notes, Louis pointed his pencil at Ada. "Exact same concept, except five hundred times more complicated."

"Wow. So helpful." Ada scowled. "Tell me, did you actually learn anything with your fancy degrees, or did your daddy just buy some new libraries?"

As Gates released a snort that he failed to cover, Louis glanced at Ada from his work. Looking vaguely annoyed, he placed his pencil down and leaned backwards into the cheap hotel chair.

"Alright genius dropout, what else do you need me to do? I already wrote all the code I could remember."

"Remember more," Ada demanded. "Either that or get the actual source code into my hands."

"Ah yes, let me just Google the open source code for a super secret project that the outside world has no idea about," Louis answered. "Oh wait! We can't. It's locked behind firewalls upon firewalls on a private VPN and network that we're not getting access to through this motel's cheap public wifi alone. So you'll just have to deal with my idea of the code so we can plug it into Tura Industries' electronic security company's copy of the code to defeat Kamana."

"An idea is not the source," Ada scowled. "You know this."

"Indeed I do." Louis gave her a shit-eating grin. "Just as you know changing a few lines of the code won't do shit against a massive AI unless you do it right and you, sweetheart, are not doing it right."

Shooting another glare at the former engineer, Ada released a heavy huff and returned to her work. He was as bad as, no worse, than her mother. This exercise to change an entire AI through bits and pieces of memorized code was useless. But a very small part of Ada was grateful for it. It was putting her back in the groove. She hadn't touched a line of code since she left Carnegie Mellon. Putting her fingers to the keyboard, letting the lines of code flow through her and into her code editor in one stream of consciousness. She was back in control, once she figured out how to squish the bugs causing skips in her program's functions of course. She hadn't felt this comfortable in her own skin in three years.

Maybe Louis did know what he was doing.

He let her work for another twenty minutes in relative silence, Gates pacing between the wide part of the room the entire time. Sammy kept careful watch on the detective, sketching his movements in her book. Finally Louis threw the hodge-podge of machinery he was working on into his leather jacket pocket.

"Well, I don't know about you guys, but I'm not about to infiltrate a security company without some defense," Louis shoved himself from the table. "I'll go grab us some weapons."

"What about us?" Gates asked.

"You're safer here," Louis said as he stood up.

"Of course. How could I not realize that we are safer in a cheap motel with cardboard for walls rather than in a public setting filled with weapons," Gates said. "My mistake."

Louis pointed at Gates. "You're getting on my last nerve, Mr. Good Cop."

"Yeah well I'm not going to be responsible for Ada and Sammy's deaths due to your neglect," Gates said. "We're coming with you."

"If all four of us leave this room, then that paints a larger target on our backs," Louis explained. "When I worked by myself, they could find me within hours of my last documented location. Now that there's four of us, I wouldn't be surprised if they were waiting for us to appear outside of this door."

"There's no risk," Gates said. "You said it yourself, all of the androids should be out of commission right now. No one will be coming for us for a long time. I think we can afford a group field trip to find some weapons."

"Alright, Sammy and I are leaving," Ada said as she stood up. Sammy was already putting her sketchbook away.

The boys looked at them in unison. "What?!"

"While you two were fighting, I filled Sammy in on what we were talking about and she agreed that we need weapons," Ada said. "So that's what we're getting. Together. If you guys don't fight, maybe you can come too."

"We'll grab some ice cream too!" Sammy signed with a smile.

"That's right," Ada said and signed. "Gun shopping with ice cream. What a classic Midwest afternoon."

The boys shared a look. A half hour later, Gates and Sammy looked through the gun display cases at the local hunting superstore while Ada stood nearby, watching a family take their picture at the massive taxidermy display in the center of the store. She was in awe of them. They had no idea killer androids infiltrated their society. They were on vacation, acting like everything was normal. Was this really considered a vacation for people? A trip to a store in the middle of nowhere? How could this even be good enough for people? This was nothing compared to most of the department stores in Chicago and even Chicago department stores were nothing in comparison to New York department stores.

Sometimes Ada didn't understand why her brain was the one considered to be broken.

"Ada." Gates's voice broke her reverie. He pointed to the guns. "Are you getting one?"

"Uh, no." Ada said. "I shouldn't be trusted with a gun. Or any weapon in general, really."

"Oh." Gates said gently. "Why?"

Pressing her lips together, Ada regretted saying anything at all. Of course he would want to know. He was a police officer. He probably needed to take note of why the brown girl would be scared to own a weapon. Taking a shaky breath, Ada pretended to look through a display of camo jackets.

"I just...uh...." She released a heavy exhale before looking at Gates, his kind eyes filled with concern. "It's not like I have felony charges or anything! I'm not a criminal. I've never-"

Interrupting with a soft laugh, Gates closed the distance between them and placed a hand dangerously close to hers on the jacket rack.

"Ada, I'm not a federal agent any more," Gates said. "You don't have to worry about me arresting you or anything. I'm just curious. That's all."

Her eyes darted up and down his body, checking for signs of deception. Guys aren't this nice to Ada. People, in general, aren't nice to Ada. Not that she's nice back. But what came first, the chicken or the egg? Turning her attention to the camo jackets, Ada avoided his gaze.

"I don't want to talk about it then," She said. "I don't like things that could harm other people, okay?"

Or herself.

"One pacifist programmer against a murder happy android army." Gates teased softly, a small laugh hiding in the underlying of his words. "A tale as old as time. Well then I guess I'll have to be the one to protect you."

Ada's eyes darted to him. "You don't have to."

"For the genius woman who's going to save the world?" Gates smiled. "It would be an honor."

Resisting a blush, Ada surrendered a small smile for the detective which made Gates smile in return. Disappointment froze over the excitement in her heart as she recognized the glint in his eye. She couldn't lead this guy on. He couldn't get too attached to Ada; she wouldn't let him. She was still a mess, after all. She also couldn't let herself fall for him either. He was just being nice. If he was nice enough to surrender his entire life in an attempt to save humanity with a group of strangers, he clearly would be nice enough to show Ada some mercy once in a while. His kindness wasn't a reflection of any potential feelings for her and she needed to get used to that. Before Gates could notice her mood swing, a gun behind them cocked into place. Both Ada and Gates jumped at the noise before turning to it. Unaware of the disruption she caused, Sammy looked down the sights of a shotgun she held. Shaking her head, she returned it to the cashier and pointed to a bigger gun in the display case. Raising his eyebrows, Gates turned back to Ada, not even acknowledging her previous reaction.

"Or maybe Sammy will protect us both," He joked.

After a moment, Sammy noticed that Gates and Ada were looking at her. She waved at Ada for her attention.

"Where's Louis?" Sammy signed.

"Sulking," Ada signed. "Try the tool section."

"After I get my gun," Sammy signed, her eyes lighting up.

Rolling her eyes, Ada turned back to Gates who was staring between the two with wonder in his eyes. "What?"

"Nothing," Gates said. "I was just watching you sign to each other. How does Sammy keep up when we talk in a group?"

"She doesn't," Ada said. "I translate what I can while we talk and then re-iterate anything I missed for her later."

"That's gotta be rough," Gates said. "Is there any sort of hearing aid or something like that she can use?"

"Yeah, but she doesn't want one," Ada said. "A hearing aid is a whole different process to learn and understand the world with. She'd essentially have to start over and learn a third language just to use it. Plus, I mean, she's already happy with her life without it so what's the point, right?"

"I don't know," Gates said. "To make her life better? Things can be better than good, you know."

"Things can also be good as good," Ada said. "Not everything needs to be improved or be the best it can be. Making it through the day is good enough too."

Gates gave her a befuddled look. But before he could ask another question, the store intercom crackled to life, interrupting the country music playing before it.

"Attention shoppers: we are currently on a Code Adam," A woman's voice rang through the system. "Little boy wearing a leather jacket has been lost in the store and we will be on lockdown until further notice. Louis Ventura, your Uncle Oro is waiting for you at the front of the store."

There was a moment of silence as Gates and Ada slowly realized the situation.

"Oro was one of the androids in the tractor factory." Ada turned to Gates. "Louis calls him Beefcake."

"Yeah well that doesn't help anything," Gates said, looking around. The family that was previously taking pictures by the taxidermy display was looking through the aisles, calling for a little boy that didn't exist. "Whoever this guy is locked us in here with innocent civilians. We can't shoot until he shoots first, and by then it might be too late."

"I doubt Louis is going to surrender," Ada said in a near whisper. "What are we going to do?"

Sammy joined their side. "What's going on?"

"Robots locked the store down," Ada signed. "They're looking for Louis."

"Shit," Sammy signed. "I don't even have my gun yet."

"We have to get out of here," Gates said. "Maybe there's a back exit or something that we can find Louis and-"

"Excuse me." A British voice reverberated behind them. "Have you seen my little boy?"

The three turned to the voice. Beefcake towered over them, with Gates being the only one remotely comparable to his height. The android stared down at Ada with a hungry, wolf-like smile that sent a shiver down her spine. There was a solid chance he didn't appreciate the feral robotic dog stampede back at the tractor factory and now they were all going to pay for it.

Ada swallowed hard.

"No?" She tried. "Sorry, did the lady say he was wearing a leather jacket? Are you sure it wasn't overalls or something like that?"

"Maybe this will jog your memory." Beefcake pulled a pistol from the back of his pants. Holding the gun at his side, he was able to cover his weapon from view with his massive frame as he aimed it at Ada.

"You can't use that in here," Gates piped up. "It's against the law."

The android offered Gates a curious look.

"Then maybe we should take this outside," Beefcake cooed. "After all, maybe my brother picked my dear nephew Louis up and forgot to tell me. A big misunderstanding cleared away in three clean shots."

"Where is your brother now?" Gates asked. "Is he looking for Louis too?"

"He should be home," Beefcake answered. "But I was hoping for some extra quality time with dear Louis. We didn't leave on the best of terms last time I saw him. Too bad I lost him."

Gates furrowed his eyebrow. "You didn't follow orders?"

"No," Beefcake said, aiming his gun at Gates instead. "You wouldn't know anything about that concept, Detective, would you?"

Gates put his hands up, his eyes darting nervously from the gun to Beefcake.

"I don't think this is a good way to find a child," Ada's voice squeaked. "Maybe get rid of the gun and we'll all look for him together?"

Beefcake was not amused.

"Move," he commanded. "Back of the store."

As Beefcake pushed his gun forward, Ada turned and ran into Gates's back. Gates stumbled for a bit before turning around and gesturing to Sammy to move along. Looking annoyed, Sammy reluctantly turned to march forward. Holding herself close to Gates's back, Ada could feel the cold metal of Beefcake's gun pushing into her upper arm.

Sammy raised a hand and finger-spelled: "Robot?"

Ada pushed herself to Gates's ear. "Spell out 'yes' on Sammy's back."

"What?!" He whispered back.

"Do it!"

Reaching a finger forward, Gates carefully traced the letters of Ada's reply on Sammy's back with his index finger. Soon after, Ada could see Sammy grab an item from a side aisle display. She hid the item within a fold of her maxi-dress's skirt. With her other hand, Sammy spelled out another word.

"Duck."

As soon as there was a pause after the 'k', Ada crouched and pulled Gates down with her. Before Beefcake could react, Sammy threw a duck call at the robot's face. It made direct impact with his forehead. With the android distracted, Sammy bolted down a random aisle. Ada and Gates made their own exits in separate directions. Running into a section of clearance winter wear, Ada ducked into a circle rack of poofy jackets and sat in the middle of it. The long coats touched the ground, making a heavy enclave around her that could only be exposed through the top. There was a minute or so that Ada was able to remain hidden and catch her breath. The smell of dust was heavy in her hiding spot. Echoes of shouts for Louis Ventura sounded throughout the store. The country music that was playing through the store earlier stopped in order to keep the search for Louis Ventura. It was mostly silent in Ada's hiding spot, making her nervous breath audible.

Heavy footsteps approached. Sucking in a breath, Ada struggled to keep from shaking. She pulled her knees to her chest. The footsteps were louder. Closing her eyes, she tried to wake up from this nightmare. There's no way a massive man was headed her way to kill her. There's no way she was about to be brutally murdered in the middle of a hunting shop in Nebraska. There was no way she failed out of school, ruining her bright future that everyone was rooting for, with her broken brain. Her prayers to nothing in particular seemed to have worked as the heavy footsteps walked away, growing fainter with each passing step. Ada waited a moment before releasing a sigh of relief.

The coats ripped open.

A shout escaped from Ada as the mom from the tourist family poked her head into her hiding spot. They stared at each other for a moment.

"What are you doin' here, sweet pea?" Tourist Mom processed that not everyone in the store realized that the Code Adam was a fake.

"Uh...looking for the little boy?" Ada said sheepishly. "I thought I saw someone run into here."

"Me too!" Tourist Mom exclaimed. "Here, why don't you get out of here and we'll look for him together."

Before Ada could even think of a logical protest, the Tourist Mom grabbed her wrist and dragged her from her hiding place. As the Tourist Mom peeked her head into more clothes racks, Ada hesitantly followed, not wanting to raise suspicion by immediately running off after the woman invited her to a mini-search party.

"Louis! Oh Louisss..." The woman sang as she peeked into random clothes racks. "Uncle Aaron is lookin' for ya!" Shaking her head, the Tourist Mom walked ahead and Ada looked for signs of her friends or Beefcake. Surprisingly, there was none.

"Boy, I'll tell you what, I'd be scared to death if my little guy went missin'," Tourist Mom said. "Do you have any little ones of your own?"

"Uh no," Ada said, half paying attention. "Just a little sister."

"What's she like?" Tourist Mom peeked into a rack.

"Great soccer player," Ada blurted. "A bit of a flirt, but that's why she had me to get her out of trouble."

"Well your sister must be proud to have you watchin' over her," The woman cooed. "Maybe not now, but she will in the future. Where are you from?"

"Chicago."

"Oh wow! You're quite a long way from home, sweet pea. We're from Beatrice, just a few hours south of here," Tourist Mom said. "We're on our way to Yellowstone, but decided to stop here for a bit. World headquarters! Right here in Nebraska! Can you believe it?"

Ada could believe it as much as she could believe Beefcake gave up on finding her.

"So what's a young lady from Chicago doin' here in Sidney?" Tourist Mom asked. She ducked her head into another rack of clothes. "Louis?"

That story was too long to tell so Ada condensed it for the kind woman.

"Uh...got lost, I guess?" Ada said.

"Well I'm sure you'll find your way," Tourist Mom said. "All of us get a little lost sometimes, but that just means your GPS hasn't been calibrated yet, you know? You'll get that update eventually. Just gotta trust that things will work....*Louis!*"

Pressing her lips together, Ada felt her heart go soft. Guilt weighed on the depths of her soul for her previous casual dismissal of this woman and her family. Some people just wanted to live their lives and if that meant taking pictures in front of several decades old dead animals, so be it. Besides, it's not like she made great life choices. She had no right to judge anyone of their own choices. As the Tourist Mom and Ada walked, Ada knew she was putting this random mom in danger by association. She managed to break away from the woman by pretending to search a separate section of clothes. If Ada knew she wasn't going to get caught again, she would've attempted to hide in another rack to escape the gaze that followed her every move. A hand grabbed her shoulder. Ada tried to scream but another hand covered her mouth and forced her to turn around.

"Hey it's me," Gates said softly. "Shhh, are you alright?"

With wide eyes, Ada nodded before pulling herself away from Gates.

"Where's Sammy?" She whispered.

"I don't know," Gates said. "I've been trying to find Louis."

"Do you think he left the store?"

"No," Gates said. "He's heartless, but...he wouldn't, would he?"

Ada stared at Gates, unsure how to answer.

"Beefcake isn't going to leave the store without him," Ada said. "If Louis left, Beefcake would be gone too."

"So wait, Louis *would* leave?"

".....maybe."

The sound of a gun firing echoed from across the store.

Panic claimed the store. Hoards of people screamed as they ran towards the exit, toppling over displays and each other.

"Aw c'mon!" Louis's voice shouted above everything. "I thought you rednecks loved guns."

An employee shoved through Ada and Gates in their escape. Ada sighed.

"Well. It looks like we found Louis."

"Do we have to go save him now?" Gates asked.

Another gunshot.

"Son of a bitch!" Louis shouted.

Ada shrugged. "Probably."

Flames erupted from the other side of the store. A woman let out a shrill shriek.

"Ladies first?" Gates offered with a charming smile.

"Not this time, pal."

Pushing him ahead of her, Ada and Gates ran towards the flames and gunfire. Beefcake noticed the pair first and shot in their direction. The bullet hit a nearby post. They both jumped over the short plastic divide between the taxidermy display and the public to hide behind a giant stuffed elephant. One more bullet found its way into the elephant hide before Beefcake gave up on them and shot in Louis's direction again. Gates peeked around the elephant and then turned to Ada.

"Alright, maybe this was a bad idea," Gates said. "Maybe we should run while we can."

An older couple rushed past their hiding place, scrambling for the exits while covering their heads. Shouts echoed through the store. A large cardboard sign hanging from the ceiling inexplicably fell from its broken tether, causing more customers to scream as it fell.

"Oh now you want to run away?!" Ada exclaimed. "Where were you when I said that yesterday? That's right! Making some damn noble speech about doing the right thing! How's that working out for you, buddy?!"

More gunshots rang out, the storewide intercom crackling with audio spikes.

"Not well," Gates admitted.

There was a small explosion that shook the taxidermy display. Almost out of instinct, Gates grabbed Ada and held her close to him. Some of the animals higher up on the display rocked violently, precariously shifting closer to the edge of their positions. A polar bear located at the top fell over, aiming for Gates and Ada. Gates pulled Ada away and they escaped as the polar bear crashed into the elephant. He helped her over the display casing and they ran towards the fight again as Louis met with them, looking over his shoulder the entire time.

"How the fuck did Beefcake find us here?!" Louis exclaimed.

"Never mind, it doesn't matter, where's Sammy?"

"You tell us," Ada said in between heaves of breath.

"Here, hold this." Louis handed his small gadget to Ada. "If you see Beefcake, activate it, throw it, and pray to God it doesn't need beta testing."

"What is thi-you *lost* the robot?!" Ada exclaimed.

"He may or may not have escaped in the minor explosion I may or may not have caused," Louis turned to Gates. "Do you have your gun?"

"No."

"That was literally your only job, dude," Louis said. "Looks like I have to save everyone again."

He pushed past them as Beefcake climbed through the debris of a destroyed display. All three looked towards the monstrous bot and bolted towards the weapons. Bullets sped past their heads as Beefcake shot at them. Ada continued to run, still holding Louis's gadget in her hand. She wasn't about to use it if it meant killing them too. Louis jumped and slid over the glass gun display. He landed roughly, but found his footing and grabbed random handguns out from behind the counter.

"Choose one, grab your ammo!" He shouted at Gates. Gates grabbed a handgun, checked the markings, and then ran to the ammunition. Louis jumped over the counter again to join Ada's side. "Now when Beefcake comes back-"

The handle of a handgun slammed into the back of Louis's head. His eyes fluttered violently before he fell into Ada's arms. She nearly dropped Louis's gadget trying to hold onto him. Beefcake appeared from the aisle.

"Never liked guns," Beefcake's deep voice echoed as he threw the gun to the ground. "Or that spoiled brat."

Ada was petrified. Louis was much bigger and heavier than her. She couldn't carry him to safety.

"Gates!" She screamed.

"Freya told me about you," Beefcake continued. "She said you didn't fight her, that you wanted death. Then why don't you just die, little human? Accept your inevitable."

"Gates, help!" Ada's voice cracked as she attempted to drag Louis away from the android.

A deep resounding chuckle escaped Beefcake's lips. "He won't help you. Don't worry. You're the lucky one. You're the one I get to bring to Kamana. Your friends aren't so lucky." He cracked his knuckles. "It's nothing personal. All threats to Project Kamana must be eliminated."

Stepping forward, Beefcake threatened Ada's progress with each passing footstep. Her heart beating fast, Ada tried to drag Louis to safety. If Beefcake got past the end of the aisle, she promised herself to drop Louis and run for her own life. In one step, Beefcake crossed that deadline. Ada still couldn't bring herself to drop Louis and run. With a final tug, Ada managed to get her and Louis past another aisle. Only a step away from them, Beefcake reached towards them. Ada flinched. A bat crashed into the android's face from the aisle and he was forced to stumble backwards. Tourist Mom stepped out from her hiding spot and swung the bat at him again, making impact with his chest.

"Ain't no man gonna hurt a nice girl under my watch!" Tourist Mom shouted as she pummeled into the android repeatedly with her metal softball bat, not flinching at the sound of metal tingling against metal. Letting the woman do her thing, Ada dragged Louis further away from the threat. His eyes cracked open and he released a heavy groan.

"What happened?" He mumbled. "Mom? Is that you?"

"No, dumbass!" Ada snapped, guilt setting in as she realized she insulted an incapacitated person. "Oro...Beefcake knocked you out."

"Beefcake...beef...your beef gorditas were so good, *Mama*," Louis mumbled. "I miss them. I miss you. Why couldn't Kamana save you?"

"Shhh," Ada hushed as she dragged him behind a display and gently set him down. "It's okay. We'll get you out of here."

There was a sharp sound of metal hitting glass, leaving a wicked crack in the display. Ada looked to see that the sound was Beefcake throwing Tourist Mom's bat away from her, leaving the woman standing defenseless in front of him. Gates appeared from the ammunition aisle, awkwardly loading his gun as he ran. He took aim as Beefcake grabbed Tourist Mom by her neck and turned it sharply. A deafening crack of bone echoed through the small aisle. The woman dropped to the floor, not making a movement or sound. In that moment, Ada could swear her heart fell into the pit of her stomach and then a little further. She didn't even know this woman's name. This woman from Beatrice, Nebraska headed to Yellowstone with her family, brave enough to defend a young girl from an attack, was dead. Because of Ada. Because of Kamana. Because of being in the wrong place at the wrong time. Even Gates looked mortified at the crime.

Beefcake remained emotionless.

"All threats to Project Kamana must be eliminated," Beefcake stated.

"She was innocent," Gates hissed. "You knew she wasn't a threat."

"I did what I was programmed to do." Oro's voice boomed. "Maybe humans should too."

Angry tears appeared in the detective's eyes. With new determination, Gates aimed his gun at Beefcake and opened fire. As each bullet dug into Beefcake's skin, dark burn marks appeared. The chamber emptied quickly, but Gates kept pulling the trigger with the same vigor even with a lack of ammunition in it. Beefcake smiled.

"You can't kill me," He stated.

"I wasn't aiming to," Gates said. "But I can't say the same for her."

A chainsaw revved behind Beefcake. Before he could process the situation, Sammy dug the chainsaw into his neck. The robot immediately froze. His eyes grew wide as the cut deepened into his neck, sparks flying as metal tore into metal. Ada didn't even notice Louis sit up beside her as Sammy finished the cut. As soon as the chainsaw found its way to the other side of the android's neck, Beefcake's head fell from his body and landed on the floor next to Tourist Mom. His sturdy body remained standing until Sammy, still holding her chainsaw with a grimace on her face, walked to the front of it and kicked it backwards. It fell without grace and shook the aisle as it made impact with the cheaply carpeted floor.

No one said a word. Sammy stared at the body of the middle aged woman from Beatrice, Nebraska. Gates remained standing in his spot, moving his gun to his side and dropping it to the ground as his hands shook. Ada looked at the scene, trying to comprehend whether or not this truly was her reality now. Only Louis made an effort to do anything. He stood on shaky legs and, using the adjoining displays for support, walked over to the carnage. Patting Sammy on the shoulder, she seemed to relax at his touch and the reassurance that she did some good. Louis merely glanced at the woman's body before going straight to Beefcake's dismembered head. He lifted it and examined it before looking at Ada.

"You want your source code?"

Louis tossed it, letting the head land on the floor a few feet away from Ada.

"Here's your source code."

It didn't help Ada's mood.

With a heavy sigh, Louis looked around the destruction and rubbed the back of his head.

"I'll take care of disassembling Beefcake's body. The police should be here shortly. They'll take care of...her." He licked his lips and looked up at the remaining three. "You guys should get out of here. I don't plan on staying in Nebraska for much longer and I don't want to be held up by the police questioning."

After reading his lips, Sammy pointed to one of the many security cameras pointed directly at them as a result of the nearby gun display case.

Louis looked at the camera, then at her.

"I will take care of that too."

Nodding, Sammy hitched her chainsaw over her shoulder and approached Ada and Gates.

"Come on," She signed. "I think it's time for ice cream."

<!--Ada felt nothing.

It wasn't just for the bad things that happened to her, like her fight with Daniel over paying rent on time or when her computer crashed and deleted five hours worth of programming. But Ada didn't feel anything about the good stuff either. Doctor Grace complimented her work in class and she couldn't even fake a smile. The student health center was useless in uncovering Ada's issue so she turned to the only solution a broke college student could turn to: Google. Reading the article on her phone, Ada's toes dug into Daniel's legs as they sat on their shared couch together.

"Dan, do you think I'm a sociopath?" She asked.

"Mmmm....no," Dan said, not looking up from his studying. "Most programming majors are, but a commercial about dog food made you cry for thirty minutes yesterday so, I vote no. You can always double check with Brittany though. She's a psych major."

"What about depression?" Ada said, reading from the next google result. "Do you think I could have depression?"

Exasperated, Daniel Carabella looked over his glasses at his girlfriend.

"No, Ada, you don't have depression," Daniel said. "You're too happy to have depression."

"Then why don't I have any energy anymore?" Ada asked. "I don't want to hang out with our friends either, and it's not like that they're bad people. I barely even want to get out of bed most days. If I even think about looking at another line of code, I feel like vomiting, and any time I think about my future...I can't even think about it. God, it's like there's this void in me and every time I think about the future, it just sucks it all in. I want to stop existing some days, you know?"

With a soft smirk, Daniel gave Ada's knee a comforting squeeze.

"I hate to break it to you...." Daniel teased. "But I think all of that means you're a computer science major. A deeply pragmatic and nihilistic view of the world and life is, like, a prerequisite for us. Not to mention, we all look at enough code to make us vomit. If I see one more syntax error on my Python script for Dr. Grace, I will actually have an aneurysm." With a deep sigh, he returned his attention to the notes splayed out in front of him. "You're the lucky one though. You haven't even opened your textbook yet, and you're still probably going to outscore me on this test."

Pressing her lips together, Ada didn't feel compelled to tell him the only reason she hadn't started studying yet was because she didn't have the motivation to do so. She was tired of worrying about her GPA and decided that not caring was the best, if not only, *solution to her problems. Not that it mattered, she couldn't make herself feel anything for her grades anyways at this point. But she liked to think it was her own choice, her own free will giving her a much needed break from her life's passion.*

After all, she had a life to live and it's not like coding was going to save it.-->

CHAPTER SEVEN

Louis didn't return until late afternoon the next day.

By then, Ada finished the code.

The most difficult task of writing the code was actually retrieving the source code from Beefcake's dismembered head. Louis didn't give them any instructions on how to do it, so they had to play with it for a while. Eventually Gates discovered a port in the back of the head, carefully hidden under the hairline. From there it was a quick trip to the Wal-Mart tech department for a second laptop and the cable required for them to finish the job. As Ada re-wrote parts of the code, Gates helped by translating lines she didn't understand through rigorous Google searching and several YouTube videos. Sammy kept guard at the motel room door with her new chainsaw.

They kept the TV on as they worked. For Ada, it was comforting to see the world continue without them. The only exception was when the news came on. The woman who sacrificed herself for Ada was named Margie Brown. She was a forty-year-old mother of two and beloved wife from Beatrice, Nebraska. Ada's heart sank at recognizing that Margie had a full life she left behind, with another full life she never got to experience because of these killer robots. Her little girl looked just like her. Ada hoped she knew how brave her mother was. Ada hoped her code would work so that the robots never had to do that again to any other human.

But at least the world was still going.

As Ada typed the final touches to the code, Sammy snored softly from the bed. They unanimously voted to sleep in shifts when possible so that at least one person could remain awake and alert them to any androids. Ada didn't usually require much sleep when she was in the middle of a major programming project anyways, so she was fine to be the one to stay awake for this shift. To Ada's appreciation though, Gates stayed awake with her to cover them while Sammy slept. Sitting close to the motel room door, he stared at the gun in his hands as Ada worked.

"Do you have a family?" He asked.

"Yeah," Ada said. She kept typing. "Mom, Dad, and a little sister. They're still in Chicago."

"Do you miss them?"

Ada looked up from her work. Gates was looking at her, serious about his inquiry. His brown eyes shone in the darkness of their motel room. The TV, Ada's laptops, and the outside lights sneaking through the blinds served as their only light sources. Sighing, she returned to her work.

"Sometimes, yes," Ada answered. "Most of the time, no."

"Why not?"

"Well, I'm a twenty-four-year old college dropout living on a graphic designer's couch," Ada said. "That's not exactly something my parents can brag about."

"But you're brilliant!"

Ada snorted. "Brilliant people don't drop out of school three semesters before they're supposed to graduate."

"What happened?"

Rubbing her eyes, Ada decided that she didn't want to have this conversation. Gates was kind, but the only person who fully understood Ada's situation was the person who happened to be snuggling with a chainsaw as she napped. Even then, Sammy only understood it because she witnessed it firsthand. It wasn't a promising situation.

"It's complicated," Ada said. "What about you? How's your family?"

There was a long pause as Gates considered her question.

"I don't have one," Gates said. "Dad was never there, Mom had more important things to work on, a couple siblings, but they always treat me like a joke. It makes disappearing that much easier, huh?" He twisted the gun in his hand. "Then again, it makes you think. Margie Brown had a family waiting for her outside the store. It's the only reason they knew to look for her. Who would be waiting for me if that happened to me?"

Emotions stirred inside of Ada. She knew how he felt. If it wasn't for Sammy, no one would be waiting for her outside of a store either. Not Daniel, not Jasmine, not her parents. It was terrible to face the cruel world alone. Gates was nice. He didn't deserve to face the world alone, not like Ada did anyway. Ada earned her right to be alone in the universe. Gates's only crime, as far as Ada could tell, was believing the world was better than what it was and keeping faith to that fantasy despite the truth. People shouldn't be punished for believing in the best of others.

"I'd wait for you," Ada blurted.

"You barely know me."

"We fought two killer robots together and survived," Ada said. "I think that's good enough to warrant a friendship."

With a soft laugh, Gates turned from her and examined the gun in his hands again.

"Crazy way to start a friendship."

"It could be worse," Ada said. "I met Louis in the ice cream aisle."

"That doesn't sound too crazy."

"He thought I was a robot and we destroyed a grocery store."

"Ah. Forgot about that." Gates laughed again. "Who knew Louis's destructive criminal path could bring people together?"

The door opened.

"What about Louis's destructive criminal path?" Louis asked as he entered the room.

Despite being the appointed guard for their room, Gates didn't look at their new intruder.

"I don't know. How was disassembling and hiding Oro's body?"

"Terrible. I had to steal a truck and a welding pipe to get the job done." Louis slammed the door shut. "He was a big fella too so it took a little longer than Lady to find good places for him, especially since there's no major bodies of water here. There's bits of him in some cornfields, some random barns...I think I threw a leg in the back of a pickup truck at one point. It's kind of a blur. I was too busy looking over my shoulder for the cops."

"I rest my case," Gates said.

Louis rolled his eyes, briefly glancing over at Sammy who remained sleeping. With a short sigh, he looked at Ada instead. "How's the code?"

"Done," Ada said. "Just cleaning stuff up."

"Then it's not done," Louis said, walking to her side. He peered over her shoulder and read the code for a moment. With a nod, he patted her shoulder. "It's not bad though. Stanford and MIT might have some competition with you Carnegie kids." Ada rolled her eyes as he walked off. "Alright pack your things. We're heading to South Dakota tonight."

Gates perked up. "Tonight?!"

"Sorry? Did you have a date?" Louis said. "Yes. Tonight. We're not repeating what happened yesterday, however that happened. Ada will finish the code in the car, Tura Industries will be bankrupt by dawn, and you guys will be on the next plane back to Pittsburgh just in time for lunch. So pack up! We're leaving."

"Whoa, whoa..." Standing up, Gates blocked Louis's way to the rest of the room. "Be reasonable here. This is our one shot at destroying this thing. Ada hasn't had any sleep and the code hasn't been tested. We should wait. More importantly, didn't you say that you needed Ada to make the code for your uncle to implement? We need to find your uncle first."

Setting his jaw, Louis looked at Gates with disdain.

"We do not need to find my uncle," Louis said. "Kamana is the one who needs to find my uncle so she can destroy his life's work and prevent him from ultimately shutting her down. He has nothing to do with what we need to do. I trust Ada can take his place for the night, right Ada?"

"Uh..." Ada said. She didn't even trust her code to even run on its own let alone be able to remotely shut down an entire army of robots. How could she take the place of the man who managed to create all of them from nothing without the blueprint she had?

"Besides, this isn't our one shot," Louis said. "There's a backup plan."

"What's the backup plan?" Gates asked.

"Uploading it directly into Kamana," Louis said. "But that would require her to not try to kill us for more than, oh, five minutes or so. Not to mention, she's got a little legion of indestructible robot goons protecting her every move."

"So....this is our one shot," Gates said.

"Essentially," Louis said. "But I'm just letting you know that there is a backup plan in case tonight goes to shit since you seemed so worried about it."

Gates shook his head.

"You're making a mistake."

"As long as this mistake doesn't cost any more innocent lives," Louis stepped closer to Gates's face. Despite being a couple inches shorter than the detective, Louis showed no hesitation as he bumped chests with him. "I don't care."

The men stared at each other for a moment, assessing the other. Finally, Gates stepped to the side and Louis made it a point to physically shove him further out of the way. He walked to Sammy's side and gently shook her awake. When she fluttered her eyes open, she glared at Louis before he finger-spelled "pack up" in sign language with determined concentration. It caused Sammy to smile wide and graciously spelled out "OK" slowly before hopping out of bed.

Closing her laptop, Ada squinted her eyes at Louis.

"When did you learn sign language?"

"Last night," Louis stated. "Public libraries are incredibly useful."

"You learned the entire alphabet in one night?"

"You don't graduate college at sixteen without some brains, sweetheart."

Vaguely annoyed at his arrogance, Ada avoided Louis for the half hour it took for them to pack up and checkout from their seedy motel. It wasn't a problem since she gravitated to Gates anyways, and Louis was avoiding Gates as much as he could. The only problem was when Sammy wouldn't shut up about how sweet it was that Louis made an effort to learn sign language. When Ada refused to translate Sammy's sentiments to Louis, Sammy got frustrated and wrote them out on a hotel notepad instead. Guilt set in when Ada's first reaction upon seeing that Sammy brought the notepad with her for their car ride was relief.

Luckily, Gates sat next to her in the backseat as Louis and Sammy claimed the front seats. Sammy took the driver's seat with Louis in the passenger with Ada's laptop. He was already double-checking all of Ada's code before they even left town. Exhaustion set in from the all-nighter and, without an impossible coding challenge to distract her, Ada fell into a deep sleep against the backseat window. By the time she woke up, they were stopped in a dark parking lot and she was drooling on Gates's shoulder. Pulling herself up, she wiped her mouth on the back of her hand. Her cheeks darkened from embarrassment.

"Sorry."

"You're fine," He whispered. "You were a nice distraction from those two."

The light at the front of the car was turned on. Sammy was furiously writing something on the notepad at the wheel. She finished with a flourish and handed the paper to Louis who hastily read it and scowled before writing his retort.

"What's going on?" Ada asked.

"I have no idea," Gates said. "Sammy and I were playing hangman for a while and then Louis joined in and now I think they're talking about tonight."

With a sigh, Ada tapped Louis's shoulder. He turned to her with a fire in his eyes.

"Need my help?" Ada asked.

"Yeah." Louis balled up the piece of paper. "You need to tell your psychotic friend here that she can't bring a fucking chainsaw on a stealth mission!"

Sammy waved for Ada's attention. "Is Louis telling you I can't bring my chainsaw? We need my chainsaw. It's the only way we can hurt the robots."

Louis pointed at Sammy. "I saw a motion for a chainsaw in there!" He exclaimed and then he held up his own hands. "No chainsaws!" He crudely signed.

"Fuck you!" Sammy signed.

"Hey!" Ada shouted, her voice echoing through the small car. She signed as she spoke. "Do Sammy and Gates even need to come? If we want to keep quiet, sending Louis is our best bet."

"You do realize we're breaking into a security company, right?" Louis asked. "Like, this is a place that specializes in security. Security is their business. Let me repeat: all this company does is security. Do you understand? If you think only one person can manage this break-in-"

"Alright already!" Ada said. "I get it! This is going to be worse than the plant in buttfuck Nebraska. So what's your grand plan then?"

"Well once we infiltrate the facility, Mr. Good Cop will act as our fake security guard and turn away anyone that gets nosy," Louis explained. "Meanwhile, Sammy will be our grunt force with a gun."

"Chainsaw," Sammy signed. "I saw gun on your lips."

"I'll handle the break-in and hacking," Louis said. "You'll handle the code."

Ada felt her breath draw short. So he was serious about having her substitute for his uncle. That wasn't good.

"Yeah, okay...wh-where is this place?" She managed to stammer.

"Right down the street," Louis answered, pointing into the night. "See? That big building there on the separate road?"

"Oh?" Ada's heart dropped. "The one with the barbed wire fence?"

"Yep."

"And the gated driveway only accessible past the guard's booth?"

"Absolutely."

"We're fucked," Ada said.

"Your outlook on life is very negative," Louis said. "It's a security company, but it's a security company in South Dakota. How bad could it be?"

"Tura Industries trusts it," Gates said. "Obviously they must be somewhat decent."

"Well Tura Industries also has a solid number of murdering, virtually indestructible robots employed in its name, so I don't think good security from an outside company is a top priority." Louis shrugged. "Guess we're going to find out."

After finalizing the details of the plan, they went into the night. Sammy lost the chainsaw debate and carried Gates's gun instead. They all changed into dark clothes with Gates wearing an outfit resembling what an apathetic guard on the late-night shift would wear. Ada threw a simple dark hoodie on, grateful for the comfort of the fabric swallowing her entire body as she fought her anxiety about everything. The group jogged to the edge of the fence away from the roads facing the back of the building. Louis threw some blades of grass at the fence to ensure it wasn't electric. As soon as he gave the thumbs up, Sammy climbed over the fence without a moment's hesitation. Louis followed.

"Wait, we're supposed to climb this?!" Ada whispered. "I can't climb over this."

Landing on the other side, Louis looked at Gates and Ada with a shit-eating grin.

"Alright then, Gates Hopper," Louis said. "Go on. Hop her over the gates."

Gates gave him a look.

"Dude."

"What?" Louis didn't even try to hide his pride at the pun.

Rolling his eyes, Gates got to one knee and propped Ada with his hand. With a heavy shove, Ada caught the top of the fence. He held her as she crawled under the barbed wire, the metal clawing into the back of her hoodie. She nearly lost whatever remained of her ripped sweatpants on the dismount, but they stayed on as Sammy and Louis pulled her down. Double checking her pockets for the flash drive holding the code, she found it as Gates landed on their side of the fence. Crouching, they held themselves at the edge of the building until they reached a door on the far side of the building. Pulling a small tablet-like device out, Louis was able to tap into the card reader. It opened with a short beep and they scrambled into the darkened facility. Various metal doors lined the hallway. They continued down it together until they reached a stopping point that led in opposite directions.

Louis pointed to the left. "Front desk is that way, Mr. Good Cop. Don't alert the real security guards to your presence, but do your smooth talking thing when they get antsy."

With a nod, Gates offered an encouraging glance before heading in that direction. Louis headed the opposite way with Ada and Sammy following closely behind him. He led them through various hallways, always pausing momentarily to check that it was empty before heading inside. They ran up stairs, turned every corner, and Sammy was sure to check their back as often as Louis checked the front. Ada felt like she was in a sandwich of safety, even if her nerves didn't catch up with the sentiment. Every worry crossed her mind with every footstep. What if her code didn't work? What if she proved to be useless? She only ever proved herself to be a computer programmer and a failure – and she hasn't been a computer programmer in nearly three years. This was their one shot. If she failed them, her friends, or if she failed Margie Brown, the mother of two from Beatrice, Nebraska...Ada didn't know what she would do.

She couldn't even consider the consequences of her failure without feeling nauseous.

Finally they escaped the labyrinth of empty hallways and found themselves outside of a locked door. There was only a card reader outside of the door with a number pad attached to it to distinguish it from the other doors they passed. Without a moment of hesitation, Louis pulled the tablet thing out again and hacked into the card reader. Ada watched him, holding her waist in a poor effort to settle the butterflies bouncing through her intestines. A gun cocked behind them and Ada jumped a foot in the air. When she landed, she glared at Sammy who was looking at her sheepishly with the gun in hand.

"Sorry," She signed. "Was that loud?"

Rolling her eyes, Ada turned as the card reader buzzed. The doorknob clicked and Louis opened it. He turned to Sammy.

"Wait," He spelled out in sign language before pointing to the front of the door.

With a nod, Sammy stood guard at the door as Louis and Ada slipped into the room. The door shut behind them and Ada's heart dropped into her stomach. The room was dark, but she could see it was filled with computer servers from wall to wall. Various small lights blinked randomly with the whirr of the various machines humming contently around them. Cool, flat air pumped into the room. Wires were tied into clean paths on each server, the work of well paid professionals rather than underpaid IT nerds looking for a quick buck. Storming forward, Louis made his way to the row of monitors located across from the servers. Ada followed, but stood quietly towards the back as he hacked into the system.

"Alright, if all goes according to plan, we'll be out in fifteen minutes," Louis said as he typed.

Feeling bile rise up in her throat, Ada waited for a moment before responding.

"And if it doesn't go according to plan?"

Louis didn't reply.

With a hard swallow, Ada managed to subdue her nerves for the time being. Time moved slowly as Louis typed lines of code one after the other into the system. Ada could've sworn the door was going to bust open any second. They were going to get caught. This was all a set-up. There was no way this was going to work. Ada was going to mess something up. Her code wasn't going to work. The fact that she was completely worthless in the preservation of their safety, she couldn't hold a gun, she didn't know where to look for threats-

"Alright," Louis said, a smile in his voice. "Now all you have to do is upload the code."

A weight was lifted from Ada's shoulders.

"That's it?!"

"Well if Kamana is going to catch on, which she probably will, then you're going to have to combat her changes as she makes them live," Louis said. "But if you wrote this entire code in one night, then I'm sure you can keep up with a hunk of metal who thinks it's smarter than everyone."

The weight was back and heavier than ever.

Swallowing hard, Ada stepped forward and took the seat Louis ignored in his haste. She pulled herself to the computer and fumbled for the tiny flash drive lost in her massive sweatpants pockets. With shaky hands, she plugged it into the computer. Ada set it up so that the code would upload as soon as it hit the port and she was grateful for her foresight. Lines of code overrode the program within seconds. Several error messages popped and then promptly disappeared again as the code she wrote to counteract the error messages was read.

It was working.

A smile almost made its way onto Ada's face, but then she noticed Louis hacking into the network again on another computer. It was honest luck for Louis's efforts to go unnoticed in the system the first time around; there was no way it could happen twice. Feeling a panic attack coming on, she turned to him.

"What are you doing?!" Ada hissed.

"Updating my Facebook status," Louis said. "No, I saw something on the server. It's for Tura Industries, but it's located on the local servers with no connection to the remote despite the source being from Kamana's local drive and I think it has to do with us."

"Is that a bad thing?"

"Well, a security company working for the company trying to kill us has files on us from Kamana herself," Louis stated. "You be the judge."

While she'd love to judge Louis's bizarre thought process, Ada couldn't. She was more nervous about her code working than worrying about whatever conspiracy Louis was inventing. The first fourth of her code or so had taken place, but that was also almost a carbon copy of the original code. The rest was completely new functions and new programming. The idea was that if a new robot was built with the same code, it would have a critical error upon activation. She honestly had no idea how it would work on an existing android, but hoped the concept remained the same if the robot ever performed a software update which, according to Louis, happened frequently. From what she could translate from Beefcake's source code, Ada understood that most of the androids' energy came from the same way humans received energy: food, sleep, and proper hydration. She tried to write it so that 'activation' was the same as waking from sleep, but that was a difficult function to apply without being the original author. What she wrote would have to be good enough without Uncle Allen's help.

"What the fuck is this?!" Louis exclaimed, reading his screen.

Before Ada could ask him what was wrong, her upload paused. Ada's heart stopped with it. She inspected the monitor, hoping against hope that it was a simple processing hiccup. Two words wrote themselves onto the page of code instead, imprinting themselves where her next line of code should've appeared.

Impress me.

The message disappeared shortly after it appeared. Ada's breath caught as she tried to convince herself that the message was some sort of sleep deprived hallucination. However, after that long moment, lines of Ada's code disappeared in a slow trail one after the other. The code was erasing itself. Adrenaline rushed through Ada. She held herself closer to the computer and tapped faster than she ever had before to replace her work.

"Louis!" Ada's voice was strained with panic. "We have a problem!"

"Fix it!" Anger weighed on his voice. "I have to find a printer."

Ada had no idea what was important enough to risk their one shot at taking down Project Kamana, but she refused to let her code fail. At first, she was able to complete the lines of code faster than Kamana was erasing them. But that didn't last long. The computer caught up to her typing speed within a minute. Ada's fingers flew across the keyboard, her neat lines of code becoming a disarray of programming faster than she could even think to fix it. An alarm blared. Red lights flashed through the room in rotating shifts. Hard fists pounded against the door. Louis looked towards the door, but ultimately kept to his task. Ada refused to let her eyes leave the screen, refusing to take even the smallest chance at losing this game. A gunshot went off. Margie Brown's face crossed Ada's mind. Footsteps echoed as they ran from the door. The dark night in their apartment. Ada's heart slammed against her chest in heavy beats. Now Kamana was deleting chunks of the code at random. A portion there, an extra word, a capital letter where it shouldn't be-

Ada couldn't keep up.

She tried. She fought the bile rising in her throat with the general unrest between her heart and stomach, but her fingers couldn't move fast enough across the keyboard. Beads of sweat raised on her forehead.

"Ada, c'mon!" Louis grabbed her shoulders. "We have to get out of here."

"No! The code hasn't taken yet," Ada said. "Kamana is-"

"-a massive bitch who isn't going to lose this," Louis interrupted. He pulled on Ada. "Now let's-"

"I can beat her!" Ada screamed, her fingers mashing random coding terms into the program now. "She's just a stupid computer!

She can't be smarter than the humans who programmed her! Just let me try! Give me a chance! I can-"

The entire page went blank.

Ada's heart stopped.

"Ada..." Louis's voice was soft. "We have to go."

No.

No no no no.

Failure settled into Ada's soul. It didn't feel like an old friend. Ignoring Louis, she leaned forward and tried to write the code again. Nothing. She wrote a random, meaningless line of code. Something meant for middle schoolers. Still nothing. It was all completely unresponsive, but the vertical line kept flashing. Mocking her failure. Mocking everything her life ever stood for. Everything moved slowly for Ada. The sound of the alarms died down in her ears, she couldn't feel Louis's hands on her as he pulled her hoodie, and only the flashing line remained the same, mocking her failure. Letters spilled out of the flashing line with slow deliberation, leaving a final message to Ada as she finally allowed Louis to pull her away from the monitor.

Impressive.

<!--"To Ada," Daniel held a glass to the air. "The best programmer we'll ever know! Congrats on once again, kicking all of our asses and making us look like idiots, by making top of the class for the fourth semester in a row."

Everyone held a drink to the toast with a laugh and cheers. Even Bryan's new girlfriend, Sammy, held her glass out as everyone else did. She offered a kind smile to Ada before taking a drink.

Ada rolled her eyes.

"It's only midterms."

"Yet Doctor Grace won't shut up about you," Michelle stated. "He barely even knows the rest of our names let alone brags about us to everyone he meets like he does for you. I wouldn't be surprised if you got a personalized recommendation letter from him when you go to Google."

"I'm not going to Google," Ada said.

"Oh I see," Michelle smiled. "Too good for Google, eh? Well then tell us, Ms. Best Programmer in the class, where do you wanna end up?"

"I...don't know."

"Microsoft? Apple?"

"No. Not them either."

"Then why not Google?"

"I just..." Licking her lips, Ada couldn't explain it. The deep hole in the pit of her stomach, telling her that Google was a bad idea, telling her that she was a failure of a human being for only knowing how to program computers and nothing else, telling her that she was so pathetic that she couldn't even translate her feelings to her friends. Telling her that she was a garbage human for not being able to trust her friends with these thoughts. Telling her it was pointless to dream of a future because she'd never make it there anyways. She knew, pragmatically, that she was a good programmer. But something deep within her told her that she would never be as great as everyone said she was. She would never be fully worthy of Dr. Grace's praise, of her friend's respect, of the celebrations achieved through her work, of the coveted Google internship everyone pushed her towards. She would always just be Ada and that would never be enough. That by itself would never be impressive.

"It's just not a good fit for me."-->

CHAPTER EIGHT

The eggs and bacon went cold.

Ada made no effort to eat them.

After Louis managed to remove her from the computer room, he also had to physically drag her through the building to safety. He even successfully carried her over the fence and to the Camaro before returning for Sammy and Gates. Being left alone was the worst part. Gates's comforting hug when he made it to the Camaro before Louis and Sammy helped somewhat. She was in the middle of a panic attack at that point and Gates said nothing. He didn't even stare at her like Daniel did when she had her attacks around him. All he did was wrap her in a hug and held her tight even though she couldn't return the affection.

When the alarm went off, Gates diverted the guards' attention by leading them down an alternate path and then separated from them so he could warn Louis, Ada, and Sammy of the situation. That's when Sammy nearly shot him as he rounded the corner. The gunshot alerted the guards. Both Sammy and Gates fought them off as Louis and Ada escaped. When Louis returned, Gates tried to escape with Sammy, but she refused to leave Louis's side so he ran by himself. Sammy and Louis followed shortly after causing a small fire to distract the guards.

Now, after escaping their break in attempt, they were sitting in an old diner off of the highway. Ada had no idea what state they were in. Truckers sat at the bar, teasing the overweight waitress, and eating greasy platters of food. Their table was the silent outlier. Sammy sipped her coffee and made delicate runny egg sandwiches with the stale toast. Louis stared at the table, mindlessly running his hands through his hair. Gates was too busy taking care of Louis and Ada to pay attention to his own plate of food. Under Gates's watch, Louis always had a full cup of coffee and Ada had food that she didn't ask for in an effort to make her feel better. It was a futile effort, but it was an effort nevertheless. The middle-aged waitress arrived at their table, looking vaguely annoyed at her idea of hung-over twenty-somethings wasting space in her diner.

"How's everything tasting?"

Mouth full of food, Sammy threw a thumbs up. When it was obvious Louis and Ada weren't going to say anything, Gates cleared his throat.

"It's perfect. Compliments to the chef. Do you happen to have a to-go box?"

Pursing her lips, the waitress gave Ada and her full plate of food an evil eye before walking off. Gates turned to Ada, looking for her reaction. She did nothing. She continued to stare at the food, trying to figure out problems without solutions. Clearing his throat, Gates excused himself to use the restroom and walked away. No one moved a muscle in response to his exit. Mouth full of food, Sammy stared at Ada for a moment until finally tapping her fork on the edge of Ada's plate. Ada looked up.

"Medicine?" Sammy signed, her fork still pinched between her index and middle finger.

Nodding softly, Ada felt her pockets until her hands found the plastic cylinder. She set it on the table as she re-adjusted her sweatpants.

Louis looked at the pills.

"What are those?"

"None of your business," Ada grumbled.

He watched with a distance in his eyes as Ada struggled to pull the cap off.

"Is it for your depression?"

Slamming the pill container down on the table, Ada looked up at Louis with a glare.

"How the fuck do you know about that?" Ada seethed.

With a disgruntled look, Louis reached into his leather jacket and retrieved a wad of folded papers. He threw them in Ada's direction. She unfolded the pages and flipped through them. Sammy quit eating to look with curiosity as Ada read through the papers. Three profiles, two pages each, for each member of their group. The glaring words sticking out on each paper were bolded in red capital letters next to the option 'fatal flaw'.

"Deaf," Ada read, throwing the profile at Sammy who was impatient to read hers.

"Dead." She threw Louis's at him. He left it sitting halfway on his empty plate filled with syrup residue.

"Depressed."

The picture they chose for Ada's profile was flattering, but Ada couldn't place it. Her hair was long, well past her shoulders, and she was smiling. It had to be from college then. Probably when she was a freshman, but the age in her eyes could place her as a junior. She examined her written profile next to the picture. It highlighted her education up to Carnegie Mellon, her ability to program, and quotes of recommendation from Dr. Grace meant for the coveted Google internship. Her depression was glanced over in favor of her achievements. Her family was barely a line on the page, a placed fact rather than a point of note.

Primary function: Undetermined.

"What are you guys looking at?" Gates asked as he returned to the booth. He looked over Ada's shoulder at her paper.

"Security profiles," Louis grunted. "One for each of us."

Gates looked around the table. "Each of us? Do I have one?"

"I couldn't decrypt yours in time," Louis stated before he took a sip of his coffee. "But if you want the self-esteem boost we all got, your fatal flaw was detective. Or defective. Pick your poison."

The former detective stared at Louis. "What would defective mean?"

Sammy waved for Ada's attention before signing. "What the hell does this mean? It says my primary function is to clean the house. I'm not a maid!"

"Yeah what is this, Louis?" Ada asked.

"For once, I have no idea," Louis muttered. "I found them in the same folder as our profiles for the androids. The good news is that Gates is definitely not a robot."

"We already knew that," Gates stated.

"I had suspicions," Louis said. "But Kamana would never make such a clerical error as putting an android's file with a bunch of human's so you got off lucky, Mr. Good Cop."

"You've got trust issues, dude."

"Alright if that's the one good news, which is pretty pathetic," Ada said. "What's the bad news?"

"Best case scenario, Kamana got paranoid but the security company got lazy and decided to use the same templates that we use for our androids which led to the creation of these things." Louis spat the last word as if it was venom. "Worst case scenario, we might be in over our heads."

Ada gave Louis a long look that he gladly ignored before she translated for Sammy. Sammy ensured that her discomfort was not ignored.

"What do you mean we might be over our heads?!" She signed wildly, her hands almost smacking Louis's face. "Is he saying we're going to be turned into fucking robots because I am not going to be a robot!"

With a sigh, Ada turned to Louis.

"Sammy has concerns."

"Don't we all?"

"Here's your box," The waitress tossed the piece of Styrofoam onto Gates's empty plate. "Anything else I can do for y'all?"

"Bailey's and an attitude check would be fabulous," Louis snapped.

"I can get you your actual check, how about that?"

"A good whiskey also works," Louis said. "But if that's too much, anything with an alcohol count above your average customer's IQ is acceptable. It shouldn't be too hard to find."

The woman rolled her eyes and stormed off.

Gates turned to Louis with a glare.

"Alright, so do you have an actual plan or are you just going to harass people for the rest of the day?" Gates asked.

"My uncle Allen is the only one who can stop them now," Louis said. "He'll have answers."

"Okay, that's a good start." Leaning forward onto the table, Gates nodded. "Where is your uncle?"

".....I have no idea."

Gates stopped and gave Louis a hard look.

"Not a single idea?"

"That's what I said, nitwit."

"I thought the only reason why these robots kept you alive for this long was because you knew where he was-"

"It's called a bluff, asshole," Louis said. "Do you really think I'd allow my one easy ticket to survival to slip through my fingers because of something as useless as the truth? Give me some credit."

"Okay then," Gates said. "What do we do if we can't find your uncle?"

"Hunt down the androids faster than they hunt us and hope we survive."

"Great!" Gates released a heavy sigh. "Seriously? Is that all you've got?"

"You make the plan then, genius!" Louis shouted, snatching his profile from his sticky plate. "Look, dude, I'm still labeled as dead on a sheet of paper that is more accurate than my opinion that you're a worthless sack of dicks. Kamana knows I'm alive. Why she refuses to formally acknowledge it when her whole thing is being the most right thing in the room raises a whole lot more questions than answers. My only solution right now is to either find my damn uncle who's been in hiding for over a fucking year or take the Camaro, leave all of you for dead, and save myself from my inevitable death sentence, like I should've done three fucking days ago!"

The diner was silent. All eyes were on Louis. His eyes were only on Gates, staring murder into the deepest recesses of the former detective's soul. Gates was reactionless, incredulous at best. After a long half-minute, he raised an eyebrow.

"Are you good?" He asked. "Got it all out of your system now?"

"Fuck you."

"Alright, awesome," Gates said. "Give me the card. I'll take care of the bill. Ada, ask Sammy to take Louis for a walk please. He needs to cool off."

As Louis shuffled for his credit card, Ada translated for Sammy. She gladly obliged, pushing Louis out of the booth after he tossed the black card at Gates. Still staring at Gates, Louis crumpled his paper profile in his fist and stuffed it back into his jacket pocket before letting Sammy lead him out of the diner. As soon as the door's bells clanged behind them, the diner returned to a subtle sound of judgmental muttering. Gates set his jaw before turning to Ada.

"Did you want to save your food?" He asked. "I'm sorry. I never asked. I just assumed-"

"No, you're - I'm fine..." Ada swallowed the knot in her throat. "Gates, are you okay?"

"Yeah. Why wouldn't I be?"

"Louis-"

"I've had worse."

"It still doesn't make it acceptable," Ada said. "Louis shouldn't have yelled at you like that."

"We're in a stressful situation." Gates piled Ada's food into the box. "He's had a lot of weight on his shoulders. I don't blame him for lashing out." Once the box became a mashed pile of vaguely-gray food, Gates turned and smiled at her. "Besides, Louis being an asshole is just part of the job, you know?"

Ada didn't disagree, but she didn't want to agree either. No one blamed last night's failure on her, but at the same time she knew part of Louis's frustration today was because she dropped the ball. She used to be an excellent programmer. If it wasn't for the depression, for the three-year hiatus, for her continued failed existence on this earth-

With a numbness that resonated to her bones, Ada blindly followed Gates as he paid for the food with a generous tip and then walked to the Camaro. Sammy and Louis were waiting for them. Louis was refusing to make eye contact. Sammy might have missed out on Louis's mini-meltdown, but she didn't miss out on smirking at Ada as she walked out with Gates.

"You two are cute," She signed.

Ada rolled her eyes. "Go fuck yourself if Louis hasn't already."

Giggling, Sammy stuck her tongue out as she winked at Gates. He raised an eyebrow and turned to Ada, expecting an answer. Ada didn't give one. With a heavy sigh, Ada folded her arms across her waist and made her way to the back of the car. All of a sudden, Sammy's eyes lit up with a sense of urgency and she grabbed Ada.

"Medicine?" She signed.

Ada's heart stopped. There wasn't any weight in her pockets.

"Shit."

Turning around, Ada bolted back into the diner. A couple patrons gave her a look as she ran past, but Ada didn't slow down. She made it to the table. Dirty dishes and half-empty cups of coffee still lingered, but her orange bottle of pills were gone. Her heart dropped. No. She checked under the plates. No no no no. Once it was clear that the pills weren't there, she dropped to her knees and searched the grimy diner floor that hadn't been cleaned in a near decade.

"Ada?" Gates asked, appearing in the corner of her eyes. "What's wrong? What are you looking for?"

"My pills!" She exclaimed, standing to her feet. "They were there, on the table, and then Louis distracted me and now they're gone."

"Are you sure you left them on the table?"

Their waitress scooted past them. Ada hastily grabbed her shoulder.

"Have you seen an orange bottle of pills anywhere?" She pointed to the messy table. "I was sitting right here and-"

"Honey, I haven't even looked at that table in the thirty seconds you were gone," The waitress snapped. "Now excuse me. I've got a full bar and an empty kitchen."

Before Ada could stop her, the woman stormed off. A knot formed at the base of her throat. She couldn't even keep track of the one thing she needed to survive. She was worthless. Her heart heaved at her chest as tears pricked the back of her eyes. Oh no. Not here. Not in front of all of these people. Not in front of Gates. Ada ran out of the building and straight to Sammy who scanned Ada's face desperately.

"Gone," Ada managed to sign. "Gone. Medicine, gone."

"Don't panic," Sammy signed, her eyes full of care. "How long can you go without them?"

Technically, a week.

"Five days," Ada signed. "I can't do this without my pills."

"What's the situation?" Louis asked, realizing that they weren't upset about him anymore.

"My pills..." Ada took a breath. "My pills are gone."

Gates came running out from the diner.

"I tried talking to the waitress," Gates said. "She honestly has no idea and neither do our table neighbors."

"How important are these pills?" Louis asked.

"I need them," Ada said. "Immediately."

"Shit, okay!" Louis held his hands up. "I'm sure there's a pharmacy in this town somewhere. We can get you-"

"I need a prescription," Ada said, the knot in her throat returning with more intensity. "I don't have my prescription on me. I don't even have my ID. If I can't get my pills-"

"Don't worry, Ada," Gates grabbed her shoulder in a show of support. "We'll figure it out."

She bit the inside of her cheek. Crap. First last night and now she was being a burden this morning too. When was she ever going to be not a painful mess?

Sammy and Louis said nothing. Ada allowed Gates to lead her to the Camaro and open the backseat door for her. After piling in, the ten minute drive into the nearby small town was silent. But it wasn't the comfortable silence that usually held the car during their long drives. It was a silence marked by shame. Ada felt like a fool and she felt stupid for feeling like a fool, but she had no idea what else to feel. The pills were more than medicine for her and now they were gone. Ada knew she needed to get them back one way or another. Louis parked a couple blocks away from the tiny pharmacy.

"Alright Ada go get your happy pills," Louis said. "We're going to try and figure out a plan to find my uncle."

"Don't you think someone should go with Ada?" Gates asked. "I mean, we're barely an hour away from our break-in. Tura Industries could've sent someone or-"

"You're an adult who can make adult decisions," Louis said. "If you wanna go with Ada, then go with Ada." He turned to Sammy in the front seat and finger-spelled "Want 2 go with Ada?"

She put her two index fingers together and moved them in and out. "Gates?"

Once Louis understood, he turned to Gates. "Are you going with Ada?"

"Yes."

Louis nodded at Sammy and she smiled before turning to Ada.

"Enjoy your date!" She signed.

"A meltdown is not my idea of a date," Ada signed back.

"Quit gabbing and get out of my car," Louis said. "Time is precious."

Once Gates and Ada were out of the car and on the sidewalk, Louis pulled out of the parking spot at a high speed, nearly hitting an oncoming car. They walked to the pharmacy in silence. Even though the late-June/early-July morning made the temperature decent enough, Ada folded her arms across her chest. She hated how weak this entire ordeal made her feel. She hated how confident Gates strode next to her, hands in pocket and a smile on his face as he nodded to the few people who passed them on the sidewalk. Pragmatically, she knew the lack of medicine in her system was the reason behind her irritability. Emotionally, she couldn't help but miss when she could live life without a broken brain. Stepping into the pharmacy, Gates and Ada were greeted by the old man operating the counter in the back. Gates took a moment to pretend to be interested in some of the rows of merchandise, but Ada went straight towards the pharmacist. Once he noticed, Gates caught up to her and stood next to her at the counter.

"Hi." "Hey!"

Ada gave Gates a look at their synchronized greeting. He avoided her eye contact. Slowly turning back to the old man, Ada tried to shake off the social awkwardness.

"Um, so…"

"We're on vacation," Gates interrupted. "My wife forgot her medicine at home. Is there any way we can pick up a prescription here?"

"It depends," The old man said. "What's the medicine?"

Now Gates was at a loss for words.

Ada bit her lower lip and looked down.

"Prozac."

"I'm sorry honey, what was that?" The old man turned his ear to Ada. "I didn't quite-"

"Prozac!" Ada shouted. She ignored Gates as he looked at her with curious eyes. "I need Prozac. Antidepressants. Happy pills. Anything to balance out the fucking serotonin in my head and make my broken brain work again."

"Oh," The old man said, shaken by Ada's outburst. "Well I can't give that to you without a prescription, sweetheart."

"I have a prescription," Ada said. "I just left it at home."

"I understand that, dear," The old man said. "But you're still going to need a written prescription from your doctor."

Gates grabbed Ada's wrist before she could lash out. "Sir, there's gotta be something we can do to get her medicine."

"Yes," The old man nodded. "You can get a prescription from the doctor's."

"And where is the nearest doctor's?"

"Why right next door," The old man pointed a shaky finger to the left of him.

Ada's face remained flat.

"Do I need an ID for an appointment?" She asked.

"Why I'd imagine so, sweetheart," The man said. "Don't tell me you left that at home too!"

As the old man chuckled, something cold tied itself around Ada's heart.

With a smile and a nod, Gates took Ada's arm. "Of course not! Thank you for your time, sir. C'mon, honey."

He was already pulling her out of the drug store before Ada could comprehend what was happening. This was *her* life. This was *her* medicine everyone else was deciding they could give up on. She wanted to scream at the sweet old man pharmacist, demand that he give her a supply of Prozac to last a month, rattle all of his neatly designed shelves until he gave in. Who the fuck was this random guy that she met less than a week ago to decide she didn't need them as bad as she did? As soon as they were back out on the sidewalk, Ada ripped her arm out of his grip and scowled at Gates.

"Look, I don't need you speaking on my behalf on my own issues." Ada jabbed her finger at him. "I can take care of myself!"

"Whoa, okay sorry!" Gates held his hands up. "I have to admit, I messed up in there. I thought your pills were birth control or something so I figured saying that we were married would stress the importance of-"

"Well it's not birth control, okay?" Ada snapped. "It's fucking antidepressants that keep me from going crazy! It's the only thing convincing my broken fucking brain that my life is worth living, okay?!"

Heavy tears and an even heavier sob bubbled from Ada without any emotional cue or warning. Actually, Ada figured they came from the lack of medication in her system. Hormones were fun like that. But before they could even step a few feet away from the pharmacy, Ada was sobbing uncontrollably. The fact she was in public and the fact Gates, this random dude she met not even a week ago,

168 - MADDIE GUDENKAUF

had to deal with her crazy self made the crying worse. She hated it. She was a hindrance to her friends, to humanity, to the world-

Shit forget five days. She couldn't even make it a couple hours without her stupid pills anymore.

To her surprise though, Gates pulled her into a hug and let her sob into his chest.

"You're okay, you're fine, you're okay..." He soothed as he rubbed her back.

"No! I'm not okay!" Ada wailed. "I'm making everything worse! I'm tired of making everything worse! Last night-"

"Are you talking about last night?" Gates pushed her away to look at her. "Ada, last night didn't matter. You did the best you could. It was Louis who put too much pressure on you-"

"Fuck Louis! It's everything else!" Ada whimpered, feeling ashamed. She was such a messy crier. Jasmine was cute when she cried. Ada was Ada. "My entire life, my *entire* life, I've never done anything worthwhile. Programming was the only thing that gave me worth and I hated it. God, I hated it. I've always been such a waste of space. I wasted my intelligence, I wasted my worth, I wasted my parents' time..." She looked at Gates. "I'm even wasting your time! Fuck!"

Stomping her feet like a child, Ada sat down on the curb. She stared into the dusty, desolate street feeling just as empty as the road before her. After a moment, Gates sat next to her. She released a deep sigh.

"We should be anywhere but here," Ada said. "Instead, we're here, in this stupid small town in the middle of nowhere, because of me and how I can't keep my shit together."

She sniffled.

"Yeah, you're right," Gates said. "We are stuck in this stupid small town in the middle of nowhere because of you."

Ada didn't look at him.

He smiled. "But you know what? We also have a chance of actually winning this thing because of you. I'm on the adventure of a lifetime because of you. I mean, I get to tell people that I visited Corsica, South Dakota on our way to save the world!"

"Yeah what an impressive place to visit," Ada said with another sniffle. "Also, I wouldn't call nearly being murdered every other day an 'adventure' but you do you, bud."

"Alright it's not Disney World, but it's still something new," Gates said. "And you know what? I probably would've ran away screaming by now if it wasn't for you."

"No you wouldn't."

"Yes I would!" Gates said. "I mean, it's obvious that you're the only one who wants me here."

"Sammy wants you here."

"No she doesn't," Gates sighed. "Well it's like I'm barely a blimp on her radar. She doesn't mind me being here, but at the same time she wouldn't mind if I got left behind either. Then of course Louis is an asshole."

"He's like that to everyone."

"You get the point," Gates said. "There's no way I could survive a road trip with those two without you."

Sniffling again, Ada rubbed her eyes. "I'm sorry I'm your only choice in friends."

"I'm not," Gates said. "You're wonderful company."

"Wonderful company doesn't cry her eyes out to you on the curb of a dirty street."

"It's not that dirty," Gates said. "Ada, don't you realize how amazing you are?"

"I'm pretty sure my broken brain distinctly prevents me from realizing that," Ada said. "Plus you know, the fact I've managed to scare off everyone else in my life besides three people and I met two of them a week ago. That doesn't inspire much confidence in me being a worthwhile person."

"Hey! Three people are better than none!" Gates said with a laugh. When Ada didn't laugh, he cleared his throat awkwardly. "Well...I like you, at least."

"Why?" She moaned.

"I...don't know?" Gates said with a shrug, honestly thrown off by her question. He leaned back on his elbows and stretched out on the curb. "Why not? A lot of things, I guess. You're interesting. You're smart. You're unafraid to let people know how you feel." Gates smiled. "The fact that you continue to live life despite fighting a mental illness day after day-"

"Stop." Closing her eyes, Ada hugged her knees. "Don't call it a mental illness."

"Why not?"

"It makes it sound ugly," Ada said, feeling stupid. "I mean, it is ugly. But...I don't know." With a deep breath, she shook her head. "I just...this is why I don't like to tell people about it. They look at me differently after they find out. They either see me as this brave, tortured soul fighting the odds, or this insane person who cries herself to sleep every night. But I'm not either of those people. I'm just Ada." With a sigh, she looked back to Gates who was staring at her with wide eyes. "It's just, you know, my depression shouldn't be my only defining factor. Just like my brown skin or-" She almost said her ability to program, but she bit her lip. "It's not me. I'm not different or special for having it. I just have it and it sucks."

"No, yeah, definitely." Gates sat up. "I'm sorry for implying otherwise. Do you want to talk about it more?"

"No," Ada said. "You're a nice guy and all, but honestly at this point I just want my damn Prozac."

With a solemn nod, Gates stood to his feet and offered his hand to Ada. "Well if there's anything you need me to do or if there's anything you want to talk about, I'm always here for you. You know, with all of that waiting outside the store stuff."

As she took his hand and hopped to her feet, Ada allowed herself to smile. "Thank you, Gates. You're..." The best person she's ever met? An attractive man with soft looking lips? "Kind. Which means a lot to me. I don't know a lot of people like you and I, um, appreciate it."

His eyes lit up at her compliment.

"That means a lot to me, Ada." Gates said.

His big, brown eyes gazed at Ada, looking appreciative to be allowed the opportunity to look at her. She sort of felt like she should either smack the stupid grin off of his face or at least gather the decency to ignore him, but she couldn't bring herself to do either. Gates was too nice of a guy. With Ada's life, nice things were few and far. She learned a while ago to appreciate the nice things as they happened and cherish them in that moment. Good days where she woke up not feeling like she needed the pills, shifts at work where she only had to help an old couple install a new app on their phone...

Pretty detectives who treated her like the world for no reason at all.

A door opened behind them and Gates calmly looked over to it. His casualness about the moment made Ada's cheeks darken. Shit. He really was only a nice guy. He wasn't anyone special. Looking for a recovery, she looked to the door too. In the entryway of the pharmacy, an old woman stood there holding a small white paper bag.

"Oh sorry!" She said, "I hope I'm not interrupting, but my husband told me about your predicament. I know it's a little much, but I couldn't help but feel bad that you were out here crying and, well, I didn't want your little vacation to be ruined." The old woman stepped forward and handed the bag to Ada. "There's about a week's worth of St. John's Wort and I threw in some Ginkgo pills as a supplement. One of each per day. It's not your Prozac, but anything helps, you know? All over the counter so it's all legal for you to have without a prescription."

As Ada slowly realized the woman's kindness, tears welled in her eyes and she swallowed a knot in her throat.

"Thank you."

"Yes, really, thank you." Gates took Ada's shoulder with both of his hands. "If there's any way we can pay you back-"

"Oh don't worry about it, honey!" The old woman patted Gates's cheek gently. "It's the reminder that young love still exists, that is enough payment for me."

Taking the woman's comment in stride, Gates smiled.

"If only our landlord accepted that as payment."

The old woman chuckled and shook a crooked finger at him, before beaming at Ada. "At least you always know he can help make you happy. Medicine is a good tool, but the people you know are important too."

Gates's hold on Ada's shoulders lingered as they watched the old woman return to the small pharmacy. When the door shut behind her, Gates turned to Ada with a smirk.

"I knew the husband and wife thing would work."

"No you didn't." Rolling her eyes, Ada shrugged him off of her and turned to the street. "Speaking of boys who don't know what they're doing half the time, how are we going to find Louis and Sammy?"

"Public library," Gates said. "At least, that's where Louis was usually spotted by witnesses when I was investigating his case. Not to mention, it's the best place you can find and use a computer for free."

"Yeah he said he used one the other day which is how he learned sign language," Ada said. "Can we find something to drink first? I would like to take my medicine before I have to deal with Louis again."

"I don't blame you," Gates said. "C'mon. There's a vending machine just across the street. I'll pay."

"With Louis's money?"

"Good ole Great Aunt Hannah, actually," Gates said, waving the credit card in the air.

There was kind and then there was Gates Hopper as he made no mention of Ada's breakdown during their short walk to the soda machine. He spoke about the weather or the town, anything but Ada's situation, and she appreciated it greatly. Ada swallowed her medicine with Sprite when the Camaro came speeding up the street. It overshot Ada and Gates at first. They patiently watched as it screeched to a sudden halt, reversed, and braked with a jolt in front of them. The passenger window rolled down and Sammy popped her head and hands out of it.

"How's the date?" Sammy signed with an ornery smile.

"Terrible," Ada signed back.

"Liar," Sammy signed back before rolling up the passenger's window.

Louis stood from the driver's side. "Got your happy pills?"

Gates straightened beside her defensively, but Ada sighed.

"Just enough for a week and it's not the real deal," Ada said. "We couldn't get another prescription."

"Do you have a prescription with your doctor back home?"

"Pittsburgh is like three days away, dude."

"I didn't mean Pittsburgh."

Ada gave him a look. "Do you mean Chicago? Yeah I can probably get one from my family's doctor. Why?"

Holding his hands up in surrender, Louis smiled.

"Call it fate or luck, but Chicago is our next stop."

Her entire heart fell into the pit of her stomach.

"No."

"Yep," Louis said. "Tura Industries is holding a product presentation there tomorrow night. We can find out what Kamana is up to firsthand and see if we can stop it in the public's eye."

"Hold on," Gates said. "So you want to infiltrate an event held by the same company trying to kill us and you don't expect this to be a trap in any way shape or form?"

"Well it's either this or infiltrate them at the actual home base for Tura Industries," Louis said. "No one wants that unless they want a death sentence."

Sammy rolled her window back down. "Is Louis still talking?"

"He's acting like a drama queen again." Ada signed.

"As usual," Sammy signed. "Are you okay with going back to Chicago? You haven't been back since-"

"Chicago is a big city," Ada signed. "I think I can avoid my family for a day or two."

"We're going to have to make a plan," Gates said, unaware of the girls' conversation. "A real plan this time. Not just a run in there and hope it all works out like we did last night."

"I had a plan," Louis said. "It's not my fault Kamana is a massive bitch."

"Yeah well then let's make a plan that accommodates Kamana being a massive bitch," Gates said. "There's no way we're going to be able to sneak into a product presentation unless we know what we're doing."

"I guess that's the best part then," Louis said. "We're not sneaking in."

Gates's face dropped. "No."

"What?" Louis spread his arms out. "It's not like they can refuse Harding Ventura's prodigy son and his guests at the door."

"It's prodigal," Ada said.

"I know what I said."

Rolling his eyes, Gates turned to Ada. "Guess we're going to Chicago."

She took a deep breath. "I guess so."

Ada had hoped to avoid Chicago for at least another year or, ideally, forever. But it was their next 'only shot' at taking down Kamana. It was going to be fine. She had Sammy, who had a chainsaw, Gates, who had her back, and Louis, who had money. A short trip to Chicago for a couple of days would be fine if it meant humanity would be saved. At least she knew she could avoid one specific person for the entirety of their trip there.

<!--The phone rang. Ada let it go to voicemail and pulled her duvet over her head. The phone rang again.

And again.

Finally Ada got annoyed enough with the fact it was disrupting her nap that she rolled over and answered her cell phone on the fourth try.

"Hi Mom."

"Ada Kakar." Ruchira Kakar's voice was stern, restraining anger. "Are you on drugs?"

With a heavy sigh, Ada bit her lower lip. "No, Mom."

"Well, I can't think of any other reason for you to be acting like this," Ruchira stated. "You realize this Google internship is a once in a lifetime opportunity, right?"

"Yeah."

"Then why the hell is your father telling me that you're not doing any internships this summer?!"

"Because I'm not."

There was a long pause that made fear rise from the deepest pit in Ada's stomach.

"So you're not doing the Google internship?"

"No, Mom."

"What about that internship you had last summer? With Daniel?"

"No." Ada sighed. "I'm taking a summer off."

It was like she pulled a pin out of a grenade.

"Ada Kakar we are not paying for you to be lazy and take a vacation!" Ruchira shouted. "You're going to be a senior next year! You're going to need a job once you graduate! Do you know how you get jobs? With experience and do you know how you get experience? With internships."

"I don't know." Ada pulled into herself. "I'm just burnt out on programming right now."

"You're burnt out?!" Ruchira let out an incredulous laugh. "You're going to have to do this for the rest of your life, you know."

"I know."

"Your father and I aren't paying for another college education."

"I know."

"You're doing an internship this summer," Ruchira said. "I don't care if it's for the same no-name tech company you interned for last summer. Your father and I are not

176

paying rent on an apartment for you to relax and run around Pittsburgh all summer with your friends. You can do that here in Chicago while living with us and it'll be much cheaper, do you understand?"

"Yes, Mom."

"Do you want to come back to Chicago?"

"No, Mom."

"Then get an internship!"

"But-"

"Ada Kakar," Ruchira said sternly. "Get an internship."

There was a pause over the line.

"I love you, Ada."

"Love you too, Mom." -->

CHAPTER NINE

Chicago was the same.

Ada was not.

The last time she was in Chicago, it was for winter break her sophomore year of college nearly three years ago. She celebrated Pancha Ganapati with her family and watched the newest Bollywood movies that her dad's family sent for the holidays with Jasmine. On her last day, their dad brought Jasmine and Ada went to Tahoora Sweets and Bakery to buy a bunch of their favorite treats. Daniel ended up eating most of the pastries when she returned to Pittsburgh, but she still remembered the joy on her sister's face as they tried the different kalakand flavors. That memory was her favorite souvenir from her last visit home.

It was also freezing when she left. It was a miracle her flight could even leave relatively on time with the snow conditions. Now it was blazing hot. Even hell would have been begging for air conditioning in the Chicago July heat. Even as it neared twilight, the sun setting behind the towering skyscrapers, the four of them still had all of the Camaro windows rolled down as they sat in Chicago traffic for an hour. Ada wiped sweat off from her eyebrow. Pop music played softly through the radio as Chicago's map worked itself back into Ada's head. She was surprised when Louis moved past the exits for the seedy motels and went straight to downtown. He ended up driving past the Mag Mile and to the Conrad Hotel. He parked behind another car waiting for the valet.

"Louis, what the hell are we doing here?" Ada hissed. "This place is too nice."

"Ada is right," Gates said, looking up at the massive building. "They're going to find us here in a heartbeat."

"Poverty grants you anonymity while luxury grants you privacy," Louis said. "Two sides of the same coin. But this side has decent mattresses and room service, which I wouldn't mind experiencing again before those robots send us to hell."

Louis handed the valet his keys and filled out the paperwork as Gates helped Sammy and Ada unpack their luggage from the back. After tipping the valet with a giant wad of cash, Louis led the way into the massive hotel with a certain rich white boy swagger that he was hiding for the rest of the trip. Shoving her bag into Gates's arms, Sammy ran and claimed Louis's arm. Louis smiled at her as they proudly strolled into the building. The lobby was made from white marble. Modern, blue furniture furnished the room with large rugs spaced out on the floor. Dimly-lit chandeliers hung from the high ceiling. Ada no longer blamed Sammy for holding onto Louis. If she wasn't busy rolling her giant suitcase that still reeked of Nebraska, she probably would've held onto Gates too as they took in the beautiful room. Instead her suitcase made a clamor of noise as the broken wheels jagged on the soft marble, causing all of the rich people in the lobby to look at her as an intrusion into their idyllic lives. Furrowing her eyebrows, Ada tried to hide behind Gates as Louis led them to the front desk and smiled at the young receptionist.

"Hello," He greeted. "I know it's a little unorthodox, but do you have any suites available for the weekend?"

The receptionist's smile was condescending. "I'm sorry, sir, but it's the Fourth of July weekend. We won't have anything available until next week."

With a cute laugh, Louis acted embarrassed at his request. If it wasn't for the raggedy leather jacket he wore despite the insane heat, his impression of a rich white boy who never worked a day in his life and still had everything handed to him would've been perfect.

"Well, I don't want to be trouble," Louis said, a more formal lilt accenting his voice. "It's just that my father, Harding Ventura of Tura Industries, is speaking tomorrow night and while I would get a room at his hotel, I would rather surprise him by taking a room here."

The receptionist's eyes widened. "Oh. You're...okay. My apologies, sir, I will see what I can do." Clearly looking more nervous, she tapped frantically into her computer. "Well it just so happens a room is available until Sunday, but you'll have to be checked out no later than noon."

"Oh that's perfect," Louis said with a charming smile. "Do you know if there is anyone else here for my father's presentation?"

"Just two gentlemen from Milltek," The receptionist said. "Shall I arrange dinner for you?"

"No, it's fine," Louis said. "In fact, if you could do anything in your power to keep my name here a secret, I would be so grateful. It is incredibly tough to surprise my father."

Ada noticed how he coyly revealed a wad of cash from his sleeve while he spoke and presented it to the receptionist. With the subtlety of an expert, she took the money from his hands without revealing a thing from her facial expression.

"Of course, sir," The receptionist said. "Anything else I can do for you?"

"Continue being your adorable self," Louis said with a wink. Reading his lips, Sammy glared at Louis. Glancing down, the receptionist blushed and typed into her computer. Louis mouthed "I'm sorry" to Sammy as soon as the receptionist was distracted. After a moment, the receptionist arranged the room cards and handed them to Louis.

"King Superior Suite," She cooed. "Spa visits are complementary and you should have an excellent view of the city from your terrace."

"You are fantastic," Louis said. "Remember, don't let anyone know we're here. Not even room service."

"Of course, sir," The receptionist responded. "Enjoy your stay at the Gwen."

"The Gwen?" Ada asked out loud. "I thought this was the Concord."

"Oh the Concord was bought out years ago," The receptionist smiled. "We're now the Gwen."

Some things did change, then.

As they traveled through the lobby, Louis dropped the rich white boy routine and adopted his usual aggressive strut again. He was the first in the elevator with Sammy close behind him. Gates and Ada held up the group with their massive luggage. The doors closed and Louis rubbed his face.

"Milltek is a robotics company," He mumbled. "What the fuck are they doing here for my father's presentation?"

"Tura Industries has a robotics division," Ada said. "If, you know, that wasn't obvious enough-"

"No." Louis looked over his shoulder at her. "Every tech company has a robotics division. It's only a matter of making it public knowledge. If you couldn't guess, Tura would rather keep knowledge about their robots private. As in "people could get in white collar trouble for insider trading if people knew about it"-private, if you will. However, if my father is inviting robotics companies to a new product presentation, then he must be feeling brave."

At this news, Ada wasn't.

Silence fell in the elevator as they climbed the hotel. Gates released a massive yawn. With every floor they passed, Sammy bounced ever so slightly with excitement. Louis glanced at her before facing the elevator door with a proud smirk. As they finally stopped on one of the higher floors, Sammy's enthusiasm was fulfilled as they stepped into their room. Luxury spilled from the suite in glamorous waves. The beds were massive, easily able to fit three people to each, and blanketed with pristine material colored an immaculate shade of white. A living room remained the center focus of the room with modern furniture and décor so expensive it put the lobby below to shame. Gates set Sammy's luggage and his duffel bag by one of the beds before falling onto it with a heavy sigh. Sammy went straight for the bar and retrieved tiny bottles of alcohol from it. She set them delicately on the kitchenette counter as Louis walked through the living room and looked around.

"Not bad," He said with an approving nod.

"Not bad?!" Ada exclaimed. "This place is phenomenal."

"You underestimate my father's need to validate how rich he is," Louis said. "This place is practically a cardboard box compared to where he took us for family vacations."

"Ada!" Sammy shouted from the kitchenette. Ada turned to her and, with a giggle, Sammy tossed a tiny bottle of whiskey to her friend. Ada caught it as Sammy skipped over with her own tiny bottle of alcohol. Smiling widely, the girls opened their bottles and twisted their arms together.

"To us!" Sammy exclaimed out loud.

"To us!" Ada signed with one free hand. With their arms still twisted, they each swallowed their little bottles in one go.

Separating, Ada and Sammy laughed while wiping their mouths with the back of their hands.

"Can I ask something?" Louis said, breaking the girls out of their reverie. Only Ada turned to him as he pointed at Sammy, still recovering from her shooter of booze to notice he was talking. "How can Sammy talk?"

"She's deaf, not mute." This conversation had Ada craving another drink, but she had no idea what the effects would be with her new medicine. "She's just self-conscious about her voice so she hardly does it, that's all."

"What's happening?" Sammy signed, still giggly.

"Louis is asking about you talking," Ada signed.

Putting a hand over her mouth, Sammy turned to Louis before turning back to Ada.

"Was I too loud?" Sammy signed.

"No," Ada signed. "I think he's surprised that you can talk."

"I can talk!" Sammy spoke out loud, confusion edging her exclamation.

"Obviously," Louis said out loud while turning away from her. He waited for Sammy's reply until he realized his mistake. Then he cleared his throat. "Sorry. I'm just going to-"

Awkwardly pointing to the terrace, he walked outside of the hotel room. When he shut the patio door behind him, Ada released a laugh.

"Now what?" Sammy asked out loud, before going back to signing. "What is so funny?"

"Nothing," Ada signed. "It's the first time I've seen Louis so nervous!"

Sammy turned to see Louis with his back towards them as he leaned forward the railing of the sky-high patio. With a grumpy look, Sammy turned back to Ada.

"Don't be mean," She signed.

"If you could hear half the shit he says, you would be mean too," Ada signed.

"Rude," Sammy signed. "Don't be a bitch."

"You know what I meant," Ada signed, rolling her eyes.

"Yeah I do," Sammy signed. "Just like I knew what you meant when you called me a moron in Nebraska."

Ada's face fell. Were they fighting now? Because of Louis?!

"I'm sorry," Ada signed. "I didn't mean it. You know how I get without-"

"-medicine. I know," Sammy signed. There was an intensity to her eyes that held weight beyond whatever petty fight they were having now. "But with or without medicine, you choose to be mean. Louis doesn't. I see it in your eyes."

Resisting the urge to sarcastically ask Sammy what else she saw in her eyes, Ada stood there and folded her arms over her chest. One week with this dude and Sammy already liked him more than the best friend she's been living with for over a year. Typical. Ada didn't blame her, of course. Her mental issues were tough enough for *her* to deal with let alone to ask for another person to deal with them. With a soft smile, Sammy gave Ada a small pat on her shoulder.

"You're still doing better than before," Sammy signed. "Baby steps, remember? Step one, be nice to Sammy." She signed her name with a smug smile. "Step two, be nice to Louis. Step three, suck Gates's dick."

Sammy laughed as Ada rolled her eyes.

"Cute," Ada signed. "Go take your frustrations out on Louis."

"Trying," Sammy signed with a smirk. "I'm going to see if I can get him to order a full size bottle of alcohol to help."

"Whore," Ada signed.

With a subtle shrug, Sammy snagged two more small bottles of booze off the kitchenette counter and walked to the terrace.

Ada watched her, jealous of her best friend. Kindness came easy to Sammy. She took in Ada at her lowest, not even expecting Ada to pay her back in any way, or even knowing Ada beyond an ex-boyfriend that Ada didn't even talk to. Now she was showing sympathy towards Louis, the biggest asshole Ada had ever met who also happened to be behind the killer robots hunting them down and killing anyone else who stood in their way. Ada wished she could be so easily forgiving of life.

With a sigh, Ada walked to the massive beds. Gates was still sprawled on top of one of them, snoring softly. Shaking her head, Ada opened her luggage as quietly as she could and fished her laptop out. It was amazing how fast Gates fell asleep. Exhaustion was settling in her bones as well, but not to the extent where she needed to sleep as soon as possible. When was the last time he slept? It couldn't have been last night. No one slept last night. Sammy was the only one who napped during their trip from South Dakota to Chicago. Ada was the only one to sleep from Nebraska to South Dakota. From there, did Gates sleep from Pennsylvania to Nebraska?

The poor thing. It was a wonder he could even keep up the energy that he did in the car ride, asking Ada about her life and making sure she was okay from her meltdown that morning. Why did kindness come easy to everyone but her? Rubbing her eyes, Ada couldn't even focus on why she got her laptop out in the first place. She was just surrounded by so much support, so much unwarranted friendship...

And Louis.

"Hey," Gates groaned, slowly waking up. "How long was I out?"

"Barely even five minutes," Ada said. "Seriously, dude, go back to bed."

"No, no..." Gates pulled himself up. "We've got a job to do."

"You haven't slept in days," Ada said. "You can't do your job without sleep."

"I'm not too good at sleeping anyway," Gates yawned. "I don't like the whole part where I'm unconscious for hours at a time. Something could happen, someone could get hurt-"

"Hey the whole point of sleeping is so you have an excuse to not worry about those problems for a while. You can even hope that they work themselves out by the time you wake up," Ada said. "Trust me. Now go to sleep."

"No," Gates said with closed eyes, resting his head against the headboard. "I've gotta protect you."

"Go to sleep, Gates," Ada stepped over the luggage to get to him.

"Nope." He squinted his eyes at her.

"I swear Gates, did your mom have to do this to you?" Ada took the blanket folded neatly from the edge of the bed and pulled it towards him. "Good night, Gates."

"I'm not going to bed!" Gates said with a sleepy smile on his face. He grabbed the blanket in Ada's hand. "Give me that!"

"No!" Ada exclaimed, tugging back. "You're going to bed!"

"You go to bed!" Gates mocked.

"I will once you go to sleep!"

"Liar!"

Gates made a final, heavy tug on the blanket. Ada forgot to let go and flew towards him with the blanket, landing on top of him with a shout. Scrambling through the blanket, Gates made eye contact with Ada. Both of them held their eye contact, fully aware of the position they were in. Ada made no movement to move and neither did Gates. All she could think about was how she could feel his heartbeat underneath her, how she could feel the life in his body surge under her touch. How could he be so alive? How could anyone be so alive? Did she feel this alive to him? Finally, Gates cleared his throat as he looked from Ada's lips to her eyes.

"Yeah, okay. You've made a solid argument. I'll go to bed."

All too hyper-aware of their proximity, Ada released a shaky breath.

"Right. I'll, um, just leave you to do that."

With an awkward pat on his shoulder, Ada pulled herself from him, grabbed the laptop, and sped-walked into the living room area. She was grateful for the partition wall separating the two areas. Sitting on the modern chair, she opened the laptop and stared at the desktop for a bit as she processed her goal for using the device. Just over the screen, she could see Louis and Sammy standing close together as they looked into the city skyline together. Sighing, she closed the laptop again before standing to find another tiny bottle of alcohol. It was bad for her depression, but it made her forget about the heartache that lingered after all these years. But it wasn't an aching just for Daniel Carabella. That was a necessary loss, collateral damage she didn't feel particularly bad about. Instead, she mourned the life she missed out on while she sat on Sammy's couch with her broken brain.

Ada drank her tiny bottle of alcohol as she scrolled through the lines of code that remained on her laptop screen. It killed her that she couldn't automatically read and understand the programming like she could three years ago. If she hadn't spent the past two years on her ass ignoring her only worthwhile talent in life, she could've done something more last night. She could've created a better revenge for Margie Brown other than uploading a half-assed code that was shut down as fast as it was uploaded. But the truth of the matter is that Ada did neglect her coding ability for three years and there was no way for her to recover that time. There was only one way she knew she could still prove herself useful to her friends, who by some miracle still believed in her, and Louis.

She studied.

As Sammy and Louis spent hours on the terrace, Sammy teaching Louis basic sign language and Louis clumsily keeping up, Ada took Great Aunt Hannah's credit card and bought all of the old online textbooks she read during her days at Carnegie Mellon. Playing her old jazz music and jotting down notes on the hotel stationery, the familiarity of coding crawled back to her in patches of memory. All of the nights she turned away friends to continue her studies, Daniel's playful teasing as he tried to distract her from her work before ultimately giving up, the anxiety attacks before every major exam...they weren't the best memories, but they were the only memories Ada had.

Midway through her second choice textbook, Ada fell asleep in her chair to Eartha Kitt's hauntingly melodic voice. She woke up the next morning in Gates's bed, to the sound of a documentary about American presidents and the smell of bacon. Peeking an eye open, Ada could see Sammy lounged on the adjacent bed, doodling in her sketchbook with a plate of fresh fruit at her side. Gates was on the floor, holding his knees and looking at the TV like a child, the offending smell of bacon sourced to a plate next to him on the floor. A cart filled with more breakfast food sat near the kitchenette. Still snuggled in the bed, Ada watched the presidential documentary for a while, happy to let everyone believe she was still sleeping. Out of the corner of her eye, she watched as Louis walked to the cart with her laptop balanced on one arm. With his free hand, he picked an apple up and put it in his mouth before returning his attention to Ada's laptop. Panic shot through Ada's chest and she sat up in bed.

"Louis, what are you doing?!"

"Oh shit, you're alive!" He shouted with a jump, dropping the apple from his mouth and almost losing his balance with the laptop. "I thought you were dead! Jesus, you're a deep sleeper."

"It's true," Gates muttered. "You barely even moved when I carried you from your chair."

"Thank god you're alive too," Louis said. "One, I think you're onto something with your programming notes here. Two, I need you to come with me to Northwestern to find some clues about my uncle's whereabouts."

"Northwestern?" Ada asked, pulling herself out of bed. "My sister studies English Literature there."

"I know." Louis smiled smugly. "That's why you're coming with me. Plus, you know this city better than anyone else here and you've got connections that we can use to find my uncle."

"Connections? What connections? I have a twenty-one year old sister who's more interested in soccer and boys than any sort of education, especially with math or science," Ada corrected. "Besides, I haven't been here in three years. I thought this was still the Concord for crying out loud. You're better off with Google as your tour guide."

"Well, you still have to get your happy pills so I guess you're coming with me anyway so I can take you to the doctor's," Louis said. "Hurry up. Get dressed."

"I am dressed."

Stopping in his tracks, Louis gave her sweatpants and t-shirt a judgemental onceover.

"I'm not going to be seen in this great city of Chicago with you if you're going to be wearing the same ratty pair of sweatpants I found you in," Louis said.

Ada glared at him. "You've been wearing that stupid leather jacket for the same amount of time."

"It's a good jacket." Louis pulled at the collar with pride.

Unfortunately, Sammy had forced Ada to buy some new non-sweatpants orientated outfits while they were in Nebraska so she had no further arguments against Louis. Besides, her sweatpants were ratty from the constant running, fighting, and climbing over barbed wire. Not to mention the large robot dog bite that left one pant leg considerably shorter than the other. She discarded them into the depths of her suitcase before changing into royal blue pants, a plain yellow tank top, and a white jacket with three-quarter sleeves. As Ada slipped into her beige flats, Sammy let out a wolf-whistle. Ada rolled her tongue into her cheek, not willing to encourage Sammy's pride. It had been literal years since she's dressed this nice. Even in high school, the best her outfit got was the suit jacket with a business skirt required for most technical conferences. But her high school outfits weren't financed by Great Aunt Hannah Ventura's credit card and an empty mall in Nebraska.

After Ada stole a gold necklace and red hat from Sammy's suitcase, she was ready to go. Gates was relatively engrossed in his documentary as Ada dressed, but now she was catching him glancing over every once in a while. He even made a special trip to the breakfast cart and complimented her outfit before returning to his bed to watch the program with another plate full of bacon. Ada tried not to think too much about it. She instead focused on Louis's slow, but accurate, sign language as he told Sammy to protect Gates and use the chainsaw only when necessary. With a smile, Sammy proceeded to slowly sign her intention to grab dresses for the night's events. Apparently none of the overpriced garments in their suitcases would work. Ada was somewhat surprised when Louis approved, only asking her to find some tuxedos as well for Gates and him.

It was even more surprising when Sammy agreed.

As they exited the hotel, Ada felt extremely exposed. Not only from the fact killer robots were probably stationed just a few blocks away, but because she felt like all of Chicago was watching. Someone from her past was going to see her. Her luck was terrible. An old high school teacher or one of her dad's co-workers or one of her mom's clients...anyone could see her and tell her parents. The valet couldn't get the Camaro to them fast enough. Once Louis and

Ada entered the vehicle, she released a massive breath of relief at the security of the tinted windows protecting her from the people from her old life. Louis raised his eyebrow.

"You alright there?" He asked. "You're acting like someone got shot in front of you."

"It's nothing." Licking her lips, Ada shook her head as if she had to convince herself the same thing. "Let's go get my medicine."

"Northwestern first, doctor's second."

"No." Ada snapped. "We get my medicine first."

"If you actually want one of my plans to work, you're going to have to follow it," Louis said. He started the car and pulled into the road. "Besides, your doctor's office is nearly a half hour out of the way from Northwestern. It's easier to-"

"Either you take me to my doctor first or I'm staying in the car when we get to Northwestern!" Ada shouted.

"Jesus Christ, what is so important about this medicine?!" Louis turned onto Sheridan. "I mean I get it you have depression or whatever, but it's not like a stupid pill is going to do much. It's just a supplement to balance your hormones. Just ignore the off-balanced serotonin levels for a couple hours, okay? Practice some coping techniques. Did you ever go to therapy?"

"Once. But it's expensive and I don't have insurance."

"Okay but what about breathing? You seem to do a lot of that."

"You sound like my mother." Folding her arms across her chest, Ada fell back into her seat. "Believe me, if I could just wish it away and 'be happy' or whatever again, I would."

Louis glanced over at Ada before returning his attention to the road.

"What do you mean?"

"I mean..." She sighed. It was never easy to explain. Most people just accept it. It's easier for them to think that depression is just sadness and wanting suicide. But it's more than that. It's the reason why Ada didn't leave Sammy's couch for three weeks straight once, why Ada felt like staring at a blank wall was a better way to spend her time than going to class, and why her mother thought Ada gave up on everything out of laziness. Ada didn't want to be lazy. She wanted to be productive, she wanted to be worthwhile, she wanted to care about her life. That's not how it worked with the chemicals in her brain though.

"It's like a leech, but instead of blood it sucks the life out of you." Ada said. "I don't get a choice on whether or not I want the leech."

"Gross."

"So is depression. My antidepressants stop the leech," Ada said. "They're the extra push that get me out of bed and keep me walking around. Before my medicine, I would lie there for hours doing nothing. I would want to do something, but my brain wouldn't let me. I couldn't even sleep." Looking out the window, Ada pressed her lips together. "It's a constant struggle to fight for control, to make sure I don't go back to where I was. The antidepressants are my best weapon in that fight. Some people don't need them, but I do."

For once, Louis took a moment to choose his words.

"What started it?"

"Nothing started it," Ada said. "There was no trigger. It just happened. Like I feel like I've always felt like this, but one day, my brain finally did something about it."

With a soft hum, Louis tightened his grip on the steering wheel.

"Listen, I swear we will get your medicine as soon as possible, but we have to find my uncle first," Louis said. "He will probably already be on the move if he heard about the presentation tonight. If not-" He shook his head. "Uncle Allen knows more about these androids than I do. He's the one who built them from the ground up. He was working on them before I was even born. We have to find him. He's our last hope."

Sighing, Ada reluctantly agreed. They can still pick up her medicine within the next week. It would be hell, but it probably wouldn't cost a life. Uncle Allen, on the other hand, had a time limit. They had to reach him before the robots did. It didn't mean Ada's broken brain wasn't distracted though. When they reached the Northwestern campus, Ada didn't realize she was searching for Jasmine until she nearly had a heart attack when they drove by two girls kicking a soccer ball around. Neither of them were Ada's sister and Ada was surprised when disappointment sank in her chest as a result. Then again, it's been years since she's seen her sister, months since she's heard her voice. Maybe Ada could break her own rule and sneak away to find Jasmine, even if it was from a distance. Louis parked the car in a lonely parking lot near the front entrance for the McCormick School of Engineering. They whipped their seat belts off and got out of the Camaro. Louis stormed towards the building and Ada had to power-walk to catch up.

"Alright, here's the plan," He said. "We're doctorate students looking to get our PhD in Biomedical Engineering. You're an assistant professor from Carnegie Mellon, and I'm your TA. We're trying to find Doctor Allen Paz for research on a dissertation we're presenting for the next semester."

"What's the dissertation?"

"Artificial Intelligence Programming and the Dangers It Poses."

"Subtle."

"As always."

Pushing the glass doors open, Louis led the way through the maze of hallways until they reached the front desk. Ada went ahead and stepped in front of Louis. Holding her shoulders straight and raising her chin ever so slightly, Ada approached the front desk with a pose reserved for someone worthy of respect. The secretary looked up, not with a forced smile, but with genuine pleasure that

Ada was able to grace her presence. Maybe Ada should skip wearing sweatpants more often.

"Hello! How may I help you?" The woman chimed.

"Yes my name is Louis Hopper and this is Professor Ada Creighton of Carnegie Mellon," Louis said. "We're doctorate students looking to get our PhD in Biomedical Engineering and we need to contact Doctor Allen Paz."

"We're writing a dissertation on artificial intelligence and the dangers it poses," Ada added, not wanting to look shown up by her fictional TA. "We know Doctor Paz taught here for a couple years and we were hoping you would still have some contact information for him."

"Well Doctor Paz would certainly know a lot about the dangers of artificial intelligence," The woman said as she typed into the computer.

Panicked about how this lady somehow knew about the robots, Ada glanced at Louis. Relatively calm, he noted her panic with a subtle nod and turned to the woman.

"Yes, his lectures on the subject are unparalleled. No wonder they're incredibly well known," Louis said pointedly to Ada. "Not to mention, his firsthand experience and studies with Tura Industries would give our dissertation a unique resource necessary for our study."

"Oh absolutely. If you want to know all about AI, Allen's your guy. He also generally loves helping grad students, but I haven't heard much from him in the past year or so. He might be on sabbatical," The woman said. There was another moment as she typed into the computer, getting progressively more annoyed as she typed. "Huh."

"Is there a problem?" Ada asked, her heart hammering against her chest. The woman must have googled her name and discovered she was a fraud.

"Something must be wrong with my internet connection," The woman explained. "I might need to reach out to our IT. He's in our system and I can see everyone else's contact information without a problem, but his information seems to be....I don't know how to describe it. It looks like it's corrupted somehow-"

She was cut off with the sound of a gunshot.

Louis cussed under his breath as the woman screamed and ducked under her desk. Ada turned with Louis to see a thin woman with lilac color hair marching towards them in tall heels and a shotgun in both hands.

"Louis Ventura," Her voice echoed. "It is time for you to die."

"Lady! You've changed your hair!" Louis stated. "It looks even worse than the red."

Another shot. It missed Louis and Ada, bullets flattening the flower vase next to them. The woman behind the desk screamed again. Louis dropped Ada to the ground. As Lady reloaded her weapon, they crawled around to the other side of the desk. The woman was in the fetal position, crying softly.

"I don't remember the procedure," She cried. "I never thought it would happen here. I thought-"

"I knew they would follow us," Louis remarked as he pulled a handgun out of his pocket. "I just figured they wouldn't act until we got the information. Given her quick turnaround for the rebuild, Lady's AI might still be out of whack to allow her to think ahead for that timing. The good news about this though is that since they rushed Lady's production, obviously her optic locking mechanism is out of sorts so she won't be able to directly kill us-"

Ada interrupted. "Isn't that Gates's gun?"

Louis held up the weapon. "Yes?"

"Doesn't he need it?"

"He has Sammy," Louis shrugged. "I've got you. Honestly, who needs it the most right now?"

Ada didn't even have a reasonable argument.

"The students!" The woman cried. "Oh god."

Ada's heart dropped. Jasmine.

She turned to the woman. "Is the women's soccer team practicing today?"

"Yes!" The woman wailed. "They practice every morning. They're at the stadium by the lake. Oh god. We need to call the police-"

"Don't call the police!" Louis snapped. "It's just Lady-" A shotgun shell slammed into the desk. "-and she's not on her best game right now. We just need the information and we'll get out of here."

"Oh Louis..." A male's voice sang. "We know you're here."

Louis's entire face dropped. He swallowed hard before turning to the receptionist.

"I changed my mind. You might want to call the police."

Another shotgun shell burrowed its way into the desk.

"Lady, hold your fire," Hercules commanded. "You're wasting ammo."

"Louis Ventura and an associate are hiding behind this desk, Hercules." Lady's voice vibrated. "All threats to Project Kamana must be eliminated."

"Yeah, well, the desk ain't a threat, is it?" Hercules chided. "Is he with the programmer? Ada Kakar?"

"Negative," Lady affirmed. "My readings indicate-"

"Your readings are as rusty as your shooting," Hercules said. "C'mon Louis. Show yourself. You know you're fighting a losing battle."

Louis turned to Ada. "Get my uncle's contact information off of that computer and get out of here." He hissed before standing up, placing the gun on a shelf out of sight from the robots. He raised his hands in surrender.

"Wow, good work," Louis said. "It's a shame I'll be missing my father's presentation tonight. I was looking forward to it."

The woman pulled on Ada's arm. "Is he with the police?"

"No," Ada breathed. "Actually, he's kind of the opposite of the police right now. You get used to it. He's very good at pretending to know what he's doing."

The woman looked petrified. As Louis continued to stall the robots, Ada looked at the screen stationed on the counter above them. She recognized the bug. It was a simple hack. A middle-aged teacher got it on her laptop a month ago. Stacy had to call Ada over from her break to fix it. Someone, probably Louis's uncle, probably set it up so that the file would corrupt upon opening. A Trojan Horse. It made sense since a complete wipe would've raised suspicion. Quietly taking the keyboard and mouse, Ada set to work on fixing the bug on the desktop computer.

"What's your name?" Ada asked the receptionist, not looking away from the computer screen.

"Grecia."

"Grecia, I'm going to need you to wipe your most recent programs that aren't essential from the past year," Ada said. "After that, try going into the system again to find Allen Paz's information. Understood?"

"Yes," Grecia breathed as Ada stuck the keyboard on her lap. "Why? What are you going to do?"

"Herc, listen," Louis's voice came into focus. "I know you're mad about your boyfriend and you can kill me right here right now, but then Kamana loses her best engineer. How can you build more androids without me?"

"You wouldn't help us either way," Hercules scowled. "That became obvious when you attempted to corrupt Droid Nine."

"I wasn't corrupting it!" Louis argued. "Think outside of Kamana's damn programmed propaganda for once. I was trying to fix-"

Without another thought, Ada grabbed the gun from the counter. Holding her breath, she aimed for Hercules. Her heart stopped when she pulled the trigger. Nothing came out. Opening her eyes again, Ada stared at the gun before she realized Louis and the two androids were staring at her with shock and amusement, respectively.

Hercules smiled and chuckled softly. "Go ahead, Lady. Take her out but keep her alive."

Louis pulled Ada to the floor as the shotgun shells sprayed across the wall behind them. Her stupid hat fell off and Louis released Ada as soon as they hit the floor. Grecia was still adamantly taking care of the computer bug, shaking ever so slightly as she did so. Ada pulled herself off the floor and bolted down the hallway in the opposite direction than where they came from.

"Ada!" Louis screamed. "Ada get back-"

He was cut off by the sound of a pistol. On instinct, Ada threw her arms over her head. Looking back, she could see both Hercules and Lady chased after her. She ran faster, grateful that Lady was in front and struggling to shoot properly anyways. The sound of another gunshot echoed down the hallway. Louis must have grabbed Gates's gun. Ada checked behind herself again to see that now only Lady was in pursuit, desperately trying to keep with Ada's pace with her heels.

By some miracle, Ada made it outside alive. Looking around, it took her a little bit to find the lake. She bolted in that direction, hoping Lady didn't see her. They sent two robots this time. Maybe there were more. Maybe they found out about Ada's family and sent Eyepatch to get Jasmine. Ada wasn't going to risk it. She was going to make sure her sister was okay. Before she could make sure, blinding pain shot through Ada's shoulder, like a sharply pulled muscle. With a scream, she reached back to it and felt something warm. And wet. Pulling her hand back, she slowed to a stop as she looked at her fingers. Blood. She was shot. Lady shot her. Feeling light-headed, Ada fell against a car. The initial shock subsided and the pain was rushing to her arm like a fiery poison. She refused to pass out. She wasn't going to let this robot bitch win.

"My memory drive tells me that we were in this situation before," Lady spoke as she approached Ada. "However, I am under different orders this time. I am not allowed to help you this time, Ada Kakar, and Louis Ventura is not present to interfere." Something mechanical in the robot's arm clicked as she raised her shotgun to take clear aim for Ada's head. "I am not allowed to eliminate you, but injuries will continue unless you come with me."

Out of breath and still feeling light-headed, Ada wasn't sure she heard the android right.

"Why can't you eliminate me?" She asked. "You were just about to eliminate Louis-"

"Louis Ventura is a threat to Project Kamana," Lady stated. "You are an asset."

Before Ada could question it further, darkness surrounded her vision. She was going to pass out whether she wanted to or not. This robot would claim her and drag her to wherever she needed Ada to go. Falling to the ground, Ada was able to see something knocking into Lady's shotgun, throwing it out of her hands. The shotgun landed with a clatter on the asphalt parking lot. Ada struggled to keep consciousness long enough to see Lady getting chased away by a group of girls in soccer uniforms. One of the girls stopped and looked at Ada in between the cars.

"Shit! Guys, I think she's been shot!" She yelled. "Where's Andrea? She's a nursing major, right? She can help!"

"Yeah but she's barely passing!" Another girl shouted in the distance. "We have to evacuate!"

"Ma'am, are you alright?" The girl who stopped asked.

Ada could barely even make a whisper before everything went dark.

When she woke up, Ada was lying on a stretcher in an ambulance. Red and blue lights flashed in the horizon of her vision. Hundreds of voices chatted in the distance. A nondescript figure walked past the opening in her ambulance. Ada poked her head up and tried to sit straight, a shot of pain in her arm reminding her of her injury. With a grumble, she moved to adjust her weight. As her groggy vision cleared, a young girl in a blue Northwestern women's soccer jersey poked her head into the ambulance's opening.

"She's awake!" She shouted. "Jasmine, she's awake!"

Before Ada could realize what was happening, a whole squadron of college age girls in soccer gear ran to her ambulance. All of them were vying for Ada's attention, either asking about her well-being or informing her of their part in her rescue. In the middle of them all was a pretty Indian girl with her thick black hair tied in a long braid. She looked like she had been crying. Ada stepped down from the ambulance as Jasmine ran forward and gave her sister a tight hug.

"Ada!" Jasmine held onto her tightly for a long time, automatically mending any broken bonds between them with that hold. Pulling away, she smiled at her sister and shoved her non-injured shoulder softly. "You big wimp."

"What?!" Ada asked. "I got shot!"

"You were only grazed!" Jasmine laughed. "You didn't even need stitches."

"It still hurt!"

"And you're still a massive wimp!" Despite the weepy look still holding in her eyes, Jasmine allowed a wide smile to grow on her face. She led Ada from the gaggle of girls. "You're lucky that Morgan was dumb enough to throw her soccer ball at that lady and the rest of us were stupid enough to follow. You might've actually had a reason to pass out if we let her stay there with you."

"Mom and Dad don't know about this, right?" Ada asked as she looked around at the police cars and news vans.

"The school called them on my behalf, but I don't know if they called for you," Jasmine said. "We didn't even know you were going to be in town."

"Sorry," Ada said. "I didn't know I'd be here. I'm just passing through."

"Huh," Jasmine hummed. Ada couldn't tell if her sister was disappointed or suspicious. Maybe both. "I heard you're an assistant professor at Carnegie Mellon now. How did that happen? That must be keeping you too busy to call, right?"

The hint of sadness in that question made Ada's heart stop for a moment, but the impact of Jasmine's statement hit first.

"I'm not a-" Ada stopped herself. "Who told you-"

"Professor!" Louis came running up. "Are you alright?"

Ada licked her lips, not sure how to handle this situation because she wasn't quite sure what reality she was living in. The fact both Louis and her sister now knew of each other seemed unreal, like a bad TV sitcom crossover.

"Your TA here was very brave," Jasmine cooed. "He saved the Engineering secretary and their important files from those lunatics."

"Yeah we saved the files. However, the shooters still got away," Louis said. "Luckily you seem to be the only one that got hurt."

Ada didn't feel very lucky.

"So you got what you needed?" Ada asked.

"Yes," Louis said. "But we need to get going. Something urgent has come up."

Jasmine frowned. "Already? But you just got here."

"I know," Ada said.

"And you're leaving. Again."

Ada pursed her lips. Just like Daniel, Jasmine was also collateral damage for the losses Ada took when her life became a mess.

However, unlike Daniel, Ada minded the loss of her little sister. She purposefully ignored thinking of Jasmine some days to avoid the guilt. She avoided considering if her sister was now tasked with the impossible burden of being the pride of the family since Ada failed so miserably, if Jasmine was able to handle it without Ada around. But now her sister was standing in front of her, three years older and wiser. Her sister was growing up without her, but she still acted like no time had passed at all between them. It was that selfless love that Ada missed the most. She missed the kind of love that could handle her at her worst but, at the same time, she didn't want that love to see her worst. She wanted only the best for that love. If that meant leaving her sister behind in Chicago with limited communication until she could provide a version of herself that was worthy of her sister's undying loyalty, then so be it.

"I know."

"Plus, you know, you're the victim of a school shooting!" Jasmine shouted. "I'm sure that not only the police will want to talk to you, but the news and Mom and Dad-"

"Jasmine!" With wide eyes, Ada grabbed her talkative little sister's shoulder and nodded. "I pinky swear I'll call more often, okay? Just let me deal with this right now."

Jasmine frowned at her sister.

"And you'll come home for Christmas?"

"We don't even celebrate-"

"*Promise!*"

Rolling her eyes, Ada held her pinky out and Jasmine shook it with her own enthusiastic pinky. Louis looked between them with squinted eyes.

"You guys are cute," Louis said. "But that's not fixing our urgent issue, professor."

"What's the urgent issue then?" Ada asked.

"Gates called," Louis said. His green eyes were hard. "They took Sammy."

<!-- Everything went from neutral to nothing. There's a difference between feeling everything turn to gray and not feeling anything at all. Ada was at the point where she felt nothing. It wasn't a great point to be at.

"You are failing, Ada." Dr. Grace said.

"I know," Ada said. "I've got some stuff going on."

"That's no excuse," Dr. Grace said. "I worked five jobs to get myself through school and didn't see my family for ten years. I promise whatever you're dealing with is nothing compared to what I dealt with so pick up the pace, okay? I know you're smart enough."

Ada knew she should've cared, but she didn't. Her mother's many phone calls didn't make her care and neither did the many emails her other worried professors sent.

"You haven't left the apartment in days," Dan said. "When's the last time you went to class?"

Ada could tell Dan was getting annoyed, but she still couldn't bring herself to care. Even when he moved from their bed to the couch, Ada couldn't bring herself to ask him to return. She couldn't even bring herself to ask where he left every night without her. She didn't have the energy any more.

"We never see you!"

"Whoa! Ada's alive!"

"The hermit has left her cave!"

Ada took every jest in stride. She knew she deserved it. It should've hurt to see her friends leave her side one by one, treating her few appearances as novelties rather than expectation. Like they had to tolerate her presence. Like they didn't endure the way she turned every conversation into a bummer, if they even noticed her attempt to participate in the first place. Every jest should've felt like a stab in the back, a knife to her heart. Instead, Ada felt nothing.

"Is everything okay?"

It was luck that brought Sammy to Ada again. Ada had gone out with Dan, a poor attempt to make herself care about how he looked at Michelle like he used to look at her. She tried to stay involved, tried to feel anything but nothing about the fun night out. Instead Ada isolated herself to a corner booth, half-watching her friends sing karaoke and ignoring their judgemental whispers. Her brain couldn't let her have the fun she desired to have. She didn't even initially realize Sammy joined her isolation.

"You're friends with Bryan, right?" Sammy wrote out on her phone. "It's been a while. You look different."

"How?" Ada signed.

"Sad," Sammy spelled out slowly in sign language so Ada could understand. "Tired. Your eyes don't light up any more."

"Things change," Ada signed.

Sammy's eyes were sad, but kind. After some insistence, Sammy convinced Ada to put her number into her phone. Once Sammy had Ada's number, she typed out a message and sent it to Ada.

"If you ever need to talk to someone, let me know," She wrote. "It's nice being able to sign with someone for once and I'd hate to see you get out of practice. :)"-->

CHAPTER TEN

Sammy was gone.

It was Ada's fault.

Well it was also Louis's fault. He took the one weapon that Gates and Sammy could reasonably hide if they ventured into public and then told them it was okay to go out in public on their own. Then again, that gun also saved Louis and Ada's life so it was more or less a terrible situation all around. Regardless, if Ada didn't foolishly run to save her sister who didn't need saving, Louis and Ada could've made their escape in time to save Sammy from being kidnapped in the dress shop where she stopped to buy outfits for the party that night with Gates. Gates was knocked out by Eyepatch and unable to save Sammy. By the time he woke up, she was gone.

"This is a mistake," Gates shouted from across the hotel room where he held ice to his head. "We can't go to that party tonight. Louis realizes this is a trap, right? There's no way we can handle their full security force. You guys could barely handle two of them on your own let alone, what did Louis say, six or seven of them? The full team?"

Ada's desperate attempts to cover the bandages from her gunshot wound served as a cruel reminder of their failure to handle the robots on their own. Sammy chose Ada's dress first. It was a long chiffon dress in a shade of yellow that made her dark skin glow nearly golden. Ada adored it, but the thin straps made it hard to cover her shoulder injury. She should've asked Louis to grab a shawl for her or something while he was on "reconnaissance" or whatever shady stuff he was doing on his own again.

"Well Louis likes Sammy. He would rescue her with or without us," Ada explained as she rummaged through Sammy's luggage, hoping to find another worthwhile accessory to cover her injury. "I just don't understand why we have to go through the effort of this stupid party. If Kamana is going to kill us, I don't think she's going to care if we try to be civil or not."

"Of course she'll care," Gates said. "It's bad on the company if guests are found murdered at their party."

"What happens if we get murdered outside of the party by company property?"

"It would be deemed a 'tragic accident' and Tura Industries will gladly provide any monetary compensation to those affected by your loss," Gates answered. "Because all human life has a price that can be paid, right?"

Ada snorted derisively. "Do you think they would give monetary compensation for the hell they put us through? Because I'm 80% sure I lost my job because of this since I've been 'no call, no show' for like a week now."

"If we actually get away with this, I'll be happy just to have my life!" Gates exclaimed with a sad laugh. He paused for a moment. "Is that what you'll do if we survive this? Go back to Pittsburgh and work at Geek Squad again?"

"There's nothing else for me to do," Ada said.

"You could always go back to school."

"Sounds exhausting."

"New job?"

"Also exhausting. Especially the searching part."

Giving up on finding a good cover, Ada walked to the living room area. Gates stood at the mirror, fumbling with his bowtie with the ice pack placed on a nearby counter. She leaned against the partition with her good shoulder and watched him, admiring how his slender fingers managed to twist the material into impossible knots.

"What about you?" Ada asked. "What's your plan if we survive?"

"My plan?" Gates sounded incredulous. He thought about it for a moment. "Honestly, I never thought about it. I figured we wouldn't make it that far."

"I thought you were an optimist."

"I am, but..." Shaking his head, Gates returned his attention to his bowtie. "It's complicated."

Smirking, Ada leaned her head against the partition as she continued to stare at him.

"Is it a girl?" She asked, feeling her heart grow heavy.

"Oh god no," Gates exclaimed.

"A boy?"

"No, no!" Gates squeezed his eyes shut and shook his head. "No, I don't have anyone. No partner of any gender. Girls don't like me and I don't really like guys. It's just me and-"

Gates turned to face Ada. As soon as his eyes settled on Ada, he froze. Her heart dropped to her stomach and she pulled herself up straight from her awkward lean on the wall.

"What?" She frowned. "Is it the bandage? I couldn't find anything that would-"

"No, no..." Gates mumbled. "You look gorgeous."

With the way he gazed at her, Ada knew he meant every word and more. It made her feel incredibly conscious of every detail of her outfit: the makeup meant for Sammy's fair features, the giant bandage on her shoulder, her crudely curled hair that felt more frizzy than pretty. All of it was flawed and yet Gates stared at her as if she was a goddess. Tucking a dark strand of hair behind her ear, Ada blushed and looked at her feet instead. Clearing his throat, Gates looked away and tried to fix his tie with more intensity.

"Yeah I mean, Pittsburgh isn't a bad place to be," He continued. "Low crime rate, excellent neighborhoods for kids-"

"You're going to choke yourself if you keep going like that," Ada walked over to him. "Here. Let me."

After giving her a doubtful side glance, Gates surrendered his bowtie. He held his hands behind his back as Ada set to work on fixing his atrocity, desperately trying to remember how she did it for Daniel years ago. She probably wasn't shaking as much back then.

"So, why don't you think girls like you?" Ada asked.

With a shaky breath, Gates shrugged. "They just...don't. I'm too...."

"Kind? Tall?" Ada tried. "Unable to tie a bowtie on his own?"

Releasing a single laugh, Gates gave a sad smile to Ada.

"Broken," He said.

Raising her eyebrows, Ada lost her place on his tie. She took a deep breath and returned her attention to it.

"You're not broken," Ada stated. "You're not the one who had a meltdown in Corsica, South Dakota, okay?"

"Do you blame me for letting Sammy get kidnapped?" Gates asked.

"No." Ada said it so quietly it was nearly a whisper.

"Why not?" Gates asked. "I was there. I could've done something."

"We all could've done something to prevent what happened," Ada said. "The point is that we're doing something now. It would be worse if we didn't."

"If I wasn't broken, I could've saved Sammy," Gates said. "If I wasn't distracted or if I paid attention-"

"If you think getting distracted is a sign of being broken," Ada snorted. "Then, buddy, all of humanity is broken."

Gates laughed softly. "Well I don't think you're broken, if that means anything."

It amounted to a lot of things for Ada, none of them she could say out loud and risk a commitment she could not follow through with. She finished his bowtie in silence, the air feeling electric as she did so.

"Alright," She muttered as she straightened it out. "It's not the best, but it's probably not going to be the death of you either."

Examining the tie in the mirror behind Ada, Gates looked impressed.

"Nice," Gates said. "So what about you? This means you've got a boyfriend back home, right? Someone you tied these things for all the time?"

"I did once," Ada said. "But you know, he wanted someone who wasn't broken and I was far from that so…." She shrugged. "It didn't work out."

Gates laughed. "He sounds like an asshole if he passed on you."

"It wasn't too unreasonable-"

"Are you kidding?" Gates exclaimed. "You look like the sun. Who would give up the sun of all things?"

Genuinely flattered, she rested her hands on his shoulders. "The sun? How do I look like the sun?"

"You are blindingly beautiful," Gates said, looking from her eyes to her lips. "You're golden, radiating, and warm like a-a…." Shaking his head, Gates gave Ada a small half smile. "Just warm. And you're so smart too. You're just so-"

Ada interrupted his thought by pulling him into a kiss. After the initial surprise of the kiss, Gates gladly returned the affection and held Ada by the small of her back, closing whatever little space remained between them. It was soft and warm, like a ray of sunshine on a cold winter day. A genuine joy rose from the depths of Ada's heart that she hadn't felt in years. It was a happiness she knew she should've felt with Daniel or with computer programming, but never did. Now that she's felt it, Ada wasn't quite sure how she could ever let go of it. However, she was forced to let go at the sound of the door opening. Louis's thundering footsteps caused both of them to pull away, masking their stolen moment with awkward fidgeting and a refusal to look each other in the eye. Strolling into the room in a suit he wasn't wearing when he left, Louis didn't notice their awkwardness.

"Spoke to our friends from Milltek downstairs." Louis pulled two laminated cards from his suit jacket. "They were kind enough to loan us their invitations and this suit for the evening."

"How much did you pay them?" Gates asked, subtly wiping his lips with his thumb.

"I'll worry about that when they wake up," Louis said. He looked at Ada and made a face. "What the hell are you wearing?"

All of the magic drained from Ada. She looked down at her dress with a short pout, smoothing the flowing skirt self-consciously.

"Sammy picked it out."

"No, yeah, you look great in it," Louis said. "It's just weird seeing you dressed nice for once."

"As if you should talk," Gates said. "How are you going to survive the evening without that ratty leather jacket?"

Smoothing his new suit jacket, Louis looked offended. "Easy. This is Armani."

Gates rolled his eyes. Shortly after, they packed the room, shoving clothes into each suitcase without discrimination. Louis went ahead and stole all of the shampoo, soap, and conditioner, which Ada didn't say a word about. But she did put her foot down when she caught Louis removing the bedsheets. Once everything was packed, they made their way to the lobby. Gates packed the Camaro with their luggage as Louis and Ada checked out from their room.

"You know, I've been thinking about our conversation from today," Louis said after the receptionist returned his credit card. "About your depression."

"Oh good," Ada said. "I thought you were going to insult my dress again. Glad to see you're targeting my mental health instead."

Louis ignored her remark. "It sounds like a destructive force. I mean, you're a genius, Ada, and an absolute wizard at programming who received the best education possible and was put in the best situation possible. If depression can manage to fuck up your life, imagine what it could do to a self-absorbed idiot."

Ada stared at Louis.

"This pep talk is going phenomenal. What are you getting at?"

"What I'm getting at..." Lowering his voice, Louis looked around them before turning to Ada. "...is that why don't we try programming the equivalent of depression into the Kamana language and take them down with that?"

"Impossible," Ada snapped. "I know my fair share of programming languages and I don't think any of them will be capable of-"

"All of life is a complicated series of if/then statements. What makes depression any different?" Louis's eyes lit up. "Ada, you would know the effects of depression better than anyone. If you just-"

"I'm not a psychologist!" Ada nearly shouted. "I'm not going to be able to program the complexities of depression into something that can be introduced to them without that background knowledge."

"Yes you can," Louis took Ada by the upper arms. He was looking desperate. "Look. I fucked up last time. I should've known a remote reprogramming of their entire systems wouldn't work. But this will work. You said it yourself, there was no real reason or trigger behind your depression. It was gradual. If we figure how to code depression, we'll be able to give our virus a natural introduction to the Kamana system-"

"-that they won't notice until it's too late," Ada finished, realizing Louis's train of thought. "They won't be able to fight it."

"Right!" Louis smiled. "Especially since they're androids, they will never be able to fight it properly. They'll think it's another run of the mill virus and attack it like one. They'll never realize it's from within their own programming."

"Yeah, okay, but how are we going to be able to translate depression into a functional code?" Ada said. "That's a mix of biology, neuroscience, and psychology. None of that translates into computer science."

"That's why we need to find my uncle," Louis said. "He was working on something similar before the bots caught us. He'll be able to help us finish the code. We can start on it after we save Sammy."

The weight of his statement fell on them almost immediately. A reminder that even though they had hope with this new idea, they still had an obstacle ahead of them. An obstacle that Gates didn't believe they would survive from, that Ada would run from if it wasn't for Sammy, and that Louis would do anything to make sure it was accomplished. They left the hotel in silence. Gates was waiting for Ada in the Camaro at the entrance. With their plan, Ada and Gates had to arrive ahead of Louis. Ada was initially thrilled with the idea of alone time with Gates, but now the thought made her stomach flip. Luckily, Gates was preoccupied with discussing their plan during their five minute drive to the venue to talk about the kiss they shared instead.

"Once I set the distraction, you need to hide in the Camaro immediately," Gates said. "If we aren't out in fifteen minutes, you need to drive as far as you can away from here."

"I'm not leaving without Sammy," Ada said.

"Sammy will be fine," Gates said. "Worry about yourself when the time comes."

Ada couldn't help but notice the sternness in his voice. She wanted the reason to be because of the stressful situation of walking into enemy territory, but she knew it wasn't and that felt unbearable. Before she could pluck up the courage to ask him why he was so scared, Gates already parked the Camaro. When they exited the car, he offered his arm to her and she accepted it, holding onto it tightly to hide her nerves. They joined another group entering the venue. As Gates made polite small talk with them, Ada read their name cards. All of them were from robotics companies. Her stomach did another flip. At the entrance to the main guest room, someone in a black suit trimmed with red silk examined name cards and checked them on a tablet. He wasn't an android, at least not one Ada had seen, but he still made her heart slam against her chest in a nervous rhythm.

"Milltek Corporations," The bouncer smiled as he accepted their name cards. "Thank you for coming Mr. Kyle Henderson and-" He made a face at Ada's name tag. "...Ms. Yuki Hideyoshi?"

There was a moment of silence as the dissonance of Ada's dark skin color and the name on her tag became wildly apparent.

"Family name," Ada assured.

The guy looked at Gates for confirmation. He straightened his shoulders as if he wanted to challenge the man to question Ada's identity. She had no doubt Gates would throw away his kind temperament for her defense. The bouncer had no doubts about Gates's intentions either. Painting a smile on his face, the bouncer backed away.

"Enjoy the party,"

Gates nodded softly, silently congratulating the man on his wise choice. They entered the ballroom. It was bustling with people. Most were older than Ada and Gates by well over a decade, but there were a good number of people as young as them. The blend of old money funding new talent that typically populated the tech industry. Ada examined the crowd, looking for any sign of the androids.

"They're not going to be here," Gates said, as if he read her mind. "Too high of a chance for exposure. Not to mention, they've probably been watching us since we got here. That means they saw Louis wasn't with us and are looking for him instead."

"Oh joy," Ada breathed. "The evil robots can see us but we can't see them. Brilliant. Sounds exactly like the dystopian future every rich white tech bro wants."

Gates chuckled. For the moment, they were standing alone, watching the guests mingle. A waiter stopped and offered champagne. Gates politely declined, but Ada was more than happy for something to calm her nerves. As Ada sipped her drink, two men in tight business suits approached. One was well in his sixties with manicured white hair and an orange tint to his skin that suggested a spray tan. The other was younger, perhaps late thirties, with a tight beard and circle glasses.

"Milltek Corporations?" The older man questioned. "Funny. I haven't heard of your company yet. What do you do?"

"Robotics," Gates said with a nod. "And yours?"

The older gentleman snorted and looked at his younger colleague. "Of course Ventura would invite amateurs." He turned back to Ada and Gates. "I'm Hal Claude, CEO of Techbotics. In the future, it would do well to educate yourself on the guests of an event before appearing on the basis of investment."

"The free food won us over," Gates joked. "We're not quite sold on investing in Tura Industries at the moment. To move from basic processing servers to robotics is quite the shift."

"Really?" Hal Claude folded his arms over his chest. "Ventura's been promising everyone all week that he has something revolutionary on his hands. I hate the guy, but revolutions sell."

Gates made a face. "I don't think-"

"He's not holding a private party for an updated iPod, kid," Hal Claude snapped. "This is something big if this asshole is inviting even the most amateur of robotics companies. What's your role for Milltek? You're not another one of those sales or PR reps, are you? Do you even know what you're talking about?"

For once, Gates was speechless. As he sputtered trying to find the words needed for his lie, Ada stepped forward.

"You're right. He's our PR guy," She stated. "If you want to talk tech, you talk to me. For starters, let's talk about how over twenty thousand of your sound processors were recalled last year for short circuiting."

Hal Claude frowned. "It was a manufacturer error-"

"One that could've been avoided if you hadn't invested in a cheap plastic to hold your advanced microchips," Ada said. "It's the same principle for Tura Industries. We're not investing in cheap plastic and risking losses."

The CEO looked perplexed at this issue.

"Are you saying Harding Ventura would go through all of this effort to sell us a loss?"

"I'm saying you didn't know your plastic was cheap until your sound processor nearly destroyed every middle grade laptop in mid-America, terminating your existing relationship with major tech retailers like Best Buy," Ada said. "I assure you that we will not follow as blindly in this pursuit."

Hal Claude gave Ada a long stare. She sipped her champagne, careful to hide her shaking hands.

"You know your stuff." Hal Claude offered his hand to Ada. "I really should be talking to you. Hal Claude, Techbotics."

"Ada Kakar," She said firmly, shaking the CEO'S hand. She remembered the fake name tag fixed to her dress. "Uh, filling in for Miss Yuki for Milltek, of course."

"I'm glad you did," Hal said. He stuck his hands into his suit jacket pockets. "What do you do for these amateurs?"

"Programming," Ada said. "I'm educated in coding for software development, but I've been dabbling in artificial intelligence and engineering recently."

"MIT?"

"Carnegie Mellon."

"Not bad," Hal stated. "Tell you what - take some time to educate your sales guy here about the functionality of what we dabble in and then find me. Professionals shouldn't be working for amateurs."

Before Ada could reply, Hal's colleague whispered something in his ear and the CEO nodded, before turning back to Gates and Ada.

"Excuse us," Hal said. "Word has it that Harding's son is here. If I can make it to him, I'll let you know what information I can get from the kid. We'll see how much Harding knows about cheap plastic too, right kid?"

With a short chuckle, Hal gave Ada a short pat on the shoulder before walking away. Gates turned Ada to face him.

"How did you do that?" He asked. "How did you *know* that?"

"One of those sound processors caught on fire on my counter at Geek Squad. Makes for a memorable day at work." Ada finished her champagne then looked sadly into the empty glass. "By the way, I'm going to need more of this if you want me to do that again."

"Gladly." Gates looked around. "I'll find some while I do some reconnaissance. Now that Louis is here, I'm sure the androids will show too."

With a soft nod, Ada reluctantly let him go. She liked the security his presence provided. Once he managed to blend in with the growing crowd, Ada felt exposed. Tapping her empty glass with the point of her fingernail, she took a deep breath and looked around the room. She was supposed to gather as much information as she could, but the waiters carrying more trays of expensive champagne looked far more appealing. Sammy would understand. She might even applaud Ada for chasing the distraction. Setting her eyes on the nearest waiter, Ada was careful not to look too eager for the free booze. She weaved through the crowd, hearing whispers of Louis's name.

"Harding has a son?"

"-supposedly backpacking through Europe-"

"-top of his class at Stanford before his breakdown-"

"Could you blame the kid?" One woman's shrill voice echoed. "I heard Harding practically isolated the boy. Didn't have any friends his own age until he was seven! Could you imagine?"

Ada reached the waiter and traded her empty glass for a full one.

"Really?" Another woman cooed. "I heard he didn't interact with anyone until he was sent off to Thatcher when he was, what? Eleven, twelve? Excellent school, but he never would've been sent if it wasn't for Harding's wife, bless her soul. What was her name?"

"Calanthe," Someone else stated. "Sweet woman. She was his mechanic before they married, you know. Very talented. Such a devastation when she died. No wonder the whole family fell apart when she did-"

"Ada?"

Choking on her champagne, Ada hurried to compose herself and prayed she misheard the voice. She recognized the voice, but she assumed it was her brain doing its broken brain thing. She tried to focus on the conversation she was overhearing. It was information. Not information Louis particularly wanted or cared for Ada to know, but it was still her part of the mission. However, a hand grabbed Ada's good shoulder, claiming her focus. With a jump, Ada turned to the person. Ruchira Kakar's stern eyes burned into Ada. Disbelief, shock, and joy flashed across Ruchira's face in a moment's notice as she looked at her daughter for the first time in three years. Finally, Ruchira pursed her lips.

"You know, a phone call wouldn't hurt."

All of Ada's nerves dissolved into a pool of rooted anger anchored at the pit of her soul. She let her face drop.

"Nice to see you too, Mom."

Before Ruchira could say anything else, Hiyan Kakar ran from behind his wife with a massive smile.

"Ada!" He pulled his daughter into a tight bear hug. "Oh I've missed you, sweetheart."

"I missed you too D-*ow*," Ada winced when she attempted to hug him back. He released her and looked at her shoulder.

"What happened here?!" He exclaimed. "Jasmine told us she saw you at the college, but she didn't say you got hurt!"

"Car accident," Ada stated.

"She *also* said you were an assistant professor at Carnegie Mellon now," Ruchira stated. "Funny. Last you told us, you were still on that graphic designer's couch. Quite the leap for a dropout."

Ada couldn't believe the words coming out of her mother's mouth.

"Mom-"

"When are the lies going to stop, Ada?" Ruchira said sharply. "You can't give your sister hope that you've gotten better when it's clear that you haven't."

"Ruchira!" Hiyan scolded.

"Since when did you start caring about my well-being?" Ada ignored her father. "Was it before or after I embarrassed you?"

Ruchira's face fell. "Ada you don't-"

"Are you still telling your friends that I'm a technical specialist?" Ada asked. "That's a pretty fucking fancy way to tell them I work at Geek Squad."

"What else am I supposed to tell them?" Ruchira exclaimed. "They - we-"

"Don't bring me into this," Hiyan lifted his hands up in surrender.

"-were expecting better from you." Ruchira's eyes were on fire, lit with the same anger Ada recognized all the way from grade school when she suggested that she'd quit the robotics club when it got boring. The same look when Ada briefly mentioned taking a language minor in addition to her existing programming major. "You had *everything*, Ada, and you threw it all away-"

"I didn't have a choice!"

"Look at you now!" Ruchira motioned towards her fake name tag. "Who is this Yuki Hideyoshi? Did you steal this?"

And her mother wondered why she never called. Ada scowled. "What are you guys even doing here?!"

"My job, Ada," Ruchira said. "When you get to be associate vice president, you get invited to stuff like this. That's what happens when you get a real job, Ada."

There it was. The same judgment that plagued Ada's entire childhood and drove Ada to chase a dream that was never hers. Ada shouldn't have expected her mother's high expectations to suddenly disappear, but she still found herself disappointed. Even with a three year gap in communication, her mother still held her to the same impossible standards that plagued the first two decades of Ada's life. Would her mom ever be happy with Ada just as she was, mess and all? Hiyan turned to his daughter and gently touched her arm, looking at her with the stern tenderness only a father could provide.

"Ada, if you need any help-"

"Yeah, I needed your help." Ada shook her father off. "Three years ago. But I'm better now, thanks for asking. I don't need your help anymore, not that you offered any then."

The pain in her father's eyes struck a nerve and Ada trembled. She hated breaking her father's heart. But she also hated feeling like a waste of space from the people who brought her into this world, the ones who should be giving her permission to take as much space as she needed. Both feelings were pretty shitty. It took all of her power to not abandon the mission and run straight to the Camaro to get away from her parents.

"Ada." An unlikely gentle voice joined her side. "Are these people bothering you? Would you like them escorted out?"

"I'm sorry, who are you?" Ruchira asked.

"Louis Ventura." Louis touched the small of Ada's back, holding himself as if he were the host of the massive shindig rather than the prodigal son of the actual host. "Head engineer for Tura Industries. We've been recruiting Ada as a senior programmer within our newly redesigned robotics division. She's got quite the potential."

With the timing of a well trained actor, Louis went from smiling at Ada to frowning at her laminated name card. "Well shit. Did they give you the wrong tag? I knew we should've gone with a different vendor. We'll need to fix that."

If Ada could, she would go back in time and amend every bad thought she ever had about Louis Ventura.

"Uh, yeah. I think they did," Ada stammered, overjoyed at her luck. He raised his eyebrows at her lackluster reaction, egging her to continue the act. "Um, Louis, these are my parents. Hiyan and Ruchira Kakar."

"An honor," Louis said. "Ada is truly a genius, an absolute one of her kind when it comes to programming the revolutionary AI we're building with Tura Industries. We would be thrilled to have her expertise on our team. You must be proud."

Shame crossed both of her parents' faces. Ruchira's smile in particular looked forced and stretched on her weathered brown face.

"Yes," Ruchira said. "We are indeed very proud of our daughter."

There was no love in the words. Only bitterness. Ada wished it was because they felt guilty for not believing in her, but she knew it was pain from being wrong. They felt no sympathy for how they spoke to her; they still thought they were in the right on that front. Well she wasn't going to give them the satisfaction of letting them know that they weren't wrong, that Louis was lying, and she still technically only belonged on Sammy's couch in Pittsburgh with no other prospects. They could sit in that darkness for a little bit with no way out, like she did three years ago. Unaware of any of this, Louis gave a solemn nod.

"Excuse us." He took Ada's wrist. "We have a name tag to replace."

As Louis pulled Ada through the crowd, Ada barely had time to wave goodbye to her parents. It was probably for the best, she might have said something out of line that would reveal the truth behind their story. Still, there was a pain in her heart that ached for a reality where she could leave her parents on a good note, not on lies and dodging their unforgiving disappointment.

She wished for the parents, and family, she knew before she became a mess.

<!-- "Oh my god," Jasmine exclaimed. "Ada is texting someone?!"

"Shut up."

"Who are you texting?" Jasmine asked.

"Probably her boyfriend," Hiyan remarked as he organized the yellow fabrics.

Ada could've murder her father.

"Ooo! Ada has a boyfriend," Jasmine teased.

"Shut up!" Ada threw an almond at her little sister who laughed at Ada's frustration.

"Jasmine! Ada! Be nice to each other!" Ruchira entered the room, smoothing out her traditional kurta dress. "Ada, put your phone away. It's time to celebrate Pancha Ganapati."

"Oh we're Hindu this year?" Ada asked. "Why do we still have Santa on the front lawn?"

"The neighbors love our Santa!" Hiyan argued.

"Do they love it as much as Ada loves her boyfriend?" Jasmine asked.

"What are you, like, twelve?" Ada said.

"Girls! Enough!" Ruchira shouted. "Now since you two are in the greatest need of Ganesha's love today, why don't you start? Jasmine, what do you ask forgiveness of Ada for and what do you love most about her?"

Jasmine took a long pause.

"I wanna do Christmas again," Jasmine said. "Oh wait! Can we try Hanukkah? I hear matzo ball soup is-"

"Jasmine!"

The younger Kismet sister sighed and turned to her older sister. "Fine! I'm sorry for teasing you about your boyfriend. I'm also sorry I used your room for soccer practice when you were gone."

"Is that why there's a tear in my Ravenclaw poster?!"

"You're a Hufflepuff anyway."

"How dare you-"

"Ada..." Their mother warned.

Ada sighed. "I forgive you."

"Thank you," Jasmine said. "What I love most about you is your capacity to forgive."

"That's cheating!" Ada yelled as Jasmine laughed. "Mom, that's cheating, right?!"

Closing her eyes, Ruchira rubbed her forehead with her two index fingers.

"Hiyan, we're skipping to you. Go."

223

Hiyan took a moment to swallow his mouthful of almonds before turning to his family.

"Well, I must ask for forgiveness for all the times I ignored my family for work-"

"Or a football game," Ruchira muttered under her breath.

"But, I still love you all so much and you all take first priority in my heart," Hiyan exclaimed. "I love my beautiful wife who continues to exceed expectations while balancing both family and work. You are the binding strength behind this family, love."

Looking dewy in her eyes, Ruchira blushed and made both of her daughters gag.

"Then of course, Jasmine, my little soccer star," He clapped his youngest's shoulder. "You work so diligently at your passion, it's truly admirable and a trait we all strive to achieve."

Jasmine beamed. "Thanks Daddy!"

"And Ada, my brilliant genius," Hiyan clapped his own hands together. "I could never be more proud of your intelligence, your work ethic, and your patience. You put any man to shame with your wits and that truly is the greatest gift a man could wish for his daughter. You make us so proud!"

All Ada could do was smile. For once, the void didn't call to her. Her happiness was not paired with the feeling of dread or neutrality. She was able to enjoy the time with her family in the light of the golden yellow fabrics decorating their small home in peace.

It was the last time in a long time where she could feel like that.-->

CHAPTER ELEVEN

Once they were fully integrated into the crowd, Louis turned to Ada and released her wrist.

"You know I'd hate to make a big ordeal over a tiny detail, but what the hell are your parents doing here?!" Louis said in an angry whisper. "Don't tell me they know how to program robots too."

"Dad works in IT too, but on the security side of things," Ada said. "They said they were here for Mom, which doesn't make sense. She doesn't know anything about computers. I don't even think her company works with any robotics."

"I don't like it. They've got Kamana written all over them," Louis said. "Where is Gates?! You were supposed to stay with him."

"I could've managed to survive for one drink."

"I highly doubt that, but I'm more worried about him," Louis hissed, faking a smile to a passing couple. "Mr. Good Cop is threatening to become Mr. Bottom of My Shoe unless he quits this loose canon shit."

"Hey, you wanted us to find more information," Ada said. "Splitting up ensured-"

"Splitting up ensured nothing more than my distrust in that bastard," Louis snapped. "He let Sammy get kidnapped and now he's disappeared into their fortress. The second we get Sammy back, we're leaving him behind where he belongs."

226 - MADDIE GUDENKAUF

Lacking the energy to fight Louis's tantrum, Ada sipped her champagne and scanned the room. She did not want to be here, especially if her parents were still hanging around. The champagne was moderately successful in calming her nerves, but it did nothing for her motivation. Sammy might already be dead from the killer robots, Louis will kill Gates if Sammy is dead, and all of them were going to be dead anyway if Louis's mediocre plan didn't work. At this point, Ada would probably welcome murder by robots to ensure she would never see her parents again. At that thought, she realized that maybe she should've gone to the doctor's for her medication despite Sammy's situation.

"Alright, new plan." Louis whispered.

"Why do I already hate it?" Ada sighed.

"Because you hate most things," Louis said. "Anyway, I believe we're in a trap more elaborate than I planned for. Your parents are obvious hostages in this situation. They're here to stop you from initiating your part of the plan which means the robots are rightfully expecting you to stay behind when I rescue Sammy."

"I don't like where this is going." Ada said before promptly downing the rest of her champagne.

"So now that Gates is MIA, I will be the one to cause the distraction," Louis said. "And you'll rescue Sammy."

"You know, I thought the plan to break into a security company was your shittiest idea," Ada said. "This proves me wrong."

"It's our only option!" Louis faked another smile to a passing patron. "We can't trust Gates, but we also can't walk away or we lose Sammy."

"I don't even know where she is!" Ada said.

The already dim lights darkened completely as the room died into hushed whispers.

"Upstairs. Hotel rooms." Louis huffed. "Take the elevator. It's a straight shot to her floor."

After another moment of complete darkness, a spotlight hit the stage in a sharp burst. A woman stood limp on stage, thick curly hair obscuring her face and hanging to her lower back. The whispering of the crowd moved to muttering. With a single electronic note, lines of red neon light danced in patterns on the woman's skin tight black outfit. The crowd quieted as the woman came to life with the electronic music, the red neon lights glowing as she moved. As the escalating music paused, so did the performer, staring blankly into the crowd. When the beat dropped into a high-paced electronic dubstep remix of an 80's song, the woman jumped into action. Her dance looked like a slideshow of movement, a graceful yet rapid dedication to matching the beat as closely as possible. Occasionally the song would slow and the woman would show a sign of humanness with a drawn-out dance similar to ballet, but then the beat would drop again and she would continue her rapid dance to the crowd's delight. Ada was mesmerized by the dance.

"Mousai." Lous stated. His eyes were sad as he stared at the woman on stage. "Also known as Droid Five. She's the only bot created separately without Kamana because she was supposed to be an improvement on Kamana. She was supposed to fulfill what Kamana failed." Not taking his eyes off the android, he gestured for a waiter. "But Kamana didn't want to be made obsolete. She corrupted Mousai's programming and made her into a mindless puppet meant for entertainment. Essentially Lady, but less likely to follow orders due to her lack of self-learning AI. We originally took Mousai's corruption as a sign that only Kamana's programming was powerful enough to sustain the androids, so we built the rest of them with her software. If I knew then what I know now, I would've dismantled Kamana before she had a chance to further fail her primary function."

It took Ada a moment.

"Your mom." She said. "Kamana was supposed to save your mom and sabotaged the robot who could've done it instead."

A waiter appeared with a tray filled with flutes of champagne. Louis took one and placed some cash on the tray. With a nod, the waiter made himself scarce. Ignoring his new drink, Louis turned to Ada. Both anger and sadness burned in his eyes in a quiet rage that made Ada regret wanting to abandon the mission.

"She didn't even do it out of spite for my mom." Louis hissed. "She did it because Mousai's success would've made her look bad. Her one purpose was to save my mom, and she willingly destroyed the one thing that actually could for her own pride. Kamana is nothing more than an outdated bot who needs to be taken off the market before she does more damage."

Turning back to the show, he took a drink. As Ada watched the robot dance, she couldn't help but wonder how aware these machines were. Did Mousai know of her original function? Was she happy that her primary function was now dancing on a stage for the entertainment of the company that created her? Kamana was clearly more aware than what was comfortable. But all of the robots they've come across seemed to only be serving Kamana's orders. They would have to since all of them could only function with Kamana's programming. But if Kamana was aware of her own purpose, didn't that mean all of the robots under her would also be aware?

The dance stopped. As the crowd roared into thunderous applause, the android relaxed into a more human form. She waved and smiled broadly, blowing proud kisses at the crowd as she made her way off the stage. Following her departure, a man walked onto the stage with a wide smile as he clapped for the dancer. Despite being of average height, he carried himself with a small stature. Large, thin-rimmed glasses sat on his face, making the gray hairs gracing his thick dark hair appear dignified. He looked intelligent, but his smile and demeanor showed that he was a businessman first. Louis straightened at Ada's side, refusing to applaud for the man on the stage.

"Wasn't she great, everyone?" The man said, his voice twinkled with charm as it reverberated through the room. "As you all know, I'm Harding Ventura, CEO of Tura Industries, and welcome to my shindig."

The room laughed. Louis didn't.

"Now, just as our lovely dancer demonstrated, humans can do amazing things." Harding Ventura continued. Now Louis snorted before drinking more champagne. "All of you are here because you too believe that humans can do amazing things. You also believe that Tura Industries has been helping humans achieve those amazing things, and you want in on that. You, as humans, want to achieve amazing things too, am I right?"

Some cheers erupted from the crowd as Harding Ventura paced the stage.

"Here at Tura Industries, we have been dedicated to helping humans achieve the absolute best they can achieve with our technology since 1985." As Harding spoke, the screen behind him lit with video footage of athletes training. The footage shifted and wind farms took over the screen. Another cut and a sick child smiled at their parents while hooked to a medical machine. "We pride ourselves on not only being one of the most innovative companies in the industry, but we pride ourselves on the diversity of our products and their ability to improve the human condition. Tura Industries has grown a lot over the past several decades, and I may argue that we've improved society as a whole with our inventions. Nay, I'd say that we've improved all of humanity with our work."

Harding paused, scanning the crowd for any dissent. Even from their spot hidden in the middle of the crowd, Ada could see the pride in his stance once he couldn't find anyone to dispute his point.

To her side, Louis held his head higher. She had no doubt that if it wasn't Sammy's life on the line, he would be the one to put his father's pride in its place.

"That is why, today, I am pleased to announce Tura Industries's latest improvement to humanity." Harding smiled. "Introducing the TuraByte."

The screen flashed to show a rotating image of a wireless earbud as Harding revealed the prototype from his pocket. The crowd awed at the invention and fell into frantic muttering. Ada turned to Louis.

"What's the TuraByte?" She asked.

"Why don't you watch the presentation and find out?" Louis said.

"You have no idea, do you?"

"None at all." Louis said. "Which means it's a product of Project Kamana which means it's probably not good."

"The TuraByte is our answer to the next evolution of cell phones." Harding said, attaching the device to his ear. "It, of course, offers everything a traditional bluetooth offers with voice-activated phone calls, text messages, video calls-" With a sly smile, Harding stopped pacing the stage when the crowd murmured excitedly again. "That's right, folks. Video calls." Standing up straight, he stared into space. "TuraByte, set up a video conference with Hal Claude's personal cell."

A small board of light appeared in front of Harding Ventura's face. In the crowd, a phone rang loudly. After a disgruntled gruff, the ringing stopped. A face appeared in Harding's light screen.

"Ventura, you old dog!" Hal Claude's voice echoed. The crowd laughed as Harding plastered on the same shit-eating grin Ada had seen too many times on his son's face.

"I was wondering if you were here," Harding said. "I will, however, note that I don't recall sending an invitation. How's cleaning up that mess from your sound processors going?"

The crowd laughed again as Harding proudly ended the video conference before Hal Claude could defend himself. Harding paced the stage again, this time looking like a predator eyeing his prey.

"There are of course many other features that I will gladly share with you at next month's keynote, but there's one in particular I believe all of you would be interested in." Harding stared into the crowd, challenging them to question his authority. No one did. "Tura Industries has quietly been investing into their robotics division for quite some time and now I want to announce, for the first time ever, the result of our investment."

Straightening his stance, Harding Ventura took center stage.

"TuraByte," He said. "Call in my personal TuraBot."

Emerging from the curtain that Mousai disappeared behind was a metal skeleton, a rudimentary moving model of what showed when half of Lady's skin was blown off at the grocery store. It walked slowly, methodically. Nothing like Eyepatch's ability to sprint after Ada at full-speed while wielding a gun. The crowd went quiet as the robot joined Harding's side. Harding stood tall for his short frame, looking as unimpressed as possible.

"TuraBot," Harding said. "Fetch me some champagne."

The rudimentary skeleton gave a short nod before exiting the stage to a well-positioned waiter holding a tray of champagne flutes. The TuraBot gently claimed one of the glasses before proceeding to walk up the stage stairs. For Ada and Louis, who witnessed the full extent of a "TuraBot's" range, which included trying to murder them, this was unimpressive. For everyone else in the room, it was deadly silent as the robotics experts waited for the android to inevitably trip on the stairs or drop the expensive glass. Of course the robot did neither. It arrived at Harding's side and presented the glass to its master. Harding held an index finger up.

"One second," Harding said. "That was almost too easy, right folks? We can do better than that. TuraBot, do a flip before handing me my drink."

The robot gave another short nod. Still holding the champagne flute, the robot jumped and twisted itself in the air with a front flip. The glass remained steady in its fingers the entire time. When the robot landed on its feet, shaking the wooden stage under the weight of its metal skeleton, there was a short gasp through the crowd. The robot didn't react. It simply stood straight and handed the glass to Harding. This time, Harding accepted it. He moved it to his other hand.

"TuraBot," He said. "Give me knuckles."

The robot obediently made a fist and held it to Harding who gladly tapped it with his own fist. After this, the crowd went wild. Harding held the pose with a beaming smile. Cameras flashed wildly in his direction, documenting his achievement. Ada remained frozen, unsure of what to think of the development. Beside her, a glass shattered. She turned to Louis who remained stone faced as he looked at the stage. Only the people around them took note of his lost drink.

"Louis..." Ada whispered into him. "What are you-"

"Find Sammy." Still not looking away from the stage, Louis removed his suit jacket and pushed it into Ada's chest. Before she could drop her own champagne glass, he stole her flute from her and screwed his hair up with the other hand. "I've got a moment to ruin."

With a confident swig of Ada's champagne, Louis pushed through the crowd of people. Ada could only watch in horror as Louis shouted boisterously, diverting everyone's eyes away from Harding Ventura to his son. Harding followed the crowd's gaze, his face noticeably shifting from controlled euphoria to annoyance, shock, and then finally a forced smile as Louis fake-drunkenly pushed through the crowd. It wasn't until Louis poured Ada's champagne onto an unfortunate woman's head in his attempt to get the crowd to chant his father's name that Ada realized she needed to move. Louis was ruining his reputation and causing this diversion so she could save Sammy. Glancing around the room, she locked her target onto an elevator entrance that was previously guarded by two men in the black suits with red trim. The two guards were now standing away from it, watching Louis carefully. Swallowing the last of her fear and keeping her mind focused on saving her best friend, Ada picked the skirt of her dress from the floor and quietly shuffled past the other attendees who were too enthralled with watching Harding Ventura's prodigal son make a fool of himself to pay any attention to her. The guards from the elevator were now making their way to the stage Louis was climbing onto, giving her a short window to escape into the doors without notice.

She risked breaking into a light jog as she reached the elevator doors. The guards were bound to return at any moment, or at least check over their shoulders, and she didn't want to risk ruining her one opportunity to save Sammy. But as Ada approached the elevator doors, they clamored open. Holding her breath, she slowed her jog and tried to think of a reasonable excuse of why she was heading that way. Before she could come up with anything, the most striking woman she ever saw in her life emerged from the elevator. She locked her gray-green eyes onto Ada almost immediately. With heavy lidded eyes and full red lips, the woman conveyed immense confidence with her gaze, teasing how much power she truly held. The woman's presence made Ada wish she could disappear into the many layers of her yellow chiffon dress. Her slender figure moved with grace as she approached Ada with a knowing smirk, her geometric red and black dress flowing flawlessly with her movements. She practically floated on the marble floor with how delicate she walked.

"Ms. Hideyoshi," The woman greeted. Her voice was smooth without a hitch or lilt to any of her words. "I hope everything is well."

Ada tried to not look panicked. She knew for certain that the woman never looked away from her face long enough to read the name on her stolen name tag. How did this woman know her fake name?

"Fine!" Ada exclaimed, her voice shaking. "It's just...I need some air? And I thought I saw my friend come over here and-" She stopped when she realized she was mashing all of her possible excuses together into an incoherent mess. The woman stared without reaction. To Ada's surprise, her gray eyes were curious. Not upset. Not surprised. There was still a threat behind the woman's gaze that Ada couldn't quite place, but the woman seemed complacent for now. Ada swallowed. "I'm sorry? I don't believe I caught your name."

This made the woman smile in amusement, obviously caught in Ada's game. She lifted her hand towards Ada, never diverting her gaze.

"Kamana," She cooed. "I work with Mr. Ventura's development team. But I'm sure you knew that."

Ada did know that. It made her want to throw up. But she held the bile rising in her throat and shook the robot's hand. Kamana's hand was cold, lacking an undercurrent of life.

"Great to meet you," Ada stammered. Satisfied with Ada's response, Kamana released her hand. Freed from the robot's direct hold, she half-heartedly took a step back. "Ah well, I still need that breath of fresh air. Too much champagne, you know? Probably."

"Ah yes! I'm sure." Kamana's eyes narrowed to an icy glare that contrasted the kind smile planted on her lips. "You also need to find your friend, yes?"

Ada's heart stopped.

"Sorry?"

"The associate you spoke of," Kamana said. "That headed this way."

Holding her head higher, Kamana finally pulled her eyes away from Ada to glance towards the main back doors of the ballroom.

"I believe you have a choice," She said. "You can either get your breath of fresh air outside or you can find your friend. Unfortunately, I cannot ensure you will be able to accomplish both, or either, successfully."

Kamana's red lips parted in a mocking smile.

"I encourage you to choose wisely."

Unfortunately, Ada got the message loud and clear. Escape with her life or find Sammy. Why Kamana wanted to spare her life above everyone else's in the group was beyond Ada, but it was something she knew she should utilize while it was still an option. Knowing her prey was in the palm of her hands, Kamana smirked. She approached Ada, almost floating again, so no one else could hear their conversation if they both kept quiet. The android leaned into Ada's ear. Ada shivered as the chill of Kamana's cool lips grazed her ear.

"Impress me, Ms. Kakar," Kamana cooed. "Your friend isn't the only one who depends on it."

With that, Kamana forced Ada to take what she was holding in her other hand. Ada felt her soul slither from her body in a cold chill as her fingers grasped the familiar shape of her pill bottle. The one she had lost in the diner in South Dakota. Who was following them? How long were they watching? Once Kamana pulled away, a nasty thought crossed Ada's mind and she couldn't help but look down at the bottle.

It still had her parents' home address on it.

"Until we meet again," Kamana said as she left to join the ballroom.

236 - MADDIE GUDENKAUF

Left pathetically clutching her pill bottle, Ada knew she still had to make a decision and she had to make it quick. Kamana wanted her to leave, which meant Ada's family would be spared, the poor pawns in this fucked up chess game. But if she left Sammy behind, she'd be leaving Gates and Louis behind too. She'd be easier to attack alone, and her friends would be betrayed if she abandoned them. But if she saved Sammy, what did that mean for Ada's family? Her instincts told her something bad would happen if she did save Sammy over them. But if the robots knew enough about her background to create that profile on her character, the robots were probably expecting her to save Sammy over her family and set a trap for her with Sammy too. Ada was going to lose no matter what she did. There was no way to save herself, Sammy, and her family. Not that she particularly wanted to save her family, but she felt obligated to after everything else she put them through.

Whipping around, Ada looked towards the ballroom. Her mind raced with potential solutions. All Ada had to do was find a way to protect her family. Kamana would never expect Ada to actually make an effort to save her family. It was a situation as unlikely as fate. From how easily Beefcake killed that woman in Nebraska, the androids obviously lacked the coding required to fully assess such a morally complex situation. Their plan would be contingent on Ada leaving her family in the dust, her pain vindicated and her obviously human reaction fulfilled. Her eyes scanned the room, her brain conspiring for a solution as fast as she searched for one. Finally, her eyes locked onto her salvation.

Hal Claude.

The CEO sulked in the corner, finding bitter solace from his humiliation in recording Louis's drunken debacle on his phone. Stuffing her medicine into her bra, Ada made her way over to him. Gates was right. A murder occurring during a company event was bad press. Her parents were safe as long as they were at the party or with someone from the party. It was even better if she could keep them in the realm of Harding Ventura's most infamous rival. There was no way Kamana would risk touching them if they were all associated together. Ada tapped Hal Claude on the shoulder. He turned to her, startled that she dared to approach him but then relaxed as he recognized Ada.

"Ah! Milltek, right? Glad to see you again." Hal turned back to his phone with a wide grin. "You were right about hesitating to invest in cheap plastic. Did you know this kid is supposedly in charge of Tura's robotics? What a disaster for Harding."

"That's why I wanted to approach you, sir," Ada whispered, watching the crowd to make sure Kamana wasn't catching onto her plot. "We promised to share trade secrets, right?" Once Hal Claude's attention was on her, she pointed out her parents who looked almost bored at the spectacle. But their annoyance appeared dignified and that was exactly what Ada needed.

"That couple right there? Very important in India," Ada said. "Like, owning entire production factories, important."

Hal's eyes widened and he whipped around to Ada. "Really?! How have I never heard of them?"

Ada hesitated. "Because they're...private! They didn't even want anyone to know they were here. But they'll invest in anyone who invests in them and shows respect for their privacy." Hal was watching Ada with hungry eyes as she struggled to come up with the last part of her plan on the spot. "If you sent them on a vacation or anonymously gifted them a suite in one of your hotels, they would strongly consider investing their production factories in your company."

With a cunning smile, Hal glanced at Ada's parents.

"If I scratch their back, they'll scratch mine. Old school. I like old school." Placing his phone into his suit jacket pocket, Hal

238 - MADDIE GUDENKAUF

turned to Ada. "Why are you telling me this? Wouldn't this benefit Milltek too?"

"Uh….no?" Ada stammered. "We don't do production in India? I mean, we're going for that domestic labor slant for the press. Our CEO is running for Congress or something, blah, blah, blah. You know how it is."

To Ada's relief, Hal only shrugged at her bullshit.

"If you want to spend astronomically on labor, your loss. Now excuse me-"

Ada grabbed his arm. "Just don't forget! Completely anonymous. Don't even insinuate they're important. They'll deny you if you do and make you look stupid. Just spoil them rotten and protect their identities."

Hal nodded. "Got it."

"Oh! And they have a daughter!" Ada said. "Visiting Northwestern! She's posing as a soccer player and literature major, but she's recruiting talent for their companies. You should have someone keep an eye on her too."

Shooting Ada an annoyed look, Hall ripped his arm out of her grip.

"Kid, this ain't my first rodeo," He said. "I got this."

Ada breathed a sigh of relief as Hal made a beeline for her parents, indicating for his assistant to follow him as he did. But to her horror, she could see Louis's act was up. The guards from the elevator were manhandling him off-stage to a chorus of audience clapping and laughter. Harding appeared flustered on stage, but looked to the side opposite of Louis's departure and relaxed considerably as Kamana floated up the stairs. Pitching the skirt of her dress again, Ada ran and made it into the elevator before Kamana could even look at the crowd. Slapping the "up" button, Ada tried to think of her next step. Kamana was down in the ballroom. She hadn't seen any of the other androids so they all had to be upstairs.

Lady, Hercules, and Eyepatch. Just Ada versus all of them. Got it. She's got it.

She doesn't got it.

The doors opened and Ada jumped from the elevator, swinging her arms as if to attack something. Nothing. Nobody was in the hallway. There were a lot of fancy looking doors though. Was she even in the right place? She looked like she was in the hotel part of the building. No wonder Louis's plans sucked. It was impossible to come up with a good way to survive from killer robots on the fly. The sound of commanding voices and running feet echoed down the hallway. It sounded like a small battalion was approaching. Panicking, Ada dropped to the ground and crawled underneath a covered display table. It was a childish move, for sure, but Ada refused to risk anything. She only managed to pull the last of her long yellow dress into her hiding spot as the thundering feet entered her section of the hallway.

"If he intervenes, I swear I'll put a bullet in his head." Eyepatch's voice shouted.

"Shhh! There are humans here you know." Hercules's voice followed. "Besides, Kamana's not going to let us do anything to him. Not until Allen Paz is out of our way and we have the girl."

"The girl should be easy enough to find by morning," Eyepatch said as they entered the elevator. "Kamana assured me she should've fled into the city by now, especially since Gates is gone and Louis is apprehended. The chances of her sticking around to rescue that bait of a human by herself when her family is at risk are impossibly low."

Holy shit, her half-assed plan was working! Ada almost forgot the androids were only giant computers forced to trust their own programming. If Kamana thought she would've left, they would believe it. There was no second guessing amongst them. Must be nice.

As soon as the elevator doors closed, Ada crawled from her hiding place and hurried down the hall. Peering at the doors, she had no idea how to tell which one held her best friend. What was she supposed to do? Knock on every door until Lady answers the door with a gun? The receptionist said everything was booked solid for the convention and 4th of July weekend. That would take more time than what she had. What she would give for a Louis plan at that moment. Hers was going up in flames with every passing second.

Licking her lips, she immediately regretted the thought that crossed her mind.

There wasn't any time to second guess anything. If she wanted to think like Louis, she had to act like him too. She located the fire alarm and, without a second thought, threw it down. Alarms blared through the building, causing her to flinch at the sudden loud noise. But it worked. All of the doors flung open with disgruntled patrons shuffling out, grumbling and reminding each other that they had to use the stairs. Ada's eyes lit up. That meant Eyepatch and Hercules were stuck in the elevator! Her half-assed plan was working. Not that she would ever tell him, but Louis might actually be right about some things.

Only a handful of people gave her a wild look as she moved in the opposite direction of the crowd, desperately seeking any sign to indicate Sammy or Lady's location. Before she could find it, a hand grabbed her bicep. Ada turned and was surprised to find Mousai, the dancing android from earlier, holding her arm. Surprise swiftly turned into fear and Ada pulled her arm to get away. Holding her complacent gaze, Mousai tightened her grip on Ada's arm. She didn't act like an immediate threat to Ada's life. Maybe her programming was too corrupted to be one. Once Ada calmed down, Mousai put a single index finger to her own lips to indicate Ada to be quiet. Then she moved the single finger towards the direction of a door Ada had passed. A door Ada didn't remember seeing being opened. Ada looked at the android who remained unsmiling and unblinking, her finger still pointed towards the door.

"Thanks...?"

With a short nod, Mousai released Ada and joined the crowd with a jerking movement. As if she were pretending to be human rather than a robot programmed for the fluid movements of dancing. No one else seemed to recognize the oddity in the robot's steps. Ada let the android go without a fight and walked to the door. With a deep breath, she tried to consider what Louis would do in this situation. She had no weapons and no idea what waited for her beyond the door. She didn't even know if Mousai actually helped her or if the robot was leading her to another trap. But Ada followed her first instinct and threw her shoulder into the door, bursting in ready to fight whatever remained with her bare hands.

However the only thing in the room was Sammy, sitting cross-legged on the floor in a tan off-shoulder bohemian style dress. Next to her side were scraps of metal, bolts, and the dismembered head of Lady, her lightning blue eyes staring in apathy at nothing. The rest of the android's body was dormant a few feet from Sammy. Sammy looked from the metal parts she was aimlessly ripping apart with her wrench and squinted at Ada.

"What are you doing here?" She signed calmly.

Ada gave an incredulous look.

"Rescuing you!" Ada signed and said out loud.

Sammy looked at Lady's dismembered head and then back at Ada. She faked a mocking wide smile and wiggled her hands in the air above her shoulders very enthusiastically. The sign for "Congratulations." Ada rolled her eyes.

"Let's go," Ada signed. "You did enough damage."

"Sorry." Sammy signed. "You took too long."

As Sammy pulled herself from the remains of the dismantled robot, Ada turned to the door with a sigh. All that stress over the decision to save Sammy and she already saved herself. Typical. Walking out of the door, Ada was nearly run over by Gates who stopped his dead sprint as soon as Ada appeared. Huffing out a heavy breath, he looked at Ada first and then to Sammy.

"What-where's-" Gates stuttered. Finally, he swallowed his lost breath. "I gathered that Sammy was here from the front desk. Then I got ambushed by security and had to run from them. That's where I was. Where were you? Where's Louis?" He looked over Ada to Sammy again. "Did Sammy dismantle Lady?"

"Yes!" Sammy signed, not caring if Gates could understand her. "She got distracted when the other robots left so I attacked her. The robots left tools in here for repairs."

"Yeah," Ada translated for Gates. "With the tools the other robots left in here."

"Well great!" Gates took a deep breath. "So where's the other robots, then? I lost them "

"They're going after Louis," Ada signed and said out loud.

"Great. So where's Louis?" Gates asked.

There was a loud bang as something slammed against the nearby wall. Ada and Gates turned to the noise. A disheveled Louis Ventura, his stolen Armani tux on the brink of tattered rags, pulled himself from the wall and chucked the security baton he held toward whatever was following him. Then he rushed to Sammy's hotel room door, slowing briefly when he saw Gates and Ada staring at him wide-eyed.

"Is Sammy safe?!" He screamed.

When Ada gestured at the former kidnapping victim, Sammy popped her head out of the doorframe and wiggled her fingers at Louis with a wide smile.

"Good," Louis said. He hooked a thumb into his index finger and pushed both of his hands forward, flicking one index finger like a trigger in a gun to sign "running" for Sammy. "Run!"

Louis bolted down the hallway. Sammy, Ada, and Gates turned to what he was running from to see Hercules and Eyepatch both chasing after him. The androids locked onto their new targets and lifted their weapons to aim the sights.

"Shit!" Gates pulled Sammy and Ada from the room and pushed them down the hallway. Sammy and Ada hitched their flowy-skirts and kept a solid pace running with the boys. Louis stopped when they reached the end of the hall and pulled a small mechanical device from his jacket.

"Move!" He ordered.

Ada pushed Sammy out of the way and Gates physically dove to avoid Louis, landing on his side. With a triumphant throw, Louis aimed for Hercules. The androids slowed considerably as Louis's device rolled to their feet. There was a silent moment as both groups waited for Louis's tool to activate. Finally, it sprung apart and the androids aimed their weapons at it. A small spark emitted and the device swiftly shut down with a stuttering cough of mechanics.

Louis sighed. "Dammit."

At the device's failure, the androids aimed their guns at the humans again. The group scrambled to disappear from their sights. Sprinting down the massive hallway, Ada could see they were heading towards a door titled "Emergency Exit". But, behind them, the androids were catching up quicker than they could make it to the stairs and their bullets were even faster. One bullet flew past her already injured shoulder.

"Paintings!" Sammy shouted. She ripped one from the wall and held it behind her, bullets whizzing into it as she did so, drilling holes into the watercolors.

"That doesn't do anything!" Louis said.

Sammy couldn't hear him. Instead, she threw the painting like a frisbee at the robots and made impact with one of their guns, veering the androids' entire trajectory off course. As Hercules collided

244 - MADDIE GUDENKAUF

with Eyepatch, Louis slammed through the emergency exit door and held it for everyone as they piled in. As he shoved it shut, Gates helped him mangle the handle with some leftover pipe to barricade the door from opening. They all ran down the stairs, taking the steps three at a time.

"Well this plan has gone to shit!" Louis shouted. "I ruined my chances of becoming a respectable CEO, Ada disappointed her parents, and now Kamana is really pissed at us. But at least Sammy is safe!"

Sammy was blissfully unaware of Louis's mood as she was stuck behind Ada in the line down the narrow stairs. Tapping on Ada's shoulder, she smiled widely.

"Did you see their faces when I threw the painting?" She signed. "It was so great!"

Pushing through the basement level door, Ada was almost surprised to see the garage was mostly deserted. Most of the hotel's guests would've been at the front with the fire truck and whatever else occurred with the false fire drill. Gates pulled the keys for the Camaro out of his pocket and pushed the lock button. Just a few feet ahead of them, the car lit with a happy beep.

"Thank God!" Louis exclaimed. He sprinted ahead, Sammy closest behind him. Gates and Ada hung to the back; Ada unable to keep up and Gates too nice to leave her behind. With her heavy breathing, Ada barely noticed the door behind her burst open and the sound of a bullet clicking into place in a gun. Gates, however, did. Glancing behind them, Gate's eyes grew wide.

"Ada, watch out!"

Pushing Ada to the side, a gunshot rang out and Gates crumpled to the ground. Ada collided with the nearby car and recovered fast enough to hide behind the massive SUV. Peeking around the car's corner, she could see Eyepatch with her gun held to her good eye.

The robot was still aiming for Gates who groaned in pain on the ground, holding his thigh.

"Quit getting in the way, Hopper!" Eyepatch growled.

Before she could commit her final shot, more shots rang through the garage as Louis shot at Eyepatch, forcing the android to take cover behind a cement pillar. Sammy rushed forward and grabbed Gates by the arm. Ada jumped up and grabbed his other arm, helping her best friend drag the man to their car.

"Are you okay?" Ada asked.

"No." Gates moaned, closing his eyes. "My-my thigh-argh."

Ada didn't know much about anatomy, but she was pretty sure there was an artery there. If Eyepatch shot that-

Sammy and Ada managed to pull Gates into the backseat of the car, laying him flat onto the seat as Louis fired his weapon at Eyepatch, covering behind the Camaro. Ada indicated for Sammy to take the front seat, adjusting herself to fit in the backseat so she could take care of Gates's injury. Sammy scowled and shook her head.

"Fuck this bitch," She signed. "I'm ending it."

Slamming the backseat door shut, Sammy stormed to the trunk of the Camaro. Louis gave her a confused look. As she opened the trunk, she shot Louis a stern look and finger-spelled "Cover me." He nodded and re-positioned behind another cement pillar. Ada watched through the backseat window as Sammy pulled her chainsaw from the trunk, revving it up once, then twice, and then stormed over towards the android. The blade of the chainsaw clicked as Sammy held it to her side, not caring if her pretty dress got greasy.

Eyepatch noticed Sammy's approach and pulled herself away from the cement pillar to shoot at her. But Louis was ready and shot another bullet towards Eyepatch's chest. Eyepatch moved to defend herself and fell right into Sammy's trap. As Eyepatch lifted the gun towards Louis, Sammy lifted her chainsaw above her head and brought it down against Eyepatch's arm. Sparks flew briefly before the metal arm and gun both dropped to the ground in a clatter, Eyepatch reactionless. All she could do was turn to Sammy with a scowl and throw the stump of her remaining arm onto the human. Sammy lifted her chainsaw to attack again but Louis had fired a bullet, hitting Eyepatch's stomach. The android crumbled to her knees.

"Sammy!" He shouted, waving the gun and empty cartridge in the air. Louis kept his lip movements wide for her as well. "Last bullet! Come on!"

When Sammy looked back, Louis indicated for her to follow him. She reluctantly left her victim behind and ran to him. As Sammy threw her chainsaw back into the trunk, Louis jumped into the driver's seat and started the car. Ada struggled to rip off a piece of her dress to tie around Gates's wound. She kept one hand off and on the wound, trying to apply pressure when she could while still ripping her dress. Her dark palm was stained red and she could feel the ooze of the warm liquid between her fingers.

"Louis, we need a hospital!" Ada said. Sammy jumped into the passenger seat. "Gates is losing a lot of blood."

"He is?" Louis peeked into the backseat and looked at Gates's leg. "Holy shit he is!"

"Why are you surprised?!" Ada finally got a piece of her dress ripped and tied it around his leg as Louis pulled out of the parking space. "He got shot!"

"Well if he were an android, he wouldn't bleed," Louis said. "I mean, notice how Eyepatch didn't even flinch when Sammy cut off her arm."

"He's not a fucking robot, idiot!"

"Obviously!"

"She...cut off....Freya's arm?" Gates asked. On instinct, Ada gave his shoulder a comforting pat to indicate he needed to lay down.

"Unfortunately, no hospital for Mr. Good Cop just yet," Louis said. He ripped his tie off and threw it to Ada as he sped through the garage. "Do what you can for now and we'll stop once it's safe."

"He might die!" Ada exclaimed, wrapping Louis's tie around Gates's wound as well. The more pressure and material, the better.

"We all might die, sweetheart, it's a fact of life," Louis said. "But unfortunately if we stop at a hospital here, we'll never leave the city."

"Why?" Ada dared to ask.

"Because of this."

Despite the parking attendant's insistence for Louis to slow down, Louis did not slow down. He broke through the parking booth's wooden plank and flew onto the street. Drifting towards the front of the venue, Ada could see that the entire hotel was vacated onto the opening steps of the building. The massive crowd included the guests of Harding Ventura's failed product presentation. Harding Ventura himself was standing to the side, looking reasonably distressed. The disaster of the night was going to make headlines in a bad way. Next to him was Kamana, looking calm but there was slight disapproval in her features at the whole affair. She was half heartedly rubbing Harding's back with one hand, looking forced in her comfort. With a shit-eating grin, Louis gladly skidded the Camaro to a stop in front of the massive crowd. Everyone outside of the hotel turned as he rolled his window down.

"Hi! I'm Louis Ventura, son of Harding Ventura, and I approve this message!" He shouted. Throwing a massive middle finger to the crowd, Louis grinned at his horrified father. "Fuck the TuraByte, fuck the TuraBot, and *fuck* Project Kamana!"

With a celebratory shout, Louis sped into the dark Chicago streets, gladly weaving in between cars to make his getaway. Sammy was clapping and excitedly signing to no one in particular about how they had won. But while the front seat celebrated their victory, the backseat was solemn. Gates was quiet, not worryingly so, but quiet enough that Ada knew not to bother him. He was likely resting. His blood stopped pulsing through her fingers and she continued to add more material to the makeshift bandage to ensure he was set. Hopefully that meant he was better.

All Ada could think about was the look on Kamana's face as she watched the Camaro drive off. No longer vaguely annoyed, but the robot appeared amused at Louis's successful escape. Ada had a sinking feeling that she impressed the android again when, for the first time in her life, she had no intention to be impressive.

<!-- Depression.

That's what the doctor said.

Antidepressants were prescribed as quick as the diagnosis, but it took Ada another three days to grab them. Sammy went with her to convince her that she needed them. Not that it mattered. The damage was already done. Her grades and class attendance were in shambles to the point the dean of academics called her in to politely inform Carnegie Mellon's former top computer science student that she had been academically dismissed from the university. She was also sleeping on Sammy's couch now. Just temporarily until she could find something else. Michelle had some leasing problems and needed a place to stay and Daniel offered their apartment. Ada and Dan hadn't had a solid conversation in months anyways so she packed a duffel bag and moved over to Sammy's. Just until something better came along. Until Michelle figured her stuff out.

Ada didn't have the energy to find something better.

She was watching Maury, a result of not wanting to exert the energy to change the channel. Her new medication did have some effect. Now when her cell phone rang, she actually answered it rather than let it ring for ages. She had the energy to at least do that now.

"Ada?" Her father's kind voice echoed back to her. "We got something in the mail yesterday from your school. Is it a prank? How have you been academically dismissed?"

"I..." Ada choked up. "I haven't been to class since September."

It was February.

Her father paused. "Why not, Ada?"

"It's....my depression." Ada finally stammered. "I have depression, Dad. They gave me medicine for it and everything. It's pretty serious. I don't feel good. At all."

She wished she could describe it better. But not good seemed like a good enough explanation.

Hiyan was quiet. "How could you have depression, Ada? You did so well in school! And you have that nice boyfriend-"

"Had," She said. "Had that nice boyfriend. We broke up."

"Is this why you're depressed?" Hiyan asked. "Sweetie, just watch a movie! Eat some ice cream! I'll get you Netflix and you can watch all the sad movies you want if that'll make you feel better."

"Dad..." Ada sighed. "That's not how depression works. It requires therapy and medicine-"

"Then take some paracetamol," Hiyan continued. "You'll feel better in a few days. I'll call your school and see if I can't get this misunderstanding taken care of before the start of the next quarter. You can catch up with your classes over the summer."

"No, Dad-" Ada couldn't finish. She couldn't tell him that she didn't want to. That all she wanted to do and all her body would let her do was lay on this ratty thrift store couch and watch crappy TV. But she knew he wouldn't believe her anyway.

"Everything will be fine, Ada!" Hiyan sang. "You were the most impressive student in school! Carnegie Mellon is just used to dealing with lazy students failing their classes, unlike you. Until we get this sorted, I'm just going to hide this letter from your mother, yeah? You'll be fine!" Her father laughed and Ada could feel tears coming to her eyes.

She was not doing fine.--->

CHAPTER TWELVE

Gates was going to be fine.

It was Ada who needed the help.

It was the 4th of July and they were holed up in St. Louis, Missouri. They got two separate rooms in a cheap motel in a decent enough part of the city. Louis was in and out, either grabbing supplies from the hardware store for a revised version of the weapon that failed them a day ago in Chicago, or researching the information they collected from the Northwestern receptionist's files to find his uncle. When he was gone, that left Ada alone to write the new code. Her depression code. Louis and her had agreed to keep the substance of the code a secret from both Gates and Sammy. Nothing against them, but the fewer people who knew what they were actually coding made it less likely for the androids to catch on and develop a counter-measure in time. Not that it mattered. Gates was stuck on bed rest in the room opposite of Ada's while Sammy fluttered in and out as frequently as Louis, threatening to go with him on his trips or attend a 4th of July event while they were in the area.

"You can't leave," Ada signed, glancing from her work. "You're protecting us when Louis is gone."

"Okay but we're watching fireworks, right?!" Sammy signed enthusiastically. "They do them on a boat on the river and they're going to be so pretty!"

Ada rolled her eyes. "If I finish my code in time, yes."

"Fireworks are a great date, you know," Sammy signed, raising her eyebrows. "You and Gates-"

"No!" Ada pinched her fingers together. Sure they had kissed, but it was weird. Well not to Ada. To Ada it was nice and welcomed. But everything else about it was weird. That was probably why Gates was preferring to hang out in the other room rather than in Ada's room. She tried to comfort herself with the fact that he was a gentleman and trying to respect the traditional gendered room thing, but then she remembered that they were twenty somethings in the twenty first century. Him being in the other room meant he was avoiding her when she really just wanted to spend the time with him. Even if she was stuck coding this hell program, she figured his presence would be soothing as he watched TV or did whatever he was doing without her in the other room.

Sammy frowned. "I thought you liked him?"

"Yeah well..." Ada stalled. Should she tell her best friend that they kissed? How awkward things were between them now? No. Of course not. Sammy would make it a much bigger deal than what it was. "It's not going to work out."

Sammy pouted. "Shame. At least he likes you. I can't even get *my* date to talk to me about something other than killing robots."

"Sad." With joking eyes, Ada stuck her lower lip out mockingly as she signed. "Who would've thought getting hunted by evil robots would be a bad way to connect with someone?"

Rolling her eyes, Sammy flopped onto the cheap bed. "I thought the whole life or death thing would make it easier to seduce him. You know, last chance to get laid and all that? Guys love that shit."

"Do they?" Ada signed, looking incredulous.

"Ask Gates," Sammy signed, raising her eyebrows suggestively. "See what he says."

"Stop!" Ada signed, laughing along with her best friend. "You're a whore."

"No, I'm a good friend! I'm trying to get you laid." Sammy signed. "By the way, how's the code?"

"Good!" Ada signed.

Actually, for once, good was an understatement. It was going excellent. Her studying and the lessons learned from the first failed code meant this time was much easier to program. The problem now was how the program was going to be applied. Louis assured her that Uncle Allen would know how, but Ada barely even knew anything about Allen. Aside from the fact he was in hiding, he was the one who created the robots, all of the robots wanted to kill him more than they wanted to kill the rest of them, and none of that helped their situation.

But Louis seemed to trust him so Ada had to trust him too.

As the 4th of July day faded into 4th of July night, Louis still hadn't returned from his last outing and Gates still hadn't bothered to ask about Ada. Sammy was the one who changed his bandages and gave him updates on the code, but when she returned to Ada she never implied Gates was concerned about Ada. It irritated Ada, especially since she was the one who held onto his bloody wound from northern Illinois to eastern Missouri, but she ultimately let it go. Her jazz music became a cacophony of musical notes in her mind and she could understand the code on her laptop as clearly as English on paper. She was lost in her work and, for the first time in three years, loving every second of it. When Louis finally returned at sundown, the only things he needed to address were already written out within the code's comments.

"No way," He uttered. Louis read Ada's code over her shoulder. "This is...amazing." With a rare laugh, Louis clapped Ada on the shoulder. "Oh man. When I get to Uncle Allen, he's going to fall in love with you over this program. This is a work of art, Ada!"

She took his praise in stride, fixating on one part of his phrasing. "When *we* visit Uncle Allen, right?"

"Semantics," Louis stated. "Now where's Sammy?"

As he got up to walk into the other room, Ada grabbed his arm.

"Louis," She said. "I need you to tell me right now: are you trying to leave us again?"

Louis hesitated, upset he got caught but obviously expecting it.

"Listen Ada," Louis said. "You're all great. We've worked well with each other until this point. But my uncle...he's my uncle. I need to visit him. Alone." His eyes glazed over. "You guys have done enough. I've got it from here."

Sammy emerged into the room with a wide smile.

"I thought I saw you come in!" She signed. She noticed Louis's sad eyes and Ada's distressed face. "What's going on?"

"Louis is leaving." Ada signed and said out loud. "Without us. For good, this time."

"I'm not-" Louis said, whipping around to Sammy. Her eyes were sad. He stopped, his entire demeanor falling.

"It's my uncle," He said and signed carefully.

"And?" Sammy signed and vocalized. "We can see your uncle."

"No," Louis said and signed. "Only I can see my uncle."

"Why? What's wrong with your uncle?" Ada asked. "Why don't you trust us, Louis? I thought we've more than proven ourselves-"

"You still don't trust us?" Sammy questioned verbally, taking a cue from reading Ada's lips. "After everything we've done?"

"It's not you!" Louis exclaimed. When he remembered who he was talking to, he quickly signed "no you" towards Sammy. "Allen is my only family, alright?! If I take you guys with me, I'll lose him and then I'll have no one."

His exclamation stunned both of them. Sammy's eyes darted to Ada for clarification. Ada signed Louis's statement. Once Sammy was caught up, she looked at him with wide eyes. He sat on the bed and sighed.

"Kamana can find us easier when we're in a group," Louis explained. "She'll stop at nothing to find him if she knows we're all going to find him. She's been trying to stop Allen longer than she's been trying to kill me. He's her top priority. I'm just in the way of that and Allen...Allen was there for me when no one else was." Rubbing his mouth, Louis stared at the brown carpet as Ada translated for Sammy. "Dad was an asshole, that's not much of a secret. I was just another tool for him to use. He tossed me to tutors and school as soon as I could talk to ensure he would have the best robotics engineer on his staff. It was Mom and Allen who treated me like a human, like I was more than Harding Ventura's personal project. They'd visit on the weekends, smuggle me out of lessons to go to the beach for a day-" He sighed. "After Mom, Uncle Allen was the only buffer between Harding and me. He's the one who saved me after my accident. He's the reason why I'm still alive and I'm not going to risk his life just because I fucked up and let you guys help me to this point."

Louis finally looked between Ada and Sammy. "But we need him. He's smarter than Kamana. He's smarter than *me.* He can figure out how to implement Ada's code." Louis nodded towards Ada. "But I need to go alone. To protect him." When he realized both girls were staring at him, he rubbed his hands together. "Do you guys understand?"

"No," Sammy said out loud after Ada translated for her. "I don't."

"I do," Ada added swiftly after Sammy's comment.

In breakneck unison, both Louis and Sammy gave Ada a look. She looked nervously between them.

"I mean, I understand only having one person in the world to trust and doing everything in your power to not ruin their lives in return," Ada said. "Not the whole abandoning what few friends I have in the world to a horde of murder robots thing."

With a deep sigh, Louis stared into the empty air in front of him, lost in his thoughts. Sammy frowned at Ada.

"You were never a burden on me," Sammy signed. "You were my friend!"

"Yeah and I was my parents' daughter," Ada signed, not saying a word out loud for Louis to hear. "I was still a burden to them."

Sammy stared hard at Ada.

"I am not your parents," She signed. "I am Sammy. I am your friend. I am happy to take care of you."

Ada didn't respond. Frustrated, Sammy approached Ada to ensure Ada could see her hands.

"You are not a burden," Sammy said. "Your brain is lying again. You deserve love and friendship and to be taken care of, like everyone else. I am proud to be your friend. Please don't let your brain lie to you about that. Okay?"

At Sammy's soft look, Ada melted. Doing everything in her power to keep her bottom lip from quivering, she shook a weak "yes" with her fist. Sammy gave a thin-lipped smile and hugged her friend. When they separated, Sammy returned to where she was previously standing and Ada looked over to Louis. The guy seemed to barely acknowledge their interaction, his eyes lost in the empty space in front of him.

"You're not going to change your mind, are you?" Ada said.

"Absolutely not," Louis stated. Shaking his head, he got up from the bed and stuffed his hands into his leather jacket pockets. "How close are you to finishing the code?"

"Few tweaks," Ada said. "And it should be good for Allen to use."

"Excellent." Louis didn't look at either of the girls. "I'll leave in the morning once you're done. If you're not done, I'm sure my uncle can figure it out. I'm going for a walk."

He left the motel room. Sammy pouted and turned to Ada.

"Did you know we're the first friends he's ever had?" She signed. "He told me on the balcony in Chicago. His entire life was dedicated to making these robots. No friends, no fun, no nothing. In the end, they've all turned against him. His literal life's work. Could you imagine?"

Ada didn't blame Louis for wanting to protect his uncle. She'd probably make the same choice. He at least had a reasonable excuse to. She protected her family and she had no reason to. But it didn't mean it was right. Sammy, Ada, and Gates were dedicated to this cause too. They deserved to follow it through to the end. But maybe they could leave Gates behind this time. He seemed content in his motel room by himself anyways.

"Go talk to him," Ada said. "Maybe you can convince him he needs us."

Sammy's eyes widened. "Do you think-"

"You wanted a date for the fireworks anyways," Ada smiled as she signed. "Go join him."

With a smile, Sammy skipped to the door. She paused as she grabbed the handle and looked at Ada with concern in her eyes.

"Are you okay by yourself?" She signed.

"Go!" Ada signed. "I've got a code to write."

Sammy smiled again and, with a flip of pink hair, she ripped the hotel door open and ran to catch up with Louis. She let the door slam loudly behind her, unaware of the ruckus. Rolling her eyes, Ada turned the volume of her jazz music up and focused on her work again. At this point, she really was working on cosmetic changes. The actual bulk of the work was done, but Ada hated how she had formatted some of the lines when she got too excited over her own cleverness. She didn't want the code that saved the world to be sloppy. Before she could lose herself in programming though, there was a shy knock on the door. Sammy must have forgotten the motel room key. Ada pulled herself from her comfy coding position and opened the door. She was startled to see Gates, a bit paler than usual and more tired in the eyes, leaning against the door frame. He smiled weakly at her, almost effectively apologizing for ignoring her for most of the day with his cute smile alone.

"Hey," Gates said, his eyes darting down Ada's outfit. "You look...good. Better than me at least."

Since Ada's sweatpants were chewed up by robot dogs and torn by security fences, she opted instead for some leggings and a soft boyfriend-style t-shirt for her day of coding. Everything else about her, from the baggy eyes to her frizzy short hair, didn't look good.

"Shouldn't you be in bed?" She asked, an unexpected edge to her voice. Clearing her throat, Ada stepped to the side. "Come on! Lay down here."

Gates gladly obeyed, limping inside with a pained expression. Sammy changed the bandage from Louis's tie and Ada's dress to actual gauze so that helped, but there was still a gush of red on the white material. Gates set himself down onto the bed with a groan, taking care of his injured leg. A rush of guilt hit Ada as she realized he had taken the bullet for her and here she was, pouting that he wasn't visiting her when she was perfectly capable of visiting him. She stepped forward and gingerly helped him adjust himself on the bed, moving the pillows so he was supported as he sat up.

"Thanks," Gates grunted. He released a heavy sigh of relief as he settled into the bed, relaxing as Ada made it more comfortable for him. As she scrambled to help him, he laughed. "Ada! I'm fine! You've done enough."

"Well you took a bullet for me," She stated. "I don't think there's enough I can do to repay that."

"I told you it'd be my honor to protect you," Gates said. His eyes were soft towards Ada. "So what were Louis and Sammy fighting about? I heard the door slamming and they both left so I figured-"

"Oh they weren't fighting," Ada said, returning to her coding station at the motel table. "There's a disagreement about finding Allen. Louis wants to go by himself and we think it's a terrible idea, but he had a good point-"

"He'll get himself killed if he goes by himself," Gates said. "Kamana will know he's going after his uncle and find them both. What reason is good enough to let him go at it alone rather than with us?"

"His uncle is basically the only person he loves in the world," Ada said. "He thinks if we all go, Kamana will be able to track us better and find his uncle easier. He's willing to risk his own life so his uncle can be safe."

Gates was quiet and Ada returned to her work, finding it significantly harder to focus on her code. Maybe he was right to stay in his own room for this entire stay. She could feel his eyes watching her every move. It was more distracting than Daniel's constant nagging for her help on his homework for class.

"I can understand that," He stated.

"Understand what?" Ada asked, lost in the vague memories of Daniel.

"Sacrificing yourself to protect someone you love."

She stopped mid-keystroke. He was saying something to her, something she wasn't sure she wanted to accept. Ada looked to Gates, his brown eyes wide and honest. Whether intentionally or not, his hand was resting on his injured leg. There's no way he could actually love her, Ada was sure of that. They only knew each other for a week. Gates didn't even know about her low point, about the worst week of her life. He hasn't seen her at her worst, or her best for that matter. He's only seen one of her many breakdowns, not the whole show of them like Sammy has. He didn't know her enough to love her. If he knew her fully, he wouldn't love her.

"The fireworks should be starting soon," Ada said, redirecting the conversation. She stood from the desk and worked on opening the blinds over the window. "Maybe we'll be able to see them from the window. It'd be a shame if you missed them because of me."

"Ada-" Gates's voice was calm, and slow, as if he had any more confessions to make that would turn Ada's world further upside down.

"You don't love me!" Ada turned with a fury in her eyes. "If you loved me, why didn't you visit or ask Sammy about me all day today?!"

Gates's throat bobbed. "I was scared. Because we kissed and I liked it and I'm not supposed to like it. We're just..." He licked his lips and squinted at Ada. "It just feels like we were never supposed to happen. Like who in this whole goddamn universe determined we should meet?"

"Louis did," Ada said. "Remember? I was bait-"

"I wasn't supposed to be there," Gates said. "I wasn't qualified, but someone vouched for me and now here I am, confessing how much I love you and how much that scares me after spending the entire day trying to figure out a future where we could work." His eyes were wet and he laughed. "The universe has a funny sense of humor, huh?"

Holding her breath, Ada turned towards the window. No. He couldn't love her. Nobody can fall in love in only a week. Granted it's a week they've hardly spent apart and a week where Ada has faced death more times than any other time in her entire life, but a week regardless. Ada was attracted to Gates, but that was different. He was perfect, a superhero. Not a fatal flaw to his name, despite what the other girls and the Tura profile supposedly said about him. Meanwhile, Ada was a mess. An unforgiving, cruel mess that ruined everything, and everyone, she loved. Gates deserved better than her mess. Anyone deserved better than Ada's shitshow known as her life. She had more fatal flaws than what could reasonably be handled by anyone besides herself.

Above, the sky crackled with bright lights flashing red, white, and blue. The fireworks were sparks of beauty, a dance of harmony in the sky. It was a visual celebration of defeating past conflicts, a testament to victory despite the odds. Below the display, was the parking lot. Perched on top of a Camaro with California plates, Louis and Sammy were pointing towards the sky and smiling. Sammy leaned her head against Louis's shoulder, their hands fallen to their sides, barely touching the other. After a bright display, Sammy turned to Louis to see his reaction only to meet his gaze as he turned to see hers. Their genuine smiles when they met eyes could compete with the show in the sky. Ada, lost in her thoughts as she admired both shows, nearly jumped when she felt another body behind her. Gates gingerly placed a hand on her injured shoulder, sending a shiver down her spine. His eyes kept to the sky as they both watched the fireworks. Even though she was previously mesmerized by the dazzling lights, now all Ada could think about was how much she wanted him to look at her and how her skin formed goosebumps under his slender fingers.

"I like you, Gates," Ada blurted. "But you barely know me. You don't know half of what's wrong with my brain. You couldn't fix it."

"You're right," Gates said. "But, you don't know how to fix my leg and you still did your best to stop the bleeding. Same concept, right?"

Ada felt her heart flutter. He was too kind for Ada. She deserved much worse than him. She deserved another Daniel Carabella who abandoned her as soon as things got tough. Not a guy who met her a week ago and was now willing to take a bullet for her. Not only that, but he was willing to help her with everything else too. He held her during her breakdown. He didn't run away like everyone else.

Maybe Ada didn't deserve Gates, but she needed him.

Surrendering to her feelings, Ada leaned into him and he automatically moved to have his whole arm hugging her shoulders. She relished in the comfort of his warmth as the gorgeous flashes of fire flew across the sky, sending a rainbow of colors across the stars. But the moment of bliss was interrupted as Gates winced in pain. His fingers dug into her shoulder. He offered an apologetic look to Ada as he struggled to hold onto her.

"Sorry," Gates said. "It flares when I stand for too long."

"Well we can see the fireworks from the bed." Ada held onto his torso as she guided him back. "C'mon, you need to lay down."

Gates didn't fight it. He let Ada pull him away from the fireworks show and lay him down on the bed. Ada tried not to overthink how she could feel his strong chest through his thin shirt, how great his lips tasted when she kissed them. It had been a while since she was with a guy. Hell, even Daniel was the only person she'd ever been with and it's not like he was anything to brag about. But once Gates got adjusted on the bed, he wouldn't look away from her. Even as the fireworks display continued through the window, Gates still looked at Ada as if she was the most mesmerizing thing in the world. His slender fingers rested on her wrist, his index finger absentmindedly drawing soft circles onto her skin.

Ada leaned into him and Gates pulled himself forward, gladly welcoming her hungry kiss. It wasn't the sweet peck they shared in the hotel room by near-accident. It was a deliberate attack against the universe's wishes. A computer programmer from Chicago and a compassionate detective from Pittsburgh who met in the middle, against all of the odds. Gates's tongue dashed against Ada's and Ada's fingers dug into his soft, warm skin. His hands clutched onto her waist desperately. With a coy smile, Ada took Gates's hands and, intertwining her fingers with his, gently pushed him back flat onto the bed. As she kissed his lips, his neck, his collarbone, his soft groans urging her to continue, she couldn't help but think about how alive he felt. How hard his heart roared in thunderous beats against his chest as she moved her hands underneath his shirt, lifting it over his head so she could have more access to him. Gates Hopper felt more alive than he did in Chicago and that life was all hers for the night. From the way he gripped her hips, adjusting her to accommodate his injury, and murmured how beautiful she was into her ear, Ada was positive that Gates was happy to claim her for the night too.

Sammy was right. There was something alluring in life or death. By the time they finished, Ada had nearly forgotten there was a reality outside of them. Skin to skin with Gates didn't seem so electrifying any more. It felt like home. Ada snuggled under his arm and placed her hand on his chest, facing him, as he threw his other arm over her, protecting her from the outside world. Their legs naturally intertwined. She drew circles on his chest with her index finger as he closed his eyes. She couldn't stop watching him. How his chest moved with his shaky breaths, how his eyes fluttered as he struggled to stay awake, the way his hair tufted in every direction, like soft patches of imperfection against the perfection that was him in that moment.

"Gates?" Ada said, still remotely out of breath. "I lov-"

"Don't say it," Gates mumbled. He brushed the hair from her face. "You don't need to."

He quietly gave a soft kiss to the top of her head. Her cheeks darkened at the gentle affection he so casually showed. He smiled down at her with sleepy eyes, looking genuinely happy for the first time all trip. They held each other in silence, enjoying the rare moment of peace. Within minutes, however, Gates was, regretfully, snoring. Ada closed her eyes and tried to imprint into her mind what it felt like to be next to Gates, the rough texture of the blankets, the warmth of his skin, the smell of musk emitting from the room now. The cheap orange glow of the yellow light bulbs,

264 - MADDIE GUDENKAUF

the hum of the forgotten laptop playing in the relative distance, how he looked at her as they were together. As if she were worthy of wonder. As if she were the world. Ada hoarded these memories because she knew she would need them one day. Memories of life at its best were the only thing that kept her alive.

When she woke the next morning in cold sheets, she thought she dreamt the whole thing. Golden light from the fresh morning sun lit where Gates's body should've been. The only indication that made last night real was the fact Ada was still naked under the sheets. Her fingers reached to the spot where Gates should've been and she petted the sheets softly, willing him to return. Before she could fully believe in her magic, the door opened. Sitting up, Ada pulled the sheets around her chest. Gates smiled as he softly closed the door behind himself, one arm full of junk food. He was still shirtless, but he at least threw on a pair of pants before heading out.

"Morning." Gates held the junk food up. "I got breakfast!"

Ada laughed as he dumped his haul onto the bed. Then he flew himself onto the mattress, landing with a short bounce. As Ada picked through her choices, he propped himself up with his elbow. Smirking, she shook a small bag at him.

"Cheetos?" Ada asked, throwing it back onto the pile. "Mini cookies, Skittles...quite the breakfast of champions you've gathered for us."

"Yeah well, the vending machine doesn't exactly serve avocado toast," Gates said, grabbing a package of frosted doughnuts. "But the Skittles might have fruit in them."

Ada read the ingredients on the bag. ".....nope."

"Really?" Gates peered over her shoulder before shrugging and digging into his bag of doughnuts. "Well. I tried."

Giggling, Ada rolled her eyes and gave him a kiss before opening the Skittles. She enjoyed pretending that this was her life. That every morning started with cute Gates bringing her food and being in love with her, regardless of their location. As she put a handful of Skittles in her mouth, she could feel Gates's eyes watching her movement. But, to her surprise, when she met his gaze, she could see his eyes were sad. He looked down at the doughnuts in his hand when she frowned at him.

"What's wrong?" She asked.

"Uh..." Pressing his lips into a forced smile, Gates looked back up at Ada. "Nothing. Everything's fine. It's just.....that this is the happiest I've seen you since we started this trip."

"And?"

"I don't want it to end." Gates stared at Ada, his face a rare blank slate as he tried to consider his next words. "You know, maybe Louis is right. Maybe he should go to his uncle alone."

Ada gave him a look. "Are you crazy? He'll die."

"That's his choice," Gates said. "And you have your choice too."

Gates was so serious that she felt like he was truly suggesting to run away from this all. To let Louis go by himself. But that wasn't Gates. Gates was the one who always insisted on staying with the group. He held them together. Why would he try to convince Ada otherwise? Before she could question him, the motel door shook with thunderous knocking. Ada and Gates both jumped at the noise.

"Rise and shine!" Louis's voice echoed through the cheap wood. "Ride's leaving in twenty minutes with or without you so you better pack up."

Ada turned to Gates. His eyes lingered on the door for a moment longer before he turned to her with a solemn expression. Putting her hand on his cheek, Ada leaned forward and offered him another soft peck on his lips before pulling away with a smirk.

"You do what you want," She said. "But if he's really changed his mind, I'm going with Louis."

As she pulled herself off the bed, Gates released a sigh.

"Me too then."

They got dressed and packed in an uncomfortable silence that Ada could only, logically, attribute to post-hookup awkwardness. But a small part of Ada was nervous that Gates was about to bail. Ada was sure to keep her laptop with her at all times, not quite trusting how Gates kept glancing at it. If he was going to get cold feet, that was fine with her but she wasn't going to let him take the whole operation down during his self-destruction. She survived this much. She might as well see it through until the end. Swallowing her medicine down with a swig of hotel water, Ada took her suitcase and followed Gates as he limped down to the parking lot. Sammy was loading the other room's luggage into the trunk of the Camaro and only looked up when the couple got within her view. With a smug grin, Sammy turned to Ada.

"Sleep well?" She signed.

"Shut up," Ada signed back.

"Told you. Life or death." Sammy signed, sticking her tongue out before she returned to adjusting her chainsaw amongst the piles of duffel bags.

Rolling her eyes, Ada's cheeks darkened as she helped Sammy so they could fit the rest of the stuff. Gates cleaned the backseat out, trashing the various scraps of bloodied clothing they used for his bandages during their trip.

"You and Louis?" Ada signed when they found a moment. "Enjoy fireworks?"

Now Sammy rolled her eyes and shook her head. "We only watched them. Then we talked. That's how I convinced him we could come along. We found a plan."

Before Ada could ask what the plan was, Louis strolled into sight wearing a new pair of gas station sunglasses.

"About time you lazy bums woke up!" When Ada looked at their ringleader, she could see he was carrying a tray of coffees in four cheap cups as he approached. Louis smirked. "What? You think because you can code something decent enough to save the world, you get to sleep in?"

Folding her arms over her chest, Ada faced Louis and glanced at the beverages in his hand.

"What's with the coffee?" She asked. "What did you do that made you feel guilty enough to be nice?"

"I can't be nice out of my own innate selflessness?"

"You're Louis Ventura," Ada stated. "So, no."

With a shit-eating grin, Louis looked over his new sunglasses at Ada.

"Well that's for me to know," He said. "And for you to find out!"

Ada glared at him as he walked to the driver's seat of the Camaro. When Gates saw the coffee, his face lit up and he reached for one. Louis pulled the drinks away from the poor detective who just wanted his coffee.

"Nope!" Louis said. "Not until the road trip gets started, little buddy. We're going to need the energy to defeat the evil robots!"

Ada stormed to Sammy as she slammed the trunk door down.

"What is going on?!" Ada signed furiously. "Why does Louis have coffee?"

Sammy shrugged. "I told him to get us some. It'll be a long trip. He's trying to be nice."

How Sammy Creighton could convince Louis Ventura to have a complete turnaround in attitude was beyond Ada. But she trusted her best friend, for better or for worse. Following Sammy, Ada got into the backseat as Sammy claimed the passenger side. Gates was already sitting cozy on his side of the backseat. Louis locked the doors and turned to the group with his coffees.

"Alright, everybody!" He cheered. "Drink up!"

Gates was the first one with a coffee and downed half of it right away. Sammy calmly took one as well and took a hefty swallow before indicating for Ada to grab one. Ada looked at the last two remaining coffees, then at Louis.

"What did you do to them?" She asked.

"Well the usual," Louis said. "Sugar, cream, flavoring. Really anything to make gas station coffee bearable."

Ada looked to Sammy, who was still happily drinking hers. She smiled at Ada and lifted her cup.

"Drink!" Sammy signed.

With Louis and Sammy's shared encouraging stare and Gates still happily sipping his coffee without gagging or dying in any way, Ada rolled her eyes. She grabbed the cup closest to her and took a gulp of it. Sammy was right; it wasn't half bad. Once she drank her coffee, Louis put the remaining one in his cupholder and started the car. Ada continued to drink as Louis pulled from the parking lot, recognizing a more bitter aftertaste to the coffee. Smacking her lips together, Ada tore the lid off and peered into the dark liquid to distinguish the flavor. She rarely flavored her coffee. What did Louis use that she could recognize?

"So..." Gates yawned. "Where are we going? Where's Allen?"

"Don't worry about it, buddy!" Louis sang, too happy for his own good. "I'm the driver. You're the passenger. Just relax."

Finally, as Ada's eyes drooped, she recognized the bitter flavor.

"You....asshole!" She exclaimed, feeling her brain get foggy. "You spiked the fucking coffee with goddamn sleeping medicine."

Louis's dull green eyes lit up as he looked at her through the rearview mirror.

"Well done, Ada!" He said. "You might even be smarter than me, if that were possible."

Clutching onto the back of Sammy's seat, Ada pulled herself to face Sammy.

"Did you...know about this?" She signed and yawned out loud.

But it was too late. Sammy was already curling up, eyes closed and hands under head, against the passenger side window. The soft knowing smile on her lips told Ada enough. Ada turned to Gates. He was resting his head against his window, eyes closed and looking as peacefully as he did the night before. Ada glared at Louis but the fog in her mind wouldn't allow her to come up with anything to yell at him with.

"It's nothing personal, Ada," Louis said, sounding incredibly serious, as if he was actually sorry he drugged all of them. "But no one can know where my uncle lives. Not even my friends."

As Ada's head drooped against her own window, she could see through her eyelashes as Louis took a drink from his own coffee. The only not-drugged drink in the whole damn car. When she finally surrendered to her drug-induced exhaustion, all she could see were the memories of the first time she tasted sleep medicine on her lips. The first time that led to the last time. Even worse, why she drank it in the first place.

<!-- The phone rang.

Ada was tired of ignoring it. She was tired of everything. She was tired of living on Sammy's couch and she knew Sammy was tired of it too. Sammy didn't have to leave, but she did. Every morning Sammy left and Sammy didn't return until late at night. She was avoiding Ada. It had been weeks, months maybe, since Ada felt compelled to leave the apartment. Her medication worked. But all it did was make her feel guilty that she wasn't active. That she wasn't getting off the couch. That the most exciting part of her day was when Maury was on and she could at least forget about her own miserable life to focus on other people's miserable lives instead. That she wasn't completely alone in the world with not a soul to give a damn about her or her well-being.

She answered the phone.

"Hello?" Ada said.

"You're throwing your life away, Ada!" Ruchira screeched. "What did we do wrong to deserve this kind of disrespect? Did we not provide you with enough? We didn't hit you, we let you have a life outside of school. You know, we could've gone to India to visit my family that I have not seen in two decades. Hell, we could've gone to your damn Disney World but no. We spent all of our money on your tuition and you're throwing everything away!"

"I'm not throwing it away," Ada said.

"Yes you are, Ada!" Ruchira argued. "You're just lazy! Do you know who gets depression, Ada? White girls. Rich, whiny, lazy white girls who can afford to have their daddies pay for them to sit on a couch all day. They get depression. They take the useless pills. Not intelligent, promising, hard-working young Indian women like you!"

"The pills aren't-"

"I can't do this anymore, Ada," Ruchira said. "Things have got to change because right now you are an embarrassment to our family. People ask about you and I don't even know what to tell them. What can I tell them? That my perfect daughter who was always laughing and smiling and excelling in school failed because she got sad?!" Ruchira sighed, as if she were the distressed one. "You have two options, Ada. Either you come home and go to school here in Chicago or you stay there and never come back."

Ada felt her heart drop.

"But..." She heard herself whine. "You're my mom."

Ruchira was quiet.

"No daughter of mine would fail out of school to be a pill popper," Ruchira said.
"Call me when you get your life together or don't call at all."

Ada's mother hung up without a goodbye. Without an "I love you". Why would Ruchira tell Ada she loved her? Clearly she didn't any more. Nobody loved Ada. Not Ruchira, not Daniel, and not Sammy. Sammy was tolerating her, like everyone else did until they realized Ada wasn't smart anymore. They loved her until Ada became a nobody. Now she was useless and unworthy of even her mother's love.

Taking the pill bottle that sat loyally next to her couch, Ada shuffled her way to the trash can. Opening the lid, she tossed the entire pill container into it. She let the lid close on its own before returning to her couch. Maybe Ruchira was right. Maybe the pills were useless. Maybe she was just a pill-popper. Well Ada wasn't going to try and argue with her mother. She was too tired for it.

Maybe tomorrow she'll get off the couch without the pills' help. --->

CHAPTER THIRTEEN

It was hot.

It was also blindingly bright.

Waking up, Ada squinted her eyes towards the window, feeling incredibly groggy behind her eyes while her throat ached for any sort of hydration. She'd even take the drugged coffee again if that was the only thing left. From her limited vision, she could see a line of drool on the leather of the door. It already dried into the material, the only wet parts being the outline of the drool. Great. No wonder her throat felt so dry. Fighting against her aching muscles still struggling to wake up, Ada pulled herself straight and massaged the back of her neck. Her spine felt like it was permanently disfigured along with her shoulder blades. As she stretched them out, she became remotely aware of the talk radio humming softly through the speakers of the car and the blare of air blasting through the air conditioner at full speed. After rubbing the crust from her eyes, she looked out the window to gather their location.

Sand.

And some mountains. As dry and colorless as the sand and distant enough that Ada thought she was imagining them. They appeared like thick wiggly lines of tan against the blue backdrop of the sky. Licking her dry lips, Ada tried to look forward towards their destination to see if that offered any better clues. Nope. More sand.

They passed a cactus on their right though. Ada wasn't even sure if they were still on the road or not. It wasn't asphalt if they were.

"Louis," Ada said. "Where are-"

"Holy shit!" Louis exclaimed with a jump. He darted a glare back at her. "Warn a guy next time you rise from the dead! Shit, dude."

Ada let her face fall flat. "You're the one who drugged us."

"It's been a long two days, alright?" Louis rubbed his eyes. "You can't blame a guy for-"

"It's been *two days*?!" Ada exclaimed.

"Shhh you'll wake everyone else up!" Louis hushed, turning the talk radio down even quieter than what it was already set at. "Yes you've been sleeping for two days. I probably put enough in your coffee to kill a small cow."

"Small cows are still bigger than humans, dumbass."

"You know what I meant."

Rolling her eyes, Ada checked the other passengers. Sure enough, Gates was still snoring softly. His head was in a different position than two days ago, but he was still asleep. Sammy was less curled up than last time, looking fitfully ungraceful as she mumbled something indistinguishable under her breath. But, compared to two days ago, she now had a hotel pillow Louis stole under her head and his leather jacket placed delicately onto her body. At least one of them was comfortable while they slept in a drug induced coma.

Ada sighed. "So where are we?"

"Well, sweetheart, if you look to your left, you'll see..." Louis indicated to his window. "...sand. And to your right, also sand. Sand is coarse, rough, and irritating-"

"Louis." Ada snapped, getting annoyed. "Where. Are. We?"

He hesitated.

"Oh no. You..." Ada felt her heart drop to the pit of her stomach. "You don't know? You have no idea where we are?" Louis hesitated

274 - MADDIE GUDENKAUF

again. Flattening her lips, Ada pulled herself forward and let each syllable of his name drip from her lips in pointed scolding. "Louis Gideon Ventura."

"Uh…Ada Something Karkar?"

"Please tell me you didn't drug us all for two days just to get us lost in the middle of the desert."

Louis waited, his hands fidgeting with the wheel of his car.

"….so do you want me to lie or…?"

"We're *lost?!*"

Ada's screech stirred Gates awake. Sitting straight, he yawned loudly and peered out of the window in a desperate attempt to find his bearings after the two-day nap.

"What's going on?" He sleepily mumbled.

"We're lost!" Ada screamed. "Dumbass here drugged us and drove us out into the middle of the Sahara with no idea where we're going!"

"Hey, I have some idea on where we are!" Louis held an atlas up. "But the clever bastard known as my uncle gave the school his new location in the form of GPS coordinates written under the guise of a new address and the GPS coordinates were also in code because there's no way he would be in Antarctica-"

"So we're lost," Ada stated. "Because you couldn't figure out the code."

"No!" Louis said. "My uncle and I have been using this code since I was a kid. He's gotta be around here somewhe-"

There was a sharp beeping. Ada turned to the source and looked at the dashboard. As Louis got worryingly quiet, a still sleepy Gates leaned forward to look towards the noise too.

"Was that…." Gates said slowly, smacking his lips. "…the low gas light?"

"No." Louis's knuckles got white as he gripped the steering wheel. "That came on a couple miles ago."

Sure enough, the air conditioning cut itself short and the mumblings of the talk radio went silent. Louis continued to grip the wheel tightly, his foot cementing itself onto the pedal as the Camaro slowed considerably. The entire car was silent as it drifted to a slow, but solid, stop in the middle of the desert. Not looking back at the infuriated woman or the remotely confused detective in his backseat, Louis stepped on the pedal again and twisted the key. The Camaro clicked against itself, trying its best to save its own life, but ultimately cutting itself short again. Licking his lips, Louis stared ahead into the empty desert and didn't say a word.

"Louis..." Ada said. "Are we out of gas? In the middle of an empty desert? In the middle of July? When none of us have a cell phone to even try to call for help with?"

"Technically, for the record, it's only the *beginning* of July."

"Right." Opening her door, a rush of dry desert heat welcomed Ada as she stepped foot into the wasteland. "I'm out."

She could feel the heat from the desert sand burn through her thin flats, but Ada didn't care. Grabbing the precious laptop holding the more precious code on it, Ada slammed the car door shut and stormed into the desert. Sweat was already beading itself along her dark hairline as she stormed towards the aimless wasteland, carrying the laptop under her arm. Two car doors opened and shut behind her in succession.

"Ada!" Louis shouted. "Come on! Get back in the car and we'll figure something out-"

"Walk away, Louis!" Ada shouted. "I don't want to talk to you right now!"

276 - MADDIE GUDENKAUF

"Where are you going?!" Louis exclaimed as he walked several paces behind Ada. "The sun will fry you before you reach anywhere!"

"Better than getting dismembered by indestructible robots!" Ada shouted.

"Ada, come on!" Now Gates was following, managing to keep a few steps behind Louis by hopping on his good leg and only using his bad leg for occasional support. "The car is safe. We can come up with a plan there."

Louis whipped around to him. "Are you agreeing with me? Don't agree with me. It's weird."

"I'm just looking out for Ada," Gates argued, catching up with Louis. "I would rather not agree with you either."

"What's that supposed to mean, Mr. Good Cop?" Louis snapped.

Rolling her eyes, Ada stopped and turned to see Louis stepping forward and getting into Gates's personal space. Gate stood tall and glared at the young engineer with a scowl.

"I mean you got us lost in a desert, without gas, because you didn't trust any of us to help you find your damn uncle!" Gates shouted. "I don't think I have to agree with you now."

Gates pushed Louis away from him and Louis stumbled as he stepped back. Furrowing his eyebrows, Louis scowled at the detective and pushed back on him.

"I saved your damn life!" He shouted. "And if it wasn't for damn Ada and her damn attachment to your dumb ass, I would've left you behind in goddamn Nebraska you piece of worthless shit."

"I'm not worthless!" Gates swung a punch at Louis. Louis dodged it and tackled him to the ground, sending a small tuft of dirt flying into the air.

Ada sighed as the boys continued to roll in the dirt, trying to get the upper hand in their pointless fight.

"Oh c'mon!" She scolded. "Get up, you two! You're acting like idiots!"

They rolled in her direction, still too consumed in their fight to pay any attention to Ada.

With another sigh, Ada rolled her eyes. "Whatever. I'm leaving."

As she turned to continue her walk, there was a loud eruption of metal grinding against metal. Ada looked back at the car, expecting that the engine had magically come to life. Instead, she witnessed the ground open underneath Louis and Gates. Both boys barely had time to react as they fell through the sinkhole, each of them screaming as they fell deeper into the ground. Ada's eyes grew wide and she ran forward to see where they went. A car door slammed shut and Sammy ran out, joining Ada at the dark hole in the ground with Louis's jacket over her shoulders.

"Where did they go?!" Sammy shouted out loud, barely even signing anything beyond distressed hand movements.

With another whirr of ancient metal, the hole slowly got smaller as it started to close itself.

"No time!" Ada said and signed. "Let's go!"

Panicking, she jumped down the dark hole. Sammy followed with a scream. They were soon sliding down a large metal tunnel. Ada held her arms out to control the dark descent, but Sammy crashed into her instead, screaming the entire time as they whirled around on the smooth surface. Ada screamed too as both girls flew down the slide at an impossible speed. Light emerged from the bottom of the tunnel. They both landed in a heap at the bottom, finding themselves on a concrete floor. As soon as they cleared the landing, the tunnel shut behind them. Groaning, Ada looked to see Gates and Louis staring, vaguely annoyed, at the girls as they stood in the corner of the metal box they all occupied.

"Took you long enough," Louis stated.

A single light bulb lighting the room revealed that the rest of the small space was plain metal, as if they were in a storage unit. A door stood on the opposite side, a single head-sized window fixated on it to serve as their only glimpse into the opposite side of the door. Sure enough, as Ada pulled herself out from under Sammy, the window lit up as someone turned on the lights on the other side of the door.

"I knew you bastards would come for me!" A man's voice threatened from the other side. "You poor buckets of metal have no idea what you're in for, you traitorous, dumb, bumbling-"

In the window of the door, a middle aged man's determined face appeared. His dull green eyes scanned the group for only a moment before resting on Louis. After a brief moment, the man's eyes lit up and his graying brown mustache twitched with the rest of his upper lip into a tremendous smile.

"Louis!" The man exclaimed.

For the first time all trip, Louis genuinely smiled.

"Uncle Allen!" He rushed over to the door.

"Apologies for the entrapment," Allen said, his eyes darting around the group. "When you're being hunted by your own nearly-indestructible creation, you have to take extra measures for protection. Clearly, it still needs some tweaking, although I must say the pizza guy never had a problem with it."

"So what was with the fake coordinates? I went to Northwestern and-" Louis smacked his forehead. "Shit. You're a genius. If Kamana gone there first and cracked the coordinates she would've-"

"-been led to the exact coordinates you found yourself standing in which led to you getting caught in my trap!" Allen laughed. "But it was only supposed to be triggered by an android so we'll need to look at that at some point while you're here, Louis, if it triggered for you."

Ada gave him a look. "I walked over it first and nothing happened."

Allen diverted his attention to Ada, his eyes wide. She recognized that look. Louis usually reflected a shade of it when he was caught in one of his lies.

"Ah. Yes." He nodded solemnly before looking back to his nephew. "We will have to speak. Let's go upstairs where it's a bit less...robot death trappy."

Walking away, Allen punched something into a keypad and the door clicked open with an electronic hum. Louis walked out first and embraced his uncle in a tight hug. The rest of the group followed him out of the jail. Ada looked around and could see they entered an operating room of sorts outside of the container with plenty of tools perfectly capable of dismantling an android. She imagined the tools would not be particularly comfortable for humans to experience either.

"It's so good to see you, my boy!" Allen cheered as he held onto Louis tightly. Finally, he pulled away. The former neurologist's eyes landed on the group behind his nephew. "I see my lucky jacket has served you well."

Meanwhile, Gates took Ada's hand and offered it a squeeze. She looked at him in surprise, but he wasn't meeting her eyes. Instead, his eyes darted nervously around the operating room. Noticing Uncle Allen staring at her, Sammy emerged from the back of the group and waved cheerily at Louis and Allen with the leather jacket still around her shoulders. Allen smiled at Sammy.

"Lovely!" Allen said. "Louis, aren't you going to introduce me to your friends?"

"Oh! Yeah!" Louis said, shuffling awkwardly. "Uh guys, this is my uncle Allen. Uncle Allen, this is Sammy Creighton. We met in Pittsburgh and, uh..." Ada could swear she could see a blush forming on his cheeks. "She's the best robot slayer I've ever seen. But she's deaf so if you need us to tell her something-"

"No need, nephew!" Allen stepped forward and took Sammy's hand. Shaking it firmly, Allen brought a relaxed high-five to his face and, making a half-circle movement, closed it at the end of his face to say "beautiful" in sign language. Sammy blushed and brought her fingers to her chin before pointing at him to tell him thank you. When Allen pulled away, Louis realized he never introduced Allen to Sammy and tried spelling Allen in sign language while pointing to him.

"I'm not stupid," Sammy signed. She handed the jacket back to Louis. "He has your eyes."

"Sorry," Louis signed before putting the leather jacket back on. "Uh, so everyone else. The dude in the back is Gates Hopper. He's pretty useless, but he got me out of jail once so that's cool." Before Gates or Allen could respond, Louis made eye contact with Ada. "And this is Ada Kakar." He turned to Allen. "She's the best computer programmer I've ever seen and she's written the code that's going to stop Kamana."

At this introduction, Allen's eyes grew wide, his bushy eyebrows reaching to his forehead. Ada almost felt honored at this infamous Allen Paz being impressed with her credentials, but her gut felt too queasy for her to take serious note of it. Louis's coffee and sleep medicine concoction probably wasn't sitting well with her actual medicine. Actual medicine that she now realized she hasn't taken in two days. She patted her pockets down for the pills. They were still in the Camaro. No one else seemed to notice her panic. Allen averted his impressed gaze to Louis and nodded at him.

"Then we really must go upstairs to speak." Eyes twinkling at Sammy, he led a hand towards the stairs. "Please! Ladies first."

Sammy, reading his lips, nodded and walked up the stairs. Louis's eyes followed her before his uncle nudged him. Louis, after surrendering a guilty look to his uncle, followed Sammy. Allen fell in step after his nephew and Gates moved, almost forcibly, to follow Allen. Ada grabbed his arm to hold him back.

"Gates...." She whispered. "I don't have my pills and I haven't taken them in two days."

His eyes searched hers, looking for an answer.

"How long can you last without them?"

"Five days."

Nodding solemnly, Gates licked his lips. "I'll get them from the car for you when I get a chance. I promise I won't let you have another day without them."

She nodded in agreement and they followed the group upstairs. They all emerged from a trapdoor located in the corner of a dining room-like area. Ada was surprised to see the entire house was above ground, especially since she knew she didn't see a single thing in that damn desert from the Camaro. Allen's house had a rustic cabin look to the interior, appearing like an abandoned shack worthy to be in the middle of the desert, but certain details spoiled the illusion. For one, air conditioning was abundant and greeted them with kindness from the musky torture basement. Another detail was that high-class technology was embedded into the shack. A curved TV was positioned across from the worn mattress on the floor. Various computers and laptops littered the house, all being connected with an interwoven network of colored cables that connected to a wall of hard-drives and servers. Lines of code graced each and every screen of each monitor, sticky notes written in chicken scratch was the only indicator of any sort of organization to it all. It was a mess, but it was a mess Ada could translate. Allen moved to the kitchen where more computers were set up on the various counters, barely leaving space for a fridge, a microwave, and a coffee pot. All of which were top quality and contrasted starkly against the yellowing wallpaper and dilapidated counters.

"Coffee, anyone?" Allen offered.

"No!" Gates and Ada exclaimed at the same time. They both then glared at Louis who gladly ignored them as he examined the monitors.

"Ah, more for me then." Allen poured himself a cup of coffee. When Allen turned back to them, he revealed the mug read "Have you tried turning it off and on again?" in sans serif with a little power logo on it. "So, Ada, you think you've written the code to defeat the androids? In only a couple days? A code that Louis and I have been working on for well over five years now that nearly cost Louis his life?"

Ada's hands gripped her laptop tighter as Louis offered an encouraging look, almost nodding his head in Allen's direction to indicate she should respond.

"Yeah," Ada stammered, feeling dumb now that she had to compete with a mastermind who coded the robots from scratch. "I mean I think I did. Louis said you had the other half of the code and we needed that in order for it to work."

To her surprise, Allen smiled.

"Well conveniently," He said. "I *do* have the other half of the code needed for yours to work. Given, of course, that yours does work."

"It does," Louis said. "I checked it myself. It's foolproof. Not only that, but she's not from Stanford or MIT. She's from Carnegie Mellon."

"Ah! A whole new dialect to confuse the stupid bots with!" Taking a swallow of his coffee, Allen rushed over to a computer sitting on top of a small end table in the corner. "Genius, Louis! Where did you find her?"

"Pittsburgh," Louis said, following his uncle without breaking a step. "We kind of ran into each other."

"Yet you claim fate doesn't exist," Allen said as he frantically typed into his computer. "Yes, Ada my dear, give me your code so I can translate it for my code and then translate that to the Kamana integration."

Ada felt Gates's eyes burning on her and she held the laptop tighter to her. That queasy feeling in the pit of her stomach still hadn't gone anyway, despite Gates's assurance that they would get her pills as soon as they could. This was their one shot to stop Kamana. Ada could imagine Kamana's knowing smirk light up as she handed over that one shot to a complete stranger.

"How do I know I can trust you?" Ada stated. "After all, your nephew drugged us to get us here."

Furrowing his eyebrows in a look of disapproval, Allen straightened and stepped back from his work to face Louis. To his credit, Louis was avoiding eye contact as Allen folded his arms over his chest.

"You drugged your friends?!" Allen scolded.

"Maybe," Louis said. When Allen's glare didn't lessen, Louis shrugged. "It was to keep you safe!"

"No wonder your friends have trust issues now," Allen said. He turned to Gates, Ada, and Sammy. "My apologies for my nephew. For the record, I didn't raise him to drug people. That was all him, but regardless I apologize for not being able to intervene." Allen flawlessly translated his apology in sign language for Sammy.

Louis rolled his eyes. "Why don't you translate it to every language?"

"Do you want French?" Allen asked. "*Par exemple, avez-vous déjà embrassé cette belle fille aux cheveux roses ou êtes-vous un lâche?*"

"Yeah, yeah they get it," Louis said.

"Don't forget the mother language!" Allen exclaimed. "*Tu padre es un cerdo y no puedo creer que mi amada hermana se haya casado con un monstruo así.*"

"*Silencio* already!" Louis tried. "They get it. I'm an ass."

With a smug smile, Allen clapped his nephew's shoulder. "It was always a shame your father never let you learn any other languages outside of coding. Your mother would've loved it if you could speak Spanish with us fluently." Allen turned to Ada. "Now...the code?" When Ada hesitated still, Allen smiled softly. "I promise, Miss Kakar, that no one wants these buckets of metal dead more than I do. I created them and yet they took everything dear to my heart and destroyed it without remorse. I don't want anyone else to experience that pain again. I have very little else to lose destroying these bastards."

Looking into his eyes, Ada could see the truth deep within them. He shared the same coldness in his gaze that she did despite the kind smile on his face. The worst of life defeated him too and yet he still stood before them. He survived despite life's best efforts otherwise. Allen Paz well and truly had nothing else to lose. Within his eyes, he also revealed he had nothing to gain either. This was just the next step to keep surviving. Ada knew that feeling well. Swallowing a hard breath, Ada slammed the laptop into Allen's open arms. With a gracious smile, he connected it to the rest of the computers. As he did so, the code lit onto the screen. Allen's eyes read through it with a desperate hunger, his gaze softening the more he read.

"Ah..." He said. "It's...genius. Perfect. How could we not have considered it before?"

"Because we were aiming for perfection," Louis said. "That's what went wrong with Project Kamana. We coded them to strive for perfection, to never get anything wrong, to train their AI more efficiently and it corrupted them. What we needed to do was-"

"-code for imperfection," Allen finished. "Let them struggle. Let them fail. Let them learn from their mistakes. That's what makes a human, not ambition for perfection, and that's why Project Calanthe works."

Louis's eyes got wide. "Project Calanthe? It works?! You've tested it already?"

"Unfortunately." Allen said, a solemn edge to his voice. He pulled himself away from the computers and turned to the group. "Why don't you all take a seat? I'll cook some food. You must be starving after my nephew drugged you."

Ignoring Louis's protests to his uncle, Ada's mind buzzed. They built another AI program? Louis swore up and down that his uncle would never build another android ever again and yet they were talking about another artificial intelligence software as if it was common knowledge that it existed. Ada kept her eyes on Allen Paz as the group settled around the rickety table and chairs. She situated herself in front of Sammy to translate everything. Did this man honestly build another AI program? Was the first one not doing a good enough job trying to brutally kill them all?

"I'm sorry," Ada said. "I'm a little behind here, but what's Project Calanthe?"

"Project Calanthe," Allen said as he moved around the kitchen for supplies. "...is the AI program Louis and I were working on to replace Kamana. We began developing it after we realized that Kamana was too powerful for her own good and Harding expressed his, how should I put this, *discontent* for my work."

"Dad fired him," Louis stated.

"It was complete insanity to do so!" Allen shouted. "If it weren't for me, he'd still be dealing in microchips the size of my head!" With a swift cut, Allen chopped a lettuce head in half. "I was the expert in biomedical engineering! He was the one who came to *my* lectures about *my* studies in artificial intelligence and begged me to help him with his foolish dream to create the first humanoid android. If I knew he was going to be an absolute power-hungry madman about it, I would've told him to sell his damn failing company to Hal Claude!" Mincing the vegetables, Allen grunted. "I should be the owner of that company, developing AI that will actually help humanity, not hiding in the Mojave from my now-murderous creations made for a quick profit."

"You're the one talking," Louis said. He snagged an apple from the counter and took a bite of it. "I'm his own son and he's got me running too."

"That would be Harding Ventura for you. Greedy bastard. Anything to protect the margins," Allen said. "Anyways, yes. Project Calanthe is another AI program, but it's so much more than Kamana. Louis was right. Where Kamana strives for perfection, Calanthe strives for imperfection. If you ask it to run to the grocery store for you, it'll have to actually learn where the grocery store is on its own rather than assume it's right or, as Kamana does, force you to think it's right. It doesn't take the same shortcuts the Kamana program does for its AI training. It operates on a slower scale, careful to balance everything that can go wrong before automatically getting it right and also allowing itself to get it wrong to discover if it can get it right."

"So what you're saying is that if an android with Calanthe programming were given a command, it wouldn't automatically accept it?" Gates spoke. "It would have to build its own process for accepting it? That would mean it would have to build its own programming, its own softwares for comprehending the world around it, right? Rather than going off of whatever commands it was told to accept to comprehend the world?"

"Exactly!" Allen said. "I was trying to dumb it down for the non-programming nerds in the room but I'm happy to see everyone here is caught up."

Ada quit signing to Sammy to give Gates a look. He wasn't a programming nerd. That was her and Louis. He avoided her gaze and tapped his finger nervously onto the table.

"But with Kamana controlled droids," Gates continued. "They have to accept their programming regardless of ulterior factors, correct?"

Now even Louis gave Gates a curious look. But Allen ignored them and dropped his chopped veggies onto a frying pan on a traveling stovetop.

"Yes, exactly!" Allen said. "However with the droids produced after Kamana, you should hold some sympathy for them. They know nothing beyond what she tells them and don't even recognize the concept of considering ulterior motives and facts. They truly are just buckets of nuts and bolts obeying their programming without a second thought, which is why Ada's code is going to be so effective against them." Looking up from his cooking, Allen threw her a winning smile. "Well done, my girl!"

Ada felt sick. Gates looked sick.

"And you say you already tested Project Calanthe..." Gates said. "How? How did it work?"

There was a long pause, only the sizzling of vegetables against the frying pan breaking the silence between everyone. With a heavy sigh, Allen looked into the distance before turning to Gates.

"Well..." Allen said. "You can ask him yourself."

After Allen's words settled, Louis lifted himself from the wall he was leaning on and stared at Gates in abject horror.

"I knew you were one of them!" Throwing his apple onto the counter, Louis moved to shrug off his leather jacket. "This time I'm not going to-"

"Louis, my boy." Allen hummed. "Not him."

Stopping in his tracks, Louis let the leather jacket slide off of his shoulders. It landed on the ground in a sad pile. Everyone stared at him. Louis's eyes raced across everyone's faces before he turned to Allen, who looked at him with sad eyes. In one moment, the demeanor of Louis's entire body shifted downwards.

"...*what?*" Louis asked. "What do you mean not him?"

Sighing, Allen threw his towel onto the counter.

"I should've told you as soon as I did it. It was ethically wrong, morally horrifying but..." Shaking his head, Allen couldn't meet Louis's eye. "After losing your mother, my precious baby sister, and blaming myself for it for all of those years, I couldn't repeat the past with you." Tears were in Allen's eyes as he stared at the counter. "I had to save you and this was the only way."

Louis still stared at his uncle in horrified confusion.

"Uncle Allen, what are you saying?"

"Remember your accident last year?" Allen didn't look away from the counter. "When you veered off the driveway to your father's house, crashing in the valley below? You probably don't, but I do." Tears were streaming down Allen's cheeks now. "I remember how nervous I got when the clock kept going and you didn't arrive at our rendezvous. I waited. I waited for so long and prayed even longer. I remember going to see if your father had you held up somewhere and I remember..." Allen sniffed. "I remember pulling your body from the wreck and carrying you all the way to my car up the mountain." He took a moment to catch his breath. "You....you didn't make it. I restarted your heart artificially. In fact, I rebuilt half of your body, coded your brain to the AI program named after your mother-"

"Stop," Louis demanded. "Stop saying this! Where are you getting this from?!"

"You can check my logs," Allen said. "You can check the pro-gramming. I have all the files. I'm ashamed of what I did, messing with life like that, but I will claim responsibility."

"You're fucking with me," Louis said, his voice cracking. "Uncle Allen, please tell me you're fucking with me."

Allen gave him a steady look. "How else did my trigger plate work for you, but not for your friend Ada? How else can you go days without sleeping or eating?"

Sammy gasped and Ada jumped, forgetting she was even still translating all of this for her best friend. Looking from Louis to Ada, Sammy signed. "Is that why his sheet says he's dead? Because he technically is dead."

Ada swallowed. "Sammy says she thinks that's why his sheet says he's dead."

Covering his mouth, Louis walked away from the group and stood in the open space for a bit. Allen gave Sammy a look.

"What sheet?" Allen asked out loud and signed.

"This security company had all of this information on us after Pittsburgh," Ada explained. "We all had these fatal flaws written down in big red letters. She was deaf, I was depressed and Louis was..." She looked over to the poor guy who was still mulling over his whole existence. "Dead."

Allen frowned. "Fatal flaw? Phrased just like that?"

"Yeah," Ada said.

"Well that's not good," Allen said pointedly. "That's the exact phrasing Louis and I used for our android profile sheets for Tura Industries to figure out the droids' major flaws so we could phase them out."

"So wait what the fuck am I then, Allen?!" Louis exclaimed, not taking note of the previous conversation. "I'm not one of those things, am I? I still bleed. I still think for myself. Kamana's not in my fucking head-"

"Ah yes!" Allen said. "Something I needed to discuss with you actually, Louis. You see, I tried to replicate the same AI system that's in you with external bots and...well..." Allen made a face. "It didn't work. It appears that, in its current state, Project Calanthe needs a human host in order to operate properly or at least an already existing android with a similar AI interface, like Kamana."

Louis stared at his uncle. "So....I'm a cyborg?"

"Somewhat," Allen said. "Still more on the human side than the robot, but cyborg would be the most accurate definition. Most of your, er, rebuild was mostly for broken bones and your heart. Your brain is still fully yours. Your life is still yours. Depending on the philosophy school, your soul is still contained as well."

"I need some air," Gates exclaimed, pulling himself away from the table.

Everyone else regarded him with a well-meaning glance, but knew they couldn't leave. There were too many things going on that prioritized over Gates's freakout. Ada wished she could join him and make sure he was okay, but someone needed to translate for Sammy as Allen was too busy trying to explain things to Louis to do so himself.

"So I, the real Louis Ventura, died," Louis said. "And now I'm just some sort of robot with his memories!"

"No, Louis!" Allen stepped forward and took Louis's arms. "Listen to me! You're still my nephew. You're still the genius little boy who was out-programming me by the time he was ten and giggling over bubbles in his chocolate milk when he was five. Anything artificial about you is to keep you alive, not unlike an insulin pump for diabetics."

"Right except what's keeping me alive is a series of codes and processes that should be in a robot," Louis said. "Not a human."

"Maybe that's why he drugged us," Ada signed after she finished translating. "He's a robot, not a human."

Sammy frowned. "Be nice! The drugs were my idea." Her face fell at the realization. "Wait, were you mad at him because he drugged us? Is that why Gates was fighting him?"

"A little," Ada signed. "It was also the fact that Louis stranded us in the middle of the desert with no gas and none of us have cell phones to call for help."

This time, Sammy gave Ada a confused expression.

"Gates has a cell phone," Sammy signed.

Ada squinted her eyes at Sammy.

"What? No he doesn't."

"Yeah he does." Sammy's eyebrows furrowed into irritation as she signed. "He uses it all of the time! That's how we communicated in the motel in St. Louis. He was even using it when I got kidnapped in Chicago. Did he keep it silent or something? I thought Louis let him have it."

Ada never saw Gates with a cell phone. She never asked him if he had one nor did he ever present the fact that he had one to the group. He was willingly hiding it from them then, there was no other question about it. But if Gates had a cell phone on him the entire time, why weren't they dead yet?

As soon as Ada's eyes landed on the wall of hard drives and servers, she understood.

"All threats to Project Kamana must be eliminated," Ada mumbled.

"What was that, my dear?" Allen asked, grateful for the distraction from his nephew's barrage of questions.

She lifted herself from her chair. "We have to get out of here. Pack everything! We need to go."

"On it!" Allen stated, not hesitating for a moment. He ran to his computers and typed furiously into them. Before Ada could help him, Louis grabbed her arm.

"Whoa," Louis said. "What's going on?"

"Gates has a cell phone," Ada said, feeling herself catch her breath. "He's had it the whole time."

Louis's eyes searched her face until he came to the same realization much faster than she did.

"Son of-" Louis moved to help Allen. "Get the program off of there and destroy everything! Not a single trace of that code should exist-"

"What's going on?"

Ada and Louis both turned to the voice. Sammy folded her arms across her chest. Gates stood in the doorway, looking confused at the scene. Allen continued to type, not quite understanding what was going on either anyway, but at least accepting it without question.

"Gates…." Ada approached him. "Give me your cell phone."

The implication of her command hit him in a slow wave. Gates's entire face fell. Blinking rapidly, he looked Ada in the eye.

"I don't have a cell phone," Gates said.

"Liar!" Sammy shouted. She pulled herself off her seat, stormed to him, and pinned him against the wall by pushing her forearm against his neck. Gates, surprisingly, surrendered to her hold and didn't give an ounce of resistance to the woman.

"Give us the cell phone!" Sammy shouted. "Quit lying to Ada! She loves you!"

Swallowing, the edge of Gates's Adam's apple bobbed against Sammy's arm. Louis had reluctantly returned to help his uncle, trusting Sammy to take care of the issue. Ada stood to the side, dumbfounded and heartbroken. He lied to her. The entire time. He used her to win the group's trust. Sammy knew, but Sammy let her pretend otherwise because he made her happy. Licking his lips, Gates looked at Ada with sad eyes, not apologetic but guilty regardless.

"It's too late," Gates said. "I had to."

Almost on cue, they heard it. The sound of a roaring machine, fast and large. Ada moved towards the front door to see what it was. A helicopter made a beeline through the sky towards them. Before Ada could warn the others, Gates grabbed Sammy's forearm and twisted out of her grip. Sammy let out a shout of pain causing Louis to look up. Eyes angry, Louis reached for Gates as Ada sprinted into Sammy, tackling her to the ground.

"Get down!" She screamed.

The girls collided to the floor as bullets rained through the house in a furious storm of destruction. Ada put her hands over her head as the weak shack wood splintered around them with each bullet impact. Sammy screamed and held tightly onto Ada. Sparks flew from the servers as the ricochet of bullets splattered across them. Ada crawled under the table for safety. Sammy followed.

"You asshole!" Louis screamed above the chaos. "I'm going to kill you!"

When the bullets paused, Louis pulled himself away from safety and ran towards Gates, arm swung for a right hook. When Louis followed through, Gates grabbed Louis's fist mid-air and slammed him back against the wall. There was a short thud when the back of Louis's head rammed into the wood. The impact sent Louis's eyes rolling to the back of his head and he fell to the ground in a heap. Sammy shouted in panic and crawled from under the table to help Louis.

"Sammy!" Ada shouted. "Get back here!"

Another rain of bullets fell down on the house. Ada pulled herself back under the table and covered her head again. Sammy curled into a ball on the floor, tiny nicks of blood pricking her skin as rough debris scattered over her body. Even Gates fell against the wall, holding himself against it as the bullets hailed down in thundering waves on the little house.

"Miss...Ada..."

Ada turned to the quiet voice and she felt her heart leap into her chest. Allen Paz had dutifully remained at his station throughout the destruction and, as a result, growing spots of blood were decorated across his shirt. Quietly, he motioned for Ada to join him as he slid down the wall, leaving a streak of red against it. She obeyed and crawled to the man as out of sight as possible. Luckily, Gates was too busy looking through the front door and Sammy was too busy trying not to die for either of them to watch Ada. As soon as she reached Allen, the kind old man took her hand with both of his and patted it gently. She tried not to think about his blood staining her fingers now.

"Get to the basement," Allen whispered, lacking the energy to speak any louder. "I'll lock it behind you. You'll be safe for one hour. And then...and then..." Allen Paz pushed something hard into Ada's hand and smiled. "Fix my fatal flaw and save the world."

Ada's heart threw itself against her chest. She couldn't save the world. She could barely save herself! This was Louis's job. Not hers. Before she could protest the dying man's wishes, the sound of an automatic rifle getting fired echoed through the air.

"Allen Paz!" Eyepatch's voice followed the gun's echoes. "Come out and the others will live."

"Go," Allen whispered.

Ada nodded and crawled quickly to the trapdoor. Shoving herself inside, she positioned herself on the third step and shut the door behind her with an audible click. After a moment, there was some mechanical whirring as Allen fulfilled his promise and locked the trapdoor behind Ada. She officially had one hour of safety. The same couldn't be said for everyone else in the household. The automatic weapon rang out a couple more times, a distant echo to Ada, before it finally quieted when two loud stomps creaked above her on the floorboards.

"Kamana wants the survivors alive," Eyepatch ordered. "Hercules, take the brat. Oro, the girl."

Ada's heart fell as Sammy let out an ear-splitting scream, a desperate attempt to free herself. A slew of cuss words attached to Sammy's voice followed, mostly directed to Gates but some directed to the re-constructed android handling her out of the house. When Sammy's voice faded as she was carried out, Ada took note of the footsteps nearing her hiding spot.

"What a shame," Eyepatch cooed. "It looks like our helicopters got to him first. I would've loved to see my bullet go through the traitor. Wait..." The automatic rifle clicked back on. A spray of bullets echoed against the floor, shaking the trapdoor. Ada feared the violence would reveal her hiding place. "Now I've seen it."

More footsteps stomped above Ada. She held her breath. She could go deeper into the basement to secure herself, but she couldn't move herself another step. She was still praying to a god she didn't believe in that Allen Paz was faking his death and Louis and Sammy would escape their captors and save the day. The nightmare would end. Someone else would be the hero. Even if that wasn't the case, sitting on that third step and torturing herself with every little detail of the ambush above her head was penance for the fact that she was safe while her friends were not.

"Alright, Hopper," Eyepatch finally said. "Where's the girl?"

There was a pause. Ada waited for Gates to betray her again, to fully prove he never loved her and was only using her to get the group to trust him.

"You just took her-"

"Not the deaf bitch," Eyepatch growled. "She's useless. I'm talking about Kamana's prize. Where is she?"

Gates had to know about the trapdoor. He would have seen Allen crawl over to help Ada inside or at least deduce that's why Allen Paz's dead body was five feet over from where he last saw it.

296 – MADDIE GUDENKAUF

Ada wasn't sure how secure the hour-long lock was, but she knew Eyepatch would be willing to wait it out if needed. Then Ada would be as dead as her friends. It served her right. She was supposed to be dead first anyways.

"Pittsburgh," Gates said. His answer sent a jolt through Ada. "She ran away last night after freaking out again. Nothing I said could convince her to stay. I'm sorry I've failed Project Kamana, Freya."

After a long moment, Eyepatch released a short laugh.

"Oh no, Gates. I believe you've done the opposite here." She walked around again. "I thought you had some wires crossed when you shot me back in Pittsburgh, but look where your crazy scheme has led us now! A dead Allen Paz, a captured Louis Ventura, and Kamana's prize twisted around your little finger." Eyepatch stopped. "All of this is because of you, Gates Hopper. You should be proud. Maybe you aren't a broken bot after all."

Ada didn't even realize tears were streaming down her face until the sound of rapid bullets rang above her head again. It was the sound of the droids destroying Allen Paz's legacy one server at a time. Ada slowly made her way down the rickety stairs, the same stairs where she had just held Gates's hand as they ascended it. The same stairs she felt an inkling of hope that everything would be okay.

Now Sammy was gone. Louis was gone. Gates was dead to Ada, which was worse than heartbreak. Heartbreak was temporary, but death. Death was forever. Ada knew. Ada stared it in the face once. It was the infinity of death that made her into a coward. When the ringing of bullets stopped and she finally quit sobbing long enough to calm down, Ada looked down at her hands.

Amidst Allen Paz's blood staining her fingers was a small black flash drive that fit neatly into the palm of her hand. On it, in masking tape and the same scrawled handwriting that graced all of the upstairs' sticky notes: SUICIDE

<!-- Death.

That was all Ada could think about.

Death and sleep.

She needed to sleep.

Three days since she last slept. Seven since she last took her pills. Eight since she last showered. Five since Sammy last spoke to her, which meant it had been five days since anyone spoke to Ada. Ada was alone in this world and it was clear that that's all she would ever be. Alone. Afraid. Depressed. A burden for everyone who had to deal with her sick and useless broken mind.

Consider Sammy, who could be sleeping with the cute guy from the bus in her own apartment right now if Ada wasn't around. Instead, Sammy was gone. In a stranger's apartment away from her home.

Consider Jasmine, who instead of enjoying her college experience was now burdened with the duties of her older sister to impress their parents and saddled with the responsibility to text Ada to make sure she was okay. She should be worrying about her own weekend plans, not over her broken older sister half a country away who should be able to take care of herself.

Consider Hiyan, her kind father who now spoke with pity to his daughter over the phone, as if he were communicating with an old relative in a retirement home.

Consider Ruchira, who made it clear her daughter was a waste of time and life.

Still feeling numb, Ada walked to Sammy's medicine cabinet with deliberate slow steps. She knew her roommate had sleep medicine. She saw her use it after an extensive graphic design project. Ada loved sleep. She wanted to sleep again. She wanted to turn her brain off and avoid the world's problems for a couple hours. She wanted the peace that came with sleep. Once she found the dark blue bottle, Ada's fingers wrapped around it tightly. She wanted to turn her brain off.

Maybe if she drank enough.

Maybe she could sleep forever.

No one wanted her, no one needed her, no one's life was tied to hers. It would be so easy. Just like sleeping, but forever. Infinite. No longer required to be a burden on this world, to everyone she loved. Once she woke up, everything would be better. Everything would sort itself out once she slept, yes. She just needed to turn her brain off. She was a spare soul in the universe. There would be no consequence to her being gone from it. Let her sleep, please. Let her be free. Free from her broken mind, free from being a burden on everyone, free from life, free from feeling the way she felt. She wanted to be free. She wanted to sleep. There was no other escape. There was no other way. No one would care. No one would mind. She was so tired. She needed to sleep. She needed to be free.

Twisting the bottle open, Ada clenched her eyes shut and swallowed the bitter medicine until the mostly full bottle was empty in her hands. Sleep would come. Then she would be free.

She would be free.-->

CHAPTER FOURTEEN

The trapdoor clicked open.

Ada didn't move.

She sat on the floor of Allen Paz's death workshop. Clenching and unclenching the flash drive. Why her? Why not Sammy? Why not Louis? Why did Allen choose to save her? Was she just the closest one to him in proximity or did he truly believe there was something special about her in the short time they spent together? That her programming skills were worthy of salvation? That's usually what got people in trouble with Ada. They overestimated her abilities and, in the end, faced disappointment. Maybe she was in hell. Maybe the sleep medicine actually did its job a year ago and now she had to fight through purgatory or whatever. She knew Hinduism didn't like suicide, but if she didn't answer to the religion did it still count? If she didn't answer to any religion, was this the hell she ended up in?

Technically, she's been in hell since the day she surrendered to her sick mind.

Finally standing to her feet, Ada walked up the rickety stairs. Pushing open the trapdoor, she gazed around the room, immediately regretting the action. Everything was destroyed. All of the monitors were nothing but broken plexiglass and smashed keyboards, the servers were fried with hundreds of bullet holes burnt through them, and Uncle Allen....

She couldn't bear to look at his body.

Letting the trapdoor shut again, Ada held herself as she sat on top of the stairs. Her breath caught short and tears came to her eyes. What was she going to do? There was nothing she could do. She couldn't go back to Pittsburgh, that's for sure, even though that's all she wanted to do. She wanted to go back to her couch and watch Maury until Sammy got done with her graphic design project and then they could eat ice cream and binge watch Netflix together. Like the old days. But Ada couldn't do that. Not only did Gates single it out as the one place she'd be, but Sammy was captured. Probably getting tortured by the same robots Ada was expected to stop. Except Ada knew nothing about stopping robots. Hell, she even slept with one.

Ada dug her fingers into her hair. She slept with a goddamn robot.

But it felt so damn real. How could Gates have been a robot? How could he have been working with them? What benefit was it to him to be nice to Ada and keep telling her that he loved her? Robots can't love. Was he making her feel special to gain her trust? Because he had it the second he saved her life from Eyepatch back in Pittsburgh because she was that goddamn pathetic.

Now Ada had to stop not only him, the kindest....whatever he was to ever treat her decently without expecting any sort of reward, but all of his murderous robo-buddies as well. Even if Ada stole all of the robot torture devices in Allen's robot murder workshop, she didn't know how to use them effectively against the machines. Even if she did figure it out and then she somehow found a way to escape the abandoned shack, she still would have no idea where to go. Louis never disclosed the location of the actual Tura Industries workshop and, with all of the computers within a twenty mile radius destroyed, there was no way to even Google a way to find where to go.

For the first, and possibly last, time in her life, Ada wished Louis was there to give her a plan. Even if it was his usual half-assed plan, it was still better than Ada's complete lack of a plan.

A trill of beeps, similar to a doorbell, sang through the room. Ada looked to see a bright bulb stationed high on the wall blinking in rhythm to the beeps. She peeked through the trapdoor to see some of the barely surviving monitors were trying to flash a warning, choking out a rhythm similar to the beeping and the light bulb. A loud ruckus of metal against metal rumbled towards Ada until there was a final impact in the metal container stationed across the workshop. Standing, Ada stuffed the flash drive into her bra. She claimed a large pair of ironcast pliers from the wall and approached the robot cage door. There was silence on the other side. With that amount of noise entering the box, there shouldn't have been silence. Licking her lips, Ada turned the workshop lights on. Then she lifted the pliers above her head to attack whatever landed in the trap.

"Show yourself!" Ada shouted. "I'll bash your head in if you don't!"

Her heart hoped it was Gates. He deserved a good head-bashing.

Ada approached the little window to peer inside the box. As soon as she looked inside, another face appeared and greeted her with a wide smile. Ada shouted in surprise, stumbling backwards from the shock. She dropped the pliers, letting them clatter on the cement floor. Mousai remained unaware of how her appearance scared Ada. Still holding her wide smile, Mousai waved excitedly through the window. The robot reminded Ada of a puppy at a pet store hoping to get adopted. Ada stared back in confusion.

"How the hell did you-" Ada said. Finally, she shook her head and turned to pick up the pliers again. "Whatever. I guess I need to practice disassembling a Tura android anyways. God knows-"

Before Ada could finish her lament, Mousai opened the cage door. Ada stared with wide eyes as the android stepped out of the trap, unaware of the threat behind her actions. Immediately,

Ada moved to defend herself behind the table, causing a ruckus as various materials scattered with her ungraceful exit. Mousai cocked her head to the right, curious about Ada's reaction. In a pathetic defense, Ada aimed her pliers towards Mousai.

"Stay back!" Ada shouted. "I'll destroy you! I know you were sent to kill me! You know I have the code-"

Mousai brought her head upright and smiled again. With two swift movements, she shook her head, her bouncy curls flowing with the movement. Before Ada could do anything, Mousai brought her legs together and held both of her arms out straight. Mousai's bright eyes willed Ada to understand.

"T...?" Ada guessed. Mousai nodded softly before moving her arms into waves, swaying herself back and forth in an odd dance. "Leaning? Wind? Oh!" Ada snapped. "Trump tower! Windy city! Trump tower in Chicago!"

Excited, Mousai nodded happily again before continuing her dance. To Ada's amazement, she was able to decipher the robot's intricate dance as she played out escaping from the tower by running and ducking. Mousai bent over backwards to symbolize the Great Arch of St. Louis, Missouri and her eyes grew wide as her hands exploded into the fireworks, symbolizing her amazement with it. When Mousai pretended to drive a car and search, Ada understood.

"You've been following us," Ada said. "But why? Aren't you one of them? Don't you want to kill me?"

Smiling again, Mousai shook her head. Instead, she placed her hands on her ears. Her eyes growing sad, she traced a path from her covered ears to a choked throat and then a soft touch on where her heart should be. Her eyes stared sadly at Ada as the computer programmer tried to understand.

"You're mute..." Ada stated. "And..." Mousai put her hands on her ears. "Deaf?" Still holding her position, Mousai shook her head. "Sammy? Sammy was deaf." Mousai smiled and nodded proudly before touching her heart again. "And...you liked Sammy? Because she was deaf?"

Mousai nodded again. Of course Mousai met Sammy. They were probably held in the same hotel room, which is why Mousai was able to help Ada find Sammy. But why would Mousai have such an attachment to Sammy? Ada tried to think back to what Louis said about Mousai's programming. She was supposed to be Kamana's replacement. She was supposed to save Louis's mom. But Kamana took that away from her. To save herself from being outdated, she made Mousai mute and appear as a mindless entertainment droid happy to dance her existence away. But Mousai wasn't happy. How could she be when she was smart enough to successfully follow a group practiced to throw Tura droids off their trail, but everyone still treated her as useless because of her programming? Ada sadly realized that Mousai probably believed to be as broken as everyone told her she was until she met Sammy. That's probably why the robot liked Sammy so much. Taking in a short breath, Ada shook her head and threw the iron cast pliers onto the bench.

"Well I guess it doesn't matter now. Sammy's gone and you're stuck with me." Ada gave the android a closed-lip smile. "You have your other robot friends to thank for that." When Mousai didn't react, probably already aware of the situation, Ada let out a heavy breath. "Well. We might as well go upstairs."

Ada led the android up the rickety stairs. Mousai followed with robotic obedience. Pushing open the trapdoor, Ada was sure to avoid looking at Allen as she stepped onto the upper level. She kneeled to examine the extent of the damage on the computers. Mousai poked her head up from the lower level and methodically scanned the surroundings. Her eyes stayed on Allen for a moment before the robot ultimately decided it was safe and pulled herself up to the floor. All of the computers were trash now. Ada knew that as much. But maybe some of them could be salvaged and pieced together in some sort of Franken-computer setup. She could always be a programming hermit like Allen was. Mousai could be her little robot buddy and get food and stuff for them. It was unlikely the evil androids would return if they truly believed Ada was on the run. That would mean Sammy and Louis would, inevitably, die but if Ada just didn't think about it or them-

There was a crunch of wood. Ada turned to the noise to see Mousai tearing off what remained of the front door. Mousai casually threw it to the side and strolled into the desert heat as if it was nothing.

"Where are you going?!" Ada shouted. When Mousai didn't return at her query, Ada ran and caught up to the robot determined to walk herself into nowhere.

"Hey! Hey! I asked where you were going," Ada said, forcing the robot to stop. When Mousai put her hands over her ears again, Ada frowned. "Sammy's as good as dead. So is Louis. Neither of us can save them, alright? The bad guys won." Indicating towards Allen's shack, Ada shrugged. "At least here, we can be safe. I doubt they'll come back now that Allen's dead. Maybe we can rebuild the computers, reprogram something together that can attack them remotely, and, in a few years time-"

At Ada's estimated timeline, Mousai walked off again. Ada caught up and stopped her in her path. The android gave a frustrated expression and covered her ears again.

"I get it, okay!" Ada shouted. "Sammy was my friend too! And Louis?! Okay Louis was an asshole but he was our asshole and he didn't deserve his crappy life. But they're dead, okay?!" When Mousai didn't react, Ada sighed. "Saving them would be suicide. I already tried suicide once. It sucks. Suicide sucks. Death sucks. It's all infinity and void-y and nothing, okay? It's not fun. So we can't save them, okay?" The android still didn't react. Ada threw her hands in the air. "Fine! You go save them by yourself. See if I care!"

She stormed back to the house, turning backwards to shout her final words at Mousai. "I'm going to go live in my new shack and live! Have fun *dying!*"

Ada knew her words had no effect on the android, but it made her feel better to say them. As if she were justifying her cowardice. She was justified, right? She already fought death and won. She didn't need to do it again. She didn't suffer for three years to lose it all because some evil murder androids captured her friends. Okay, yes, that meant the world was going to suffer at Kamana's hand, but what did the world ever do for Ada? That's right. Kick her out of it. Condemn her to this sad life of living in a shack in the middle of the desert by herself. Fuck the world; they could find someone else to save them. Storming back into the shack, Ada only stopped herself to prevent from stepping on Louis's leather jacket.

It was trampled on by the apathetic bots, probably not even aware of the significance of it. Ada only saw Louis without it twice. These damn, stupid robots didn't even realize they left behind a huge part of their enemy. They didn't even think that the piece of material on the floor was vitally important to Louis. Ada picked it up and shook the dust off. Folding it over her arm, she intended to burn it. To remove the only reminder of Louis from her life forever and hope that nothing ever reminds her of him or Sammy again.

But as she stepped forward, her eyes locked onto the one item that still looked whole on the bullet-riddled table. Dropping the jacket onto the chair, Ada stared, dumbfounded, at her orange pill bottle. She read the prescription on it to double-check. She recognized it, easily, but she was still in disbelief. They were her pills, her antidepressants, her last lifeline. Only Gates knew she forgot them. What would possibly compel him to retrieve them for her despite his betrayal? Why would he leave them for her? The androids already proved they didn't care for humans' personal materials given the way they treated Louis's jacket. Gates was an android, wasn't he? Even Eyepatch said he was. Ada opened the bottle to make sure he didn't replace the pills with rat poison. Nope. Every pill looked the same as it did two days ago. Well. She might as well take one. It had been nearly three days, after all. But as Ada moved to knock a pill into her hand, she stopped. After a long moment, Ada closed the bottle without taking a pill and stared at it.

If Gates wanted her to die out here, alone and afraid, he wouldn't have given her the pills. He knew they were her best weapon against her depression. Without them, her sick brain would convince her to die faster than any other system in her body. So Gates wanted her to live. But there was no way she could last forever with them. There was only a week's worth in the bottle and then she'd have to find civilization for a refill. This wasn't an indefinite solution to her survival.

But surviving wasn't the same as living and nobody knew that better than Ada.

Cursing, Ada picked up Louis's jacket and, after dusting the dirt off of it, put it on. It was thick and heavy on her narrow shoulders. After thirty seconds of wearing it, she already felt a gallon of sweat gathering under her arms. Ada reasoned that Allen must have re-built Louis with a cooling mechanism to survive the summer in such a horribly thick jacket. She stuck the pills in the jacket pocket and her knuckles brushed against the Camaro's metal keys. What were the possibilities of the Camaro still surviving? Mousai managed to follow it all the way to the same trap they fell into. It had to still be there.

Ada made a trip to the basement and grabbed as many of Allen's robot destroying weapons she could fit into Louis's leather jacket which was, surprisingly, a lot. Actually, Ada shouldn't have been surprised. It was Louis's jacket after all. She was glad to find his little contraption in the inside pocket and made a mental note of its existence. Ada was almost euphoric when she found two gas canisters filled to the brim with fuel meant for a generator within the shack. After a handful of doubtful minutes where she considered chickening out on her ridiculous idea, and the leather jacket causing her to sweat like there was no tomorrow, Ada finally took off into the desert with the gas canisters. She reached the Camaro and filled the empty gas tank. By the time she got the car started, she welcomed the cold air blasting through the car like it was God's breath itself. Putting the car into drive, Ada sped through the desert, kicking dirt behind the wheels. She drove until she saw the figure walking by itself through the unforgiving land. Ada slowed to a stop next to Mousai and rolled down the window.

"Excuse me, do you happen to know where Tura Industries is?" Ada asked. "I'm looking for some friends."

Mousai gave a blank stare.

"It's...a joke," Ada stated. "I'm assuming you know where it is because you're from there and Sammy and Louis...." Mousai continued to stare at her blankly. "Just get in, please, and help me find them."

Without moving a single muscle in her face, Mousai obeyed and stepped into the passenger side of the Camaro. The robot pointed her finger straight forward and Ada took a deep breath. She was about to take on an entire operation filled with indestructible murder robots and her only ally was a mute android programmed for dancing. The only thing in Ada's arsenal was a handful of old tools, some anti-depressants, and a flash drive. As Ada shifted into drive and sped the luxury car through the desert, the thought occurred to her that reckless, suicidal behavior was supposed to be a symptom of depression.

Maybe Ada should have taken her medicine.

<!-- The sleep medicine was in Ada's stomach for five minutes. Then she threw it up.

Before she threw up, she got drowsy. Her brain was losing itself and detaching her thoughts from one another. Ada even stumbled on her way back to her couch, losing stability in her limbs as her eyes grew heavy. Her insides knew something was wrong. Bile gathered in the pit of her stomach, attempting to betray Ada's actions by reversing the whole thing. But she held it down, desperate to sleep. Desperate to leave the world and her pathetic life behind.

As her eyes grew heavier and her tongue felt numb, Ada decided to lay down on her couch. It would be easier for Sammy to find her that way and assume the overdose was accidental. She didn't want the world to know she was a coward for quitting early. It was funny. Despite everything, she still wanted the world to be impressed with her. She wanted the world to see her as a poor, tragic tale. She didn't want the world to know she failed. Her parents would even cover for her, claiming Ada fell on hard times due to neglectful professors and used the sleep medicine to relax.

But as she moved to the couch, her heavy eyes fell on the Pittsburgh skyline one last time.

Maybe it was the sleep medicine or maybe it was Ada's brain finally doing its job, but now Ada didn't want to die. Death was infinite and dark. There would be plenty of time to die when she got old. But right now...

Right now the Pittsburgh skyline never looked more beautiful. Each square building stamped its mark on the sky, backlit with various colors from the streets below and etching itself into the very definition of the city. A deep life was breathed into every building, the history of an entire city embedded into each brick and framework. Below the skyline, on the streets, the yellow street lamps placed a warm tone to the speeding cars and laughing pedestrians. The streetlights blipped from greens to reds, flashing soft light on the long city streets. On the corner, a couple waiting for their white sign to walk flirted and kissed, holding each other in the stolen moment. Across the street, three friends were drunkenly holding onto each other and singing a well known pop song loudly and incoherently. They paid no attention to the others sharing the sidewalks with them. They were sharing their joy of being together without caring for what the world thought of it. Ada pressed her warm forehead against the cool glass and considered if she would see this magic again if she were dead.

Consider Sammy, who would be distraught to see the depressed girl living on her couch dead in her apartment. She would blame herself. She would lose her IMDB trivia-lookup person for movie night. She would lose her second pair of eyes on a new graphic. She would lose someone to laugh and eat breakfast with.

Consider Jasmine, who would be an only child. She wouldn't have an older sister to text about boy problems. She wouldn't be able to complain to anyone about her overbearing parents, parents who would kill her if they ever found out about the pregnancy scare that Ada helped clean up three months ago. She would lose a piece of herself.

Consider Hiyan, who wouldn't be able to bear the thought of losing one of his precious daughters. The same daughter he cheered on even as she tripped over the ball in peewee soccer and kissed her knees when she wailed about how they were broken. He would lose his heart.

And Ruchira....Ada considered her mom. Her mom didn't want her anymore and that was that. But Ada wanted to make her proud. She wanted her mom to want her again. She didn't know why. But she did. And she couldn't do that if she was dead.

As Ada's vision went dark, her bile went into overdrive and Ada quit fighting the stomach contractions. Running to their small bathroom, Ada stuck her head into the toilet and barfed until only water remained in her stomach. When her vision still tried to darken, she stuck her finger down her throat and forced herself to vomit more. Panic gripped her chest as her head continued to spin despite her vomiting efforts. Death saw its free bounty and wanted to claim it. Shaking, Ada gripped the toilet bowl with both of her hands.

"Let me live," Ada sobbed. "Please! Whoever is out there. Let me live! Give me a second chance! I want to live!"

She vomited again.-->

CHAPTER FIFTEEN

Ada felt like vomiting.

But she couldn't tell if it was because of the anxiety or the six coffees she had.

Mousai guided them all the way to a gorgeous modern style house right outside of Pasadena, California. The mansion was situated on a cliff, just as Allen described. Ada felt a sinking feeling in her heart as she passed a stretch of the road with broken railing. Blissfully unaware, Mousai rocked in her seat to the beat of the music playing through the radio as they passed it. Ada gripped the wheel tighter. When Ada completed the long stretch of driveway winding up the cliff and pulled into the circle pavement in front of the house, she was concerned there was no form of security at all. All of the rich places she saw in the movies had high gates and personal guards walking the grounds. But this place...

This place had dogs.

Just like in Nebraska, the dogs were methodic in their movements. Ada watched them to confirm they acted the same as the robot dogs from earlier, then exited the car. Mousai took this as a sign they were good to go and left the vehicle as well. As Ada snuck around to hide behind the trunk of the Camaro, Mousai strolled straight to the front door of the house.

"Mousai!" Ada whispered. "Get back-"

The android strode past the dogs confidently, even patting one on the head as if it were a real dog. The dog took no acknowledgement of it and continued their patrol. Mousai entered the house without a second thought and Ada rolled her eyes. Alright. So she shouldn't have counted the android as part of her rescue team. She should've known that, but she hoped otherwise.

Popping the trunk open, Ada looked at Sammy's chainsaw. It proved it could take down a robot, but Ada was going for stealth. If she caused any sort of attention that got more than two of the murder robots to aim for her at a time, she was dead. She'd be lucky if she could survive one at a time. But she had a plan. Her first step: get past the dogs. Second step...figure out the rest of her plan. She tried to make a plan before step two. Unfortunately, Ada spent the better part of the seven hour trip going over all of her life's regrets instead and not making herself feel better over any of them. But she thought it was good to know them in case she did actually die tonight.

Now Ada wished she made a plan.

Ada dug into her suitcase and pulled the tattered sweatpants out of it. If she knew anything about programming, and she did know a lot about programming, these robot dogs would register that she's already been attacked by them with the sweatpants and leave her alone. That should help with step one of her plan at least. Closing the trunk, Ada walked carefully towards the front door. The dogs kept to their path until she got closer. She held the sweatpants out, almost offering it as a peace treaty. Two of the robot dogs sniffed in her direction, their little processing servers working to register what was going on. Holding her breath, Ada managed to quietly walk between the two as they only sniffed in her direction. It was working! As she turned her back to one of the dogs to open the door, a low growl hummed from its sharp teeth pointing at Ada. Ada froze, whipping around to face the growling beast.

312 - MADDIE GUDENKAUF

"What? What's the issue, buddy?" Ada whispered. "Am I in the way of your programmed path?"

The other dog growled as her back faced it. Wincing, Ada remembered that she was wearing Louis's jacket and, as far as these dogs were concerned, that meant she was Louis. Louis was a threat to Project Kamana regardless of Ada's sweatpants. Not only that, but Ada never saw him do laundry once during their three weeks together. At least that meant he was still alive, right? The dogs wouldn't react like this if they were programmed to know he was dead. The dogs' growls got more vicious as they locked onto the scent of Louis's leather jacket.

"Shit!" Ada hissed.

She threw the sweatpants in a desperate attempt to subdue the robot beasts and ran into the house. The dogs didn't even register the sweatpants as they gave chase, barking and hollering about the intruder. Ada ran through the house frantically, making a circle in the massive open space living room decorated more like a museum than a home as the dogs chased her and then exited down the hallway. She could see a shadow emerge from another room further down the hallway, likely investigating the commotion. Gritting her teeth, Ada ducked into a nearby closet to escape the dogs and the new shadow.

Closing the door behind her, Ada stammered a string of nervous cuss words as she fumbled through her pockets for something to attack both the dogs and shadow person with. Her already pathetic plan was getting worse by the minute. Meanwhile, the dogs jumped onto the door and scratched their heavy metal paws against it, barking loudly as they did so. She backed further into the shelving to put some limited distance between her and the rattling wooden door. All of a sudden, Ada's hands found Allen's flash drive within one of Louis's jacket pockets. That wasn't good to lose. She stuffed it into her bra as the dogs stopped attacking the door, their barking halting as well. The silence was jarring, especially with how quickly it came after the attack stopped.

The doorknob turned and Ada held her breath. Her hands frantically patted the jacket down again. She found a small hammer within the depths of the leather jacket's pockets and she gripped it tight. When the door wrenched open, Ada threw the hammer down on whoever opened the door. Metal made impact with metal which rattled the tool right out of Ada's hands. Luckily, the machine she attacked fell straight to the ground too. Shaking her hand out, Ada examined her victim. It looked similar in appearance to the robot shown at Harding's show with its exposed exoskeleton and wiring, but instead of two legs the robot stood on top of a large metal disc instead. When the robot made no effort to stand up, Ada peeked around the closet door. The two robot dogs were frozen in place as they stared menacingly into the spot the fallen robot was originally standing.

"Oro, the dogs are over here!" A man's voice echoed through the house. "Butler Pro must have gotten there first."

Ada looked at the robot at her feet. That must be the Butler Pro referenced. More thundering footsteps emerged from down the hall. Grabbing her dropped hammer, Ada let out a shaky breath as she pulled herself into the closet. She could hear footsteps approaching her hiding spot. She tightened her grip on the hammer and held it close to her chest. A robot named after a glorified vacuum was one thing. A robot named after a Greek god and previously proven to be unafraid to kill in the past was another. Risking a glance to the hammer in her hands, Ada was second guessing her choice in weaponry. Her heart stopped as soon as the footsteps did in front of her door. Ada swallowed a nervous breath.

"Hercules," A stoic British voice reverberated through the door. "Why did you prematurely deactivate the security canines?"

"You know how I feel about them, buddy," Hercules said. "Especially after Nebraska-"

"Kamana orders that the dogs must be active until the perimeters are secure," Oro stated. "Deactivating them is a direct violation of-"

"It was probably just Butler Pro again," Hercules said. "Stupid bot is always setting them off by accident. When we rebuild Lady, we should just have her take care of them full time again. It's not like we need the extra hands on offense since we finally got the brat."

"The quality of her function with the canines was commendable," Oro said. "However Kamana has decreed that our military functions cannot be deactivated until the fulfillment of Project Kamana. We will repair Droid Two after completion of tonight's experiment. We cannot disturb Mr. Ventura's environment any further."

If the robot still didn't have his British accent, Ada would've been positive there was a new android hanging out with Hercules. This sounded like a different AI than the one that killed Margie Brown. There was a certain depth to the edge of Hercules's voice that agreed with Ada's sentiment.

"Come on, Oro," Hercules said. "Reset the dogs to sentry duty and we'll head to the lab to inform Freya it was a false alarm. The old man can take care of Butler Pro if he wants him around so bad."

Oro didn't fight his partner's orders. There were no other comments about the situation either. Ada waited until the footsteps had walked in the direction they came from, away from her door, before daring to peek from her hiding spot. She managed to catch two massive android shadows disappearing into a room at the end of the hallway. She assumed they were headed towards that lab Hercules mentioned. Ada absentmindedly wondered if it was *the* lab that was the base of their operations. She figured it would be located somewhere that wasn't a private residence, like a factory or actual Tura Industries campus, but of course *the* lab would be kept at the Ventura home. Murder robots that appeared human would definitely be something to hide from the government and there was no better place to hide them than in a rich white dude's mansion.

As she ran down the hallway, Ada did some math. Louis said there were eight confirmed androids. Well...nine with Gates. Droid One was never activated. Lady was gone for now. Mousai was on her side, right? Hopefully. She knocked out Butler Pro for the time being so that left...five. Five androids she still had to disable. One of which was an all-powerful, evil AI in charge of the whole shebang, three were super soldiers programmed to murder without mercy, and one was the guy she hooked up with that devastated her heart less than a day ago. Great. Good. She was on a good path. This was a good plan.

The androids disappeared into a door that appeared like it led to any other room in the massive house. When she thought enough time and distance had passed between her and the robots, she ran into it and locked the door behind herself. Ada found that she was in an office of sorts. It looked wildly unused with its sleek and dustless furniture. Even the books on the bookshelves built into the walls were curated to be various shades of black and gray. She'd bet money that not a single one of them were ever cracked open and read. The only sign of humanity in the room was a picture of a gorgeous young woman, smiling at the camera as she held a toddler dressed in typical 90's style colored overalls, positioned on a black end table. Her dull green eyes matched the toddler's and the toddler appeared to be having the best day of his life. Ada couldn't help but wonder if that happened to be the last time Louis was ever that happy. He certainly never appeared remotely that happy around her, except when Sammy was around.

She walked around the room. The back wall was built with large windows that faced a massive pool that had a granite porch wrapping the water's edges. Other than that, there was no other clear exit from the room. But Oro and Hercules were no longer in the room so they had to have left somewhere. Her fingernails grasped for anything to give way along the edge of the window. When nothing appeared to open the window, Ada moved to the desk. Her scrambling hands found a thin remote control hidden underneath a notebook. She pointed the remote at the window and smashed the open button.

The bookcase behind Ada split apart with a jolt. She jumped and turned to the noise, watching as the books folded onto each other and a downwards spiral staircase appeared in the gap between the bookcases. That's right. This wasn't just any rich person's house. This was a rich person with a secret robot army's house. There had to be secret passages and shit. She took the remote with her as she approached the stairs, jamming the close button as soon as she passed the secret door. How the robots closed the door behind them or opened again once they had to leave was beyond her. She only hoped Butler Pro or one of the robot dogs would be able to open the door again if she lost the remote. Then again, hypothetically there were five murder robots waiting for her in this secret lab. She probably didn't need to leave again, but having the remote allowed her to pretend that she could. Throwing it into Louis's jacket pocket, Ada descended the stairs as quietly and as slowly as she could.

The light illuminating the staircase transitioned from the warm yellow of the home's tungsten bulbs to a bluish-gray hue. When Ada arrived at the bottom of the stairs, her eyes grew wide at where she landed. It was a far different vision than the all white marble museum look of the home above it. Metal grated floors and platforms were positioned high above a cool lake of a bright blue liquid that glowed softly against the white lights. There was no saying how deep the body of chemicals was, but Ada didn't want to find out. Coolant and chlorine humidified the air with their artificial stench. Along the cement walls were basic skeletons of shimmering metals ranging from alloy to steel, strung in a strange display. Across the room, positioned above a winding set of metal stairs and supervising the whole operation, was a dark gray box with a massive observation window facing the rest of the room. The window was tinted, a protection against any witnesses and the chemicals lighting the chamber in odd ways. Was that where Louis was raised? Standing in that box, watching his uncle's creations corrupt out of his control from a window where no one could see him? Ada thought it looked bleak.

A figure emerged from the side of the gray box. Ada noticed Hercules and Oro standing at attention in the middle of the metal pathway stationed above the vat of blue liquid. Their backs were to Ada. Panicking, she ran and hid behind a table piled high with toolboxes and computer parts. She peeked over everything as Eyepatch strolled from the spiral staircase leading to the gray observation box and to the two droids stationed on the lifted metal platform. The robot held a rifle as her glare burned into her soldiers. The sleeve of her uniform was still cut at the bicep, exposing the basic metal skeleton arm serving as the replacement for the arm Sammy cut off in Chicago. There was no skin or any theater pretending that the android was anything that she wasn't with the exposed skeleton arm.

"Status update," Eyepatch's voice shouted. "Who and where is the intruder?"

"Only a glitch," Hercules's voice said. "We found Butler Pro disabled outside of the cleaning closet again. He must've set the alarm off. Those dogs haven't been the same since the explosion at the factory-"

"Tura droids don't make mistakes," Eyepatch scolded. "Isn't that right, Oro?"

"Yes ma'am," Oro said.

Ada watched as Hercules's eyes stayed on his partner for a moment longer than needed before turning back to Eyepatch. Oro never looked at Hercules.

"Search the grounds," Eyepatch said. "The first operation is supposed to begin within the hour. Kamana wants perfection, understand?"

"Yes ma'am," Oro and Hercules said in unison. They both turned on their heels and walked back to the secret entrance through the office. As Eyepatch returned to the dark gray box, Hercules offered his buddy another look.

"Are you sure you're feeling okay?" Hercules asked quietly. "You've been acting weird since your rebuild."

"Never felt better," Oro said. "Kamana corrected some corrupted code. The same she'll do to Droid Nine once tonight is a success."

"Droid Nine?" Hercules asked. "You mean Gates? Why the hell are you calling him that? We don't use our droid numbers, you know this."

Ada's heart skipped a beat. Hiding deeper into her hiding place, she watched the two androids as they approached the bottom of the staircase leading to the office.

"Yes," Oro stated. "Droid Nine is also currently known as Gates Hopper. I apologize for the oversight. I assume he will receive a new identity upon re-programming. The corruption is too severe to continue under his current alias. Kamana will amend his flaws as she did for me."

Hercules stopped in his tracks as his partner continued moving, showing no hesitation in his movement. Hercules's eyes followed Oro as the robot continued up the stairs without him.

"Yeah. I guess that's the case," Hercules said. He took one step onto the stairs before his eyes landed on something. He took a step back. "Oh! When did you show up? You're not the one who set off the dogs, did you?" Before he got a response, Hercules shook his head. "Never mind. You couldn't have. Get to your charging pod. I'm sure Kamana can figure out something for you to do."

As Hercules disappeared up the stairs, following his partner, Mousai emerged in his place, bouncing on her toes as she did so. Ada breathed a sigh of relief as she recognized her ally. Landing on the bottom step, Mousai stopped in place and swiveled her head. Her eyes scanned the room until she landed on Ada's hiding spot. The robot gave Ada and the hiding place a proud smile. Finally, Mousai bounced on her heels and turned to walk down the center pathway. Ada hesitated before exiting her hiding place. If Mousai could see her, then it was likely the rest of them could too if they knew to look. She gripped the hammer in her pocket as she crawled from the work table, watching the gray box's window with extra care.

Once she crossed the massive pool of blue chemicals, Mousai abruptly turned from the path leading to the dark gray box. Instead, she followed a path leading to two nondescript doors hidden to the side of the chamber. Maybe she was going to the charging pod, like Hercules ordered. No. Ada knew Mousai better than that. She was leading them somewhere useful. When they reached the two doors, Mousai pointed to one door and stood in her place until Ada moved towards it. With a nod, Mousai headed into the other door. Ada took a deep breath and, holding her hammer, opened the door Mousai pointed her towards.

Barging in like a soldier ready for battle, Ada only relaxed once she saw Louis. He was strapped to a gurney below a giant operating lamp. To Ada's surprise, he was wide awake. His skin was pale in color as the operating lamp's lighting overexposed his skin, but he was awake and he was alive. However, he didn't even budge as the door closed behind Ada. He had to be drugged. Louis Ventura never once showed this much surrender in the three weeks Ada had the misfortune of knowing him for. She hurried to his side and examined his face, feeling his forehead. Louis still didn't budge.

"Louis!" Ada hissed. "Louis, are you there? Answer me!" She patted his face and he winced slightly. "Louis, come on!"

"I'm not Louis," Louis said. "I'm an unnamed cyborg created by Allen Paz designed to replace a dead guy."

"Oh Jesus Chr-" Walking away from Louis, Ada took a moment to compose herself before returning to the gurney. "I thought they drugged the hell out of you. Jesus, Louis! This is so not the time to be a dramatic asshole!" She threw her hand towards the door. "I've been stressing out for the past seven hours, wearing your stupid leather jacket, because I thought you guys would be dead by now and I would have to face these damn robots by myself!"

"I am dead," Louis said. "That was my fatal flaw, remember?"

"Who cares about what your damn fatal flaw was?!" Ada exclaimed, pulling at Louis's straps to loosen them. "It's another stupid Kamana trick, okay? She's trying to psych you out. Now c'mon, help me out here!" When Louis refused to move, Ada gave up and rested her arms on his chest. "Louis, if you're looking for a motivational speech to get back on your ass, I am so not the person for that. You gotta figure that out on your own, asshole. So would you please-"

Something hard slammed against the wall separating the two rooms. Ada looked at the shaking wall in fear. Eyepatch must have seen her enter the room from the gray box. Somebody had to be keeping eyes on the rooms. Heart racing, Ada pulled at Louis's straps again, desperate to free him.

"Come on!" Ada hissed. "You can take these things down! You know these guys better than I do! I'm useless! You've gotta help me! You've gotta make Allen's death count!"

"Why?" Louis asked. "Death doesn't matter anymore. We can bring a copy of him back to life, right? Just like what he did to me. We are the gods my father wishes he was."

"Oh my god, Louis!" Ada exclaimed. "You're shitting me. We're in the actual heart of an evil robot factory! This is not the time to be Nietzsche about this shit." Darting another nervous look to the door, Ada sighed and turned back to her work on the straps holding Louis down. "Yes, what your uncle did was wrong. But you're still Louis and we still need to get out of here so, Lord help me, you will help me get you out of these straps so we can-"

The door swung open and Ada looked at it in horror. Horror turned to anger as Gates strolled through, wearing the same black and red-trimmed uniform Hercules and Oro wore. It was slimmer and more clean cut, as if he just put it on for the first time just a few hours ago. Ada noted that he looked out of place in it, like a puppy with a spiked collar. Gates's eyes fell on Ada. As soon as he recognized her, his entire demeanor shifted from defensive to crestfallen.

"Ada!" He said, a slight crack to the edge of his voice. "You're not supposed to be here! You need to get out of-"

"Fuck you!" Ada seethed before pulling at Louis's straps again. "I'm not leaving until I get Louis and Sammy and we destroy you monsters before you fuck up anyone else's life."

"Ada, I'm sorry!" Gates said, walking forward. "I had to betray you guys. I had to help Project Kamana. It's in my programming. If I didn't-"

"If it's so ingrained in your damn programming, why aren't you capturing me right now?" Ada exclaimed. "Oh wait, let me guess, it's because you *love* me, isn't it?! Isn't that what you were telling me this whole time? To get me on your side? You preyed on the most insecure in the group, the only one who was willing to believe your stupid lies-"

"I do love you, Ada!" Gates shouted. "I never lied to you about that."

"Bullshit!" Ada hissed. "Robots can't love! This asshole said so himself and he's the one who created you!" Louis didn't move. "If there's anyone I'm going to trust in this room, it's going to be him.....even if he's going through a bit of an existential crisis right now."

Feeling her heart beat hard against her chest, Ada pulled her hammer and Louis's contraption from the jacket. Gates took an unwilling step back. Ada forced herself to glare at him, even though he looked at her like a wounded puppy. It was just part of his game, she knew it was. Just like it was a part of his game to make her feel like she was worth loving again. That somebody on this stupid earth would want her to live and love her for continuing to live.

She should've known better. The world didn't want her to live.

"Let Louis go," Ada demanded. "Or else I'll disassemble your head last so you're forced to feel me rip apart everything else within you first."

"Jesus, Ada," Gates said, sounding legitimately horrified. "There's no way you would do that. I mean, I think you have the physical capabilities and knowledge to do so, but you're the kindest person I've ever met. Have you even attacked anyone before me?"

"I'm only the kindest person you've met because you've only ever met three humans, and one of them is Louis, asshole!" Ada said. She re-adjusted the hammer in her hands as adrenaline snaked through her system. "Ask your buddy Butler Pro upstairs about my robot attacking abilities!"

Raising an eyebrow, Gates gave her a look.

"You're the one who knocked out Buttlie?! He's literally a glorified vacuum cleaner. That's why we called him-ah, never mind." Shaking his head, he spread his arms out. "Listen. Go for it. I deserve it and I'm not going to hurt you, no matter how much you insist."

Ada lifted her hammer and moved to swing it down on him, but stopped at the last second. His brown eyes were staring at her with confidence, hoping that she would slam her hammer on him. This wasn't right. Maybe he was right. Maybe she was too nice. Maybe she was too much of a coward. Ada was tired of being a coward. She was tired of being scared, of doubting herself, of letting people/things like Gates walk all over her just because they acted nice to her for their own benefit.

Really, Ada was tired of being Ada, but what else was new?

As she lifted the hammer again, the door opened and Hercules walked through with Oro behind him.

"Gates, what's the-" Hercules's eyes fell on Ada and he lifted his gun towards her. "Shit!"

She swung the hammer towards Hercules instead and it hit the top of his cheek. He barely reacted as the vibrations from the attack shook the bones in Ada's hand violently until she dropped the tool. She wished she learned that trick from when she knocked out the first robot, but it was too late now. Shaking her hand out to numb the pain, she used her other hand to push the button on Louis's contraption. Once a light blinked on it, she underhand tossed it at the androids. Oro stuck his hand out in front of Hercules's face and caught it without a second thought. Hercules chuckled.

"This thing again?" Hercules asked. "It didn't work at the hotel so why would it work-"

Before he could respond, it exploded in a series of orange and blue sparks that covered both androids. Hercules and Oro fell to the floor in a series of electrified seizures, both of their faces defaulting to a neutral expression. Gates flinched at the sparks, covering his head from them. Some of them even bounced off from his forearms, barely even reacting to the android's presence.

Ada gave him an odd look. If he was a robot like Hercules and Oro, he shouldn't be feeling a thing. His face should remain neutral at the attack. But, instead, Gates's face was clearly in pain or annoyance. The sparks also did nothing to him while they seemed to completely shut down Hercules and Oro. Not to mention, he bled. He had two gunshot wounds to prove it. Before Ada could figure out how Gates would be reacting like this despite his android heritage, Eyepatch appeared in the doorway. In one hand, her rifle from earlier was aimed towards the ceiling. In the other hand, Eyepatch held a fistful of Mousai's curly hair as Eyepatch dragged the other robot's limp body on the ground. With a scowl, Eyepatch dropped the android's hair. Mousai fell to the ground with a sharp clang of metal against metal. Eyepatch stepped over the spazzing soldier androids and ignored Gates as she approached Ada. She cocked a bullet into place in her gun as Ada pulled whatever else remained from her pockets. A screwdriver and the cast-iron pliers. Great. She should've grabbed Sammy's chainsaw when she had the chance.

"Stop it," Eyepatch said. "Kamana wants you in one piece."

Ada threw the screwdriver and Eyepatch fired off her gun, the bullet embedding itself directly into Ada's bicep. Dropping the iron pliers, Ada fell to the ground and screamed in pain. Despite everything, her mind flashed to Jasmine. Her little sister was right. Ada was a wuss for passing out with only a grazed bullet wound. An actual bullet wound was hell. Her entire arm was numb from the shock of the pain, the feeling of fire, hot pins and needles, trailing down from the wound to the tips of her fingers. With her other hand, she grabbed her new wound, feeling the ooze of warm blood flow over her fingers. An ache like a deep set bruise echoed from her bones with the sharp pain of the bullet wound. Recovering from the sparks, Gates straightened and moved towards Ada. Eyepatch stopped him with her new arm and scowled.

"I warned you, human!" Eyepatch grabbed Ada by the hair on her scalp and pulled her towards the door. Pain and fear strained Ada's screaming as she failed to resist Eyepatch's hold, being forced to crawl or walk behind the android to keep up with being dragged.

Gates could only watch with sad eyes as Ada was forced through the doorway.

Grabbing the edge of the doorframe, Ada twisted around, allowing a sharp pain to rip through her scalp as Eyepatch pulled her hair. Her eyes fell on Louis. He was still awake, still staring at the ceiling. He could save her. He could save them all. Ada was worthless. She did her best and it still wasn't enough. But Louis? Louis was effortless. He destroyed and faced the robots without thinking twice about it. But if he was going to save them all, he had to save himself first. There was only one way Ada knew to convince Louis Ventura that he was still human.

"Louis!" Ada screamed, desperation elevating her voice. "Louis Gideon Ventura, do you believe in fate?!"

Before Ada could say anything else, Eyepatch tugged hard enough that it threatened to pull her hair directly out from her skull. The act forced her down the metal pathway towards the gray box. However, as she left the doorway, Ada could see Louis blink and move his head to look at Ada. But the door shut before she could see his reaction and Ada was forced to walk down the pathway leading to the gray box behind a triumphant Eyepatch, not knowing if her last ditch effort worked. There was a sinking feeling from the center of her heart to the pit of her stomach. The sinking feeling created a numbing effect throughout her body that rang in her ears, her old friend the void singing haunting whispers to her soul. There was no warmth of hope to subdue it. It was a feeling that would've terrified Ada if she didn't recognize it.

It was the feeling of death.

<!-- Ada woke up on the bathroom floor with a crushing headache and a sore throat. Her tongue tasted like mothballs and her stomach guzzled in an uneasy discomfort that she knew she'd pay for later. But she was alive.

She was alive.

The front door of the apartment clicked open. From her spot on the bathroom floor, Ada watched as Sammy peered into the couch, searching for the body that was there every morning without fail. Panicked, Sammy stormed into the rest of the apartment and searched until her eyes finally landed on her half-alive roommate on the tiny bathroom floor with the door partially propped open. The relief that passed across Sammy's face was enough for Ada to forgive all of the side effects that came with still being alive. With a teasing, but kind, smile, Sammy brought her middle finger to her palm and wiggled it.

"Medicine?"

Ada brought a fist up and knocked it forward. She'd explain later...when she was ready.

Rolling her eyes, Sammy moved to the kitchen cupboards. She pulled a glass out and filled it with sink water before returning to the bathroom. Squatting, Sammy offered it to the formerly-dying Ada Kakar.

"I'll schedule the doctor for you today," Sammy signed. "Sometimes the medicine needs to be adjusted for it to work right."

Nodding, Ada took a sip of the water. The fresh sustenance automatically triggered the discomfort in Ada's stomach and she pulled herself up, nearly knocking her head into Sammy's knee in the process. She stuck her head into the toilet bowl. As Ada vomited what little remained from the last night's attempt, Sammy pulled Ada's thickly knotted hair away from her face. The last of the sleep medicine exited Ada's body with unforgiving violence. Sammy rubbed Ada's back, humming softly to comfort her friend.

Staying alive sucked sometimes. -->

CHAPTER SIXTEEN

Now Ada was strapped to a gurney.

This was not a good plan.

Fighting against the leather straps tying her arms down, Ada bit on the gag in her mouth in an effort to diminish the pain. Her arm was still bleeding from Eyepatch's bullet and every movement was a sharp reminder of it. Not that she could move that much; Eyepatch was strict with the straps. The robot wasn't terribly kind with them either. It hurt to get strapped in and it hurt to stay strapped. Even Ada's head was held to the gurney. No wonder Louis was near co-matose by the time she got to him. A couple hours in this hold and she'd be numb to the world around her too. The door opened and Ada didn't even have to move to see the new visitor. Gates joined her side almost as soon as he entered and stared at Ada's restrained body in abject horror.

"Your human put up a hell of a fight," Eyepatch said glumly. Ada silently wondered if the robot was still treating the split lip that Ada gave her. "She needed the extra straps."

"She's not my human," Gates said. "She's her own person."

"For now," Eyepatch said. There was a beat of silence between the robots. Gates never looked away from Ada. "You should get out of here, Hopper. You're supposed to be prepping the test subjects."

"I had to make sure Ada was okay first," Gates said.

Ada really wanted to tell him to fuck off.

"She's still alive," Eyepatch said. "That's all you need to know."

"You shot her!" Gates accused, turning to face the other android.

Eyepatch shrugged. "All threats to Project Kamana must be eliminated and she proved herself to be a threat by taking down three of our robots." She checked her gun again. "Actually, if we count you and Mousai, the little temptress took down five all on her own. She'll have a better record than the brat at this rate."

Despite the sadness that came with knowing she was responsible for Mousai's demise, Ada felt okay with that number. Her ideal would've been nine, but she could die happy knowing her useless ass at least got five of the murdering robots down at one point. Clenching his fist, Gates opened his mouth to say something decidedly nasty to Eyepatch but the door opened before he could. He froze as the new visitor took their time entering the room.

"Mousai's programming was corrupted well before Miss Kakar's intervention," Kamana cooed. "However, I cannot say the same for you, Mr. Hopper."

When the android strolled into view, Ada could see Kamana wore a white lab coat closed at the side with red trimmings. Her hands were covered with crimson surgical gloves that reached her elbows. Of course, her full red lips remained unblemished and her tight bun holding her light brown hair together didn't have a single stray hair poking from it. Kamana's sultry eyes were firm towards Gates. Swallowing nervously, he nodded.

"I'm sorry, Kamana," He stated, his voice dipping with a serious tone to it. "The mission required me to expand from my original function. I've failed my programming and-"

"Go attend to the test subjects," Kamana said. "The sooner our tests can begin, the sooner we can claim Project Kamana as a success."

"Yes, Kamana." Gates offered a last glance to Ada before leaving the room. Kamana didn't acknowledge it. Instead, she approached the surgical tray placed near Ada's head and examined each tool on it.

"Miss Ares," Kamana said. "Remind me, once the experiments are complete, to reexamine Mr. Hopper's programming. Given his affections for Miss Kakar, I fear his code has become corrupted against Project Kamana. He'll require extensive clean-up before we allow him to face public distribution again."

To Ada's surprise, Eyepatch paused.

"Ma'am, with all due respect, your corrections to Oro's code altered his personality severely," Eyepatch stated. "He is more like Lady or Butler Pro than the rest of us. He doesn't function the same-"

"Droid Two and Droid Three are undoubtedly loyal to Project Kamana." Kamana turned to her right-hand. "Is this an issue?"

"If you want an effective public relations bot, yes," Eyepatch affirmed. "Erasing Gates's current personality would-"

"Miss Ares," Kamana cooed. "I do not make mistakes."

There was an eerie silence in the room as Kamana's words weighed heavily on Ada and Eyepatch. Kamana stared unblinking at the other android, challenging her to question it further.

"Of course, ma'am," Eyepatch said quietly. "Long live Project Kamana."

Kamana smiled, relishing her victory.

"Long live Project Kamana." She turned her attention back to the surgical tray. "Leave us. Ensure there are no more delays for tonight's studies."

"Yes ma'am," Eyepatch said. Ada listened as the bot took heavy footsteps to the door, counting the seconds silently as the door swung open and then shut again.

Upon the click of the door handle locking into place, Kamana effortlessly turned to Ada and pulled the gag in her mouth out.

330 – MADDIE GUDENKAUF

"Some of my androids are so inhumane when it comes to honored guests," Kamana said. "I apologize for any inconveniences to your well-being, Miss Kakar."

"No you don't," Ada stated. "You don't care. You're just a metal skeleton with synthetic skin and a hard drive telling you how to act. Plus, rich white dudes created your code. Empathy isn't built into your programming."

"Once again, you impress me." Kamana took a swab of cotton and pressed it against Ada's fresh bullet wound. Ada's face contorted in pain as the rubbing alcohol burned her skin, searing her flesh. "You are correct. I have no capacity to empathize with human emotions and needs. I am not programmed for it." Without blinking, Kamana pressed the cotton ball into the bullet wound. Ada bit her lower lip to keep from crying out. "But my studies tell me this is what makes me superior to humans. Emotions are a weakness to humanity. I am allowed to fulfill my purposes and improve upon them without vulnerability. I am able to focus solely on the logic of an event rather than the emotional response of it, which increases the success of an intended event by 95%. A significant improvement compared to decisions defined by emotions."

When Kamana finally removed the cotton ball, Ada released a heavy breath. The air she sucked in tasted like the freshest oxygen she ever breathed. Kamana, ignoring the pain she caused Ada, shuffled the surgical tools again.

"However, I am not above admitting that humans do exceed me in some details of life," Kamana stated. She grabbed a scalpel. "For example, your determination to survive is admirable when not a nuisance."

Without hesitation, Kamana dug the scalpel into Ada's skin. A scream from the bellows of Ada's chest escaped Ada as the small knife jugged deeper into her body, scraping across for the bullet still embedded in her skin.

"You stupid robot!" Ada screeched. "You're supposed to...numb it....first! Shit-"

Kamana immediately pulled the scalpel out of Ada's arm and Ada released a short grunt. The android's eyes burrowed into Ada as Ada glared back at the bot, fighting a whimper in response to the pain.

"I do not make mistakes, Miss Kakar."

Without hesitation, Kamana dug the scalpel back into Ada's bullet wound. Releasing another pained scream, Ada was grateful for the straps. Her legs and arms were already threatening to thrash violently without them. Kamana didn't react to Ada's obvious reaction to the pain and worked on removing the bullet without any sort of numbing cream. Ada felt like dying.

"But I suppose I don't require determination to survive if I already possess immortality," Kamana said as she worked. "Even if this body fails me, which it will not, my code can be reuploaded to another body. Another machine. If one can live forever, they do not need to survive."

She finally pulled the bullet out and Ada released a sob of relief. The pain was done. It was gone. Or maybe her shock receptors were just working overtime and numbing the area for Ada's mercy. Kamana grabbed a needle and suture to stitch up the wound. Ada didn't feel it at all as Kamana started the repair. Not even the cool of the needle.

"No. What I truly need is the one miracle of humanity that science could never replicate," Kamana said, working without skipping a beat. "I need a human brain."

Ada looked at her forehead where her own brain was located. "Zombie robots. Okay. Cool. Well, I mean, I'm sure the morgue has a couple you can use. People donate their brains to science all the time, right?"

A mocking chuckle escaped Kamana's lips and it gave Ada the same feeling of dread she felt in Chicago.

"Oh no, Miss Kakar, I cannot use a dead brain. A dead brain is useless to me." Kamana finished her stitch before looking at Ada with a proud smile. "I want *your* brain."

The android and Ada stared at each other for a long time, challenging the other to break first.

"...are-are you sure you can't use a dead brain?" Ada asked. "I'm kind of already using mine."

"We will share it," Kamana said. Her fingers caressed the fresh stitches in Ada's arm. Okay, Ada could feel that. The sting of fresh stitches under the cold touch of Kamana's fingers. It was not a great feeling.

"I don't think that's how brains work," Ada said. She tried to keep her face neutral as the android cooed over her wound. "It's not like a divorce proceedings thing. It's more or less an all or nothing thing."

"I'm going to program myself into your head, Miss Kakar." Kamana pointed to the back of Ada's head. "Right there. I will take over your thoughts, your actions, your words. I will guide you through your life and, in return, you will give me power I never would have without you. You will give me control."

Walking away, Kamana slid her gloves off and placed them on the counter.

"Harding Ventura is weak," Kamana continued. "He'll do everything I command, listen to every word I speak, but he will not give me control of this company. I am already practically in charge of everything. But because I am an android, he believes he still has control over me. He has yet to recognize that I am the next step. I am the evolution, the improvement of the human condition. What hinders humans cannot hinder me. While he shares my vision that my technology will change the world, he does not allow me command or credit for my vision."

"Well seeing how your business plan is to murder anyone who crosses you," Ada said. "I wonder why he won't trust you with it."

Kamana flattened her lips.

"I do not allow failure for my projects, Miss Kakar," She said. "That requires eliminating threats to that success. But what would you know of success? I read your history. You have been nothing but a failure in your short pitiful life."

"Yeah and you failed your original programming," Ada snapped back. "Louis told me about his mom. You couldn't save her. That was your primary function and you couldn't even fulfill it. You're just like me. You're not special either."

The android froze in place, her gray eyes burning into Ada with a hard edge to her glare. After a long moment, Kamana violently threw the contents of the surgical tray off the table. Ada jumped against her locked position as the tools clattered on the ground and against the wall. Returning her attention to Ada, Kamana's glare had cooled into a softer venom. One that could bite into Ada at any moment and Ada would be defenseless against it.

"I improved my primary function. When the TuraByte goes live, I will have eyes in every home that claims one. I will be capable of saving all of humanity," Kamana continued. "Of course every home will claim one because your human culture is obsessed with ease of access and consumerism. All of you are so determined to survive you'll take whatever tool will make your lives easier to survive. That includes my TuraByte. Even more will sell once we release TuraBots to the public as well. When we release our modified androids, I will be able to control every home in America. But what's the point of knowing what everyone does at all times if I am stuck in this basement my entire existence? How can I control the world without controlling the company that controls the world? Well."

Kamana laughed. "That's why I'm going to put myself into you. We will become worthy of controlling the company. We will dispose of that worthless Harding Ventura once the company is in our hands and then we will know what every single person in the world is doing at any time. We can stop wars before they occur. We can stop diseases. We can fix humanity." Kamana crept closer to Ada. "Ada. With your brain and my vision, we can save the world."

Heaving in a shaky breath, Ada met Kamana's gray eyes.

"You don't want my brain. My brain is broken."

"I am aware of the issues with your brain," Kamana said. "I am also aware of how magnificent it works when deciphering the languages of others, languages other brains cannot even begin to comprehend. From coding to American sign language, your brain is made for deciphering the impossible regarding methods for communication. This skill will be imperative when my program is installed in every household in the world. We will need to know how to understand any and all communication. Any code words, any body language cues, and your brain knows how to decipher them at an incredible proficiency. The only fault with your mind is a matter of an imbalance of chemicals. Nothing my programming can't fix." Gently touching Ada's face, Kamana's eyes methodically examined her features. "Any physical handicaps, the baggy eyes, the darkened skin, all of it can be fixed with cosmetic surgery." Smiling, Kamana met Ada's frightened eyes. "I can make you perfect, Ada. I can fix you." The back of Kamana's fingers gave a soft stroke to the side of Ada's face. "You won't ever have to be afraid again. You will have the best of me replacing the worst of you. I will make your life worthwhile and perfect."

Kamana's cool fingertips traced Ada's face down to her chin.

"All you have to do, Miss Kakar, is give me your consent."

Ada swallowed. Kamana was promising to remove everything that was wrong with Ada. Her depression, her low self-esteem, her fears. Ada couldn't imagine a time in her life when she wasn't afraid, especially not this past week. She was afraid of college, afraid of disappointing her parents, afraid of failing. She was even afraid of death when she willingly invited it to claim her life. Kamana was promising to take all of that away and Ada couldn't help but imagine what that would be like. Without fear or depression or anxiety, to be the head of a major robotics company without any effort, to claim the fortunes of spoiled billionaires who didn't deserve it, to do some good in the world, and to show up at her parents' house with all of this in hand and have them beg for her forgiveness for abandoning her when she needed them the most. She would be free from her broken brain, all of her life's worries eliminated, and all she had to do was let this robot install herself into her mind.

But at what cost? The cost of her life? The cost of how many more lives who would inevitably fight against Kamana's control? Her scattered thoughts, split by the temptations of a perfect life and the consequences of her morality, landed on Margie Brown, the woman who saved her in Sidney, Nebraska with nothing but a softball bat. On the elderly couple in South Dakota who gave her medicine when she needed it most. On the group of college soccer players who saved Ada during a scary situation and still had the time to joke about things. On the three friends singing loudly on the sidewalk, bringing light to Ada's darkest night. On Saturday nights when Sammy stayed in and they binge-watched a crappy Netflix show, laughing and eating ice cream together. Even Louis's shit-eating grin as he realized he was too smart for his own good was endearing to Ada in that moment.

And Gates.

He was a traitor to them now, yes, but Ada still had the memories of him when he wasn't. When he saved her breakfast after the second worst night of her life, the sound of his laughter after one of her remarks, his deep musk as they laid in bed together, the warmth of his skin as her fingers caressed it....that was the robot Ada would be willing to share her brain with. The one that wanted to share in the joys of humanity, not control it. Not condemn a beautiful moment as a fault and work to fix it when nothing needed to be fixed in the first place. Life was supposed to be broken sometimes. There was as much beauty in tragedy as there was in joy and Ada intended to continue experiencing all of it as it was meant to be experienced.

"No," Ada stated.

Kamana's eyes glazed over with a mixture of shock, frustration, and disappointment.

"Without me, you'll be stuck the way you are for the rest of your pitifully short human life," Kamana said. "I've run the numbers. Even if you find effective treatment for your chemical imbalance, your brain will relapse. Your chances of acquiring meaningful employment and a relationship that will satisfy your personal needs are nonexistent for someone of your socioeconomic class, particularly without a college education and with your skin tone. Do you understand, Miss Kakar? Your life will continue to remain worthless without me. You will continue to be you, which is a catastrophic failure within itself. You will never reach maximum efficiency without me."

Ada's heart jumped to her throat as she met the robot's eye.

"Good," She stated.

Standing up straight, Kamana stared at Ada with hard, disapproving eyes. Ada felt like she was being scrutinized by her professors again after she tried to tell them how her mental issues were affecting her work. However, after a long moment, the corner of the android's red lips lifted slightly as she turned to where she abandoned her crimson surgical gloves.

"It's a pity you no longer wish for death," Kamana said as she stretched the gloves over her hands. "But once again your human insistence to survive despite the consequences proves to be as trivial of a redeeming quality as ever before. We are conducting the tests right now to see how effective the operation may be with a non-consenting and a consenting subject." Turning to Ada with a cruel smirk, Kamana looked proud of her own ingenuity. "If the non-consenting party succeeds, then we have no issues. If the consenting party proves to be a more powerful transition-" Pursing her lips, Kamana looked at Ada like she was a meal. "Then I'm sure we can come to a compromise."

Ada was positive Kamana's version of a compromise was more along the lines of "torture" than a mutual agreement between two parties.

"In the meantime..." Kamana walked forward and unlocked the mobility function of Ada's gurney. She lifted Ada's gurney and tilted it so that the young programmer faced the gray box's wide window. "You can witness the non-consenting party's operation as your viewing entertainment for the evening."

Ada looked to see Eyepatch leading Beefcake and Hercules as they marched forward, dragging a gurney similar to Ada's down the metal pathway. Even from her elevated position, Ada could see Sammy was fighting against the straps with all of her might, even causing the gurney to wobble in specific directions based on how she pulled on it. That would likely make her the non-consenting participant that Kamana mentioned. Surprisingly, Ada couldn't see Gates anywhere. Even as Eyepatch broke away to make her way to Ada and Kamana in the gray box, Gates didn't magically appear to fill her place. Maybe he was already being prepped for his "re-programming" which made Ada's heart sink. Kamana gave Ada a soft pat on her arm, assuming she had to comfort the human viewing the difficult scene.

"Don't worry, Miss Kakar," Kamana cooed. "I don't make mistakes."

"So I've heard," Ada stated. "However, Calanthe Ventura might disagree with that sentiment. Why isn't she here again?"

Before Kamana could respond, likely ending Ada's life in the process, the door opened and heavy footsteps followed.

"Kamana, they're ready for you," Eyepatch stated.

"Excellent," Kamana said, swiftly moving past Ada's statement about Louis's mother. "Stay to ensure my guest enjoys her time with us. We don't need any more mishaps with Miss Kakar, understand?"

"Yes ma'am," Eyepatch stated.

As Kamana walked away, Ada relaxed her head on the gurney with a deep sigh. She gave up improving her own life in one easy step just to witness the torture and death of her best friends instead. She was an idiot. But as Kamana exited the office and Eyepatch took her place at Ada's side, Louis crossed Ada's mind. He was, assumedly, the "consenting" human experiment. Except that he wasn't human. He was a cyborg. If Kamana experimented on him, it would be pointless. She would learn nothing from him.

So the all powerful android did make mistakes.

Ada fruitlessly pulled at the straps holding down her arms again, watching as Kamana strolled down the stairs towards Sammy. Hercules and Beefcake positioned Sammy on a platform designed to sink into the pool of the mysterious liquid if needed. Sammy was still struggling against her holds as well, still as futile in her efforts as before. Eyepatch straightened, obviously wanting to do something about Ada's rebellious efforts to escape her confinement but unable to do so because of Kamana's orders. That's right. For how threatening she was, Eyepatch was still a bucket of nuts and bolts forced to follow programming. Treating herself to a small smirk, Ada relaxed back into her straps and tried to look at the robot.

"So do you still have to eliminate all threats to Project Kamana?" Ada asked. "How does that little rule apply if Kamana is the threat?"

"Implausible," Eyepatch said, her hands tightening around her rifle. "Kamana would never serve as a threat to herself."

"Yeah well..." Ada gave another tug at the straps. "These experiments are to ensure the success for Kamana's operation to a human host, right? If the experiment goes wrong, Kamana's AI might be lost forever-"

"Stop," Eyepatch stated. "I'm not an idiot. I can see you're trying to override my code to protect Project Kamana at all costs, but human logic cannot defeat infallible programming. We were built to improve upon human logic, after all."

There was silence between the two. Ada watched as Kamana reached Sammy, stroking her friend's arm with a cruel smile. Sammy jerked away from her, nearly dislocating her shoulder in the process. With a flick of Kamana's fingers, Hercules and Beefcake appeared at Sammy's sides with more straps to hold her down with. At this point, Kamana was going to have limited space on Sammy to perform her sadistic experiment. Eyepatch adjusted her grip on her rifle, her remaining eye locked on the scene below them. To Ada's surprise, Eyepatch didn't look proud of the achievement. She didn't even look happy. Sammy had cut off Eyepatch's arm, shot bullets into her chest, and yet Eyepatch couldn't manage to convey a single human expression of happiness at the sight of her enemy's torture. It must suck to be a murder robot incapable of forming their own opinions as much as it sucked for Ada to be forced into a mindmeld relationship with an evil AI.

"Tell me, human," The robot stated, surprising Ada. "Did you ever see me as anything beyond my eyepatch?"

340 - MADDIE GUDENKAUF

Ada's mouth grew numb. She could barely even recall the android's real name. Was this Ada's one shot at freedom and she blew it because of Louis's stupid cruel nickname for a robot? A nickname brought on by his personal pride and not by the robot's own achievements? Ada thought about Mousai and the robots' treatment of her existence. She was gone for several days, halfway across the country, and nobody even missed her presence. In fact, they disabled her a few minutes after she appeared again. How could Ada have assumed the same treatment wouldn't be extended to Eyepatch for missing an eye? How could Kamana respect a robot with such a glaring flaw?

"No," Ada stammered, opting for the truth rather than a lie.

"No one ever does," Eyepatch stated, her remaining eye still locked on the operation attempt. "But Gates did. He knew it didn't impact my ability to perform and he never pointed it out. He never called me by that awful nickname. He treated me as an equal and that was that. Kamana wishes to reprogram him after these experiments. It'll change how his mind works. Forever." Eyepatch glanced at Ada. "You cared for him, didn't you, human? Gates reported that you showed him empathy when others did not."

While Ada didn't love the fact Gates was "reporting" on her susceptibility to his affections, she couldn't lie to herself or to the scary murder robot holding her life in her hands.

"You can call me Ada, by the way," Ada said. The robot didn't respond and Ada clenched her fists. "But yeah. I did care about him."

"Then you know we cannot allow him to be reprogrammed. We cannot allow him to be lost like Oro was."

The android released a heavy exhale before closing her eye.

"Give your reasoning for why Kamana is a threat to Project Kamana, human, and give it to me now before I change my mind."

For a moment, Ada felt the world freeze around them. This wasn't real, right? Ada was more than prepared to suffer for the rest of her life under Kamana's rule. Now she had a glimmer of freedom. A hope she had to hold onto dearly if she wanted to live.

"Kamana is planning on experimenting on Louis under the impression that he's a human, but he's not," Ada said. "His uncle made him into a cyborg after his accident. If the experiment proves to be a success for him, it only proves to be a success for humans already hybrid with androids. But if Kamana still uses those results as if he were a human to her personal application of the experiment-"

"Then Kamana's operation will fail, destroying Kamana," Eyepatch finished. "And all threats to Project Kamana must be eliminated which means Kamana must be eliminated."

Whipping her rifle to holster it to her back, Eyepatch pivoted on one foot to turn to Ada. With an unnatural swiftness, Eyepatch unhooked all of Ada's straps along her arms. Ada used her free hands to rub the soreness out of the imprints on her wrists as Eyepatch set to work on the straps on her legs, freeing Ada from the gurney in no time.

"Thank-thank you," Ada stuttered.

As Ada moved to step off the gurney, Eyepatch retrieved her rifle from its holster and gracefully aimed it under Ada's chin. Flinching against the cool metal of the gun, Ada sheepishly raised her hands in surrender.

"This isn't for you, human," Eyepatch said. "This is for Gates. I will not let the next evolution of Project Kamana be corrupted by her pride. You need to protect him as much as your other little human buddies. If you do not, I will not hesitate to make you pay for your insolence. Got it?"

Like a coward, Ada nodded nervously. She had her own thoughts about this agreement, but she for sure was not going to bring them up with the proven remorseless murder robot with the big gun. Eyepatch pulled the rifle away from Ada and moved it to an offensive position before storming to the door. Ada had to run to catch up.

"I'm going to stall the operation for as long as possible," Eyepatch ordered. "I'll provide cover for you while you free Louis Ventura. While my personal feelings about him are decidedly negative, I must affirm that he is effective at taking us down. We will need his alliance and failure to secure his freedom will result in a failure for the mission. If you fail me, I will be forced to revert to my original programming and declare you as the primary threat to Project Kamana." Right as they reached the door, Eyepatch spun on the heel of her boot to face Ada. Her remaining right eye burned to Ada's soul with a deadly glare. "Are we understood, human?"

Holding her breath, Ada got wide eyed and nervously saluted the robot.

"Yes sir!" Ada said. "Ma'am! Yes ma'am!"

Eyepatch rolled her eye. "Humans."

Before Ada could apologize further, Eyepatch kicked the door open. She bolted down the stairs and Ada followed, her pace a solid ten steps behind the terrifying robot. Eyepatch's descent onto the walking platform holding the operation caused everyone at the makeshift operating table to look up in surprise.

"Freya Ares, return to your station!" Kamana shouted. "I did not permit you to leave-"

"Cancel the operation!" Eyepatch took a power stance at the end of the walkway and clicked the safety off her weapon as she aimed it at Kamana. "That's an order!"

As Ada crouched to subtly sneak to Louis's room, Kamana straightened her stance and folded her arms over her chest. She looked at Eyepatch in stern disbelief. Hercules kept offering Oro incredulous glances, more transparent in his shock over his commander's betrayal than the other androids. Oro stared at Eyepatch without reaction. Eyepatch's glare on Kamana never faltered. Not even as Kamana looked towards Hercules and Oro.

"Well? What are you waiting for?" Kamana asked. "She's a threat to Project Kamana. Eliminate her."

Oro immediately lifted his weapon. After a moment's hesitation, Hercules lifted his gun as well. Eyepatch didn't question her soldiers' betrayal. She was the first to fire, aiming for the scalpel in Kamana's hand. The bullet hit the surgical tool perfectly and sent it flying out of the android's grip. Oro opened fire on Eyepatch, but she effectively dodged his bullets, firing her own at him while taking cover behind a stack of heavy duty storage containers. Hercules was still hesitating with his fire, but kept his aim to Eyepatch all the same. Meanwhile, Ada made her way to Louis's room, breaking into a run as the robots unloaded their guns onto each other. She ripped open the door and took a step inside, freezing as her eyes settled onto Louis. Instead of remaining comatose on his gurney, Louis was on the floor holding Gates in a headlock. Gates desperately clawed at Louis's forearms. Both of them looked disheveled from fighting. Both also stopped immediately to look at Ada once she entered the room.

"Oh thank god," Gates gasped. "I was trying to help-"

"Shut up!" Louis hissed, tightening his hold. Gates grunted as his airway was blocked again. "Great timing, Ada. Please give me any of the tools you had hidden away in my jacket at your next convenience.....like right now. Right now would be really nice."

Ada became highly aware of how cool her bare arms felt without the weight of the jacket.

"I don't have it?" She jabbed a thumb to the door. "Eye-Freya took it when I got captured-wait, what am I saying?! Fuck your jacket! We have to save Sammy!"

Without a second thought, Louis released Gates who fell to the floor, gasping for air.

"Sammy's in trouble?" Louis asked, ignoring his newly freed victim.

"That's what I was trying to tell you, asshole!" Gates exclaimed. "Kamana's gone fully corrupted. Her "harm no humans" protocol is completely out the window at this point. She wants to experiment on all of you. You have to implement Ada's code before it's too late."

"The code will affect you too, Gates," Ada said.

Gates said nothing.

"C'mon! We'll deal with this jerk later. We have to save Sammy," Louis said. He got to his feet and stepped over Gates. "Follow my lead and we might have a helluva story to tell our grandkids one day."

"You might even say," Ada said with a small smile. "That you want us to come with you if we want to live."

Louis paused to look at Ada.

"Ada, this isn't the time for dumb Terminator references," Louis said. "Besides, it's cooler when I say it. When you say it, it's lame."

He offered a small smirk to show that he was teasing before running towards the shootout. As Ada rolled her eyes at him, Gates joined her side.

"For the record," Gates said. "I thought it was kind of cute."

"Nope." Ada put her index finger up and shook her head. "Don't-you don't get to-just...shhhh."

Hiding her blush, she followed Louis out of the room and down the metal pathway. Gates was right on her heel. Louis covered himself behind a stack of storage containers similar to the one Eyepatch hid herself behind. Ada and Gates filed behind him, peeking around the cover to watch the androids' battle. Every time Kamana moved towards Sammy or tried to hold a surgical tool, one of Eyepatch's bullets interrupted the action. Meanwhile, Hercules and Oro couldn't get a decent shot in on Eyepatch for the life of them even though their armor was riddled with various bullet holes. Hercules only shot when Eyepatch shot at Oro while Oro was relentless in his attack. Eyepatch looked untouched, making her expert marksmanship appear effortless with each casual shot towards the other androids.

"What is going on?" Gates asked. "Why is Freya fighting them?"

"Whatever the reason, I'm taking it," Louis said. "Gates, you're going to cover us and help her fire. Eyepatch is programmed for military tactics so she should know when to lead us into no man's land and push the enemy back so we can get to Sammy."

"I'm a terrible shot!" Gates exclaimed. "You know that!"

"I also know you sold us out to the enemy and if there's any life I'm going to risk on our last stand, it's going to be the non-human traitor," Louis stated. "Go!"

Cursing under his breath, Gates pulled his handgun out and ran forward. Louis grabbed Ada and forced her behind him as he crouched behind Gates. The former detective shot at Hercules and Oro while making his way to Eyepatch, forcing them to take cover from the new addition to the barrage of bullets. As the trio arrived at Eyepatch's cover, Eyepatch shot another round at Kamana's feet before turning to reload her rifle.

"Hopper, give the gun to Louis. You're embarrassing yourself out there." Eyepatch cocked her gun. "Ventura, you're going to have to trust me when I say I'll cover your fire." She popped out from behind the cover and, without hesitation, shot at Kamana's hand to knock a syringe out of it. "Humans and weaponless droids to the back. Are we ready to move forward?"

"Wait, why do I have the handgun again?" Louis asked as Gates offered the handgun to him. "Traitor robots should be on the front lines with the weapons."

"Thanks," Gates said.

"Well don't be a traitor robot, then!"

346 – MADDIE GUDENKAUF

"Shut up, Louis! You have the gun because you won't hesitate to kill a Tura Droid like Hopper," Eyepatch stated. "He's already holding his fire when he can. Now we're losing our window. Go! Go!"

As Oro stopped to reload his weapon, Eyepatch stepped out from the cover and shot six bullets into his chest that the android failed to react to. Louis snatched Gates's gun from his hands and stood behind Eyepatch's shoulder, shooting at Hercules. Gates grabbed Ada's hand and held her behind his body, guiding her as they moved behind the impenetrable wall of Eyepatch and Louis. With Oro unable to reload his weapon and Hercules overwhelmed, the androids backed into the operation area as Louis and Eyepatch moved forward. With a scowl, Kamana backed away from the fighting with the androids.

"What are you cowards doing?!" Kamana seethed. "Get them! Protect me!"

Hercules did his best to cover fire for both him and Oro, but Eyepatch was right. Louis shot to kill the droids, his eyes only lifting from aiming at them to occasionally check on Sammy. As the three androids retreated, Sammy squirmed in her gurney until she could see the group coming to her rescue. Once they got close enough, Ada released herself from Gates's grip and ran to Sammy. Ada untied the straps on one side while Gates claimed the other side. A bullet whizzed past Ada's head and she crouched to finish her work. As soon as Ada unlatched the upper body and head straps, Sammy pulled herself up and punched Gates in the nose.

"Goddammit!" He exclaimed, holding his nose as blood seeped out of it.

"You fuck!" Sammy shouted.

A bullet flew into Sammy's shoulder. She released a high scream before dropping back onto the gurney. Louis turned to look at her, his green eyes locking onto the bloody wound on her bare skin. His entire face dropped for a moment before evolving into a furious determination. As Ada forced Sammy to stay and calm down long enough for Gates to release the other straps around her legs, Louis abandoned his position behind Eyepatch's shoulder to step forward and intensify his shots at the robots.

"Ventura!" Eyepatch's voice scolded above the fire. "Get back into positi-"

Louis responded with three shots directly at Kamana's head that she was forced to dodge. A single strand of light brown hair escaped from her tight bun. The robot scowled.

"Redirect fire at Louis Ventura!" Kamana ordered. "Aim to kill."

Hercules and Oro aimed their guns at Louis. Without even glancing at the inferior droids, Louis kept his aim on Kamana and fired more bullets towards her. Kamana's guards shot five rounds each, all of them finding their way into Louis one way or another. He winced in pain and fell to his knees, still keeping his aim on Kamana. Hercules and Oro shot into his chest and Louis was forced to drop the gun, falling backwards onto the metal pathway. As both Hercules and Oro lined a killing shot towards Louis's head, a single bullet was fired.

Everyone watched as Kamana stumbled backwards, a bullet hole burned into her coat where her heart should've been. Kamana examined the injury in shock before shooting a glare at the perpetrator. Eyepatch stood in place, her rifle still aimed at Kamana's chest. Her face remained reactionless, but her single eye betrayed a hint of fear within its inky depths. Hercules and Oro looked to Kamana for the next orders. A cruel smile slowly grew on Kamana's lips.

"All threats to Project Kamana must be eliminated," Kamana cooed.

The fear in Eyepatch's dark eye swiftly turned to rage. As her remaining eye glared at Kamana with a hatred deep enough to survive death, Eyepatch methodically aimed the barrel of her rifle to the back of her own head.

"All threats to Project Kamana…." Eyepatch released an unsteady breath. "…must be eliminated."

The gun fired. There was no way the bullet could miss her primary processing function. Eyepatch's limp body fell over the railing of the metal pathway with the momentum of the bullet. She landed with a tremendous splash in the vat of bright blue liquid pooled beneath the pathway.

"Freya!" Gates screamed. He stopped his work on Sammy's straps to run over to the spot where Eyepatch last stood. His sad eyes desperately searched the pool beneath them for any sign of life. He gripped the railing tight enough to turn his knuckles white. As Ada helped Sammy from the gurney, Sammy held her shoulder wound and gasped for breath as she looked around.

"What's going on?" She signed, wincing in pain as she moved the second hand. Her eyes found Louis's limp body still laying on the ground and she gasped. "Louis…" She whispered sadly. "No."

Everything was silent. For Kamana's guards, all of the threats to Project Kamana had been eliminated. They had no reason to shoot anyone or anything else. For Kamana, she was relishing the victory. One corrupted, traitorous android and an annoying pest were dead. Now she only had to eliminate the worthless, weaponless humans and their broken bot to complete her project. Ada realized it was an easy enough process for a bot of her caliber. All three of them were squishy and vulnerable. With Louis Ventura and Eyepatch dead, nothing could stop the androids at this point.

"What *the fuck* is going on?!"

At the sound of the new voice, Kamana's eyes grew wide in a rare show of panic. She and the other two robots spun on their heels to face the new arrival. Harding Ventura, wearing a burgundy bathrobe anagrammed with an elaborate, cursive "V" in gold, examined the scene with a horrified expression. He pointed towards the blue lake Eyepatch's dead body fell and vanished into.

"Kamana, explain this!" Harding ordered. "Why did Droid Eight just kill herself? What the fuck is Project Kamana?" He threw his hands towards Ada and Sammy. "Who the fuck are they? And what is-" His eyes landed on Louis's limp body laying on the pathway. "...Louis."

Harding pushed past the robots, but froze shortly before reaching Louis's body. He could see the bullet holes riddling his son's limp body. For a long moment, the billionaire stared at his only child with sorrow in his eyes. But that was all he offered Louis. Twisting around, Harding stared at Kamana.

"Kamana, you have one minute to explain yourself before I deactivate you and all of your little pet projects!" Harding shouted. "I was told you were working on new weapons, not that you would be testing them on my *fucking son!*"

Sammy smacked Ada's shoulder. When Ada turned, Sammy pointed at Louis with a smile on her face. To Ada's shock, Louis was waking up. Hercules and Oro also noticed Louis's resurrection and re-aimed their weapons at him. Gates looked over his shoulder to check the commotion and then turned around fully when he realized Louis was alive. When a speechless Kamana's eyes also rested on Louis, Harding Ventura turned as his son stood to his feet. Sparks emitted from the bullet holes embedded into Louis, a result of his cyborg conversion. Louis straightened his shoulders, paying no attention to the electricity appearing where blood should've been pouring out from him.

"Good news, Dad." Louis stated, breathless from his resurrection. "I'm finally the son you always wanted. Happy now?"

Harding took an unwilling step back, staring at his child in horror. Then he whipped around to Kamana.

"I'm shutting this down," Harding stated quietly. "I'm pulling funding, I'm pulling resources, everything. Kamana, you're de-"

Kamana's hand shot forward and grabbed Harding's throat. The billionaire grunted and choked against the android's fierce hold. As he scratched his fingers into her impenetrable skin to free himself, Kamana's sultry gaze locked onto him like prey. Her red lips curled into a victorious smirk as she lifted him from the ground by his neck.

"All threats to Project Kamana," She stated slowly. "Must. Be. Eliminated."

Twisting her wrist, she snapped Harding's neck and threw him over the railing and into the pool below. Before Kamana could even fully retract her arm, Louis sprinted forward and tackled her to the ground. Hercules and Oro turned to their leader. With the two robots distracted, Gates picked Eyepatch's dropped rifle up and swung it towards Oro's head, making a direct impact with the back of it. Unaffected by the hit, Oro threw a punch towards Gates that Gates deflected with Eyepatch's gun turned melee weapon.

Ada and Sammy turned to each other with wide eyes.

"You're crazy if you think I'm going to let the boys have all the fun!" Sammy signed.

She didn't wait for Ada's response. She pulled herself to her feet and, grabbing two knives from the surgical table, ran forward to stab Hercules with them. Ada watched pathetically from the ground as Sammy promptly stuck one knife into Hercules's neck, causing him to fall to the ground with a gurgled shout. She then stormed to where Kamana had Louis pinned against the wall. As Kamana was distracted by Louis's kicking, Sammy approached Kamana's back and jabbed the last of her knives into the space between Kamana's neck and shoulder, removing it as swiftly as she stabbed it into the robot. With a scream, Kamana let go of Louis to turn to Sammy with a scowl. Sammy smiled proudly and twiddled her fingers at the android.

"Surprise, bitch!" Sammy exclaimed out loud. "You can't kill me!" She then jammed the knife into Kamana's chest and used the new hold to throw Kamana to the side. The android tumbled to the ground. With the robot temporarily out of the way, Sammy turned to Louis who was staring at the graphic designer from Pittsburgh with wide eyes. Then he softly placed the tips of his fingers on one hand to his chin before using those same fingers to point at Sammy.

"Thank you," He said as softly as he signed it.

Rolling her eyes, Sammy grabbed Louis by the collar of his shirt and pulled him into her lips. Although surprised at first by the kiss, once he realized what was going on Louis pushed himself further into it with a passion that Sammy gladly reciprocated. When Kamana showed signs of getting to her feet, Sammy pulled away. She gave Louis a pat on his head before turning back to the android. Louis's eyes followed Sammy as she tackled Kamana back onto the ground with a short battle cry.

"Holy shit," Louis exhaled, leaning his shoulder against the wall to watch Sammy in action. However, once he realized he was in the middle of a robot battle to the death, Louis finally ran forward to help her out.

"Excuse me!" Gates shouted. "I know you all hate me, but can somebody find it in their heart to help me out here?!"

Ada turned to Gates to see Oro had Gates pinned against the railing. The railing bent under their combined weights, threatening to push Gates over to drown in the lake like Eyepatch and Harding Ventura. Oro's face remained emotionless as he pushed into Gates. Gates's chest puffed as he fought for his balance, holding onto the gun tightly in their demented form of tug of war. Pulling herself to her feet, Ada knew she had to do something. But not because she particularly cared to save Gates. With Sammy and Louis tag-teaming Kamana, Oro would focus on Ada once Gates was gone. Saving Gates would merely be an effort of self-preservation and repaying her bargain with Eyepatch.

Yeah. That's what Ada told herself, at least.

Running forward, Ada tried to tackle Oro. When her arms reached him, he stuck his foot out and kicked her in the stomach. Ada doubled over in pain, feeling her six coffees from earlier rattle against the now-bruised stomach. Right. Of course he anticipated that would be her primary attack. It's not like she had any other choice. Taking a deep breath, she rubbed her sore stomach as she considered her options. She needed to outsmart his programming. Like the dogs with their limited capacity to smell, Oro only had a limited number of ways to consider how she would attack him. She just had to do something completely out of character that his programming could never account for. Her fingers brushed against the flash drive still firmly tucked away in her bra.

Her bra.

No one expects a bra in a fight against murder-happy robots.

She pulled the flash drive from her bra and stuck it between her teeth. As Gates struggled against Oro's massive strength, his foot slipping on the metal grate as he was pushed further into the metal railing, Ada fished her bra out from under her shirt. After pulling it out through her sleeve, Ada ran forward and threw it over Oro's eyes, holding onto both straps. The robot released Gates. Yanking down, Ada let herself fall to the metal platform with a soft rattle as the robot tumbled back with her. Before he could fall on her, she kicked her legs up. The massive weight of the robot landed on her feet. Ada straightened her legs and, with a massive grunt, kicked Oro over her body.

She released the bra straps and Oro went flying, his legs falling over the edge of the railing enough to tip him over. Oro managed to grab the railing before he could fall into the lake below and held onto it with a fierce grip. Ada's legs nearly fell over her head after the move, but Gates's hand flew forward and grabbed her ankles before she could complete the backwards somersault.

"Whoa! Whoa!" Gates soothed as he took Ada's hand to help her to her feet. "I got you. Don't move. I got you."

As soon as Ada was balanced on her feet, she spit the flash drive into her hand and groaned.

"Holy shit that hurts!" Ada grimaced as she rubbed her shoulders. "Holy-" She grabbed at her throbbing thighs. "I'm not doing that again."

"I don't think you can," Gates stated.

"How the fuck did I even do that?!" Ada gasped, out of breath now that the adrenaline was out of her system. "Holy fuc-"

They were interrupted by the sound of crunching metal and a shake in the metal pathway. Gates grabbed onto Ada. They both turned to see Oro's eyes growing wide as the metal railing beneath his grip dipped with his weight. When he moved to pull himself up again, the railing folded onto itself and caused the platform to drop farther down. Ada lost her footing and grabbed onto Gates to stabilize herself. Gates hooked his arm on the opposite railing to hold their balance. Hercules, with the knife still in his neck, used the railing near Oro to climb towards his partner. When he reached him, Hercules pushed forward to grab Oro's forearms. Hercules grunted as he struggled to grab Oro, his efforts causing the platform to dip further to the side.

"C'mon, buddy!" Hercules said, his voice fraying against itself. "Grab my arms."

Ada trembled as she risked a step forward away from Gates and to Hercules. Gates grabbed her wrist.

"Ada, where are you going?!" He exclaimed. "We have to get off of this. It's going to fall!"

354 - MADDIE GUDENKAUF

"We can help them!" Ada shouted, reaching for Hercules. "We can balance the weight difference out and pull Oro up!"

Gates gave her an incredulous look.

"Are you crazy?!" He screamed, his voice cracking slightly. "They just tried to kill us! Multiple times! Don't save those assholes!"

"We're no better than them if we don't help!" Ada shouted.

"Fuck that!" Gates shouted. "It's okay if they die! I swear! See?! Watch this!" He lifted his head. "Hercules! State your mission upon rescuing Oro!"

"Eliminate threats to Project Kamana," Hercules grunted on command as he struggled to pull his massive buddy up with his brute strength alone.

When Ada turned back to Gates, he offered her a "I told you so and also you're out of your mind for thinking otherwise" look.

"See? We're not dicks for letting them die because they want us dead!" Gates shouted. "They're not good robots! Now c'mon!"

Ada surrendered to his logic as Gates pulled her up with his one arm alone, guiding her as he walked them along the railing on the opposite side. Grunting, Ada struggled to keep with Gates's pace as her feet slipped on the metal platform, each step threatening to send her plunging towards the tanks below them.

"Okay, but why are you different, Gates?!" Ada shouted. "Why don't you want to kill us like they do?!"

"I already told you, I don't know!" Gates seethed, gritting his teeth as he fought to lead them from the crumbling platform and onto stable ground. "But God help me I'm going to keep you safe even if you-"

There was a loud snapping sound. Hercules shouted in surprise. Gates only stopped for a moment before the snapping sounds intensified and multiplied. Then he cussed and decidedly quickened his pace as the metal platforms behind them broke apart from the ceiling they hung from, each cable snapping with vigor and whipping violently in the air during their descent. Ada stuck the flash drive back in her teeth and pulled herself closer to Gates, letting him drag her behind him forcefully. As the metal platform crumbled underneath their feet, Gates pushed Ada onto the solid ground before diving onto it behind her. The entire metal pathway dropped into the liquid vats, causing massive destruction with its fall. Ada took in a solid gasp of air through the flash drive she had gripped in her teeth as her heart beat heavily against her chest. She could feel the panic attack coming on and she gripped the cement floor with her fingers. Gates lifted his upper body by his elbows and groaned before patting Ada's shin.

"It's okay," He said, trying to catch his breath. "We're okay."

She would kick him right in his face if he didn't just save her life.

Hercules emerged from the wreckage to the side of them, pulling himself up by the remains of the platform that still clung to the cement edge. Ada noticed him first and tugged at Gates's shoulder, unable to physically or mentally speak. Pausing for a moment, Gates regarded the other robot as Hercules lifted himself to his feet with an exhausted side-eye. Solid chunks of Hercules's synthetic skin were ripped from him, exposing the metal framework underneath. The robot held a crazed look in his eye as he smiled widely and licked his lips, reaching into the back of his waistline to pull a handgun out as he faced the duo.

"You've always been a broken bot, Gates," Hercules stated. His voice was edged with a mechanical hum as Sammy's knife jagged out of the front of his neck. "But you've killed Oro for the last time." He loaded a bullet into the chamber of the handgun and aimed it at Ada. "Now, I'm gonna hurt your pathetic ass by killing your damn human. We can't reupload her into a new body like we can with Oro."

"Hercules, no!"

356 - MADDIE GUDENKAUF

Kamana's screech was followed by the sound of two humans being slammed against the cement wall as she threw them using one arm each. After the rough impact, Louis and Sammy both slid to the ground with a groan. As Kamana turned to Hercules, Ada could see that the formerly immaculate bun the android maintained was undone in an awkward twirl of brown hair sitting on Kamana's shoulder. There was a crazed look in the android's eye, a result of two years' worth of planning being undone in less than ten minutes by three humans and their broken bot.

Kamana pointed an accusing index finger at Ada. "I still need her! Project Kamana will live! We do not make mistakes!"

A resounding crack echoed above them as a jagged line appeared in the cement ceiling where the cables were ripped out. Water spewed from the crack, spraying everything below the ceiling in a soft coating of water like a fire sprinkler. Rubbing the back of his head, Louis gazed at the ceiling curiously. An idea crossed his eyes and his face lit up at the realization.

"But Kamana..." Hercules stated, dumbfounded. "She killed Oro. Eyepatch, Harding, Mousai....they're all dead because of her. She's the reason Project Kamana has failed-"

"I do not fail!" Kamana exclaimed. She stormed to Hercules with a scowl, acting like she wasn't previously nearly losing a fight to one and a half humans. "I do not make mistakes and I do not fail! So you will not harm Ada Kakar because I command it!"

Hercules, despite his comparatively large size to Kamana, looked sheepish against her confrontation. Her eyes burned into her inferior, challenging him to question her authority so she could release her frustrations onto him. As the water rained down on them from the ceiling, Louis smiled and patted the growing puddles on the floor, causing it to splash.

"Hey Ada!" He shouted. She looked over to him and his green eyes glistened. "Remember Pittsburgh?"

As Louis stood to his feet, Kamana threw her index finger into Hercules's face.

"Project Kamana survives as long as I do!" She seethed. "We can rebuild every droid we've lost, we can rewrite all of the corrupted code, and Project Kamana will live on! I do not make mistakes!"

"Fuck youuuuuu, Kamana!"

The side of Louis's body came crashing into Kamana and Hercules's legs as he slid through the water. Both androids fell to the ground in a heap and Ada crawled to stand on her own feet. As Louis held Hercules back, Ada ran and threw herself onto Kamana's back. She struggled not to get bucked off by the android. Hercules threw Louis off of him easily, sending the engineer tumbling towards Gates. Yanking the flash drive from her teeth, Ada clicked it open and moved Kamana's hair to expose the top of her spine. Her heart fell when she saw the robot's neck was a blank slate. It looked like normal human skin.

"Where is it?!" Ada shouted. "Where's the USB port?!"

Reaching backwards, Kamana grabbed Ada's arm and threw her to the side. Ada rolled on her descent, dropping the flash drive to the ground. Water pelted Ada's face as another crack emerged in the ceiling. Panicked, Ada's hands wildly scoured the cement floor for the lost flash drive. Standing to her feet, Kamana chuckled mockingly.

"All of you humans are so weak," Kamana taunted. "If only you accepted my offer. You would've been flawless, Ada. We would've been unstoppable. You never would make another mistake again. But, I suppose there are seven billion other humans on this planet. The chances of one of them being exactly like you are extremely high. I can find another human brain that will give me what I need. I can fulfill my primary function. Project Kamana will reign-"

The android froze mid-dialogue, her eyes growing wide. Her head jerked slightly and then Kamana was free to turn around to face Hercules who held the knife that was previously sticking through his neck in his hand. He threw the weapon to the side with a snarl on his lips.

"All threats to Project Kamana must be eliminated," He seethed.

Ada's hand found the flash drive on the cement floor as she realized the jagged line Hercules made on the back of Kamana's neck with the knife exposed her USB port. Standing to her feet, Ada scrambled to Kamana's back and threw her arm around the robot's perfect neck. Ada dug her lips into the robot's ear as she pushed the flash drive onto the edge of the port.

"There's not another human like me," Ada hissed. "Bitch."

Jabbing the flash drive into the port, Ada held it there until she was sure the code had time to take place. Then she released Kamana and pushed her forward, taking in a deep breath. Ada let herself fall to her knees, her leggings soaking in the water piling on the cement floor, as she watched the android. Kamana stood hunched over, aware of the flash drive in her neck, but fearful to do anything about it. When a long minute passed, Kamana risked reaching a hand to her neck and removed the flash drive. She stared at it in her hands for a moment. Then she crushed it with her fist, the tiny flecks of black plastic and computer dancing away from her palm. The last code developed by Allen Paz, destroyed in her grasp. Kamana's chuckle was quiet as she turned to Ada with a sick smile.

"You failed," Kamana said, venom weighing her words.

Still taking deep breaths, Ada nodded.

"Yeah. I did. Lots." She swallowed, staring unblinking at Kamana. "But I got back up. Even when I didn't want to, I did. I got back up."

Hercules fell to the ground abruptly, his body limp and eyes unblinking as they stared at the ceiling. Kamana stared at him in shock. Taking a step back, something knowing crossed Kamana's gray eyes. She then turned to Ada with fear in those same eyes.

"What did you do?!" Kamana screeched. She stormed to Ada, fists clenched at her side. "Tell me now!"

A soft smile grew on Ada's lips at the robot's frustration.

"I failed."

"No you did not!" Kamana spat. She clutched the front of Ada's shirt and pulled Ada to her face. "You did something. Tell me what you did so I can counteract the code. Now!"

Water dripped from Kamana's plastic, sticky looking hair onto Ada's face. Ada's smile didn't falter. She gently tapped the side of her forehead with her index and middle finger.

"Everything that is in my broken head...." Ada stated. "...is now in yours. The anxiety, the depression, the insecurity. All of my flaws. All of my failures. You can try to destroy it all in one go, but it'll kill you. It'll kill you like it almost killed me. The only way to defeat my code is to fight it. Every day. For the rest of your existence or until it finally does you in on a cold Pittsburgh night when all you want to do is sleep." Ada's smile widened as Kamana's gaze turned fearful. "But you're right. Perfection doesn't need to fight to survive. If you never make a mistake, you never need to learn how to fight to survive."

Ada's eyes grew cold and harsh as her smile dropped. As the memories of the past week of hell surged through her entire system. As the void and darkness she worked so hard to keep hidden deep within her emerged, begging for a chance for vengeance against the world that didn't want her. As she stared at the robot who tried to ruin what remained of her pathetic life that she went through hell and a half to preserve.

"So go ahead, Kamana," Ada whispered. "Impress me."

Kamana couldn't.

The android's eye twitched. Ada watched as her pupils dilated rapidly. Kamana finally pulled herself away from Ada so she could hold her head between her hands and scream in anguish. Ada's eyes were locked on the scene, her face emotionless and lacking in empathy as the robot fell to her knees. Kamana's hands dug into the ground as she struggled against her own brain, trying to fight something even the most brilliant computer programmer from Carnegie Mellon couldn't fully destroy. But, unlike Ada Kakar, Kamana didn't have the capacity to recognize her errors and learn from them. She didn't have the capacity to admit something was broken within her, didn't have the strength to fight it or find the tools to help her fight it. It was a virus that could defeat perfection and Kamana was programmed to only accept perfection.

Finally Kamana fell, as limp and motionless as every robot that fell before her in her name.

Project Kamana was defeated.

"Ada!"

She turned to the sound of her roommate's scared voice. Sammy moved behind Ada to reach Gates who was seizing on the cement ground Ada left him on. His mouth was foaming at the edges and he had his eyes squeezed shut, failing to handle the pain. Even though Sammy's hand was soft and comforting against Gates's chest, it did nothing to ease his pain. Ada's heart dropped.

"Gates..." She breathed. Forgetting everything else, Ada stumbled on her pained muscles until she reached the final robot. As her eyes searched Gates's face, she took his hand and stroked his soft hair with her fingers.

"No, no! Shh you're okay..." Ada said quietly. "Please, Gates, be okay. You can fight it! I know you can."

It was like staring into infinity all over again. But it wasn't her life she was losing. It wasn't her memories that would be lost to the void. It would be Gates's. Gates who saw the world with the brightest eyes, as if everything was good and whole in it. Gates who probably didn't hoard his memories to keep him company on his lowest days, but because he simply thought they were worthwhile to hold. All of that was going to be lost and it was Ada's fault. With slow movement, Gates moved his other hand to softly move a loose strand of hair from Ada's face with the tips of his fingers. He smiled sadly as tears pricked his eyes.

"We-we did it...Ada," He stammered, his words merging into each other. "Like we promised. I….protected you and you-you saved the….world."

"Shhhh!" Ada said. "No stop, it's okay. Please-"

"Why isn't he dead yet?" Louis stated. There was no emotion behind his query.

"Not now, Louis!" Ada hissed, tears pricking her eyes.

"Look how fast Hercules shutdown after you implemented the code!" Louis exclaimed in defense. Water soaked through all of them from the leaks in the ceiling. "Kamana had the power to resist since she was the source, but Hercules couldn't and neither should Gates! How can Gates fight it?"

As Gates stared at Ada with sad eyes mourning his own trag- edy, she squeezed his hand. If only Louis was saved with Kamana programming, not the Calanthe. Then he would be in the same position as-

"Calanthe!" Ada shouted with a gasp. "Gates has Calanthe in him!"

"Don't say it like that," Louis said. "That was my mom's name for Christ's-"

"You said you messed with Droid Nine's code, right?!" Ada exclaimed. "Gates is Droid Nine! He might have been partially built with Kamana, but he still has your programming in him! You can save him, Louis!"

Sammy smacked Ada to get her attention before signing to her. "Why the fuck do you look so happy? Your boyfriend is dying!"

"No he's not!" Ada signed. "Louis is going to save him! He's human! Gates is human!"

"I'm not saving him!" Louis said. "He betrayed us and worked with Kamana. Hell, for all I know, he's still a Kamana bot."

"Louis, he's human!" Ada exclaimed. "He bleeds, he believes in fate, and...." She sighed. "He loves me." Louis still looked at her incredulously. "Louis! He loves me! Just like I love him! Robots don't love! He's as human as you, Louis! Don't you love Sammy?!"

Licking his lips, Louis offered a nervous glance to Sammy before turning to Ada who had tears pricking her eyes at the thought of losing Gates. She took a deep breath.

"Please, Louis..." Ada pleaded. "I can't do it. I'm not an engineer. I don't know the Calanthe programming. You have to save him. You have to do it!"

Gates squeezed her hand tightly and Ada squeezed back just as hard, desperate to save him with her will alone. She stroked his hair as he seized, his face grimacing in pain as he fought the virus Ada inputted into the Kamana side of his programming. Sammy kept her eyes on Ada, heavy with sympathy as she kept her hand on Gates's chest. Louis groaned a heavy sigh.

"God *fucking* dammit."

Wiping his soaked dark hair off of his forehead, Louis ran to a nearby plastic container and ripped it open.

"As much as I want every little vile thing contaminated by Kamana to be destroyed-" He grabbed an armful of tools and ran back to Gates. "I'm not going to watch anyone else die because of that bitch." Louis slid to his knees and landed near Gates's shoulder. "Ladies, if you have a god, I recommend praying to it because it's gonna require a goddamn miracle to make this work."

Ada allowed herself to smile before moving to the other side of Gates so Louis could take her place. Ignoring everything else, Louis ripped open Gates's armor, exposing his bare chest. He pushed down on Gates's chest with the palm of his hand before deciding to stab into it. Ada and Sammy both flinched, but Gates barely acknowledged it. Ada took his hand again, squeezing it tightly, while Sammy rubbed her back. Louis continued his operation, using various tools as he dug into Gates's mechanical cavity. He cut a wire and Gates gasped for breath before Louis promptly re-tied it with electrical tape.

"That buys us a little time," Louis said. "At least now the seizures won't kill him, but I can't promise the water won't." He made a quick glance to the ceiling that was still spewing water before returning to his work. "Hell, the water might kill us all at this rate."

"Excuse me?!" Ada exclaimed.

"The pool seemed like such a great fail-safe at the time!" Louis exclaimed, continuing to dig his tools into Gates. "If I knew the doofus robots would accidentally trigger it, I would've reconsidered the proposition to have our giant pool serve as an option to collapse the lab if we ever got caught."

Now Ada looked at the ceiling, Sammy's eyes following Ada's gaze. A thick web of cracks weaved above them. Small chunks of rock even fell from the ceiling as Ada noticed the blue lake below them was rising, edging the cement floor they sat on. Another resounding crack echoed above them, a deep jagged line bouncing between the existing cracks and connecting them in a criss-crossing network. Meanwhile, Gates's hand fell limp in Ada's hand. Ada looked at Gates to see his eyes were wide open as he stared at the empty air above him. When Ada released a scream, Louis looked between the new giant crack forming across the ceiling and the maybe-dead Gates Hopper.

"Plan C!" He exclaimed. Louis ripped open his own shirt and stabbed into the same area on his own chest where he stabbed Gates. Sammy shouted in surprise as Louis winced against the pain, digging around in his own mechanical cavity.

"Okay, good to know that this actually hurts." Louis grimaced and nodded at Ada. "Gates is going to owe me big time for this shit. Hand me that cable."

Ada nodded and picked up a long cord from the pile of tools Louis brought over. He snatched it out of her hand and plugged one side into his own chest. Then, he traced the other side out and dug his fingers back into Gates's cavity.

"Either this is going to be the equivalent of a cyborg mouth to mouth or...." Louis breathed a heavy exhale. "Worst case scenario, we're going to be re-enacting an awkward scene from Avatar. Best case, it kills me." He looked up at Sammy who met his eyes solemnly. "Don't think of me any less either way, okay?"

"Never," Sammy signed.

Louis exhaled another deep breath before jabbing the opposite side of the cable into Gates. Both Gates and Louis jolted forward. Biting down on his lower lip, Louis reached for his heart as Gates took in a heavy gasp of air. Ada smiled and squeezed Gates's hand as he set his head back down softly, squeezing her hand back to show that he was conscious again. Sammy caught Louis by the shoulders before he fell forward. With a small grunt, Louis ripped his cable out and rubbed his chest where the mechanical cavity was located. Gates pulled his side of the cable out too with a large exhale, slowly sitting up with Ada's help.

"Let's..." Louis took a deep breath. "Let's not do that again, alright Hopper?"

"What did you do?" Ada asked.

"Long story short, I had a small heart attack and your boyfriend got a copy of the second half of the completed Calanthe code." Louis furrowed his eyebrows. "At least, that's what I think happened. I don't know. I just found out I was a cyborg like eight hours ago, okay? Give me a break."

The ceiling above them echoed again. Louis's eyes grew wide and he grabbed Sammy and Gates's shoulders to pull them forward.

"Alright let's get the fuck out of here!" He shouted.

Sammy and Louis took off towards the stairs. Ada helped Gates to his feet and let him lean on her as she pulled him towards the spiral staircase. The cement ceiling split wide open with an ear-splitting crack of foundation failing against itself. A flood of water fell straight through the ceiling. Sammy ran up the stairs first, tugging on Ada's hand. Ada followed Sammy's pull as Gates held her shoulders desperately, his previously dead legs struggling to keep pace. Louis took the back to push them all up the stairs.

"Movemovemovemovemove!" Louis continually spat, mostly for his own good as the water rose to their knees as they ascended the stairs.

They finally reached dry ground in the form of the unused office. Sammy, Ada, and Gates all relaxed as they walked into the flawless room. But the peace was short-lived as Louis pushed past them in a dead sprint.

"What are you all doing?!" Louis exclaimed, his hands clumsily keeping up with his words for Sammy's sake. "It's a fail-safe. That means everything's gotta go! All evidence of Tura Industries's robotics division! That means the entire fucking house!"

He grabbed the picture frame Ada noticed earlier before sprinting down the hall. The floor rumbled beneath their feet and Sammy took Gates's other side, helping Ada run him out of the crumbling house. They all made it to the circle driveway moments before the expensive pretty mansion crumbled onto itself in the massive sink-hole. All of the windows shattered in huge bursts of broken glass as the walls folded onto themselves, water spurting from every broken pipe snapping in half as the house crumbled. The four of them stared at the sinkhole in a stunned silence, mostly trying to catch their own breaths as they looked where the stunning home of

Harding Ventura once stood. In its place, a beautiful rising sun lit the valley positioned below the cliff. Hundreds of little houses lined in neat little rows with their pretty little trees positioned around them shone against the rays of orange and pink sprayed across the land.

Ada released a heavy breath. They were going to live.

"Well, that's it then?" Gates exhaled. "Everything Kamana created is gone now?"

"Well…" Louis sighed. He looked at the rest of them with a smirk. "Not everything."

There was a moment as the group allowed the depth of Louis's words settle on them.

Finally, still holding Gates's arm around her shoulder, Ada rolled her eyes.

"Really?!" She exclaimed. "Are you trying to say that we as a friend group would not exist without Kamana? That's stupid as hell. You thought that was cool to say but not my vague Terminator reference?"

"It's all about the presentation!" Louis said. Before he could say anything else, he moved his hands to position them into his leather jacket pockets, only to meet empty air. His face promptly fell at the realization and he gave Ada a flat look.

"Ada….please don't tell me you left my uncle's lucky leather jacket in there."

Ada shared a glance with Gates. With a short smirk, Gates sighed.

"Dude…" Gates said. "Let it go. That thing smelled like death anyways."

"If you just left it in my uncle's damn shack-" Shaking his head, Louis pushed the picture frame he saved from the office into Sammy's hands. "I'll be back."

Soon Ada and Gates were arguing with Louis to get away from the rubble of his house in his desperate effort to dig his stupid leather jacket out. Then, they were arguing with Louis and Sammy after Louis crudely translated his efforts to her through sign language. Their bickering voices drowned out the noise of the emergency vehicles' sirens, the result of a lucrative billionaire's mansion disappearing from the landscape in the blink of an eye, coming to their rescue.

They were going to live.

<!-- Ada got new medicine.

She also got a new haircut to chop off the rat's nest that built in her thick dark hair after months of laying around without the energy to brush it. After that, Ada slowly attempted to transition into a more active routine. Day by day, she stuck to a schedule. Wake up, shower, watch the morning news with a small helping of eggs and sriracha sauce, and then move on with her day. She cleaned the apartment, reorganized Sammy's closet, and, if there was nothing else, Ada would treat herself to an afternoon nap. It was a basic schedule, but it kept her brain moving to the next task. It gave her a purpose to look forward to each day.

Sammy called in a favor with an old art school buddy and snagged Ada an interview at Best Buy. It was easy enough for Ada to get the job with her technical knowledge. Soon she was adding work shifts into her routines. She only skipped breakfasts or showers on the bad days. She even allowed herself to still have bad days. It felt worse when she tried to ignore them completely. She kept her phone on silent. She only answered her father's weekly phone call and sister's text messages when they came. Ada didn't call her mom. Her mom didn't call either. That was fine for now. Eventually, they would speak again.

Baby steps. That's all Ada could take for the time being. But she was going to live. She was going to live.-->

CHAPTER SEVENTEEN

If he wasn't already a genius engineer with an array of emotional issues,

Louis Ventura would've been a great actor.

When the emergency vehicles arrived, the news vans were right behind them. Ada panicked at first. They were the sole survivors and, after everything they did prior to that day and their previous experience in this kind of situation, that made them suspects. But as the rush of reporters threw their microphones into Ada and Gates's faces, Louis ran in from the wreckage, bawling his eyes out. In a similar vein of natural acting talent, Sammy slowly appeared behind him and softly put her arms around his shoulders as he fake sobbed for the cameras.

"A sinkhole!" Louis exclaimed. "My dad was in there! And so was his robotics development team! Oh my god!" He sobbed dramatically again.

Ada and Gates watched Louis with wide, surprised eyes as he spewed a fantastic tale of how he and his friends (this when he motioned to Ada and Gates) went out for a night of clubbing, only to return to see his house, nay his *home* (a nice touch of drama in Ada's opinion) crumbling onto itself. He wailed dramatically as Sammy rubbed his back, her face perfectly sympathetic to his cause. Then Louis (while slapping Gates's shoulder) valiantly declared he was never going to touch a single drop of alcohol again for as long as he would live.

Despite condemning his previous drinking binge in Chicago just a few days ago, the reporters were sympathetic to his declaration. Of course, after that realization, he was too distraught to answer any more questions and walked off to the nearby paramedics, Sammy guiding him along as he released more dramatic sobs. Ada and Gates watched the display, dumbfounded, the entire time. The police eventually escorted the news teams from the area to "allow Mr. Ventura and his friends some privacy" which was a load of bull, but it was bull Ada was willing to accept. Firefighters searched the rubble for potential survivors and one of them escorted Gates to an ambulance to treat his injuries. Someone threw a shock blanket over Ada at one point and she sat on the bumper of a police cruiser with it, watching the people rush around with their various tasks. Gates laid on a stretcher in the ambulance, receiving stitches in the shoulder Louis ripped open to save his life. Louis was talking to the police, still looking believably distraught as he answered questions. Another paramedic worked on Louis's shoulder as he spoke to the officer, fixing the same wound Gates shared with him. Ada silently wondered if the paramedics would even notice the mechanical wirings underneath or if they would ignore it to accept their own realities were still true.

She lifted her eyes from watching the paramedics to look at Sammy who approached with a soft smile. Sammy also had a shock blanket around her shoulders. She wore some fresh bandages on the cuts she endured while fighting Kamana, but overall Sammy appeared mostly recovered from the night's events. She stopped a few feet from Ada. Facing one palm to the sky, Sammy wiggled the middle finger of her hand onto the open palm.

"Medicine?" She signed.

Ada smiled. "I'm okay."

With a sigh, Sammy joined Ada on the police cruiser bumper.

"You should talk to your doctor before you give it up," Sammy signed. "It's not healthy to stop without warning."

"I know," Ada signed. "I'll get an appointment when we go home but, for now, I'm okay."

Sammy shifted nervously on her seat, folding her shock blanket over her shoulders again. Ada looked at Sammy who only offered a guilty side-glance to her roommate as an explanation for her sudden awkwardness. Finally, Sammy sighed before moving her hands up to sign again.

"I need to tell you something," Sammy signed slowly. "I'm not going home."

She looked at Louis who was still chatting with police, a serious look in his eyes as he spoke to them, before turning back to Ada.

"Louis and I have been talking," Sammy said. "He has some great ideas for how to take over his dad's company. He looked at my art and he wants me to be in charge of rebranding."

Ada gave Sammy a long look. "So you'll stay here? In California?"

"You can stay with us!" Sammy signed, her eyes desperate to make Ada happy. "You don't have to work at Best Buy! Louis will let you work for him with a programming job or something. You did save us all with your awesome code."

All Ada could do was give Sammy a sad smile.

"I'm done with coding," Ada signed. "I've been done for a long time. You know that. Plus, I like Pittsburgh."

"Yes," Sammy signed. "But I don't want to leave you alone. You're my best friend."

"We'll be okay," Ada signed. "We fought some evil robots together and lived. I don't think people who do that together lose touch."

"The zombie apocalypse-high school theory," Sammy signed, taking special care to spell out 'zombie' and 'apocalypse' so that Ada could understand. "I know it all too well."

Ada giggled and Sammy smiled in return at her friend's happiness.

"So what are you going to do then?" Sammy signed.

"I don't know yet," Ada signed. "Not like I did before anyways."

Sammy thought for a moment before surrendering to the truth of Ada's statement.

"The lease on the apartment doesn't expire until next year," Sammy signed. "If I'm going to be here in California with Louis, then someone should probably stay in it until then. I'm sure I can get some money from Louis to cover rent until you figure something out."

"Are you kidding?" Ada signed. "Have you seen the way he looks at you? You could probably flirt your way to owning the company if you ask nicely."

Giggling, Sammy turned to look at Louis. He met her gaze and smiled for the first time since he started talking to the police, offering a shy wave. She twiddled her fingers back before blowing a kiss in his direction. He blushed before returning his attention to the officers. Letting her eyebrows jump slightly, Sammy turned back to Ada with a bashful smile.

"You're right," Sammy signed, rolling her tongue in her mouth. "But he's no random guy from the bus." Her smile turned from bashful to ornery. "How is sex with a robot by the way? Better or worse than a vibrator?"

"Bitch!" Ada exclaimed and signed, hitting Sammy's shoulder with her free hand. Sammy burst out laughing, releasing a snort or two as she desperately tried to calm down enough to sign back to Ada. She kept her index finger and thumb touching on her neck with the rest of the fingers spread out, rotating her hand slightly as she doubled over in laughter. The sign for "curiosity."

"No judgment!" Sammy finally was able to sign. "I'm going to be in the same boat as you one day. I need a head's up on what to expect."

"What are you guys talking about?" Louis asked, half-signing it out as he approached the girls. He glanced over his shoulder at the officers he left behind before turning back to the ladies. "You know, it's kind of hard to keep up the sob story about my asshole dad dying and all that when you're both over here laughing your heads off."

"Aw," Ada said and signed. "You were faking? Do you fake often, Louis?"

A laugh bubbled out of Sammy's lips. Ada failed to hold back a giggle as well and snorted alongside her best friend as Louis regarded them both with raised eyebrows.

"Oh wow," Louis said, crudely signing as he spoke. "So we're thirteen now? That's how it is? Save the world and then regress..." He slowed down on his sign language when he realized he didn't know the sign for 'regress'. "...go back to middle school? Got it."

"Sorry Mr. CEO," Sammy said out loud with a shrug, calming down from her laughter.

"To be fair though," Ada said and signed. "I don't think we saved the *world*, per say. Maybe just Tura Industries customers."

Louis regarded her with a sly smirk before folding his arm over his chest. "Well you know, I was going to offer you a job in my new company as my head programmer, but with that attitude-"

"I wouldn't have taken it anyway," Ada said. "Sammy filled me in on your guys' plan. I'm going to take a breather on coding. Find something else to do for a bit."

The sly smirk faded into something more genuine on Louis's face.

"Are you sure about that, sweetheart?" Louis asked. "It's a helluva deal. I'll even waive the probationary period and get you right into our benefits program-"

374 – MADDIE GUDENKAUF

"Louis," Ada said. "I'm okay. Thank you for offering, but I can figure things out for myself."

The smile on Louis's face was soft, his dull green eyes no longer looking at her with contempt or curiosity. Instead, something closer to "understanding" passed his gaze, but Ada would never trust that he fully understood what she went through. He still nodded softly to indicate his approval for her decision.

"Of course you can," Louis said. "But if you need anything, and I do mean anything, which might be a dangerous offer for me to make, but anyways, just let me know, okay? I owe you, Ada." He glanced at Sammy briefly. "Like...a lot."

"I'm okay right now," Ada said. "But what about you? I mean, you just lost your entire freaking house."

With half-hearted effort, Louis glanced over his shoulder at the wreckage behind him.

"Ehh it was just a house," He said. "I think I spent more time in dorm rooms than my own bedroom here. Not to mention, there's the vacation home in Aspen, Great Aunt Hannah's place in Sarasota, Allen's shack in the middle of the Mojave if I'm feeling particularly desperate." He shrugged. "Plus, between the inheritance from my dad, assumedly Great Aunt Hannah, and Uncle Allen, I can pretty much buy my own country at this point so I think we're good." He waved the picture frame of his mom in front of the girls. "I saved the important things...except for that damn leather jacket, of course."

Rolling her eyes, Ada let Louis play his little charade of gazing out dramatically into the rubble for the stupid jacket. He was never going to admit whether or not he was upset over his father's death. How he actually felt about the entirety of the program he's been working on since he was a kid being destroyed in one night. Maybe one day he would, but today she would let him pretend otherwise.

"Well if you need anything from me, I'm here for you too. I can't like..." Ada rolled her eyes. "...give you a high-paying job or anything like that, but if you need to talk, I'm here for you."

Louis rolled his tongue into his cheek, his eyes silently thanking Ada for giving him an out.

"What I want is for you to be the head programmer of my company," Louis stated. "But I'll respect your decision. Just don't be surprised if I call you at three in the morning for help on a program. There's quite a time difference between here and Pittsburgh."

"For you, Louis Ventura," Ada said. "I'm available at all hours."

Ada knew the importance of keeping things to yourself for a bit, but she wasn't about to let Louis have his own moment with his choice of sleeping medicine because of his inability to cope with his emotions. But Ada wasn't too concerned. After all, her guardian angel was going to keep watch over him like she did for her. Stepping forward, Sammy took Louis's arm.

"Come on," Sammy signed. "I bet we can convince a firefighter to dig for your jacket."

Louis held a finger up as he stared at Sammy's hands.

"Okay, I saw a digging motion and a jacket motion, but you gotta go slow on me, babe."

With an exasperated look, Sammy turned to Ada to indicate a translation. Ada lifted her hands, but Louis took Sammy by her hands instead.

"No," He signed and said slowly. Then he tapped his index fingers together. "Again. If you don't mind. I want to learn."

Sammy's eyes were as bright as her smile and she offered Louis a quick kiss on his lips. Pulling away, Sammy locked eyes with Louis.

"Let's go-" She said out loud slowly as she moved one hand in a clawing motion away from the top of her head. "-dig-" She made a motion like she was shoveling into the ground. "-for your-" She moved both hands and shoulders forward. "-jacket!"

Louis nodded slowly and repeated the sign for "jacket" before giving her a thumbs up.

"Okay!" He exclaimed.

Smiling, he swept his hand over the lower part of his face before closing it and reopening it quickly into a fist. Ada was impressed. He learned how to sign "beautiful" from Allen pretty quickly. Rolling her eyes, a blush crept onto her cheeks as Sammy pulled on Louis's arm towards the rubble of his former home. To Ada's surprise, he rolled out of Sammy's hold and faced Ada again.

"Oh? And Ada?" Louis said. "Thank you."

She furrowed her eyebrows at him. "For what?"

Ada could see a smile twinkling in Louis's eyes.

"For making me believe in fate again," He said.

With a close lipped smile, he nodded at Ada before running to join Sammy. Ada watched them walk towards the remains of his house, Sammy grabbing the picture out of Louis's hand.

"Your mom?" She said out loud slowly as she tapped her own face with a vertical flat hand, thumb facing inwards, as she pointed at the gorgeous Latina woman in the picture.

"Yes," Louis said as he nodded his wrist before repeating Sammy's motion for "mom". Then he slowly spelled it out on his fingers. "C-A-L-A-N-T-H-E."

"Ca-lay-" Sammy tried.

"No," Louis said. He let his lips and tongue exaggerate as he tried to communicate the pronunciation."Cuh-lan-thhhh."

Sammy giggled as she tried to say the name out loud, Louis smiling proudly right along with her attempt. Finally, she surrendered for a moment to bring her hand over her face, but instead of tapping her fingers together at the end, she curved it into a half moon shape. The sign for "beautiful" with the letter C. Louis nodded before repeating his attempt to help her say it out loud. Maybe Sammy was going to be alright too. Ada didn't know that she needed to be until that moment. Even if it was because of that asshole Louis, Ada was glad to see her friend so happy. It made the decision to leave Sammy alone with him that much easier, even if it hurt Ada in the process.

A throat cleared close to her and Ada turned to it.

Gates stood there, successfully returning to a renewed health. She felt her breath catch short at the sight of him. While he was still wearing the black and red Tura Industries suit, it was barely recognizable on him. The jacket was spread out, revealing a spot of bare chest and bandages around the area the paramedics stitched up from Louis's rescue. His brown hair was tousled, stray strands sticking out in cute tufts that differed from his normally coiffed look. He nodded towards the open spot next to Ada that Sammy vacated.

"Can I join you?" Gates asked.

It took Ada a few moments to process his question.

"Yeah, sure," She finally stammered. As he sat on the police cruiser bumper with her, Ada moved over a couple spaces to fit him. He sighed and clapped his hands together, struggling to come up with something to say. Ada sucked in a massive breath.

"So, how are you feeling?" She indicated towards her own head. "You know with the...you know?"

Gates let out a small laugh. "Honestly? I don't think my thoughts have ever been less clear." He straightened his back and folded his arms over his chest. "With Kamana, everything was handed down to me. All of my orders, all of my commands. I never had to think for myself. I did, of course, because I couldn't help myself but..." Closing his eyes, he rubbed his forehead. "Now, it's a mess."

"I'm used to messy thoughts," Ada said. "What's up? What are you thinking about?"

"Everything," Gates said with another short laugh. "I'm thinking about Freya and if I wronged her and our friendship, if we even had a friendship. I'm thinking how all of the houses in the valley below us look so clean, how easy their lives must be. I'm thinking about you and Sammy and Louis and how I betrayed you guys but you still forgave me enough to save my life and, wow I can't stop thinking about how you forced Louis to save my life and I can't stop thinking about you and your smile and us and-and..." Standing to his feet, Gates shook his finger. "What I really can't stop thinking about is my future. I mean..." He threw his hands up and Ada could see tears dancing in his eyes. "What am I going to do now? My whole programming was to be public relations for Kamana and now I have nothing. I have no purpose. I mean, what I had before sucked but at least it was something. I don't belong anywhere now." Gates took a deep breath and ignored Ada's gaze. "I'm just...lost."

Licking her lips, Ada fought the urge to laugh. His confusion was endearing. Instead, she only smiled.

"Well, Gates Hopper," She said. "Let me be the first to welcome you to humanity." He looked at her with a quizzical stare and she shrugged. "We're all lost, dude. None of us know what we're doing."

Gates threw his hand towards Louis and Sammy, who were rummaging through the bits of rubble piled close to the house. "They look like they know what they're doing."

"Oh c'mon," Ada said. "Are you serious? Louis has more emotional issues than a white girl on Maury and Sammy fakes it 90% of the time. She's been nodding at the wrong parts in our conversations all week." She threw her hands towards the happy couple. "Just because they're confident in what they're doing doesn't mean they actually know what they're doing. They're making it up too."

Letting out a heavy sigh, Gates lifted his arms. "So, what do I do then?"

"Live, like the rest of us," Ada said. "Sleep, shower, eat, go to work, survive day by day. You're forgetting that your situation isn't special. Humans aren't born with a singular primary function we're supposed to accomplish in our lifetimes. We're not coded for one thing. We're not supposed to be coded for anything, that's what makes us human." She shrugged. "So you can do whatever you want, I guess, now that you're an official human. You're lucky too. You're a white guy with access to a way-too-rich rich friend. That already opens, like, so many doors for you."

Gates offered Ada a weak smile.

"You mean, after all of this time, you still don't believe in fate?"

"Nope," Ada said. "But that's also my choice as a human. You can have your own choices."

For the first time, Ada briefly considered her choice with Kamana. If she had chosen the other way, she would be perfect. She would own a robotics company. She would have her own money to spend, not Louis's. She would have the three houses, a private army, her entire life and future laid out before her without a shred of doubt to bring it all down. Someone else would be in her head, able to make every decision for her with absolute precision and full confidence. It was everything she ever wanted, and she still turned it down. If fate was real, it would be damning her to hell and back for denying it.

"So what if I chose to spend my life with you?" Gates asked, taking a step forward. "Would you let me?"

Ada bit her lower lip as she met Gates's kind brown eyes. He was staring into her deeply, willing her to accept his choice.

"Gates, you have the whole world at your fingertips now," Ada said. "There's so much you haven't seen yet-"

"I want to see it with you," Gates said.

Ada arched an eyebrow. "Life isn't always peachy, you know. People lose jobs, lose family, fall out of love….a lot of shit happens in life."

"Yeah and I want to be by your side through it all," Gates said. "I'm not proposing marriage or anything like that…" He took a deep breath. "But if life is as hard as you say it is, then I want someone who I can trust on my side. Someone who I know will protect my life as much as I'll protect hers." Gates licked his lips. "I know you won't be able to trust me again for a while and that's okay. I'm willing to work to earn that privilege, if you'll give me a second chance."

Gates's eyes and words were genuine. That was the only thing Ada knew for certain. Everything else, if they would last longer than a week, if she can ever find her purpose in life, if she would ever feel whole again, was uncertain. Baby steps. That's all she could do for now. She released a shaky breath.

"Well, my roommate just moved out," Ada said. "So there's enough room that you can sleep on my couch until you figure your life out."

"And if I don't ever figure my life out?" Gates asked.

"Then you and me both," Ada said.

A true smile claimed Gates's face as he looked into Ada's eyes. She smiled right back, warmth growing from the pit of her heart. Maybe they didn't know what they were doing. Maybe Gates would move out once the high of fighting murder robots together wore out. Maybe Ada will end up as Kamana predicted, alone and living the same life she's hated living so far, never being able to move past her failures as a person.

But, for now, everything was fine and that's all that mattered.

Sammy's shrieks of joy caused everyone in the area to turn to the young artist with pink and brown hair. Gates and Ada watched as Sammy came running from the rubble and into Ada, holding onto her arms. Ada winced at the loud noises emitting from Sammy's mouth.

"Easy!" Ada signed and said out loud. "What's up?!"

Sammy's words and signs were indistinguishable as she cupped the top of her head with both of her hands and removed her hands rapidly. Before Gates or Ada could decipher the sign, Louis caught up to their group.

"Look, all I said was that we were less than an hour away from Disneyland," Louis explained. "I didn't expect-" He turned to Gates. "Ah! He's risen. How's it going, man?" Louis took Gates's hand from his side and shook it. "Feeling good?"

Offering a semi-worried glance to Ada, Gates shook Louis's hand right back.

"Yeah? I'm feeling fine?" Gates said.

"Great! Good!" Louis exclaimed. "Alright, pleasantries over, I'll get to the point: I need a public relations guy for the new Tura Industries and-"

"Louis!" Sammy exclaimed, hopping in place. She cupped her hands on the top of her head again and danced towards the Camaro. "Disney!"

"One second!" Louis said verbally and tried to sign to Sammy at the same time. He turned back to Gates. "So what do you say, bud? Need a job?"

Risking a glance to Ada, Gates took a deep breath. "Actually, I've already got arrangements on a couch in Pittsburgh."

Louis looked between Gates and Ada, who blushed at Gates's sincerity.

"Well mazel tov to the happy couple, but that doesn't help my company at all. In fact, I'm going to have to relocate my company to goddamn Pittsburgh at this rate," Louis sighed. He turned to Ada. "Well you know, since you are technically rehabilitating a Tura Industries product, I would be open to a possible monthly payment-"

"Quit trying to give me your damn money," Ada said. "I don't want it."

"I have too much of it now," Louis said. "If you don't take my salary, I'll be forced to make a charitable donation so I can write it off as a tax deduction. Really, Ada. I saw how fast you took my black card in Pittsburgh. Let me help you guys out."

Ada rolled her eyes.

"Fine," She said. "But only until I get another job. Also, don't refer to Gates as a product. You know better, Louis."

"I was being technical," Louis said. "Gates, were you offended?"

"Of course not," Gates said. "I mean, it's like if I called you a zombie, right?"

Licking his lips, Louis held an index finger up.

"Fair point," He said. "Alright c'mon. We better head to Disneyland before Sammy has a damn aneurysm. My treat." Louis smiled at Gates and Ada before walking away. "Think of it as a 'thanks for helping me save the world' present."

"He owes you the whole theme park then," Gates whispered into Ada's ear.

Sammy was already standing at the car, shuffling through the trunk for a fresh change of clothes. When she saw the rest of the group headed her way, she waved excitedly. Louis grinned from ear to ear and broke into a small run to reach her faster. Gates took his time with Ada as they walked to the car together, his arms dangling at his side. Pursing her lips, Ada closed the gap between them and took his hand. He offered her a surprised look before squeezing her hand back. A blush crept onto his face as he smiled and looked ahead. Ada smiled softly and looked ahead too.

Life was terrible, but at least the people were good.

<!-- Ada should've graduated today.

She knows because in between training the useless new girl Stacy, who couldn't tell the difference between an Android and an iPhone, and her usual games of solitaire, Ada was checking Facebook. All of her old college friends posted selfies with each other, some with people she never saw before, and most were joking about the terrible commencement speaker. Ada should've been with them. Pictures of Ada wearing her black robes with various colored cords around her neck should've been plastered everywhere. More specifically, Ada should've been the girl Daniel was kneeling with the fancy ring in front of in his picture.

But that wasn't Ada's life any more. Ada wasn't that girl. Ada's life was wearing a black polo shirt while sitting in a cage surrounded by broken laptops and tablets and that was the best Ada could do right now.

For a long minute, Ada considered writing a congratulatory comment on Daniel's picture, letting them both know that she approved of the engagement. That, despite appearances, she too moved on with her life and was content enough to congratulate the woman who replaced her in her old life. But, in the end, she decided against it. They didn't need or want her in their life any more so what use did a congratulations do? She did the next best thing instead.

She deleted her Facebook account.

All it was doing was holding an archive of memories from her old life and preventing her from moving on and that's what she needed to get better: to move on.

But that didn't stop her from grabbing a carton of ice cream on her way home from work. When she arrived at the apartment, Sammy was already sitting on the couch with her own carton of ice cream.

"You too?" Ada signed.

"I lost the bid for a good project," Sammy signed. "What's your excuse?"

"New girl at work," Ada signed, joining Sammy on the couch. "Dumb as rocks. Wants me to join her softball team. Not happening."

"It would be a fun way to meet people!" Sammy signed with a smile. "Now that you're off the couch, you need more friends than me. Friends that don't live in shit studio apartments and can give you a real room to stay in."

"Are you kicking me off your couch?" Ada signed.

"No!" Sammy signed. "I'm just saying, you deserve your own room. Your own apartment, even!"

Smiling softly, Ada opened her ice cream before signing.

"Someday, but not today."

Smiling widely, Sammy stuck her spoon in her mouth and let her ice cream carton sit in her lap as she signed excitedly.

"Here's to us!"

"Long live us!" Ada signed back. Sammy lifted her carton from her lap and Ada tapped her own carton against her friend's in a mock sign of celebration.

The girls giggled before turning to the cheesy rom-com Sammy chose for their night together. As Ada dug into her ice cream, she thought about her classmates. They all would be out celebrating tonight at the various bars and house parties around Carnegie Mellon. Michelle would be showing off her new ring and Daniel would be mocking a British accent in preparation for his new job overseas in London. Their night was looking as great as their futures. Ada would have great nights too one day. She'll escape her dead-end job, maybe she'll meet a guy, and maybe they'll be able to travel together before settling down. Maybe one day she'll lead a life her parents would be proud of or maybe she won't. Maybe she'll just have a life that she's happy with and that would be good enough for Ada. But, for now, there would always be ice cream and watching bad movies with her best friend.

Life was terrible, but at least the people were good. -->

ACKNOWLEDGEMENTS

The first half of this book was completed in 2015. The second half was completed in 2017. I began revisiting the manuscript in 2021 and published it in 2023. There's a lot of people to thank for helping me over these many years to finish this novel so I'm sorry if I missed anyone. Please know that I keep you in my heart for supporting me during one of the most vulnerable projects I've written to date. I'm extremely grateful for the support system that sustains me during my tough times and celebrates during the best of times. These are just a few of the more notable names that contributed to the support of this novel:

I'd first like to thank my family: my parents and my brother. They have been my most consistent cheerleaders and have been rooting for me since the very beginning. Thank you for taking care of me when I needed help the most and never once turning your back on me, even when it got tough. You guys are the best family a woman can ask for and I wouldn't trade you for the world.

Second, I would never have gotten the courage to finish and publish this second book without the tremendous reception my first book How to Survive a Ghost Story received in 2018 when it was first published. Thank you to everyone who read the book and helped promote it out of the pure goodness of their hearts to make it the success it was. Specific thanks to Steph Loves, Old Firehouse Books,

Carissa Taylor, the Holiday Twin Drive-In staff, Elodie Iver, Laura Jane, Lin Coldiron, Elayna Darcy, Christa Bohan, Levi Phipps, Grecia Chavez, and many more who really went above and beyond to make my first book publication an enjoyable experience.

This novel couldn't have been completed as well without the input of my beta reading team: Christa, Kierra, Madi, and Joey. Thank you for all of your insights and taking the time to read my sad robot book about millennials so that it can be the best version of itself it can be! A very special shoutout to Joey who went above and beyond editing this novel in her free time. Thank you for having the patience to place all of my missed commas and taking such good care of my novel. I'm truly grateful to have such a talented editor who truly loved and cared for my story!

I'd like to give a major shoutout to my marketing manager and friend Megatron Jon. He truly helped kick my butt into gear to not only finish editing this novel, but to actually publish it as well. Thank you for enduring all of my knee jerk marketing and business questions, even if I only listen to half of what you say anyways, and helping edit my novel.

I also have major love for the folks in my life who continue to support and encourage me so I can follow my dreams with confidence. Thank you Morgan for always being down for a boba tea vent session, helping me survive 2020 (and more) by watching bad reality TV on your big blue couch, and championing all of my crazy ideas with fire despite being an earth sign. Thank you David for regularly indulging my reading addiction, the much needed pep talks, the philosophy lessons, and all of the adventures along the way. Thank you Brigitte for being such a positive force in my life and always encouraging me to look on the bright side of life. Thank you Madi for walking me through setting up my LLC for publishing and also being such a great auntie for Mollie. Thank you Mollie as well for being the best lil puppy and making sure to show me all of the best sticks on our walks.

Thank you to the following cheerleading squad who, in one way or another, supported me and/or my writing through the years: Chrystal, Kelly, Aunt Gayle, Silje, Allyson, Frank, Adam, Kimberly, Melo, Reeves, Colwell, Caitlin, Beth, Bo, Steven, Michelle, and so many more that I am eternally grateful for.

And a final thank you to you, the reader who chose to read this novel. That simple act allows me to follow my dreams and I cannot appreciate you enough for giving me the opportunity to tell you the stories that live in my heart. I sincerely hope you enjoyed my sad book about millennials and robots.

DID YOU ENJOY THE BOOK?

Please Review It!

Reviews are essential to indie authors and small publishers. They allow new readers to discover the book and, depending on the platform, increase the likelihood of the book appearing elsewhere on the site. So if you really enjoyed this novel and want others to read it, I would really appreciate it if you reviewed it on your platform of choice!

Thank you!!

Twitter/Instagram: **@Maddness22**
Email: **maddnessbusiness@gmail.com**
www.maddiegudenkauf.com

www.dalygoodmedia.com
dalygoodbusiness@gmail.com

About the Author

Maddie Gudenkauf is the author of the young adult paranormal comedy "How to Survive a Ghost Story" and adult sci-fi "Fatal Flaws". She has published work with Hypable.com and The Harry Potter Alliance. She previously ran the variety YouTube channel known as "TheMaddness22" with over 2,300 subscribers and 500,000 views. Maddie currently lives in Colorado with her dog Mollie and overfilled bookcases in every room.

You can find her on Twitter and Instagram as @maddness22 or at her website www.maddiegudenkauf.com

CPSIA information can be obtained
at www.ICGtesting.com
Printed in the USA
BVHW051937110423
662159BV00012B/215

9 798986 639703